Advance Praise for *The Land Grant*:

"Cisneros, who practices law in Brownsville, continues to impress with his sharp characterizations and thoughtful, many-layered stories." —*Booklist*

"In the troubled, dusty border region of South Texas, corruption and violence aren't isolated forces to be wrestled with and conquered by our hero but a pervasive condition. Alex is no white knight, but he's sympathetic enough that the harsh denouement will leave readers shaken." —*Publishers Weekly*

"Set in the Rio Grande Valley of South Texas, Cisneros' legal thriller paints a vivid picture of border justice with a cast of characters ranging from the Pope to Mexican narcotraffickers. A lawyer himself, the author has written a fast-paced, complex novel." —REFORMA Newsletter

D0951105

THE
LAND
GRANT

THE LAND GRANT

CARLOS CISNEROS

Arte Público Press
Houston, Texas

The Land Grant is made possible through a grant from the City of Houston through the Houston Arts Alliance.

Recovering the past, creating the future

Arte Público Press
University of Houston
4902 Gulf Fwy, Bldg 19, Rm 100
Houston, Texas 77204-2004

Cover design by Mora Des!gn

Cisneros, Carlos.
   The Land Grant / by Carlos Cisneros.
      p.   cm.
   Sequel to: The Case Runner.
   ISBN 978-1-55885-706-3 (alk. paper)
      1. Land grants—Texas—Fiction. 2.Right of property—Fiction.
   3. Mexican-American Border Region—Fiction. 4. Texas—Fiction.
   I. Title.
   PS3603.I86L36 2012
   813'.6—dc23

                                                      2012026150
                                                      CIP

♾ The paper used in this publication meets the requirements of the American National Standard for Information Sciences—Permanence of Paper for Printed Library Materials, ANSI Z39.48-1984.

12 13 14 15 16 17 18   10 9 8 7 6 5 4 3 2 1

To Janice Johnson, Frank Whigman and Michael Wheeler, thanks for all you do.

PROLOGUE

ENITO DEL ANGEL was twenty-six years old when he became a priest. Not a week after being ordained, the humble priest was assigned to his own parish—in the one-traffic-light town of Raymondville, Texas. Although he was young, Del Angel was a caring priest who looked after his congregation, even if he occasionally had to butt heads with his superiors, including Bishop Ricardo Salamanca, head of the Catholic Diocese of the Southern Coastal Counties. For more than a hundred years, the diocese's reach had stretched from Nueces County all the way down to Kleberg, Kennedy, Willacy and Cameron. Four dirt-poor counties stacked on top of each other, near the Gulf Coast, in fertile South Texas.

Although his assignment demanded generating higher levels of monthly tithing at the Cristo Rey church, so far Del Angel had spent most of his time ministering to the sick and the hungry. And instead of pushing his flock to reach deep into its pockets, he had stocked his parish's pantry with food bought with his own savings and had added an extra night a week to the soup kitchen's schedule, where he and three other volunteers fed the homeless of the poor ranching community. The faithful at his church loved Del Angel, but Bishop Salamanca was not exactly sure what to make of the young cleric's growing independent streak.

The irony of the bishop having ordered the young cleric to raise more money from his poverty-stricken parish in order to construct a larger church was not lost on Del Angel. The few good paying jobs to be had in Raymondville were at the two prisons

1

outside of town, the Wal-Mart nearby and the federal detention center housing undocumented people awaiting deportation. Why was Salamanca intent on squeezing the poor to build himself a new church, when, in fact, the diocese could easily pay for the construction itself? Or, wouldn't that money be put to better use in aiding the poor and infirm? Was Salamanca out of touch? Besides, not only was the diocese as a whole one of the richest in the entire United States, but the diocese also sent twenty-five million dollars a month, overseas, to the Vatican, thanks to its ownership of La Minita ranch—an enormous tract of land aptly named "Little Mine." With more than half a million acres rich in oil and gas deposits, La Minita was the largest single landholding in North America, and for the past forty-five years it had been titled under the Agnus Dei Foundation, a for-profit corporation owned and operated by Salamanca's diocese.

What people did not know, or had conveniently forgotten, was that back in 1960, seventy-year-old Austin McKnight, the last heir apparent to La Minita, had died lonely and heartbroken. With no heirs of his own, McKnight had willed away everything to the diocese. And now, all the major gas and oil producers—Exxon, Shell, BP, Chevron, Pennzoil—and the railroads, wind farms, shrimp farms and all the telecommunications companies held billions of dollars worth of exploration, production and other similar leases on La Minita. How much money actually poured into the diocese's coffers every year was a well-guarded secret. Anonymous sources close to Salamanca, however, estimated the earnings to be in the range of thirty to fifty million dollars a month.

It was Sunday night, and Del Angel was at the altar getting ready to wrap up the last Mass of the day. He was moving about slowly, purposefully, concentrating, as this particular night the Spanish Mass was packed. The aromas of incense and fresh flowers filled the semi dark space. The present flock was quite different from the Spanish-speaking regulars he ministered to on Sunday mornings. These were the Mexican farmhands and their families, many of them in the States illegally, from in and around Raymondville. They scratched out a meager existence on the farms and ranches scattered about Willacy County, living under the radar, far below the latest governmental poverty index.

Del Angel raised the chalice and host over his head and invoked God to send down the Holy Spirit and transform the bread and wine into the body and blood of Christ. "*Y en la noche que fue traicionado, Jesús tomó el pan y dio gracias. Y partiéndolo se lo dio a sus discípulos y dijo, 'Tomad y bebed todos de él que éste es mi cuerpo que será entregado por vosotros. Haced esto en conmemoración mía.'*"

As he knelt down for a few seconds of silence and reverence behind the wooden altar, Father Benito then took the host and washed it down with wine. He then stood up and continued, "*De nuevo, tomó el cáliz, y alzándolo dio gracias, luego lo pasó a sus discípulos diciendo . . .* "

As Father Benito continued with the holy ritual, he noticed the shadow of a man enter by one of the doors located at the side of the church. The man paused for a brief moment, appeared to be removing his hat, and slowly walked toward the center aisle, squeezing and maneuvering through the crowd.

"*Este es el sacramento de nuestra fe. Anunciamos tu muerte, proclamamos tu resurrección, ven, Señor Jesús,*" said the priest, as he stretched out his arms, inviting everyone to stand. His thoughts then turned to the bishop. For weeks, Salamanca had been promising to come and say Mass in an effort to help kick-start the capital campaign for the new church, and tonight was supposed to have been that night, thus the large turnout. Salamanca had cancelled, again at the last minute. His assistant had called and had said the bishop was the guest of honor at an art exhibition being sponsored by a well-connected political donor named Mauricio Mercado and his Corpus Christi law firm.

Once more, Father Benito raised the host slightly over the paten and facing the crowd repeated, "*Este es el Cordero de Dios que quita los pecados del mundo . . .* '"

Father Benito and the altar boy then walked to the front of the altar and took their places, ready to dispense Communion. As per Salamanca's strict rules, Father Benito was still required to place the host in the mouths of the parishioners, while the altar boy discreetly placed a small silver tray under their chins, in the event a host was dropped.

The stranger then came into view, again, walking down the narrow center aisle, toward the altar, as a line now quickly formed to receive Communion. After dispensing the holy bread and saving about thirty souls, it was now the stranger's turn. The man stopped, locked eyes with Father Benito and opened his mouth in anticipation.

"¿*Cuerpo de Cristo?*" asked the priest. But before the priest could hear the requisite "*amén*," the stranger pulled a pocket-sized, semiautomatic Beretta pistol from under the hat he'd been clutching close to his chest, and shouted, "Burn in hell, Salamanca!"

Bishop Salamanca flipped the channel on the high-definition flat-screen TV mounted above the decadent, Carrara marble jacuzzi and thought what a nice gift it would be for the Honorable Judge Remington Phillips to grant his diocese's motion to dismiss plaintiffs' lawsuit now pending in one of Kleberg County's district courts.

He'd been soaking in his jacuzzi for almost an hour, trying to relax a bad back—courtesy of an extra fifty pounds he'd been carrying around for the past years—as he enjoyed a tranquil Sunday evening in his quarters overlooking the magnificent bay of Corpus Christi. In the room next door sat a young seminary student who was there for the sole purpose of guarding his holiness' privacy and serving him snifters full of Canticle, a rare pear brandy imported from the Isle of Rhodes. The seminary student was also tasked with reviewing the correspondence and accompanying legal bills from the diocese's attorneys defending the latest attack on the Agnus Dei Foundation. For the last twenty years, various groups of heirs—claiming to be descendants of Don Arturo Monterreal, a Spanish settler who received a *porción* or piece of land straight from the king of Spain, Charles III—had tried in vain to reclaim their lands now in the Agnus Dei Foundation's grasp. Of course there was nothing small about the *porción* that Monterreal had received back in 1767. Since Monterreal was the nephew of the Count of Montealto, a blueblood with connections to the monarchy, the original conveyance was comprised of close to two million acres.

Legend had it that Monterreal, under the guidance of the Count of Montealto, had left Asturias, Spain, in the eighteenth century and headed to New Spain to serve as an *oídor*, or high judge. He was commissioned to replace Don Lino Salas, a nobleman from the village of La Pontiaga, who'd fallen ill and no longer could attend to his public duties. Monterreal had first landed in the port of Veracruz and soon headed northwest to replace Salas, who'd been stationed in Monterrey.

The Santibáñez clan—all descendants of Candelario Santibáñez, a great, great, great, great, great, great, great grandson of Monterreal—had been the latest round of heirs to mount an all-out attack on the Foundation, but so far, the diocese's high-powered attorneys had managed to delay the case for almost three years. Not all the delays could be blamed on the tactics employed by the foundation's lawyers. For starters, the first attorney handling the case had died when his Denali SUV rear-ended an eighteen-wheeler on the stretch of highway between San Antonio and Corpus Christi. Then, in a strange twist of fate, the second plaintiff's lawyer to come into the case, an attorney from Florida, had to be committed to a mental institution when the pressure from the case got to him. But now it appeared, thanks to a generous political contribution from Salamanca's Foundation to Phillips' reelection campaign—via the Vatican and routed through the Universal Trinity Alliance, a political action committee—the lawyer-less plaintiffs were about to be thrown out of court.

Bishop Salamanca's lifelong dream of becoming a Cardinal was finally within his reach. The latest directive from the Vatican was to fend off the Santibáñez group at all cost and steer clear of trouble. The last thing the Vatican needed was another story in the papers dealing with sexual abuse or bishops being kicked out of the church for fathering illegitimate children.

The portly bishop stared at his stubby hands, still wrinkled from soaking in the bathwater. Despite being almost seventy years old and having some mobility problems, Salamanca still possessed a keen mind and the resolve, along with a large war chest, to defeat the Santibáñez group. He was determined to put an end to all this litigation, once and for all. After all, his diocese had spent, unnecessarily, some fifty million dollars over the last two decades defending such frivolous claims, even claims from other sister dioceses from around the state that opined that Agnus Dei should share the gas and oil royalties. This was money, in Salamanca's opinion, that could have been better spent in other evangelical and worthy pursuits.

"Bishop Salamanca?"

Tony, the seminary student, suddenly appeared with a frown on his face. "It's the chief of police from Raymondville, down in Willacy County, Bishop."

"Take a message. I'll call him later."

"I'm sorry, Your Holiness. The chief said it was important. He said there's been trouble at the Cristo Rey church."

From the jacuzzi, Salamanca reached for the receiver and waited for Tony to hand it over.

"Now what? I should have known better than to send a novice to that church." Salamanca threw back the last of the Canticle. "C'mon, hand me the receiver, hurry! *Adeste Fideles*. What did Benito do now?"

"Looks like he got himself killed, sir," muttered Tony as he handed Salamanca the cordless phone.

CHAPTER 1

ALEJANDRO DEL FUERTE was reading the story of the Cristo Rey shootings in the local paper, while finishing breakfast at his favorite hole-in-the-wall, La Fonda Chiquita, when his cell phone went off. It was Gigi. Not six months after getting engaged, and his fiancée appeared ready to put kryptonite shackles around both his ankles. She wanted to know if he was going to join her at the Blue Moon yoga studio for their daily hour of spiritual rejuvenation and stress relief. Class was starting in fifteen minutes.

Since Alex won the Harrow lawsuit and walked away a millionaire, his stress level, instead of diminishing, had climbed through the roof. At twenty-seven, Alex could not understand if his stress had something to do with playing the stock market or letting Gigi move in with him at the Contessa di Mare, his South Padre Island penthouse.

Alex was looking at the text message with a frown on his face, when Juan, the owner, interrupted, "Let me guess . . . *la patrona*, right?"

"Would you believe it?" sighed Alex. "And we're not even married, yet. *Qué desgracia.*"

"Have you all picked the date?"

"*N'ombre, qué* date *ni qué nada*. We can't even agree on the kind of wedding we want. She wants a destination wedding . . . in Greece, of course. And I can't have no freakin' destination wedding. *Está loca.* My grandpa can't travel anymore. After eating dirt outside of Luby's, the time he broke his hip, he's been in and out of hospitals. But, did Grandpa César listen? No way, no how! He

7

had to go and have his Sunday fried-fish Luann plate. So, now I can't have the old man traveling. *Pero ella no entiende . . .* I don't know what's gonna happen."

"Let me guess—she saw 'Mamma Mia,' the movie, *verdad*?"

"*¡Claro!* It's all *pinche* Hollywood. They plant all these fantasies in their heads. I mean, Gigi can be the most effective, professional, kick-ass trial lawyer you'll ever see in action . . . but don't get her talking about the wedding. It's like . . . common sense goes out the window. The whole thing's RIDICULOUS."

"So what kind of wedding do you want?" asked Juan as he delivered a basket of warm tortilla chips to the two UPS drivers sitting at the next table.

"I don't know anymore. I thought this would be simple, enjoyable . . . fun. And now, it feels like work. Hell, I don't even know if I want a wedding . . . or even if I want to get married. The last wedding I went to was a disaster . . . "

"Oh, yeah?" asked Juan.

"Yes," continued Alex. "I was a third-year student in law school and one of our classmates was getting married at the Ritz Carlton. Twenty minutes before the guests were due to arrive at the hotel for the lavish reception, the banquet waiters began lighting the candles on all the tables . . . "

"Yeah?"

"The scented candles sat on beautiful, but flimsy, twelve-inch candleholders. One of the holders tipped over as soon as the last waiter finished setting up and exited the ballroom. No one saw it happen, but a tablecloth caught on fire. The sprinkler system went off . . . and there you have it."

"No!" gasped Juan.

"Yep, my friend, the bride was devastated. Anyway, with other weddings going on at the hotel that same night, there was nowhere else to put the party."

"What happened?"

"Not knowing what else to do, the banquet director set up a buffet table out in the parking lot, and we had ourselves a wedding out front."

Juan thought about it for a minute. "Well, you know what they say . . . it's good luck if it rains . . . and the sprinklers went off . . . so . . . "

"I guess," mumbled Alex, "but maybe I'm getting cold feet."

"What? Are you sure?"

"Right now, I should be concentrating on hitting homeruns—hitting million-dollar verdicts, getting plenty of trial experience. I should be focusing on making a name for myself. The way I look at it, a lot of folks think I got lucky in the Medina case. That it was pure, unadulterated beginner's luck. That since that trial, I haven't tried any big, important cases. Some say I can't do it again."

"So you'd rather be trying cases than getting married?"

"I guess . . . I mean," stuttered Alex, "I'm just worried this is how it's going to be. She'll want me to do everything with her . . . be together . . . all the time . . . attached at the hip. Let's go to yoga, let's go grocery shopping; let's go look at wedding dresses, check out tuxedos, bridesmaid dresses, pick a honeymoon destination, the china, registries, work on the guest lists . . . all kinds of crap. And now, we even work together. I don't know, man. I'm seriously having second thoughts."

"You're not ready to throw in the towel, are you?"

"If this is how it's going to be . . . maybe . . . " shrugged Alex. "I mean, If I'm going to do this, then let's just have Bishop Salamanca marry us at my ranch. It's not even an hour away. It's got everything . . . and everybody can attend. On one side we got the beach. On the other side, there are the rolling savannahs with all the wild, exotic animals, and then we have the 10,000 square-foot main house. Hell, we could even set up air-conditioned tents outside, with one or two stages, waiters, bartenders *y ya*. We don't have to have all the other stuff . . . bridesmaids, mariachis, a string quartet to play at dinnertime, then the band. It's too much. Just a DJ, fruit punch, cake and be done. *Vámonos.*"

"Did you finish the landing strip?" asked Juan as he cleaned in and around Alex's table. "Last time we catered the fund-raiser for Chief Justice Jay Junco, you were in the middle of building it, right?"

"Yeah, that's right. It's finished. We can now land all kinds of small planes, even Learjets. The place has everything. We could have a real nice, simple, fun wedding there . . . but don't tell that to Gigi."

Juan was now refilling Alex's coffee cup. "Just go with the flow, Alex. Try to relax."

"I'm trying. Not only is she becoming increasingly difficult, but now with the new diet she just started . . . it's getting worse. Anyway, you know what they say . . . "

"It's her day," finished Juan as he used his hands to put quotation marks on the phrase, "and she gets whatever she wants, right?"

"*Ni modo*," said Alex, shrugging his shoulders. He was now standing, reaching for his wallet to pay the bill. The conversation had moved to the cash register area.

"Are you going to make your yoga class?" asked Juan, changing topics as he took the twenty from Alex's hand and opened the cash register.

"I don't know. But I do know this," said Alex, looking down on his clothes, shaking his head, "today is the last day you'll see me wearing Isla yoga pants, Hemp tank tops and Birkenstock clogs."

"What do you mean?"

"I'm gonna let her worry about the wedding," started Alex as he collected his change, "and I'm gonna get back to work and get on with life. I miss the courtroom. And I miss getting up and putting on a crisp suit every morning. I miss trading blows with opposing counsel. I want to stop thinking about that damned wedding because more I think about it, the less I want to go through with it."

Juan extended his hand to shake Alex's, one of the most, if not *the* most, loyal customer at the mom-and-pop restaurant. "Well, that sounds like a good plan."

Alex turned to leave. "I better put my foot down while I can. If not, it'll be too late. Next thing you know, she'll sign us both up for ballroom dance lessons."

"You have a great day," replied Juan, with a grin from ear to ear, "God bless you."

"Thanks, bro," said Alex. "I'll see you around."

CHAPTER 2

T HE LAW FIRM of Del Fuerte, Fetzer & Montemayor occupied the entire top floor of the Boca Chica Tower in Brownsville, Texas. Since leaving the Cameron County DA's employ, Gigi had joined Alex and his old law school professor, Michael Fetzer, in establishing the new law firm. Alex and Michael had decided it was time to close the Artemis Square location and find a larger space. The firm now focused on high-profile criminal defense and "bet-the-farm" type commercial cases. On occasion, after a quick partners' meeting, the trio would agree to represent a few, select plaintiffs in catastrophic injury cases, where justice demanded said involvement or if the case had the potential for establishing new precedent or bring about much-needed change in the community.

Since the partners were very selective in the types of cases they handled, this allowed Alex, Michael and Gigi to lead a care-free and laid-back existence. At the present time, the firm was handling the defense of three civil cases, along with the prosecution of one catastrophic injury case in which an entire family perished when their brand-new Hybrid Hummer overheated and spontaneously combusted as they waited in line to cross the Gateway Bridge from Matamoros into Brownsville. The firm was also prosecuting on behalf of the school district five major construction-defect cases that required joining multiple defendants, including general contractors, various engineering firms, architectural firms, all the subcontractors, site managers, suppliers and even one or two surveyors.

To Alex, one of the perks of being the principal name partner was having the oversized corner office with the best view into Mexico and the beach out on the eastern horizon. He had grown to love the new space: the stucco walls with the Monterrey finish, his wrought-iron desk with the beveled glass, the Equipal leather chairs with curved willow-stick backs. In and around the office, there were three large Botero replica sculptures made out of rare black Oaxacan clay from Doña Rosa's art studio. On the glossy Saltillo tile floor there were several Oaxacan wool rugs, and on the walls, along with the watercolor paintings brought from his last trip down to San Miguel de Allende, were his law license and a framed blowup of the jury note from the Harrow trial: "Judge, when can we start awarding punitive damages?" Signed, the jury foreman.

Although it was supposed to be a law office, the eclectic space now looked more like a small private museum. With collectors' magazines strewn about on the hand-carved designer coffee table in the sitting area, the space had slowly become a shrine to the Mexican-American War of 1847.

As per Alex's request, the landlord had outfitted the wall directly across from his desk with built-in bookshelves that Alex filled with artifacts and collectibles from the Battle of Chapultepec, a bloody clash in which six of Mexico's bravest teenage cadets had perished while defending their beloved country. To prevent the capture of the Mexican flag by American forces, Cadet Juan Escutia—believed to be thirteen at the time—had wrapped himself in the Mexican flag and plunged to his death from one of Chapultepec Castle's observation towers.

Since learning about the battle at a young age, Alex had become obsessed with that particular event in Mexican history. Having spent his formative years in Matamoros and having attended elementary school in the border town, Alex had studied and learned about the Mexican-American War from his fifth-grade teacher.

A year or so after his parents passed away, Grandpa César had taken Alex on a trip to Mexico City. The highlight of the trip had been a visit to Chapultepec's Castle, where Alex viewed frescos of all the cadets and toured the grounds. During that week-long trip, he'd learned that an Aztec emperor had first lived in his temple high on top of the hills in a forest known as Chapultepec. Then, centuries later, when the French occupied Mexico, Emperor Maximilian had built himself a lavish castle on top of the Aztec temple. In time, the Mexicans expelled the French and turned Maximilian's castle into a military academy.

For years, Alex had racked his brain with questions related to the event. Why had the young cadets stood their ground against a better trained, better armed, battle-hardened enemy? Seriously, did they think they could win? And why had they failed to heed General Nicolás Bravo's retreat orders? They were outnumbered a thousand to one! Were they on a suicide mission? What kind of individual would risk everything to defend his ideals, his country? And what in the name of God would possess somebody to embark on a suicide mission?

After the office move, it had taken Alex a couple of months to fill the distressed-looking bookshelves with his favorite antique books. The topics ranged from biographies for each of the six Niños Héroes to the *Chronicles of General Nicolás Bravo*, all the way to Presidente Benito Juárez's *Cinco de Mayo: Lessons Learned from the Battle of Puebla*.

With his newfound wealth, Alex had gone about collecting originals and copies of academy manuals, military instruction manuals, Juan Escutia's admission papers to the academy, the bayonet that Vicente Suárez used in combat, along with many other items: several hundred-year-old copper uniform buttons, an authentic military saber purportedly having belonged to eighteen-year-old lieutenant Juan de la Barrera and an old pair of scuffed military boots. Notwithstanding Gigi's protests, Alex had picked up the rare items during a trip to New York by way of an impromptu visit to Sotheby's, the auction house.

It was barely 11:00 A.M., but all Alex could do was obsess about the annoying wedding. And not only were the wedding bells clanging loudly inside his head, but he'd failed to show up for yoga class again. For some strange reason, since getting engaged to Gigi less than six months ago, it seemed time was moving faster as the wedding date approached. Already, his mother-in-law had started planning Gigi's numerous showers, and the wedding was still a year away. In his lifetime, Alex had never met a bride-to-be whose social calendar included weekly wedding showers being sponsored by the best friends from high school, the best friends from college, the best friends from law school, the best friends from work, not to mention the ones put together by family members, cousins, *tías, madrinas*, grandmothers, *vecinas* and even his in-laws' *comadres*.

"Mr. Del Fuerte?"

Alex looked up to see Astrid standing at his door.

"Yes, what is it, Astrid?"

"You won't believe who's on the phone, holding on line one."

"Gigi," countered Alex, "and she sounds pissed, right? Can't I have a second to myself?!!"

"Wrong, sir. It's Paloma Yarrington De Macallan."

Alex's eyes grew wide. "What . . . ? Why is she calling me? Did she say what she wants?"

"No, you want me to take a message?" asked Astrid.

"No, it's okay. I'll talk to her. Thanks." As Alex reached for the receiver, he signaled Astrid to close the door on her way out.

CHAPTER 3

ALEX ATTEMPTED TO pick up the receiver, but was unable to move. He continued staring at the red light blinking back at him. He wondered what it was that Paloma Yarrington De Macallan could possibly want. After all, it had been at least two years since their last chance encounter at Louie's Backyard. Paloma had come up to Alex in order to rub in his face the fact that she was now over him and happily married to the great Calvin Macallan.

Since that encounter, Calvin's dad, District Judge Walter Macallan, had been forced to resign in disgrace as information surfaced that the judge routinely hired undocumented workers. And not only had he violated all kinds of federal laws, but the former judge had somehow managed to have the County of Cameron pay the tab for all the help employed at his palatial home, his beach house and the family farm. Thus, at the end of the inquiry, Judge Macallan had been ordered to repay the monies to the county and the U.S. Treasury for all the payroll taxes he'd failed to withhold from the undocumented workers' earnings. In order to avoid a lengthy federal prison sentence, Macallan's hotshot lawyers—from the white-collar defense firm of Canales, Martinez & Rodriguez— had worked out a plea agreement with the feds whereby their client would surrender his bar license, repay the monies owed, pay a hefty fine and swear to never again seek public office.

Alex picked up the receiver and, pretending not to know who was holding on the line, graciously said, "This is Alejandro Del Fuerte, how can I help you?"

"Alex?" asked Paloma. She sounded nervous, as if she'd been caught by surprise.

"Yes. What can I help you with, Paloma?"

She cleared her throat. "This is quite embarrassing, but I'm calling you for two reasons. First, daddy asked me to say hi and ask you if you'd be interested in getting involved with a case dealing with some heirs to a Spanish land grant . . . there's billions in oil and gas royalties at stake."

"I don't know, Paloma," said Alex as he shifted uncomfortably in his leather chair. "If it's such a big case, I would think the trial lawyers would be lining up around the block waiting to jump in and get a piece of the action, no?"

"That I don't know. But daddy said these people are his constituents . . . that they need help. Apparently their last lawyer quit on them at the last minute . . . and they're looking to hire a new attorney. Daddy thought of you. He also said he owed you BIG, but he wouldn't elaborate. He said you knew what he was talking about and that he sent his regards. He also said this could be the case that put your new firm on the national map, a very important case."

"Well, let me ask you. Do you know who's on the other side? Who the heirs are suing or who's defending this thing?"

"No, but daddy said he could help you get something lined up with the plaintiffs . . . a meeting or something. I don't have all the details. I don't even know what the lawsuit's about. Anyway, he wanted to know if you were interested. All you have to do is say that you'll at least take a look at it," continued Paloma, the daughter of Lieutenant Governor Rene Yarrington, the maverick of Texas politics.

"Well," conceded Alex, "I would have to double-check with my partners. I can't bring a case into the firm unless all the partners are in agreement . . . see if it's something the firm wants to touch."

"When will you know?"

"I would have to meet with the plaintiffs first, and then my partners."

"Okay, sure. Makes sense."

Alex paused and wondered why Yarrington was sending him such a case. After all, Alex had never handled any real estate matters, much less a complicated land dispute probably dealing with all kinds of heirship and clouded title issues. Hell, his worst grades in law school had been in Real Property I and II. He'd bombed not one, but both of the courses.

"So," started Alex, "what was the other reason for your call? You said you were calling for two reasons."

"Eh, yeah," remembered Paloma. "This is rather embarrassing, but . . . " She paused. "I'm getting divorced."

"Oh," muttered Alex. He did not know what else to say, so all he could add was, "I'm sorry to hear that."

"I rushed into that marriage, Alex. That's what happened. You and I . . . " she stopped, mid-sentence.

"You and I what?" Alex had propped both feet on the windowsill and was looking toward Mexico. Out in the distance, he could make the outline of UTB, Brownsville's ever-expanding college campus.

She blurted it out, "I was on the rebound, okay. You and I had just broken up. I was miserable . . . then Calvin came around and, well . . . things happened. I should have known . . . Anyway . . . suffice it to say that now we're through. I'd like for you to handle my divorce. That's why I'm calling you."

"Whoa, whoa, whoa . . . slow down. Me, as your lawyer?"

"Yes, you as my lawyer. Look, there are no children. Only a house and furnishings . . . that's all. It's a simple divorce, except for the part where I'm supposed to get half of his retirement . . . I don't know how that works."

"I've never met a simple divorce, Paloma. Besides, I don't think Gigi will let me have any part of it. Hell, I don't even want to tell her I had this conversation with you. I'm gonna have to pass, I just can't. I'm sorry. I can recommend someone else. You can also file online, you know?"

"Okay," said Paloma, "can you just walk me through it?"

"I guess, ahem . . . " Alex was scratching his head, trying to find a way to get out of this one without looking like a complete jerk. After all, there was no reason to piss Yarrington off. As it now appeared, the Lieutenant Governor was the link to a potentially huge lawsuit.

"Gigi doesn't have to know. It'll be our secret."

"Secret? *Qué* secret, *ni qué* secret. Are you crazy? Why can't you just have one of your daddy's friends help you? He's got tons of lawyer friends. They'd probably love to do it for free to be in his good graces. It'll be so much easier. Let a pro do it. File it, serve Calvin, wait sixty days . . . and presto! Be done."

"No, Alex. I want to do this on my own. I don't want to involve my father. After our breakup, I just wanted to get married, put some distance between my dad and me. So I jumped into it, and it was a big mistake, but now I realize that I need to start solving my own problems."

"So you run to me, instead?"

"All I'm asking for is some guidance, okay? I too went to college, you know? I think I can figure out how to put together a simple divorce petition, Alex. Can't you send me a sample divorce?"

"Okay, okay. I'll have Astrid email you a divorce case. If you get stuck, you can call her and she'll walk you through it."

"Okay. I really appreciate it. So, what do I tell my dad? Are you interested in the case?" she pressed on.

He put down his pen, swirled around on his chair and threw his legs up on his desk this time. "I'll talk to him about it, sure. I can't commit to anything, though."

"He'll be in Raymondville tomorrow. I know he's going to meet with some of the plaintiffs at the old Rio Boot Company Restaurant. Do you want to meet him there?"

"What time?"

"Noon."

"I'll be there," Alex said, nodding his head. "I know the place. Best chicken fried steak south of San Antonio."

"Thanks, Alex, it means a lot to me, really," she said, sounding genuinely thankful. "I'll tell him you'll be there."

"Okay, bye." He was ready to end the call.

"Wait," said Paloma, "wait one second."

Alex rolled his eyes, "What is it?"

"Are you truly happy?" asked Paloma. "Do you really love Gigi?"

The question had come completely out of left field, and it stunned Alex. He thought about it for a second, but not wanting to discuss the specifics of his love life, he simply answered, "Sure, I'm happy. Who isn't?"

"Oh, I see."

"Listen, I have to go. I have another call. We'll get you the forms."

"Okay, Alex. Thanks."

"Bye."

CHAPTER 4

FIVE SECONDS LATER, the double doors to Alex's office flew wide open and slammed against the textured walls with a loud thud. It was Gigi, and she wanted to know why Alejandro Del Fuerte, her fiancée, the most sought-after bachelor north of the Rio Grande, not to mention a "Rising Legal Star" as recently featured in *Extreme Lawyer* magazine, had failed to show up at the yoga studio.

"Hey, baby," replied Alex in his cool and casual manner as he pretended to be on the phone with a client. "Have a seat, I'll be off in a minute," he whispered, covering the receiver with his left hand. It was all an act.

"By the way, how's the diet coming along?"

Gigi sat down directly across from Alex, arms and legs crossed, observing her fiancé's body language. Alex continued to pretend he was on the phone. After about five minutes, Alex finally hung up.

"What's going on, honey? Is everything all right, *preciosa*?"

"What's going on with you?" she asked, looking perturbed. "And the suit? Why are you all dressed up? Going somewhere?"

"Not particularly. It's just the suit I always keep here in the office," Alex explained as he pointed to the massive hand-carved armoire in the corner of his office.

She rolled her eyes, completely dissatisfied with the way the conversation was going. "Why weren't you in yoga class this morning?"

"Because," paused Alex, not knowing which answer to use on his fiancée. Either way it wouldn't matter. The prosecutor side of Gigi was about to rear its ugly head. "I don't want to go to yoga anymore. I want to come to the office and work. These last couple of months, I haven't been feeling particularly useful . . . if you know what I mean."

"No, I don't know what you mean. Why don't you explain it to me, Alex," she hissed.

"Look," said Alex, "I don't mind doing yoga on occasion, here and there, once a week, maybe. But you're turning me into a granola head . . . and I don't like it. I'm getting soft in the belly, Gigi. I need to work. I've always worked."

Judging by Gigi's facial expression, it was obvious she was struggling with Alex's newfound resolve. "What are you saying?"

"All I'm saying is that one of us has to work. Now that we're getting married, if you want to be a stay-at-home mom, that's fine. But I will be working. So, don't go nuclear on me if I can't make yoga class, okay? That's all."

She couldn't argue with that. After all, that's why she had fallen in love with Alex. He was not a mama's boy, like some of her past boyfriends. The last boyfriend Gigi had dated had been such a loser that the guy's mom had come by, begging Gigi to give her son another chance, while she was in the middle of a trial and doing closing arguments in a capital murder case!

"We have a trial in less than two months on the Hummer case, and I don't remember anything about it. Hell, I don't even know if discovery's complete." Alex paused, wondering if he should bring up another hot topic. He dove right in, head first. "Speaking of clients, Paloma Yarrington called. She wanted to hire the firm to handle her divorce."

"The firm?! I doubt it. She probably wanted to hire you . . . now that's very different. Did you take the case?" Gigi snapped.

"Of course not, pumpkin, but . . . "

"But what?"

"Well, I do have a lunch meeting with her father tomorrow. He's referring some clients to the firm. Could be a big case—we'll see."

"I thought you hated that guy," she said as she shifted in her chair. She was now looking away, out the large window, as if just waiting to dismiss Alex's made-up excuses for wanting to meet with the legendary legislator.

"It's business, honey. If it's a good case, and you and Michael agree we should take it, then we'll do it. I'm not going to do anything without first discussing it with the firm's partners. I don't even know what kind of case it is. All I know is that it involves a land dispute up the Valley, somewhere."

"Business, business, my ass! It's a trick, that's what it is. It's Paloma's way to sneak back into our lives, ruin our wedding and try to lure you away from me," she shot back.

"Why are you talking this way? You're overreacting," countered Alex as flashbacks of the Mexican soap *Odio y Amor* swirled around his head. Never in a million years did he imagine Gigi would be capable of throwing such a silly tantrum.

"You're right," Gigi agreed, flushed with embarrassment. "It must be the stress from the wedding. I'm sorry, Alex. Sometimes my mind just runs away with me. I'm sorry. It's my mom, she's driving me crazy. She now has me doing the cabbage soup diet . . . and . . . "

"You don't need to diet . . . I love you just the way you are. You need to take it easy, pumpkin." Alex signaled Gigi to come around and sit on his lap.

"Just promise me that you'll talk to me before agreeing to do anything with Yarrington, okay? *¿Me entiendes,* Alejandro?" They were touching foreheads, looking deep into each other's eyes. They kissed.

Alex pulled away and looking into her eyes replied, "*Claro,* baby. *Lo que tú quieras,* Mrs. Gisela María Del Fuerte. I won't move a finger without first checking with you. I promise."

The Rio Boot Company restaurant was located in a two-story, corner building that, for the last one hundred years, housed the Rio Grande Valley's most famous boot company. Located on the industrial side of Raymondville, the building had sat abandoned for fifteen years before Mr. and Mrs. Lencho Gómez picked up the place at a tax sale and converted it into a restaurant. In time, word spread that the Gómez's chicken fried steak—developed from an old *vaquero* recipe over two hundred years old—was the best this side of San Antonio. The dish was so famous that people drove in from all over the state just to have a bite of the succulent, dissolve-in-your mouth, hand-breaded beef cutlet.

When Alex walked into the busy restaurant, the owners immediately recognized him and ushered him to a private meeting room in the back, where Lieutenant Governor Yarrington and another person were already waiting. The place was packed with farmers from in and around the area, oil field workers and other cowboys in town for the rodeo.

Alex was led to a room in the back that was closed and off-limits to the general public. He pulled back some heavy, red velvet curtains separating the two dining areas and greeted the party inside.

"Alejandro Del Fuerte," said Yarrington with his trademark affable grin, "come here, son. Let me give you a hug. It's been what? Two years?" Yarrington was wearing pressed Wrangler jeans, riding boots, a western shirt and a belt with a silver buckle the size of a Texas 1015 onion.

"At least," said Alex.

"Let me introduce you," followed Yarrington and pointed to the man sitting to his left. "This is Mr. Oscar Santibáñez, a descendant of Don Arturo Monterreal, one of the first Spanish settlers to receive a royal land grant straight from the King of Spain."

"*Mucho gusto,*" said Alex in flawless Spanish. He shook hands with the fifty-something man wearing khaki pants, a rolled up flannel shirt and weathered Red Wing boots.

"*El gusto es mío,*" answered Santibáñez, getting up and reaching across the table to shake Alex's hand. "Are you hungry?" He invited Alex to take his place at the table.

Alex sat down and a young waitress appeared out of nowhere with a menu and a paper basket piled high with steamy hot chili cheese fries. They were topped with a dollop of sour cream and sprinkled generously with chopped chives. "Can I get you something to drink?"

"I'll have some iced tea," said Alex.

"Are you all ready to order or do you need a few minutes?" she asked the rest.

Yarrington took the lead. "We'll all be having your famous chicken fried steak, right guys?" he indicated, not really caring what their response would be. When Rene Yarrington picked up the tab, you and everyone else at the table ate what he ordered. No exceptions, *punto*.

Alex and Oscar nodded simultaneously and reached for the chili cheese fries.

"Alex," followed Yarrington as he took a swig of his iced cold Rolling Rock beer, "I wanted Oscar to meet you. You may not know this, but Oscar and his family have been major supporters and contributors of mine, and they've come to me with a little problem they need help with. That's why you're here." He took another swig. "Anyway, thanks for taking Paloma's call the other day. She mentioned that you had agreed to help her with her divorce. As a concerned father, I just wanted to thank you. And I want you to know that I'll do anything for you, son, whatever it is, okay? And I mean that from the bottom of my heart."

Alex understood perfectly. After all, not a year earlier Alex had saved Yarrington's thirty-year political career by throwing him a bone: he had given him a clandestine tape recording of Yarrington and others discussing their involvement in all kinds of wrongdoing. Had Alex turned the recordings over to the feds, Yarrington would surely be locked up in a federal prison by now.

"Don't mention it," said Alex, remembering where he had hidden his own copy of that tape. "So what kind of legal problems is Mr. Santibáñez facing?"

"I'll let Oscar explain the situation to you," replied Yarrington, reaching over for a serving of chili cheese fries.

"*Mira*, Alejandro," started Oscar, "it's very simple: we're the descendants of Don Arturo Monterreal. He was my great, great, great, grandfather . . . one of the first settlers in the area."

"Okay," replied Alex as he reached for his iced tea.

Oscar took a drink of his Carta Blanca and continued. "Now, the story gets a little complicated, but I'm going to skip all the boring details and summarize it for you, okay?"

"Go for it," agreed Alex.

"In 1990, we, I mean, my family . . . we hear that the Balli heirs—the descendants of Father Nicolás Balli—sued this New Yorker named Madoff because they discovered the guy failed to pay oil and gas royalties in accordance with all the leases that he had entered into with the Ballis in the early 1930s. As the case makes headlines, various groups of Balli heirs come out of the shadows and join the fray. Old man Madoff has since died, and even though there's money in his estate, realistically speaking, the estate cannot pay the hundreds of millions owed in back-due gas and oil royalties. However, the estate is willing to pitch in twenty million and call it a day. The money is there for whoever wants to take it. Madoff's lawyers made an offer of settlement. One group of Balli heirs decides to settle with Madoff and his estate, they split the loot and also force Madoff's estate to return to them the mineral interests in the lands. The other plaintiffs take a chance, go to trial, win big, but then the Texas Supreme Court says, 'Nope, you lose, you waited too long to sue, the statute of limitations ran out long ago and it's GAME OVER for you.'"

"Sure, it's the standard defense argument that maybe what the plaintiffs are saying is right, but they waited too long to sue, and now it's too late," Alex blurted out as he handed his empty appetizer plate to the waitress, now delivering the piping hot entrees with buttered Texas toast, mashed potatoes and organically grown green beans. "What we call an affirmative defense."

"Exactly. Anyway," continued Oscar, "we hear of the Balli lawsuit and we start doing our own research and we come to discover that the *gringo* that had our lands and eventually gave them to the church never really owned the mineral estate. He thought he did, but he never did. There were some mistakes made on his deeds, but, ultimately, he never owned the minerals under the surface estate. Monterreal's descendants continue to own it to this day. That's us."

"Are you sure?" asked Alex, completely amazed.

"Yep," replied Oscar as he put a piece of chicken fried steak into his mouth, gravy dripping out the corner. "The honest-to-God truth."

"So, then you think the church might own only the surface?"

"Exactly," said Oscar, his eyes lighting up.

"But the surface is only worth so much. The real money is in the oil and gas deposits, huge deposits, worth billions and billions of dollars," interjected Yarrington.

"And the leases, they're worth some money too," added Oscar. "There's a brand-new wind farm, and the telephone companies all have transmission towers on the property. There's even a shrimp farm and gas transmission lines . . . all these folks pay rent."

"Okay," said Alex, scratching his head, "but didn't you say those outfits only have surface leases?"

"Aha, and?" interjected Yarrington.

Alex took a swig. "The church would own the surface estate. I don't think Oscar would be entitled to any of that income, not from the wind farms, shrimp farms or telephone companies, anyway."

"You may be right," interjected Yarrington, "hadn't thought of that."

"Who are the producers on the property?" asked Alex.

"The big boys: Shell, British Petroleum, Exxon, Chevron, Valero."

"So, are you saying," started Alex, "that you and your family still own the mineral rights? Is that what you all are claiming?"

"Yep. The church needs to return all the billions it has received."

"Illegally, I might add," followed Yarrington.

"Since it only received the surface estate from McKnight, they can't be keeping the oil and gas royalties. Those belong to us, my family, Monterreals' descendants. And that's why we sued."

"You've sued the church?" asked Alex, suddenly feeling a bit uncomfortable.

"Oh, yeah," Oscar answered.

"Where was the lawsuit filed?"

"Next town over, Kingsville," answered Oscar, "in Kleberg County. It has been going on for three or four years now. Bishop

Salamanca has been running us ragged, trying to get us to quit, but he knows we're right. At this point in time, we don't care if he keeps the surface estate. We just want what's rightfully ours, the black gold under the surface and all the overdue royalties."

"See, Alex," added Yarrington, "the Santibáñez clan has had two attorneys involved, at different times of course, but they were no match for Bishop Salamanca and his minions."

"Are you without an attorney? Is that where this is going?" asked Alex, as he motioned the waitress to bring him a Bohemia beer. Things were starting to get interesting, and it was time to switch to beer.

"I'd hate to admit it, but that's the truth. We need your help."

"What happened to the attorneys handling the case?"

Oscar and Yarrington looked at each other, then reached for their beers, took a drink and waited to answer, seeing if the other would take the lead, trying to come up with a response that would appease Alex.

As the waitress brought Alex his beer, Oscar asked her to collect the empty plates and bring more beer. "Our first attorney, Todd Dugger, from Austin, died in a fatal highway crash. A trooper close to the investigation said he was text messaging, didn't see the eighteen-wheeler and rear-ended it with his Denali. A friend of mine, however, told me that they never recovered the guy's cell phone. I tell you what, the guy had the church's foundation on the ropes; he was on his way to a key hearing in Kingsville when it happened."

The waitress dropped by with the beers Oscar had ordered.

Oscar continued, "Yeah, it was totally unexpected. Anyway, the judge hearing the case at the time gave us six months to find another lawyer. You can just imagine, no one wanted to touch the case—it was against the Catholic Church—and besides the Balli heirs settling with Madoff, no heirs have ever won such reclamation lawsuits."

"Well, I've heard there's been some courtroom victories here and there, right? Didn't the folks that fought for the Barroso Tract win in Kleberg County?"

Yarrington jumped in. "Yes, they did. But the defendants appealed, all the way to the Texas Supreme Court, and the justices took the verdict away. As a matter of fact, my good friends on the Supreme Court have never allowed any plaintiff's verdict to stand. Except . . . "

"Except what?" asked Alex.

"No case has been like the Santibáñez case, where McKnight never owned the mineral rights and thus could not convey them to the foundation. This case is a different breed of animal. I think the heirs do have a shot . . . that's why Bishop Salamanca is really worried."

"But what about the church claiming they've adversely possessed the land all this time, and now it's theirs, the surface, all the minerals, the whole enchilada?" asked Alex. "The Supreme Court has a tradition of upholding that argument to send everyone home, packing."

Yarrington knew what Alejandro was saying was true. In Texas, a squatter could come on your land, sit there for several years, in an openly and notorious manner, and if you let that happen and chose to do nothing and you waited and twiddled your thumbs, then the trespasser became the new landowner. For years, the courts around the country had dictated, as a matter of public policy, that lands should stay productive. If you did not intend to make use of your land and just wanted to sit on it, you might as well hand it over to a squatter and let him put it to good use.

"True," admitted Yarrington, "but I believe Oscar's case is different because as the purported true owners of the mineral estate—and remember, the Santibáñez clan just found out the church may really own absolutely nothing—it hasn't even been but a couple of years."

"So, let me see if I got this right," followed Alex. "The whole case rests on the claim that the Santibáñez are still within the time to sue and defeat the church's claim of adverse possession, because this new information just recently came to light?"

"Precisely," Oscar chimed in. "After the Balli case ended the way it ended, we went back and started conducting our research, and that's when we discovered that McKnight never owned the mineral estate. Everybody thought he did, but no one bothered to check. Everybody just assumed that because McKnight's family had been on the land for over a hundred years, they owned everything. But they didn't. So, we got excited."

"Wait, wait, wait," declared Alex, "hold your horses. The way I see it, it wouldn't matter. The McKnights have adversely possessed both estates, the mineral and the surface, for close to one hundred years. They've been, there . . . all this time . . . squatting on those lands, anyway. So, when McKnight's last heir gave away whatever it was that he'd received—potentially both estates derived from his squatting ancestors—then it could be argued that he too gave away everything he'd received, right? Which is what the foundation has now."

"But see, we're prepared to rebut that," Oscar replied, "because the trespass was not open and notorious to us, or the world. We never even knew. There's no evidence anywhere that proves that we previously had any knowledge that the McKnights weren't the true owners of the mineral estate. That just recently happened, the trespass by the McKnights just became open and obvious to us, you see? We discovered this new information just a few years ago."

"Is that what the Austin lawyer was arguing, at least until he died?"

"Yes, Alejandro," said Yarrington sadly, "but then the second lawyer also went ashtray."

"Oh yeah, you said there were two lawyers."

Oscar took a swig from his icy Carta Blanca and continued the story. "Nobody wanted to jump in after Dugger died. We had all these questions. So, we had to go with the cheaper chicken."

"What's his name?"

"Brad Worley, from Florida . . . used to litigate old Spanish land grant cases over there. He seemed to know what he was doing, until he left us hanging with several defense motions for summary judgment pending. The court's going to rule on those in forty-five days and Worley never filed responses. We're under the gun here. This could be the end for our case."

Alex knew what the next question would be, but was still hopeful he could dodge the bullet. "Can you help the Santibáñez family, Alex?" asked Yarrington, point-blank, not giving Alex a chance to think of a proper response.

Alex took a swig and struggled to come up with a response. "I'd have to check with my partners first. Give me a week to think about it."

"What do you think?" asked Oscar. "Can we win?"

"Whoa, whoa, whoa, I don't know anything about the case," cried Alex. "I don't even know if this is something I want to get involved in. Just yesterday, I was trying to convince my fiancée to let Bishop Salamanca marry us. The guy's now a family friend, since my last donation to his capital campaign to remodel the Cristo Rey church."

"Oh," said Oscar, "that reminds me, the guy that shot Father Benito . . . Mago, he's a distant cousin of ours. He just went off the deep end, wanted to exert revenge on Salamanca himself."

"Of course," Yarrington mumbled, "since Worley left the plaintiffs holding the bag and ended up being committed to a mental hospital, tensions have been running high in the family. Poor bastard was so confused, he thought he was killing Salamanca."

Oscar looked at Yarrington and nodded his head in agreement. "True, but Margarito always had mental issues since coming back after three tours in Iraq, anyway. We all knew he came back one beer short of a six pack."

"So, one of your family members was responsible for the Cristo Rey shooting?" Alex asked, totally dumbfounded.

"Yeah, but we've never really claimed Mago as our cousin."

Yarrington and Oscar suddenly busted out laughing, filling the cozy party room in the back of the restaurant.

Driving in his 1965 vintage Shelby Cobra 427S back to Brownsville, Alex was already counting the endless stacks of hundred dollar bills in his mind. Mountains of cash like in the pictures he'd seen on television, when the DEA busted a stash house used for counting illicit proceeds, with floor-to-ceiling cardboard boxes full of dollars. He was thrilled by the images floating around in his head. Not only would he squeeze his clients for forty percent of the monies repaid to the plaintiffs by the defendant, but he would also try to get some of the minerals back. If the defendant could somehow be convinced to also give some of the minerals back, then there was a slight chance that Alex and his firm could also end up owning an interest in the oil and gas deposits under La Minita. Even a tiny fractional interest in the minerals, Alex very well knew, could be worth hundreds of millions.

Alex realized that selling the idea to his partners would take some work. For starters, there would be serious legal and ethical considerations. Was there enough time to knock out a proper response to the foundation's summary judgment now pending in court? Could his firm save the day, give the plaintiffs enough to avoid getting thrown out of court and let them live another day? Did he even know enough about the case to get involved this late in the game? Could he get up to speed, particularly with a wedding looming on the horizon, not to mention the Hummer case, and having to review many documents, a lot of them in Spanish, relating to the Santibáñez suit?

Alex stepped on the gas, and the eight-cylinder engine roared. He was tearing up the highway, doing one hundred miles an hour as he made mental notes and relived the lunch meeting with Oscar Santibáñez and Rene Yarrington. He could already hear Michael asking about Yarrington's involvement. Would the lieutenant governor want a cut of the pie, in the event Del Fuerte, Fetzer & Montemayor recovered something for the plaintiffs? Was it even ethical to share fees or part of the recovery with a non-attorney?

Alex knew that even though Yarrington had never broached the topic at the lunch meeting, if the plaintiffs hit a home run and things went their way, ultimately Yarrington would be expecting something, *un regalito*. It was implicit in his invitation to look at the case, and, of course, it was illegal as hell. But Yarrington probably felt that he was helping a constituent, the constituent had a lawsuit that could make the lawyer a bunch of money and at the end, the lawyer could show some gratitude, or appreciation. If there was a favorable outcome, the reward would come in the form of a gift or cash.

Alex was now doing 125 miles an hour. He turned the volume up as Foreigner's "Urgent" came blasting out of the radio.

How did the politicians always manage to have their hands in the cookie jar? Alex wondered. And why did South Texas appear to be the favorite playground of such political animals, including a few crooked lawyers? The latest scandal had involved a guy who'd held himself to be a lawyer, owned a law firm, collected millions in referral fees from other lawyers and even claimed to possess law licenses in Mexico and the U.S.A. At the end of the day, it was revealed the guy had never even attended law school, much less taken a bar exam.

The biggest slap in the face, at least in Alex's opinion, was that the impostor, for twelve straight years, had contributed to all the judicial races from the lower trial courts all the way to the Texas Supreme Court. And not one, not one judicial candidate or a sitting judge had stepped forward and made any effort to return the tainted monies, monies that everyone knew the con man had obtained illegally.

Thinking about this and other legal shenanigans, Alex knew that jumping into the Santibáñez case would necessarily mean that Yarrington would get a cut. Maybe the way to deal with the lieutenant governor could be to simply give the politician the middle finger. Just thank him for the referral and tell him that the law did not allow for a kickback, so sorry, so sad. And if the guy insisted, and there was no way to avoid the inevitable, Alex could meet Yarrington in Vegas, see a showcase fight, have a great dinner and then head to the casinos. Alex would buy a million dollars in poker chips with his own money, suddenly call it a night, then turn over the chips at the blackjack table to his guest and allow Yarrington to keep playing his hands. If Yarrington wanted to quit while he was ahead or wanted to hang on to the million, then he could just go cash his chips. Barabim-baraboom, case closed. No one would ever suspect a thing.

But the biggest issue, the major issue, as far as Alex was concerned, was taking a case that ultimately was going to pit him against a family friend, Bishop Salamanca. Not to mention that Gigi had always dreamt of Salamanca officiating her wedding. This was not going to be an easy sell, by any means.

Right outside Harlingen, Alex downshifted and brought his shiny blue racehorse to under sixty miles an hour. He picked up his cell and put a phone call in to Michael. It was time to start lobbying the partners.

After three rings, the wise old professor answered. "Alex?"

"Yes, it's me. Just heading to the office, finished having a very interesting meeting. Want to hear about it?"

"Sure, who did you meet with?"

"Lieutenant Governor Yarrington. Guess what he wanted?"

"Can't imagine, do tell."

Alex cleared his throat. "Wants to hook us up with a major case."

"Really, what kind?"

"The kind we could make new law with, even right a wrong. It's the kind of case you like, plus we can make a bunch of money," explained Alex.

"Can't be that simple, I'm sure. Does the dog have any fleas?" asked Fetzer. "I never met one without 'em . . . there's got to be something wrong with the case . . . "

"We would be taking over, it's been touched by two others."

"No, Alex. Why do you want to go there? You know I don't like those cases. What if the other attorneys already blew some deadlines. I don't like to step in and clean up after other people's messes."

"What if I told you there are billions at stake in oil and gas royalties, and valuable lands, up to a million acres," explained Alex, as he inflated the numbers for effect.

"What are we talking about? A land grant case? Those cases are like black holes. They'll suck you up, bleed you dry and then spit you out, wasted, in tattered shreds, nothing left. Of course, they promise fame and riches. I wouldn't do it."

Alex did not like the way the conversation was going. "But this case is different. We've found a loophole, a back door, if you will, to survive the challenges."

"I don't know, but in fairness, you can bring it up at the partners' meeting on Monday," replied Michael. "We can discuss it, and then we can all vote on it. Anyway, I've got to go. There's a meeting of the board of directors in twenty minutes at the South Texas Historic Museum. We're discussing the addition of the Carlota Petrina Kennedy wing."

"Who was that?"

"A famous painter from New York. She retired down here in the Valley and continued painting up until the day she died. Not too many folks have heard about her. We just received a fabulous donation of over two hundred oil paintings from one of her heirs. Tremendous historic value—not so much on the artistic side . . . her paintings don't do anything for me, if you want to know the truth. To each his own."

Seeing that Professor Michael Fetzer had other things on his mind, Alex quickly said, "Okay, we'll talk later. Think about the case."

"I will," replied Michael, "I will."

CHAPTER 5

THE PARTNERS' MEETING had been scheduled for 11:00 A.M. that Monday morning. Professor Fetzer and Gigi were sitting in the large conference room by the time a clean-shaven Alex walked in, dressed in a neatly tailored, navy blue suit, Starbuck's coffee cup in hand. Betty, the firm's office manager, was also present; she was charged with taking notes at the meeting, then writing up the minutes and circulating them afterwards, for any corrections or changes.

"Good morning," said Alex, greeting the threesome.

"Morning," answered Michael. The sixty-year-old professor was wearing a Hawaiian shirt, beige linen pants and summer leather sandals.

"Good morning, Mr. Del Fuerte," indicated Betty.

"Hey," muttered Gigi, kind of disappointed and knowing full well what the meeting was going to be about. Not only did she not want to be there, but she was famished and ready to go home and eat lunch. She was snacking on celery and carrot sticks.

"Okay," started Alex, nodding to Betty, "today's date is July 15, 2007, present at the partners' meeting is Michael Fetzer, Gisela Montemayor and Alejandro Del Fuerte, along with Beatriz Contreras, the corporation's secretary. What's there to discuss? Anything on the agenda?"

"How are we doing on the Hummer case, Alex? Are we ready to take it to trial?" Michael asked.

35

"No. I'm going to need more time to be ready on this one. I'm afraid I've been playing hooky these last couple of months. There's no way I can try this case in two months," said Alex.

"At least you're honest," said Fetzer. "I guess you've been busy with the wedding plans, is that it?"

"Huh, yes, that's it," replied Alex as he glanced over at Gigi.

"How much time do you think we need to get ready to try the case?" the professor followed. "Can we get a continuance?"

"I'm sure," said Alex. "We're in front of a good judge."

"Have we asked for one before?" wondered Fetzer.

"No." Alex leaned back in the leather chair and looked up at the ceiling. "I can probably delay it for another six months. I want to say we still need to take the three remaining experts' depositions."

"Alejandro," interrupted Gigi, sounding antsy, "did you meet with Lieutenant Governor Yarrington? Did he have a case to refer to the firm?"

"You met with Yarrington?" asked Michael, sounding surprised, pretending he did not know a thing. "I want to hear all about this."

"Well," Alex cleared his throat. "Paloma called wanting the firm to help her with her divorce. I said no, of course." He looked over at Gigi and continued, "As an afterthought, and much to my surprise, she mentioned that Yarrington was looking for a plaintiff's firm to help out in a land dispute, up the Valley."

Michael's ears perked up. "Oh, yeah? What does it involve?"

"Whatever it is," Gigi interjected, "it can't be good, not if it's coming from Yarrington."

"Have you two talked about this already?" asked Michael.

Gigi started to explain, "Alex told me about Paloma's call and his meeting with Yarrington. We talked about it over the weekend."

The truth was Alex and Gigi had fought about it the entire weekend, but Alex refused to give more details on Yarrington's referral, stating that it merited the three partners' discussion on Monday. Things had gotten so heated and ugly back at the Contessa di Mare that Alex had stormed out of the penthouse and gone to sleep in his sailboat, *El Valiente*, moored over at the Sea Ranch Marina.

"Well, I want to hear about it," followed the professor. "Besides, I believe you would probably be a little biased, don't you think, Gisela?"

"Hey, I'm a partner, just like you and Alex," countered Gigi, "and I have a say so, just like everyone else in this room."

"I agree," conceded Michael, "but shouldn't we hear what Alex has to say first . . . be at least open-minded? See what the case involves?"

Alex gave Gigi an icy stare and waited for her reaction.

"Okay, fine. Tell us, Alex, what does the case involve?" asked Gigi, crossing her arms.

"It's a group of plaintiffs with claims to a million-acre tract of land stolen from under their noses, and now they're trying to get it back."

"Has the case been filed?" asked Michael, continuing to pretend this was the first time he'd heard about the new litigation.

"Yes, the case was filed in Kleberg County . . . in Kingsville, to be exact. This tract of land extends into four coastal counties, Cameron, Willacy, Kleberg and Nueces. The plaintiffs could have filed anywhere, really. I guess they thought since Kingsville houses a state university, perhaps the jury pool would be better," explained Alex.

"Why would you want to try a case in that po-dunk town?" Gigi asked. "It's in the middle of nowhere. There are no major airports nearby. You and the professor will have to drive back and forth, every day. That's two hours, each way."

Alex was shaking his head; he was ready with his answer. "Why would we travel back and forth? We just stay in town, there's a new Comfort Inn next to the highway, right next to a brand new Chili's."

"So, you're going to live in a hotel for an entire month? Or however long it takes to try this case? Hell, the Balli case, in case you've forgotten, took three months to try!" clarified Gigi.

"Why are we getting ahead of ourselves?" interjected Michael.

"That's right," replied Alex, "we don't even know if there'll be a trial. At this point, with a pending motion for summary judgment, it's hard to tell."

In legal parlance, a motion for summary judgment was nothing more than a tool typically employed by trial lawyers to try and get the other side kicked out of court, without having to go through a full-blown trial.

"Who are the plaintiffs suing?" asked Gigi. "Who's the target?"

"The Agnus Dei Foundation," mumbled Alex.

Gigi's jaw dropped to the ground. "You mean, Bishop Salamanca's diocese? But he's supposed to marry us, at the ranch . . . you, yourself . . . said so!"

Alex shook his head, "Things have changed, baby. I'm sorry."

Michael was enjoying the back-and-forth immensely. "How's the Agnus Dei Foundation tied to Salamanca's diocese?"

"The Catholic Diocese of the Southern Coastal Counties is the majority shareholder of the Agnus Dei Foundation, which controls all those lands," explained Gigi.

"Lands rich in oil, gas and other minerals," added Alex while grinning, "not too far from El Caudillo."

"Oh, really?" asked Michael. "Then that's right next to your ranch, isn't it?"

"Just up the roadway," clarified Alex. "La Minita's southern boundary abuts with my Caudillo's northern boundary. We're neighbors."

"And these are the folks that Yarrington wants us to sue, can you believe it?" scowled Gigi as she threw her arms wide open and then slammed her fists on the marble conference table. "It's got D-I-S-A-S-T-E-R written all over it. Besides, Alex," she continued, glaring at him, "you, yourself, admitted that you came close to failing real property in law school. If I recall correctly, you made D's in both courses. Face it. The subject is just not your forte. Why would you want to touch this case?"

Michael looked at Gigi. "Well, let's allow Alex finish with his presentation. Or better yet, what's the bottom line? What happens if the heirs get their lands back, assuming that would even be possible?"

"Let me answer your question this way, professor. Since the foundation received La Minita, they've been dutifully wiring to the Vatican their share of the pie to the tune of twenty-five million a month. That's part of their cut just from the oil and gas producers on their lands. You do the math . . . we would get 40% of any recovery."

"How much are the lands worth in today's dollars, knowing that there's huge oil and gas deposits under most of the tract?" asked Michael.

"And now there's a brand-new wind farm, too, along with all the major telephone companies holding leases, including major gas transmission companies. I'd say the tract is worth about five or ten billion . . . possibly more."

Betty was writing furiously on her yellow pad, trying to keep up with the mile-a-minute exchange.

"And we'd get 40% of that?" Michael asked.

Alex smiled and looked at Gigi. "Yep. We're talking generational wealth here. We'd be set for life. More money than you, or I, or our heirs, can shake a stick at. Maybe our fee could come out of the mineral estate as a portion of the overall recovery, which would be the oil and gas under five hundred thousand plus acres, or maybe it could be cash, or both. Not bad for a day's work."

Alex suddenly remembered a highly unusual case in which the astute lawyers had included in their fee agreements language that they were to get a percentage of "any recovery, whatsoever, from their clients' land grant lawsuit." The lawyers—even though their cut had been four million in cash—had also managed to bamboozle their own clients when they brought to the clients' attention the "any recovery" language and finagled their way to an additional 40% of all the lands, including the minerals, that the defendant had returned to the heirs.

Gigi cleared her throat. "And what happened to the previous lawyers that handled the case, Alex?"

Alex turned to face Michael. "The first attorney, Dugger, apparently had the foundation on the ropes, but was involved in a highway accident as he drove to a key hearing in the case."

"Is he okay?" asked the professor.

Alex looked at Gigi, then Betty and finally answered. "No, he died, after he rear-ended an eighteen-wheeler illegally parked in the middle of the highway."

"And the next attorney, Alejandro, please tell us what happened," ordered Gigi.

"A guy from Florida named Worley took over but had to be committed to a mental institution. The pressure got to him."

"Any other problems?" asked Michael.

"A relative of the plaintiffs, a guy named Margarito . . . went off the deep end, thought he could take vengeance on Bishop Salamanca, but instead shot and killed Father Benito in the middle of Mass at Cristo Rey. The guy had never been right in the head . . . had been deployed too many times to Iraq."

"So, what's going on with the case at the present time?" continued Michael.

Alex got up and walked over to the window. He looked out into the distance. "There's a pending hearing on the defendant's motion for summary judgment. If no attorney jumps in and files some kind of response for the Santibáñez family, then the case will be over. Done. Finito. Lights out."

Michael quickly followed up. "Well, but tell me, how come no other firm wants to touch it? There should be lawyers dying to take a crack at the foundation, don't you think?"

"You would think, right?" asked Alex.

Gigi jumped in. "I'll tell you why nobody wants to touch it. Because you'll either end up DEAD, BROKE, EXCOMUNICADO or LOCO in a mental hospital somewhere. Plus, in our case, you would be suing the same bishop who is supposed to be marrying us, and, don't forget, the supremes will take the verdict away, even if you win!"

Alex jumped to his feet and started beating his chest, trying to inject a little humor into the meeting. "*¡Los supremes me hacen los mandados!*"

Michael stepped in. "It makes sense. The Republicans on the Supreme Court will never let us keep such a verdict. First, because they are Republicans—in case you already forgot—three of the justices got elected with insurance lobby money. The other four justices were bought and paid for by the oil and gas industry. And the remaining two puppets were appointed by our illustrious Republican governor."

"Anyway, the other argument the High Court might use to strip us of the verdict would probably be the 'public policy' argument. Don't you think so, Alex?"

"I suppose" muttered Alex.

The professor carried on. "Imagine the economic instability it would create, not only in Texas and other oil-producing states, but on Wall Street and in Washington, not to mention the dangerous precedent for heirs all across the Southwest whose ancestors may have owned a Spanish land grant."

Alex hadn't thought of that. "What do you mean?"

"Well, Alex," lectured the professor, "if we start giving lands back to the rightful heirs, what happens to the oil and gas companies? The railroad companies that own tracks on the land? The wind farms and telephone companies? The utilities? Should they repay the billions that went to owner Y, instead of rightful owner X? And if they have to repay, what would that do to their profitability? To their stock? To Wall Street? What if heirs up and down the U.S.-Mexico border decided to start suing all over the place . . . they all want their lands back."

"It's the floodgates-of-litigation argument . . . I get it," replied Alex. "Not a very popular topic in state legislatures or Washington, for that matter."

"Exactly," added Gigi as she finished texting her mother and explained there was a new problem: Alex's crazy scheme. "I rest my case."

Alex then looked at Gigi. He had a frown on his face, but remained quiet. He had to admit, those were some good arguments. Besides, all that economic instability could possibly lead to civil unrest.

Alex decided it was time to abort the topic. "And you, what did you say a minute ago, Gigi? You mean you no longer want to get married in Greece? Is that what I just heard? You now want to get married at El Caudillo?"

"Maybe. I've been thinking about it." Gigi shrugged her shoulders and looked out her hands. She needed a manicure. "Since I know how much it means to you to have your grandpa attend . . . I've been thinking."

Michael and Betty were looking at each other, enjoying what had the makings of a potential truce.

"Look," continued Alex, "let's all sleep on it, revisit the issue next week and then take a vote. In the meantime, we can do some research: see if it's even worth getting involved with the case. What do you all say?"

"I second that," Michael blurted out.

Alex looked at Gigi, waiting for some kind of response. She was biting her lips, not saying much, arms crossed.

"The two of you can do all the research you want!" Gigi said. "I will have no part of this."

"Okay, then, I'll do the research," Alejandro sighed, mocking Gigi. "This meeting is adjourned. We'll visit the issue next Monday. In the meantime, I'll call opposing counsel on the Hummer case and start lining up the experts' depositions. Anything else?"

"Yes, there's something else," said Gigi. "The wedding's off, Alex!" She took her three karat emerald-cut engagement ring and tossed it across the conference table at Alex.

"Why?" asked Alex, totally surprised.

"Because you're helping Paloma with her divorce," Gigi scolded Alex. "You emailed her the forms and even told her how to fill them out. I thought you said you were not going to get involved? You lied to me!"

"What? Who told you that?"

"I've got my sources."

"No, you went through my emails. That's how you found out!" snapped Alex.

"Whatever, it doesn't matter."

Alex was too embarrassed to carry on in front of Michael and Betty, so all he could mutter was a soft, "Okay, fine, whatever."

CHAPTER 6

L A PAMPA RESTAURANT was the only authentic Argentinian steak house in all of the Rio Grande Valley and the only place in all of South Texas where one could find a wine list with more than five thousand labels to choose from. The wine list was almost as thick as the Yellow Pages directory. After a lifetime of fast food restaurants like Taco Bell, Brownsville had finally been blessed by the upscale-cuisine gods. All courtesy of an Argentinian family living in Mexico City, but now fleeing their adopted country's increasing insecurity, narco-violence, kidnappings and flagrant corruption.

The swanky restaurant also happened to showcase a dimly lit cigar room tucked discreetly in the back, where patrons could relax, sample a variety of wines and smoke their favorite cigars: Partagas, Macanudos, Romeo & Julietas and even real Cuban Cohibas, disguised as Dominican cigars.

The steak house was a lunch crowd favorite, and Alex had decided to hold the next partners' meeting there, promptly at six-thirty. The plan was for Alex to convince Gigi to quit dieting for one day, pump her full of her favorite wine, have her reconsider going through with the wedding and also bring her around on the Santibáñez lawsuit.

He needed to find a way to make Gigi understand this case guaranteed their financial independence for many, many generations to come. The case offered untold fame and fortune. And Alex wanted it, bad. Gigi just needed to come around. Who cared that they knew Bishop Salamanca. Sure they wanted the bishop to marry them, but it was not like they played Bunco with the guy every weekend. Any other priest would do. They were not that close.

Over the weekend, Professor Fetzer had emailed Alex that he was inclined to give the "nod" to the Santibáñez case, as long as Alex took the lead and was ready to take on eighteen-hour work days. As far as Michael was concerned, meaningful concessions also had to be made. And Alex was prepared to concede, not everything, but some points—whatever got the deal done. It had always been that way: Michael had a knack for helping the partners find the common ground, a compromise to give all sides a bit of what they wanted. The professor was the voice of reason.

Alex was already sitting in his favorite booth, enjoying the smoky aromas coming from the open-view kitchen and salivating over the appetizers he had ordered: *empanaditas*, wild game pâté and mushroom caps stuffed with chorizo de Córdoba. He was drinking a glass of Los Arcos Malbec, slowly sipping and savoring the earthy hints of lavender, vanilla, almonds and figs, while thinking about the Santibáñez lawsuit. As a matter of fact, that had been almost the only thing he'd thought about for the whole week . . . the lawsuit and Gigi, of course. Yarrington had been right: the Santibáñez lawsuit could easily put his firm on the national radar. In fact, the entire nation would be watching: Washington, the Texas legislature, the oil and gas companies, the Catholic Church and even Wall Street.

There was a large flower arrangement in the middle of the table, purposefully displayed as a peace offering to his fiancée. They were orchids of the Magnificat variety, Gigi's favorite. Considered by world connoisseurs rarer than yellow diamonds, Alex had his investigator Romeo spend all of Friday morning making calls to all the greenhouses in Puebla, Mexico, in order to find the orchids. Finally, after several hours of chasing leads and six thousand dollars later, Romeo managed to score five dozen of the Magenta-colored flowers. The delicate find had been quickly flown from Central Puebla to Mexico City, then to Houston and finally to Brownsville. Each orchid carefully packed in individual, auto-refrigerated, sealed mini-containers.

Michael and Gigi showed up together, and Alex waved them to come over to the corner booth in the back. The pair walked toward the back of the restaurant, and Gigi stopped and said hi to her old boss, the county's DA, having lunch with his deputy chief and felony chief prosecutor at a table nearby. After about two minutes of catching up, Gigi joined Michael and Alex at their table.

"¿Y esas flores?" Gigi asked with a warm smile as she gave the flower arrangement a look of approval. She was wearing a chic, strapless knit dress with a flowing skirt and cute T-strap sandals with half-inch heels. Her legs looked fantastic, and she knew it. "They're gorgeous." She now appeared to be in much better spirits.

"Like you, my love," Alex remarked as he patted the black leather booth, "please sit down, take a load off, right here next to me."

Soon, Alex was sitting in the middle of the crescent-shaped booth, with Michael to his left and Gigi to his right. His thigh was slightly touching Gigi's.

"I asked the waiter to put a bottle of Cristal on ice for you. It's ready . . . just say the word," said Alex, looking into Gigi's almond-colored eyes.

Michael interrupted and said, "You don't mind if I pour myself some red wine, do you, Alex?"

"Here, let me get that for you," said Alex, reaching over for the Malbec. He then proceeded to pour the professor a generous glass. As Alex and Michael drank from their glasses, Gigi started looking at the menu. Alex then signaled to the waiter to bring out the bottle of champagne for Gigi.

In an instant, the waiter, dressed in Gaucho pants, white shirt with ruffles, leather vest and riding boots, showed up at the table and popped open the bottle of champagne. Alex motioned the waiter to go ahead and serve Gigi; the champagne was for her, all of it, till the last drop.

Gigi took a sip, smiled and said, "What's the occasion, Alex? What are we celebrating?"

"I've decided," started Alex, "that I want to get married in Greece. Why not? I'll find a way to get grandpa there. He always wanted to travel to Europe, never had the chance. This might be the last trip he makes. What the hell!"

Michael was smiling as he dug into the *empanadas* and the wild game pâté. He was happy to see his pupil willing to concede an important point in an effort to get the negotiations off the ground.

"Why are you being so nice?" asked Gigi.

Alex paused, gathered his thoughts and let out a sigh. "Because I love you. And I want to marry you, and I want to make you happy. And if getting married in Greece is what makes you happy, then I can put my own wants on hold, for a little while at least, and put a smile on your face. *No me cuesta nada.* I want to be nice, that's all. Besides, someday we'll be able to take our kids to the place where it all started."

"That's so sweet, don't you agree, Professor?" asked Gigi.

"Sounds like progress to me," said Michael as he poured himself more wine. "Now you have to give something up, Gigi."

"I'm off my diet, for the night. Does that count?" she asked.

"I don't know. What do you think, Michael?" followed Alex as he looked at his gorgeous fiancée.

Gigi knew the professor was right. The flowers, the champagne, the food, the restaurant, were just the vessel to get the parties to relax and start talking, thinking, conceding, moving forward and, ultimately, putting aside their differences. She knew this because her father, Don Agustín Montemayor, had been a very successful *agente aduanal*, a Mexican custom broker, who'd made a fortune servicing clients all over Mexico. Years later, Gigi would recall her dad boasting that almost all of his business deals with major clients, such as Pemex, Cementos Cruz Azul, Teléfonos de Mexico and Grupo Alfa, had been inked at a dump of a cantina somewhere.

Gigi allowed the waiter to refill her champagne flute. She took another sip and finally spoke. "I know you want to talk about the Santibáñez case, Alex. As far as I'm concerned, I don't want to touch it. If you and the professor want to do it, so be it. I will not work on it. However, if you're going to do it, I just ask that you promise me two things."

"What are they?" asked Alex.

"You need to cap how much money you're going to sink into it. I want to nail that figure down, right now. If you hit that mark, and you've blown your budget, but you realize you need more money, then you will pull the plug. The firm's out. No excuses."

"What do you mean?"

"What I mean, Alex, is that I'm not going to stand on the sidelines and let you throw money away. These cases are expensive, and they can break the bank. I'd hate for you to lose it all."

"That's not going to happen," said Alex, "but anyway, I can live with that. What do you have in mind? Half a million?"

She laughed. "One hundred thousand. That's it."

"C'mon! Just to do a new survey of the entire property we'll probably blow fifty thousand. I need at least three hundred."

"Two hundred, Alex. That's it."

"We'll make it work with two hundred," said Michael. "We'll just have to watch every penny."

"What else?" asked Alex as he looked over at Michael. "What's your second request?"

Fetzer poured himself and Alex another glass of wine.

"Like I said before, don't ask me for help. I won't cover a hearing, do research or even make an appearance. I don't want any part of it," explained Gigi.

Alex reached for the last *empanada*. "Okay, is that it?"

"No," said Gigi, "one last thing."

"Let me hear it," said Alex, "what is it?"

"After you and the professor get poured out and get sent home packing with your tails between your legs, after the court entertains the foundation's motion for summary judgment . . . "

"Okay, that's not going to happen, but if it did," Alex interrupted her, midsentence, "then what?"

Gigi finished her second glass of champagne, reached over for Alex's lit cigarette out of the ashtray, took a drag, thought about what she was about to say and finally blew the smoke away from the table. "You will sell the Shelby Cobra, the Harley and the sailboat. I don't want to be a widow a year into my marriage because my husband died while taking one of his toys out for a spin."

"No," replied Alex, yanking the cigarette from Gigi's hand and putting it out in the ashtray. "Not the Shelby, that's my baby. Anything else, but not the Shelby, please. Look, I'll get rid of the motorbike and the sailboat, and I'll take ballroom dancing classes, even yoga, whatever. Twice a week, three times a week, but not my car. That's nonnegotiable, I mean it."

"Okay, then," Gigi said, "it's settled. You'll sell the sailboat and the bike, and I'll sign us up for dancing lessons at the college. And I expect you to be at the yoga studio in the morning."

"Wait, wait," said Alex, "the ballroom lessons would be to learn the waltz or tango for the wedding, okay? But the yoga? I need to work, I can't do it more than once a week. We've had this discussion before, Gigi."

"Fine."

Michael raised his glass. "Well, that deserves a toast." Gigi and Alex joined him and raised their glasses, too.

CHAPTER 7

AFTER THE EXQUISITE meal, Alex figured he'd head to the Sea Ranch Marina to swing by his sailboat and pick up his laptop, along with some of his personal items. Now that there had been a settlement reached by the parties, Gigi wanted her fiancée to move back home, ASAP. While they were eating, she'd hinted that she wanted to thank him in a "special" way.

The trio had left in separate cars, with Gigi driving a sleek, red Saab turbo. She headed back to the office to pick up a file she wanted to review to get ready for a hearing coming up in federal court. Since it was still early—only 8:45 P.M.—Michael got in his Range Rover and headed to the local Academy Sporting Goods store to try to find some hot fishing lures he'd heard about. The latest fishing report indicated that the snook were biting all along the ship channel, but only on the purple rubber worms with squiggly orange tails, and not on fresh mullet, squid, shrimp or anything else, for that matter. So, it was vital to find a bag of the elusive Triple Ripple lures to be armed and ready for the weekend.

Alex drove east on Rubén Torres Boulevard, feeling happy about the way things had turned out at the partners' meeting, and proceeded to light up a León Jiménez cigar. He blew a big cloud of smoke, put the radio on and was about to start humming along to Bread's "Everything I Own," when his cell phone started vibrating. He looked down at the screen, but there was no number, only the words "Private Call" flashing.

"*Bueno,*" answered Alex.

"Alejandro Del Fuerte," said the voice, barely audible, "is that you, the attorney?"

"Yes, who's this? Who's calling? Speak up," yelled Alex into the cell as he pulled his Shelby Cobra into a Stripes parking lot and turned down the radio's volume. He turned the ignition off. "Yes, this is Alejandro Del Fuerte. Who's calling?"

"This is Bishop Salamanca," came the reply. "Do you have a minute, Alex?"

Alex was startled, his mind started racing and he drew a blank. All he could mumble was "*Ah, sí* . . . I'm sorry, I didn't recognize the voice, Bishop. I was just on my way home, couldn't hear very well. But I can hear you okay now. Go ahead."

"Alex, son," said Salamanca, "I heard you were in Raymondville. How was your visit?"

Alejandro puffed on his cigar a couple of times, thinking of an appropriate answer. Could Salamanca be on to him? "Fine, Bishop. Just visiting old friends, playing catch-up, you know."

"I see," said Salamanca, clearing his throat. "Anyway, I was looking at my calendar for next year, and I see here there's a request from your office, asking me to say Mass at your wedding. I see here it's slated for the month of June. Is that still on?"

"Ahem," stuttered Alex, "there's been a change of plans, Bishop Salamanca. My fiancée now wants to marry in Greece. Looks like we're not getting married here in the States, after all."

"Oh, okay. Well, as your friend, Alex . . . and I mean this from the bottom of my heart . . . if plans should change, let me know. Do you want me to find you a Catholic priest over in Greece to marry you and Gigi?"

"Ah, no, sir. That won't be necessary. But of course, well, you know women. I guess if she changes her mind, again, I'll be calling you, I guess . . . if you don't mind . . . to come marry us . . . "

"Anything for a good friend and generous donor, Alex. Believe me, my diocese really appreciates your generous support, son. Anyway, as your loyal and faithful friend, Alex . . . and I know this is not any of my business . . . but I genuinely care for you, so I must say it. I'd stay away from Oscar Santibáñez and his crazy schemes. That guy can't be trusted . . . Just be careful, okay?"

Alex's heart started pounding faster, sweat beads forming on his forehead. He tried to gather his thoughts as he took a couple of nervous hits from the moist torpedo-shaped cigar. "I will, sir. I will. Thanks for the heads up."

"And Yarrington . . . that's another one you need to keep at arm's length. I wouldn't want to see you get hurt. Be careful, all right? *¿Entiendes lo que te estoy tratando de decir, hijo?*"

"*Perfectamente,*" came Alex's reply.

"Well, be careful on your way home, okay?"

"I'll be careful, Bishop. Thanks for your concern, really." Alex was now pacing outside his car, puffing on his cigar, still in shock and feeling sick to his stomach, the cell glued to his ear.

"Okay, son. May the peace of the Lord Jesus Christ be with you. *Abyssus abyssus invocat.* Let me know if your plans change, and if you and your fiancée would like for me to marry the two of you."

"Yes, sir," mumbled Alex, his head spinning faster than a Mexican top.

After the call, Alex went inside the Stripes convenience store, bought a can of beer and resumed his trip home. Trying to calm his nerves, he popped open the can, took a couple of swigs followed by a couple of puffs from a brand-new cigar and decided to call Michael. Several rings later, the professor finally answered.

"You'll never believe who just called," sputtered Alex, out of breath.

Michael, who was waiting in line to pay at the checkout counter, put down the tackle box, rolls of fishing line, boxes of hooks and several bags of the Triple Ripple lures. "Who?"

"Bishop Salamanca," said Alex as he took another swig from his can of beer. He was now driving past the main entrance to the Port of Brownsville on Highway 48.

"Really? What did he want?"

"Put me on notice to stay away from the Santibáñez lawsuit," Alex said as he frantically puffed some more on his cigar. "The sumbitch already knows we're thinking of taking the case."

"He said that?"

"Not in so many words, but the message was clear . . . stay away from Oscar Santibáñez . . . stay away from Yarrington . . . "

The cashier was now scanning Michael's items and he reached for a credit card from his wallet. "Are you sure?"

"Yep."

"So, what do you want to do? Are we going to drop the case?"

"Hell, no!" answered Alex in an angry tone. He switched gears, punched the gas pedal, and the engine howled to life. He was racing down the highway, doing ninety miles an hour. "I won't give that bastard the satisfaction. Who does he think he is, anyway?"

Michael finished paying, collected his bags and headed out the door. "The next cardinal, maybe?"

Before Alex had a chance to reply, he suddenly noticed a Texas state trooper, driving in the opposite direction, make a U-turn, turn on the overheads and come after him. "Professor, hold on. Looks like I'm being pulled over by a trooper. I'll call you in a minute."

"Do you need my help?"

"No, I'll be okay. I was just speeding, that's all."

"Yes, but you and Gigi drank a lot during dinner. Are you going to be okay? Should you be driving?"

"It's gonna be fine," said Alex as he tried to find a place to hide the opened beer can while at the same time taking repeated puffs from his cigar in an effort to disguise the odor of alcohol emanating from his breath. "I'll call you in a minute."

"I'll be waiting."

"May I see your driver's license, vehicle registration and proof of insurance?" asked Trooper Tom Martínez. The trooper was flashing his light in Alex's face, looking for signs of intoxication as Alex struggled to pull his wallet from his back pocket.

For the first time that evening, Alex realized that his movements seemed somewhat sluggish and clumsy as he fumbled with his calfskin wallet and tried to find his driver's license.

"Here it is," said a relieved Alex as he handed over his license and insurance card. "Hey, can you point your light away from my face?"

"Step out of the car," ordered Trooper Martínez. "Follow me back here, to the shoulder, let's get out of the way."

Alex followed the trooper's commands and walked to the shoulder of the narrow highway. He was now really concentrating at keeping his body from swaying side to side.

"So, you're Alejandro Del Fuerte, eh? The guy who won that big Medina case . . . what a small world," said the trooper as he read Alex's info off the license now attached to his clipboard.

"Yes, sir, that's me," said Alex as the light bulb brightened. He now remembered who the trooper was. "Wait a minute, you were the trooper that investigated that rollover accident, weren't you? What happened? You're no longer an accident reconstructionist?"

"I'd rather not talk about it," growled Trooper Martínez as he ground his teeth. "Have you been drinking?"

Two years earlier, Tom Martínez had come close to losing his job for snatching and referring highway accidents to a San Antonio lawyer named Jeff Chordelli. When the scandal broke, the trooper turned state witness and testified against Chordelli. After Chordelli was convicted of barratry, the sleazy lawyer was forced to surrender his law license and ended up forfeiting millions of dollars earned from case running. Rumor had it that Bishop Salamanca had pulled some strings to have the DA convince a grand jury to no-bill his nephew, Trooper Martínez, in exchange for his testimony and a significant campaign donation. Additionally, Salamanca had pitched a hundred thousand to the Texas State Troopers Association to save his nephew's job. Instead of losing his job, the trooper had been temporarily demoted to patrolman, charged with inspecting all commercial traffic at the Rivera weight station. A job as exciting as mushy asparagus.

"Yes, I had some wine with dinner, one or two glasses, why?"

"Got a call that there was a drunk driver in a two-seater sports car heading my way. Next thing I know, I see you whiz by at almost a hundred miles an hour."

"Oh, yeah, who's the concerned citizen, do you have a name?"

Trooper Martínez ignored Alex's questions. "How many glasses of wine did you say you had with dinner?"

"Look," said Alex, "I'm not intoxicated, okay. Just cite me for speeding, and I'll be on my way, ¿'ta bueno, compadre?"

"So, how many glasses of Malbec did you have?" asked the trooper impatiently.

"Hey!" cried Alex, "I never said I had Malbec. How did you know?"

"Put your hands around your back," snapped Martínez. "You're under arrest for driving while intoxicated."

"You can't arrest me . . . you son of a bitch! What are you doing? It was Salamanca, wasn't it?" Alex shouted as he struggled to avoid having the handcuffs placed around his wrists. "How long has that asshole been keeping tabs on me?"

The trooper continued to subdue Alex and, growing more impatient with Alex's questions, punched him in the kidneys. Alex dropped to the ground with a thud, like a sack of Texas Ruby Red grapefruit.

Martínez continued, "You have the right to remain silent."

Alex was on his knees, moaning and grabbing his lower back.

"You have the right to an attorney, and the right to have one present during any questioning." Another kick to the stomach.

Alex screamed in agony.

"If you cannot afford an attorney, one will be appointed to you." A swift kick to the back of the head.

The trooper yanked Alex to his feet, squeezed the handcuffs tighter. Alex felt like his wrists were about to be pulverized.

"Everything you say can and *will* be used against you in a court of law."

Finally, Trooper Martínez dragged Alex to the back of his unit, opened the back door and tossed him onto the backseat. "You can choose to make a statement, if you want . . . and if you do, you can terminate the interview at any time."

Martínez slammed the door shut. Alex screamed in pain and tried, without any success, to kick the unit's rear window out.

CHAPTER 8

THE RUCKER CARRIZALES detention facility is a grimy, windowless shoebox-like structure made of cinder block, rebar, concrete and barbed wire. It comprises approximately an entire city block. Located out in the middle of nowhere, in what used to be old man Ortiz' orchard, the detention facility houses most of the local criminal population, both men and women. Around the back of the facility, the newly arrested are brought in, first to the booking area, then to a temporary holding cell, until they see a magistrate judge. After being magistrated, the detainees are, under most circumstances, then released into the general population.

Alex was still in the holding cell and had yet to be released into the general population, when Professor Michael Fetzer and Manny, the owner of Speedy Gonzalez Bail Bonds, showed up. Together, they filled out some forms and went about posting the bonds in order to spring Alex. After facing the magistrate earlier in the morning, Alex had been advised of the charges against him and had been given relatively low bonds on the criminal charges. Since the magistrate knew Alex to be a colleague, the judge had allowed Alex to post thousand-dollar bonds for each of his three charges: driving while intoxicated, resisting arrest and, the most serious of them all, felony possession of a controlled substance. The last one was courtesy of Trooper Martínez, who'd planted a small cocaine baggie under the driver's seat of Alex's car.

"What the hell kind of mess did you get yourself into, Alex?" asked Michael as the trio walked out of the county jail.

Still too shocked to answer, Alex said, "I don't know. I got pulled over, next thing I know I'm on the ground, the guy's placing handcuffs on me."

"Are you sure that's how it happened?" asked Michael.

"I'm sure. It was a pretext stop, nothing more," lied Alex. There was no need to reveal that he suspected Salamanca was behind it. "The guy probably hates my guts," Alex growled, "since his life ended up coming unglued after the Medina trial, remember?"

The way Trooper Martínez had strategically whacked Alex would not leave visible bruises. For the time being, Alex would keep quiet about the beating. He was not about to reveal that he knew Martínez had been sent to deliver a message from Bishop Salamanca. So he tried, as best as he could, to downplay the entire incident. If he let on to either partner what he knew or suspected, for sure Michael or Gigi would pull the plug on the Santibáñez litigation. Alex had just been handed his first, major ass-whipping, and he had yet to step into the courtroom.

"Well, we need to get you a good defense attorney," Michael said as he unlocked the doors to his Range Rover.

Manny interrupted, "Mr. Del Fuerte, it will be a couple of months before your three cases actually land in court. I need you to call my office, every Monday morning, and check in with Lola, my assistant. Here's the number." Manny handed Alex a business card. "I need to make sure you have not fled the county."

"*Por favor*," cried Alex, "I'm not going anywhere. I'm not a flight risk, you know that."

"Sorry, *compadre*," replied the bonding agent, "rules are rules. I've got to go. See you all later."

Alex got in Michael's vehicle. "*Chingado*, now I have to call in every Monday. What's next? The probation officer coming by my house to make sure I'm still wearing my ankle monitor? *Sanababiche!* This is screwed up."

"C'mon," said Michael, "we need to get your car out of the pound and get you home."

The nasty front page headline in the *Brownsville Monitor* read: "Attorney Charged with DWI, Cocaine Possession and Resisting Arrest." Alex's mug shot was splashed all over the front page, and it was followed by a short paragraph explaining the events leading up to his arrest. Despite repeated phone calls into the lawyer's firm, there had been no comments at press time. Likewise, the Texas Department of Public Safety had declined to make any comments due to the sensitive nature of the charges and because the investigation was ongoing.

Gigi was reading the paper at her desk, when Alex poked his head in. "Hey, my love. How's it going?" he uttered.

"What the hell happened, Alejandro?! How long have you been doing coke? What else are you doing? What else are you hiding from me?" She threw the newspaper at him.

"I'm not hiding anything, okay?! That coke was not mine. Give me a cup and I'll give you a urine sample. Let's go. I'll prove it."

"Well, then, how do you explain they found the baggie in your car?"

"*No sé.* I don't know, okay?" Alex had a perfect explanation, but it would all lead back to Salamanca, which meant Gigi would then, for sure, disallow getting involved in the Santibáñez case.

"I don't know how you're going to get out of this mess, Alex. I just hope you hire a good criminal defense attorney. These are some serious charges, you know? If you end up with a conviction for the coke . . . well, then . . . there goes your law license, your livelihood . . . our marriage."

"Well, you still have connections inside the DA's office, don't you? Can't you make some calls?" blurted out Alex.

"Right now, I don't even want to see your face, much less make a phone call on your behalf."

"I got it, I get the picture . . . the whole picture on high def," Alex announced as he turned and walked out of her office.

CHAPTER 9

THE CALL FROM Alejandro Del Fuerte was announced over the intercom inside Yarrington's office at the state capitol. Yarrington was meeting with the head of the education committee, Senator Anna Lynda Slim, and the head of the finance committee, Senator Eddie Straus. They were discussing ways to increase funding for public schools without having to sock it to their constituents by increasing property taxes. They were in the middle of the heated discussion, when Yarrington heard the announcement.

"Excuse me," said Yarrington, "I've been expecting this call, got to take it in my office, it's important."

The lieutenant governor left the pair alone in the small conference room, went into his private office, closed the door behind him and took his place at his desk. He punched line one.

"Alejandro, how are we doing, son?"

"Not so great," said Alex. "Did you hear about my arrest?"

"No, what happened?" Yarrington asked as he hit the keyboard in his computer and googled the words "Brownsville Monitor Newspaper," trying to find the story.

"I think Salamanca knows I'm about to jump into the case. The guy wanted to send me a message," explained Alex. "He's behind the arrest, trying to discredit me from the get-go."

"Are you sure?"

"I'm pretty sure," replied Alex, blushing with embarrassment, "I'll explain later."

Yarrington found the story of Alex's arrest. "Oh, my . . ."

"Anyway, I need to sign up Oscar and his clan, all the plaintiffs, right away. Can you help me put together a town hall meeting in Raymondville?"

"I'll see what I can do," Yarrington answered. "Do you think the story ran in the Raymondville paper? We might have a hard time convincing everybody to sign up, if they now think you're a drunk and a druggie, too. Remember Worley?"

"I hadn't thought of that," admitted Alex. "I guess Fetzer and Gigi will have to take the lead at the meeting. I'll stay in the background."

"When do you want to do it?"

"This coming Saturday. We've got to file an appearance in the case and some kind of response to Salamanca's summary judgment and motion to dismiss. We've got to get going on this. I don't care if this guy's the pope. I'm not backing down."

"Okay, okay. Let me call Oscar, have him put the word out, round up everybody. Where do you want to do it?"

"How about Oscar's place?"

"Sounds good. Let me have my chief of staff track him down, and we'll call you right back with the time."

"Thanks."

The FedEx-Kinkos off the expressway was located in the Blue Moon Retail Plaza, next to the only Hooters in town. The small shopping center had a Cricket Cellular Store, a Day Spa, a chiropractor's office, an All State insurance office and a drop-off location for Comet Cleaners.

Alex was inside the FedEx-Kinko's working on some glossy brochures to promote the firm of Del Fuerte, Fetzer & Montemayor PLLC at the upcoming meeting with the Santibáñez clan, when his cell phone sprang to life. It was a number from Austin.

"Hello?"

"Alex," said the voice, "this is Louis with the lieutenant governor's office. The boss asked me to update you on the Santibáñez meeting for Saturday."

"Go ahead," Alex replied as he signaled the girl at the counter to ring him up.

"Apparently, Mr. Oscar Santibáñez has a power of attorney signed by all his relatives and all the heirs—the plaintiffs in the case—saying that he's got authority to transact in all legal matters related to La Minita. He's got full consent to speak for them."

"Oh, so we don't need to meet with every single one of the clients, then. Well, that was easy. So, when can I meet with Oscar to get him to sign a new contract with my firm?" Alex asked as he picked up his boxful of sleek and expensive brochures.

"That's why I'm calling. He's already on his way to Brownsville, wants you to get going on this deal as quickly as possible. So does my boss. Anyway, Oscar's got the POA with him and would like to meet with the lawyers sometime after lunch, if you're available . . . of course."

Alex started having flashbacks of the arrest. He could suddenly feel the handcuffs on his wrists and the trooper's kicks and punches to his body. "Huh, okay, sure. Of course. That won't be a problem. Tell Mr. Santibáñez I'll be waiting for him. I'm ready to get going too."

CHAPTER 10

THE KLEBERG COUNTY courthouse can be best described as a building that the winds-of-change forgot. Built in 1914 by a prominent Texas architect named Atlee B. Ayres, the two-story complex was designed with the Texas Renaissance style in mind. The front entrance of the building is flanked by two colossal marble columns, while the rest of the building is made of red brick, and the floors inside are made from South Texas rosewood. Despite the courthouse not being an expansive building, the entire interior space looks much larger due to its twelve-foot ceilings.

Alex walked into the courthouse and headed to the district clerk's office located on the second floor. He was there to request a complete copy of the case file and to submit his firm's notice of appearance, along with the clients' response to the defendant's motion for summary judgment and the plaintiff's objection to defendant's motion to dismiss. Along with the notices and the responses Alex was filing that Monday morning, Alex was also filing a request for an expedited oral hearing in connection with the foundation's pending motions. He wanted to send a couple of messages to Salamanca. First, he was not going to back down. And second, he was ready to get on with the show. There would be no more delays, no more postponements and no more bumps on the road. It was do or die.

After handing the documents to the clerk at the window and taking the file marked "received" copies, Alex walked to the end of the hallway to Judge Remington Phillip's courtroom. For a

Monday morning, there was very little activity in and around the courthouse, and Alex decided to stay and watch Judge Phillips call his docket. He turned off his cell phone and walked into the courtroom. He took a seat in the back, behind the family of a young man who was appearing in front of the judge, about to be sentenced for the charge of possession of cocaine.

Judge Phillips spoke up. "Mr. Tamayo, you appeared before me last month and entered a plea. Do you recall that?"

"Yes, Your Honor," replied the defendant, a young kid, not a day past twenty-two.

The defense attorney interjected, trying to refresh the judge's recollection, "Your Honor, this is the case where this young man has enlisted to go fight in Afghanistan with the Marines. The recruiter is here in the courtroom," said the attorney, pointing him out, "and he asked me to remind you that the Marines are willing to take him, if the court should consider some kind of probation and no conviction."

"You mean, like deferred adjudication?" growled the judge, shaking his head.

"Yes, Your Honor," replied the attorney and, laughing nervously, added, "in the old days the armed forces wanted the cases dismissed, outright, but now-a-days with the shortage of volunteers, they will take new recruits, even if on deferred adjudication, as long as you allow him to report by mail. We're asking you to consider it. May we approach the bench, Your Honor?"

"Sure," said Phillips, reluctantly, covering the microphone in front of him.

The defense attorney, the prosecutor and the judge started an impromptu mini bench conference.

"Judge," whispered the defense attorney, "this is the case we talked to you about in chambers, remember?"

"That's correct," chimed in the assistant district attorney. "The State is not opposed to allowing Mr. Tamayo to report by mail . . . we spoke with his recruiter, and the Marines are ready to take him, Judge . . . we're making an exception this time to the 'report-in-person' condition . . . we know the Marines will make sure the defendant keeps his nose clean."

"Do you now remember, Your Honor?" asked the defense attorney.

Judge Phillips nodded his head. The attorneys went back to their places.

"Let's continue," barked Judge Phillips into the microphone, ready to move the case along. "Now, Mr. Tamayo, when you pled guilty to the offense of possession of a controlled substance, more than one gram, but less than four grams, you understood that there was no plea bargain agreement in this case . . . and you pled cold to me, the court?"

"Yes, Your Honor . . . it was a cold plea."

"And you understood then, did you not, that when you plea cold and there's no plea bargain, I get to assess the punishment, huh?"

"Yes, sir."

"And today we're set for sentencing in your case. Are you and your attorney ready to proceed, is that what you're telling me?"

"Yes, sir. Yes, Your Honor."

The bald judge then reached for the Texas penal code on his desk. He waved it in front of the young, impressionable defendant. "And you understand that the range of punishment for this particular offense, a third-degree felony, the court can sentence you anywhere from probation to a maximum of ten years in prison. You understand that?"

"Yes, sir. I do."

"State, anything else?" asked the judge.

"No, Judge," said the male prosecutor from counsel's table. "There's no plea bargain agreement in this case; you're free to consider the entire range of punishment. For the record, the State is not opposed to probation with the standard conditions. The defendant has no prior record, no convictions, no prior arrests . . . "

"Okay, then. The court has reviewed your presentence investigation report, and I see that you have no criminal history. I see that you finished college, with excellent grades, and that you were also the salutatorian of your high school class." The judge then paused, looked up and locked eyes with Alex in the back of the courtroom. The move surprised the hell out of Alex.

"I hereby sentence you . . . " said the judge as he stared intently at Alex across the room and dropped the hammer, "to the maximum sentence of ten years in the Texas Department of Corrections, and hereby assess a maximum fine of ten thousand dollars." The judge then smirked at Alex, while the young man's relatives went into hysterics, the defendant's mother collapsing on the floor.

Phillips then finished, "Very well, anything else?"

All the young defendant was able to mutter was an anemic, "What just happened?"

The judge quickly followed with a "Good luck to you, son . . . you're hereby remanded to the custody of the Kleberg County Sheriff Department." Then Judge Phillips looked over at the bailiff keeping watch and said, "Bailiff, take him into custody."

"Judge, judge!" cried the defense attorney. "Please, I beg you to reconsider, Your Honor. This is unheard of!"

Once again, Judge Phillips avoided making eye contact with the defense attorney, the young client or anybody else for that matter. He proceeded to restore order by pounding his gavel on the bench. Again, he locked eyes with Alex. "This court's now in recess."

Alex had Astrid schedule a meeting at Oscar Santibáñez's place, days before. He'd wanted to provide his new client with copies of the documents filed by his firm, review some of the old pleadings in the court's file and discuss trial strategy in case they survived the pending motions filed by the Agnus Dei Foundation.

As Alex drove from Kingsville to Raymondville on his way to visit Santibáñez, he replayed in his head the brief encounter with Judge Phillips. Was Phillips going to make an example out of Alex, like he'd done with the defendant appearing that morning in court? He reached for the knob on the radio and was about to turn up the volume, when his cell phone started vibrating. It was a call from Mexico.

"Hello?" answered Alex as he noticed some strange clicking noises on the line.

"¿M'ijo?" said the voice at the other end of the line.

Recognizing the voice, Alex pulled his car into the rest area by the side of the highway, turned off the ignition and replied, "Grandpa? Is everything all right? I can barely hear you . . . there's static on the line."

He walked a few yards away from the car, toward the restroom area and the vending machines, until the reception improved. "I've been worried about you. Be careful, m'ijo." The line went dead.

Alex got back in his roadster and started driving toward Raymondville. Over on the east side of the highway, he could make out in the distance the silhouettes of giant windmills dotting the brush-covered landscape. He tried to forget about grandpa's worries and chose, instead, to call him back later that day. In two weeks, he and Michael would probably be back in front of Judge Phillips to argue against the foundation's motions. That meant Oscar Santibáñez and his recently hired attorneys needed to get ready.

Santibáñez lived on a five-acre farm with his twenty-one-year-old son, Art, outside Raymondville's city limits. The house itself consisted of an old trailer, with missing windows and wobbly wooden steps leading up to the front door. In the back of the property there were two dilapidated Allis Chalmers tractors and other useless farming implements strewn about the yard.

Before Alex pulled up to the front door, he sat in his car, smoking a cigarette and pondered if the heirs would ever see their day in court. Would they get their justice? Was that even in the cards? And what was justice, anyway? Was it for them to enjoy their lands, the spoils? Was it an apology from the defendant for having wrongfully occupied lands belonging to another? Or would it be a swift kick in their sorry Mexican asses? Would it be measured by way of the millions recovered? And what would it be like to receive millions and millions of dollars a month in oil and gas royalties? What would such a windfall do to the average person? Would the money be put to good use or be wasted? What kind of justice could a three-year attorney deliver?

Truth be told, even though he was glad to be helping the Santibáñez clan, deep down inside Alex had mixed feelings about the heirs' claims. And it had nothing to do with being afraid of Bishop Salamanca. Nor did it have to do with stepping into Phillips' courtroom. There were other reasons. To the casual observer reading the newspapers, these kinds of cases actually sounded like the Mexicans had been robbed of their lands by the Anglos. For years and years, stories circulated alleging that the Texas Rangers worked for the land barons and were responsible for killing or running off the early settlers in order to grab their lands. But hadn't Don Arturo Monterreal received his grant from a king who had actually stolen the lands from the American Indians? Hadn't all those other original settlers that received similar Spanish land grants acquired control of enormous tracts of land by force, by dispossessing the Native Americans of it? How come nobody ever mentioned that? Growing up, Alex had read up on the Ballis and others like them, who claimed that South Padre Island belonged to them by virtue of Father Nicolás Balli and his nephew Juan José having received their lands straight from the king. But hadn't the king really stolen something that belonged to somebody else? In the final analysis, weren't these kinds of claims ridiculous? Weren't the real owners of these lands in South Texas the Carancahua Indians? If one looked at the history, in hyper-technical terms, wasn't that the logical conclusion? Hadn't the Ballis and all the others been in receipt of stolen property? Didn't it belong to the descendants of the native inhabitants, who had been dispossessed by the Spanish, the Mexicans and then the Anglos? What happened to the old law school saying, "first in time, first in right?"

Besides, weren't these kinds of lawsuits nothing more than a tool to effectuate a transfer of wealth? A device to tilt the scales this way or that way? Weren't these lawsuits mechanisms to take from the rich and give to the poor? Wasn't that what the entire justice system was about? A way in which the redistribution of wealth, rights, even one's freedom, could be had? For example, in the criminal context, there was always the threat that, depending on whose view, the State could take one's liberty or one could lose his or her right to freedom. One party was trying to take something from another . . . the right to freedom. And in the civil context, the threat was always that one could lose one's property or money. In the end, was it about justice? Or was the system really about money? Along those lines, Professor Michael Fetzer had always said that the "closer one got to the courthouse, the farther away one got from justice and the truth."

Alex finished his cigarette, turned off his car and reached for his weathered briefcase with the copies of the recently filed motions and responses. He got out, went to the dull-brown aluminum door and knocked several times, until he heard some movement inside. After about a minute, Oscar opened the door.

"I'm sorry," said Oscar, "I didn't know you were outside. I was in the shower. *Pásale*, come in."

"Thanks, I want you to have these," said Alex, handing Oscar copies of the documents filed that morning. "I also wanted to share something else with you."

Oscar took the pack of documents and exhibits and started reviewing them. All in all, the whole packet filed that morning by the law firm of Fuerte, Fetzer & Montemayor comprised of a stack ten inches thick.

"This reminds me," said Oscar as he fumbled with the stacks of documents Alex had just handed him. "I have four or five boxes with documents from the case . . . I still need to turn those over to you."

"Oh, yeah?" asked Alex, seemingly surprised. "Where did they come from?"

"Worley's office Fed-exed them to me, after he got committed and his firm could no longer represent us . . . they said they didn't know what to do with them, that we should have them."

"Where are they?"

"In a shed, out back. We'll get them before you leave."

"Sure."

"Anyway, you were saying?" Oscar said, pointing to a small living area with an avocado green couch and a raggedy old La-Z-Boy. "Here, sit down."

Alex took his place on the couch. "I was in Judge Phillips' court this morning . . . "

"And?"

"I want to say that guy is bought and paid for by Bishop Salamanca. I have a feeling about this . . . call it intuition, a gut feeling or whatever. We'll never get a fair shot in that courtroom."

"Are you sure?" asked Oscar as he went through the stack of documents.

"Yep."

"What do we do?"

"There are two things we can do to try to even out the playing field. They may or may not work," explained Alex. "One, we get local counsel, somebody that is close to the judge, so that he'll think twice about ruling against us and his friend . . . now involved in the case."

"You mean the friend now being the local counsel?"

"Correct."

"And what's the other option?"

"The other option," Alex carried on, "is to pray that something happens to Phillips, a heart attack, a stroke, an aneurism, something, and we get a visiting judge from somewhere else. Perhaps somebody appointed by the chief administrative judge of the region . . . have him find us another judge from somewhere else . . . with no ties to Salamanca."

"Let's talk about this local counsel stuff," said Oscar. "How does that work exactly?"

Alex pulled out his pack of Camel Lights. "Mind if I smoke?"

"No, go ahead," nodded Oscar. "Mind if I drink a beer?" It was barely 9:30 in the morning.

"Go ahead."

Oscar got up, went to his fridge and pulled out a Tecate Light. He opened it and took a big swig. "You were saying."

"Look," continued Alex as he lit his cigarette and puffed a big cloud of smoke, "we could try to bring on board an attorney that knows the judge, or is close to the judge. It could be an old law partner, college roommate, law school buddy, even somebody who'd run his political campaigns, for example a lawyer friend that was his old treasurer, somebody that can talk to the judge, if need be."

"I thought none of the parties or the attorneys involved in the case were supposed to talk to the judge about the case."

"That's right, no one is supposed to have ex-parte communications with the judge. Not if the other parties in the case are not present. This is done to try to avoid influencing or pressuring the judge."

Alex got up, puffed on his cigarette and paced back and forth in the cramped little trailer. Then, shaking his head he added, "The truth is, it happens all the time. I've never had to do it, but there are billions at stake, not to mention the ownership of a half a million-acre tract of land, *más o menos*, plus oil and gas royalties and other valuable minerals. There are now wind farms on the property, even a beautiful portion of coastline that someday may be developed into a resort area. We might have to consider it, just in case."

"And who pays the guy acting as local counsel?" Oscar asked, sounding worried.

"I do. It comes out of my share. Usually the person gets 10% of the overall fee. In other words, he usually gets 10% of my 40% . . . it doesn't come out of your portion. So that's the good news. You would also have to sign a new contract allowing me to bring in this new attorney, and you approve the fee-sharing arrangement."

"That won't be a problem, if you think it's necessary or if it will make a difference. I trust you . . . "

"Honestly, in this instance . . . I think we'll have to hire local counsel. If we want to have a shot, anyway," said Alex.

"Okay, so what does the local counsel do? What's his role?"

"He helps out. He shows up at all the important hearings, he's there alongside me in the courtroom, arguing on your behalf, making his presence known to the judge. And if Raymondville is anything like other parts of the state, for example, Houston, Dallas, Austin, even Brownsville, then come Friday, the judge and our local counsel go play golf together . . . or go fishing together and our guy gives him an earful. You know what I mean?"

"Now let me ask you," said Oscar, "is that even legal?"

"More than anything, it's unethical, but it happens all the time. Hell, chances are the guys used as local counsel have probably given the biggest campaign contributions to the judge. For example, I've seen with my own eyes trial lawyers taking judges and their wives, or girlfriends, to Vegas when the big fights come to town. Just board the Southwest flight from the Valley to Vegas . . . and you'll corroborate what I'm saying. Those guys are always taking the judges everywhere. Those are the kinds of lawyers we would want to come and lend a hand."

"How's that possible?" asked Oscar in shock.

Alex popped his knuckles. "It just happens, that's the truth. Look, just to give you an idea, there was a well-publicized case out of Laredo where a trial lawyer from Houston and his local counsel invited the judge hearing their case to game four of the NBA finals in the plaintiff lawyer's own Lear Jet. The gig was up when a lawyer on the other side saw the three of them, sitting together, courtside, on national TV. That's how hiring local counsel works. It gets us, through our local rainmaker, one-on-one time with the judge. What do you think they talked about on board that jet? The weather?!"

"Why don't they stop it?"

"Our system is all about—what the critics call—'pay to play.' It happens down at the courthouse, the state capitol, even Washington. I always thought the whole thing was crazy . . . but this might be the case where we have to stoop just as low."

"I see," Oscar replied. "Dugger and Worley never really discussed it or brought it up."

"That's because they practiced law away from South Texas. Didn't know better, but it's rampant down here. Anyway, what do we know about Phillips? Anything?"

"He loves hunting and always gets invited to Edmundo Tijerina's ranch, just an hour west of here. They're *compadres*—Edmundo is godfather to Phillips' oldest daughter, Kimberly."

"Is that the same Edmundo Tijerina whose son is the attorney for the city of Rivera?"

"One and the same. The kid's also named Edmundo, like his daddy." Oscar finished his Tecate Light and got up to go fetch another one from the fridge.

"Will he be interested? I know that city attorneys in small Texas towns are usually allowed to have a private practice on the side."

"Maybe."

"That could be the guy we need. Edmundo will be expecting Phillips to throw his son a bone. Phillips will not want to piss off his *compadre.*"

"And don't forget, Edmundo's the guy with the ranch. If Phillips doesn't play ball, maybe Edmundo will resent that, stop inviting the judge to the ranch . . . no longer allow him to kill $10,000-trophy animals for free."

"It might be worth exploring," said Alex with a smile as images of Bishop Salamanca, cursing Alex for employing Tijerina as local counsel, swirled about in his head. "Two can play at this game."

"Sure can," countered Oscar. "Let's go get the boxes from the shed."

After leaving Oscar's place, Alex headed to Brownsville to discuss with his partners the possibility of bringing Edmundo Tijerina on board as local counsel. The irony of the entire situation was not lost on Alex. Routinely, people in America labeled the judicial systems in Mexico, and other parts of the world as corrupt, broken and unreliable, but the system in Texas was no different. Here he was, having to contemplate bringing in someone close to the judge in order to have sway and counteract the "Salamanca effect."

The truth of the matter was that as long as judges had to fund-raise to keep their seats, then they could be influenced by those same friends pitching them money. How could a judge rule against a friend or law firm that had just made a campaign contribution in the thousands of dollars? If he did, then next time around, when it came time for reelection, these same lawyers would probably contribute to his opponents' campaigns. It happened. Any judge that got out of line was subject to payback.

What everyone failed to see were the injustices committed on the average Joe or Jane Doe. Their cases stood no chance if they happened to hire the one lawyer that never contributed a single cent to the judge hearing their case. God forbid if they had to face an opponent with a lawyer known for running the sitting judge's political campaign.

Alex had even heard the stories about a practicing attorney who also happened to be the county judge of El Paso County. The entire time the lawyer had been in power—sixteen years—there had never been an adverse ruling made against him, or his clients, or the county. And the reason for this was simple, since the county judge had at his disposal tens of thousands of votes from a large army of loyal supporters. If a district judge angered the man, the next time the detractor's bench came up for reelection, the county judge mobilized his political machinery, threw his support behind the opponent and booted the hostile judge out of office. Everybody was afraid of him. Likewise, all the trial lawyers wanted to bring him on as local counsel to ensure the clients received more favorable treatment.

The lesson in all of this, Alex had learned—never mentioned in law school—was that justice came at a price. And in South Texas, the more money and connections one had, the more justice one got. Plain and simple. Influence and *compadrismo* always won.

CHAPTER 11

GISELA MARÍA MONTEMAYOR was trying on a fabulous Vera Wang wedding dress in front of full-length, beveled mirrors, when she heard her cell phone ring inside her Louis Vuitton. As the seamstress and the saleswomen worked all around her, making sure her twenty-five-thousand-dollar wedding gown fit her like a glove, she instructed her mother to answer the call.

Mrs. Montemayor, a sophisticated-looking woman in her fifties with Lauren Bacall looks, fumbled with her daughter's purse until she was able to dig Gigi's phone out. It took her a couple of seconds to figure out which button to push to answer and finally mumbled into the phone, "Hello?"

"¿*Suegra*?" asked Alex.

"Yes, *m'ijo*, Gigi's got her hands full. She's trying on her wedding dress. *¿Qué se te ofrece?*"

"Oh, I didn't know that."

"Did you want to speak to Gigi?"

"Yes," replied Alex, "if it's not too much of a problem."

"Not at all, let me get her on the phone."

Alex waited for his fiancée to come on the line as he sat at his desk. After driving in from Kingsville, he'd stopped at the office, only to find out that Fetzer had taken the day off to go fly fishing and Gigi had gone shopping.

"Alex," said Gigi, "where are you, *mi amor*?"

"I'm back from Kingsville. I filed my notice of appearance and our responses in the Santibáñez lawsuit, then stopped to visit our client and now I'm here at the office."

"How did everything go?"

"Fine. There's something I have to discuss with you and the professor, maybe it will help with the case. I think we might need local counsel to come on board, lend a hand."

"Well," countered Gigi, "I told you I wanted no part of this lawsuit . . . you and the professor figure it out. If you both decide to bring on local counsel, for whatever reason, then it's ya'lls ball of wax."

"All right, I'll talk to Michael. We'll leave you out of this," Alex said, dropping the subject. "Anyway, grandpa called, but we got cut off. I'd like to visit him this Saturday, take him out to dinner. What do you say?"

"I have a shower this Saturday," Gigi replied, looking at herself in the mirrors. She loved the way the dress fit and decided right there and then that she had to have it. And since Alex was footing the bill for it, she'd decided to play extra nice. "One of mom's friends is throwing a shower for me, but, it's at noon time. I'm sure we can go see your grandpa later on in the evening. It won't be a problem. Alex, you should see this dress . . . it's beautiful. I love it. I love you."

"Okay, then, it's a deal. I'll see you later. Be careful out there. Love ya."

"I will," said Gigi, "see you in a couple of hours."

Alex got on his computer and went to the State Bar of Texas' website. With a few strokes of the keyboard he was able to pull the address and telephone number for Edmundo Tijerina, He proceeded to dial the number. After several rings, someone picked up.

"Law office of Edmundo Tijerina," said the female at the other end of the line. "How can I help you?"

"Yes, ma'am," said Alex, "this is Alejandro Del Fuerte. I'm calling for Edmundo Tijerina. Is he in?"

"Yes, sir. He's on the other line, would you like to hold? Or would you like to leave a message?"

"I'll hold."

"Very well, give him a minute. He'll be right with you."

There was a long pause, and Alex googled Edmundo's name to see what would come up. There were a couple of links to the South Texas Hunting Guide, a weekly newsletter, where Tijerina's ranch was mentioned alongside photos of trophy game and the hunters that bagged the kills.

"This is Edmundo," said a loud voice, startling Alex. "How can I help you?"

"Edmundo, this is Alejandro Del Fuerte, from Brownsville, Texas. Call me Alex. I'm a lawyer down here. Thanks for taking my call. Do you have a few minutes?"

"Yes, shoot away," replied Tijerina.

"How would you like a juicy local counsel gig?"

"Oh, yeah? What's involved?" asked the lawyer.

"It's a case in front of Judge Phillips. A big case."

"The one against the Agnus Dei Foundation?"

Alex was surprised by the reply in the form of a question. "How did you know?"

"That's the only big case in the entire county. The one everyone always talks about . . . see what other knucklehead lawyer is going to croak next."

"Oh, c'mon. Is it that bad?"

Edmundo was laughing. "No, but it's unwinnable, in my opinion. Unless a miracle happens, I'd walk away."

"Look," continued Alex, "I won't beat around the bush. I'm now jumping in. And the truth is, I need your help. Come on board and help me even out the playing field. I'm going up against a formidable opponent, with a lot of influence . . . and only you can help."

"Why me?"

"You know the answer to that. Why do people approach either X attorney or Y attorney for appearing in front of this judge or that judge? Because they have a close relationship with him or her. Your father is Phillip's *compadre* . . . "

Tijerina cleared his throat. "I'm not so sure I want to get involved, Alex. Maybe you need to call somebody else. Judge Phillips is a good friend of my dad's, the family and so is Salamanca. I don't want to get in between, or put him in that position."

"It would be just for the hearing on the foundation's motion for summary judgment now pending before the court. It's only two weeks away. That's all I'm asking. Just hold my hand at the hearing," begged Alex.

"I . . . I don't know. Besides, what makes you think that there'll be a hearing?"

Alex knew this was true. The rules in Texas said that the judge on the case could decide to entertain motions for summary judgment without a hearing, in other words, by "submission" only. This meant that the court could issue a ruling just by reading the motions, the exhibits, affidavits and evidence presented without hearing formal oral arguments from the lawyers involved in the case. Although the preferred procedure was to give all the parties an opportunity to show up and argue live, on the record, and try to sway the judge one way or the other, a judge could decide to throw somebody out of court—just like that—for whatever reason.

"You're right," replied Alex. "Judge Phillips has the authority to throw me out of court without a hearing, but I've filed a request asking to be allowed to present an oral argument. Besides, the docket reflects that the foundation's summary judgment is set in two weeks from today. Maybe the guy wants to appear to be fair and impartial."

"No," explained Tijerina, "I don't think that's what that date means. I think he picked that date so that the parties could look at their calendars and know that their responses had to be filed with the court at least seven days before that date. Because on that day, he will issue the ruling, regardless. The guy does everything by submission."

"Well, I'm seriously hoping he gives us a hearing," countered Alex, the optimist. "Truth is, everybody already thinks my clients are not going to survive past that date, that the odds are a million to one. I'm willing to pay you, up front, five thousand dollars just for this hearing, to make a limited appearance just this time. Should I get so lucky and get my hearing, then afterwards you go home, and I go home. And that will be the end of that. Besides, since you seem to think that there won't be a hearing, then it will be the quickest five thousand dollars you've earned in your life. In essence, I'm paying you to do nothing."

"Why are you wasting your time with this case? It's a black hole of gargantuan proportions! Don't you get it?"

"Hey," cried Alex, "I'm going to be honest with you. My philosophy in life is to make an effort and at least show up, at a minimum, then let God take care of the rest. And I don't want to spend the rest of my life wondering 'What if I had tried? What if I had given it a shot, taken a chance? What if I had gotten lucky?' It could happen, you know."

"Okay, send me the foundation's motions, and I'll think about it, okay? Give me a couple of days to decide."

"I'll do that."

"Also send me your responses and everything else that you've filed."

"Yes, I'll send you a package with the stuff and the five-thousand-dollar retainer, just in case you decide to jump in."

Alex knew that once the attorney had the five-thousand-dollar check in front of him, staring back at him, the attorney's hand was going to start itching, and the chances to get him on board increased exponentially.

"All right, I'll be waiting for it, but I'm not making any promises. In any event, the five thousand is just for me to review the case and for the hours I'm going to spend thinking about it . . . see if I want to touch it or not."

Alex could read between the lines. Tijerina seemed to be saying that he could really use the money, wanted to take it and wanted to start spending it, right away. On the other hand, he felt bad because he knew that there would be no hearing, ever, and he was taking Alex's money for no reason, since he probably was not going to get to do anything.

"It's on its way."

Immediately after hanging up the phone, Alex got on the intercom and instructed Romeo to copy the documents and prepare a check from the operations account in the amount of ten-thousand dollars payable to Edmundo Tijerina, attorney-extraordinaire. Since the case was exceedingly important and Alex was in no mood to nickel-and-dime Tijerina, a ten-thousand-dollar check was Alex's way to sweeten the deal and make sure Tijerina would have a difficult time saying no, should the Holy Spirit intervene and sway Judge Phillips to grant Alex's impudent request for oral argument.

CHAPTER 12

O

NE, IF NOT the best continuing legal education conferences in Texas, is the one put together by the lady justices of the 13th Court of Appeals in South Texas. It's called Soaking Up Margaritas, Sun and Legal Knowledge in the Texas Riviera, and practitioners across the state flock down to South Padre Island during the last week in July to pick up some continuing legal education credits, catch up with old friends and relax during the three-day legal seminar at the Radisson Hotel. The impressive lineup of speakers often includes the brightest, most formidable trial lawyers in the state, supreme court justices, district court judges, federal judges, legislators, law school professors, famous insurance defense attorneys, prominent prosecutors, distinguished criminal defense attorneys and even mavericks adept at spotting the new trends in litigation, law office management, international law and research technology.

Alex had decided to attend the seminar, since the Radisson was just a minute away from the Contessa di Mare, and he needed to get some credit hours under his belt. Besides, it would be a good way to kill a couple of days before visiting his grandpa in Matamoros on Saturday. The last thing he needed was to stick around the office and get suckered by Gigi into a discussion of flower arrangements, guest counts, bridal showers, wedding menus, travel arrangements, gift registries, etc.

He was now sitting in the back of the spacious ballroom, along with two hundred other attorneys, listening to the chief justice of the Texas Supreme Court brag about the court's most recent opinions and their impact on businesses, consumers and the legal profession. Immediately after Chief Justice Winter's presentation, District Judge Phillips, from Kleberg County, was scheduled to speak on the topic of "Jury Charges: A Perspective From the Bench." He was the last speaker for the day. Immediately thereafter, the law firm of Foreman, Grisham & Cochran was sponsoring a happy hour up in the Quarter Deck for the lecturers, their families and the lawyers. In years past, Alex had enjoyed the festivities and had been able to network with lawyers from as far away as Oklahoma, El Paso, Beaumont, Fort Worth and Lubbock. Since learning that Phillips was also a speaker at the seminar, Alex decided to go to the mixer and try to meet Judge Phillips, in person. Feel him out.

The Quarter Deck is an outdoor lounge overlooking the pool grounds and the tennis courts of the Radisson Hotel. There are two bars and a small stage in the background. The bartenders wear sea captain hats, while the waitresses walk around serving drinks in hula skirts.

When Alex walked into the reception, there were about sixty lawyers mingling with some of the guest speakers. He headed to one of the bars and ordered himself a Cuba libre made with Havana Club rum. Leaning on the bar, Alex scoped out the place and noticed that Chief Justice Winters, Phillips and, presumably, their wives—although both females looked surprisingly young— were already sitting at a table in the corner, throwing back Hammerhead cocktails, oyster shooters and digging into a large platter of fried calamari. Everyone seemed to be having a good time. Perhaps because it was five o'clock on Friday, and there was still the weekend to come. Besides, the weather outside was perfect.

Alex finished his drink and ordered himself another one. He was still hanging around the bar area, when Jaime Rodríguez, an old friend from law school, approached.

"Hey, bro," said Jaime as he shook Alex's hand and signaled the bartender to get him the same kind of drink Alex was having. "I saw you in there, but hadn't had a chance to come over and say hi. How are things?"

"Good," said Alex, patting his old friend on the back. "Working, keeping busy and trying to figure out how to survive a motion for summary judgment now pending in Phillips' court." Alex pointed out Phillips over in the corner as he made the comment. Winters, Phillips and the girls were laughing and having a great time. Chief Justice Winters was baby-feeding a jumbo shrimp to one of the girls.

Jaime sipped on his drink. "When is it set for?"

"One week. But that's just it. It's set for submission only. Without a hearing and not being able to put my arguments on the record, I don't have a chance, not in this case anyway. It's a Spanish land grant case against the Agnus Dei Foundation."

"I see," said Jaime as he put his cell phone on vibrate. "Good luck." And putting his hand around Alex's shoulder said, "Those cases are unwinnable; you know that, right?"

"Yes. That's how I was able to convince my partners to let me take on the case. We wouldn't have to put any money into it, since we were taking it over from two others, and there was no expectation that we could even survive the foundation's motion for summary judgment already pending in front of Phillips. We know it's a shot in the dark, like getting snow in July."

Jaime threw back his drink. "The only way you may have a shot is to let somebody else hear the case. Have another judge handle it . . . take over the case."

Alex finished his second drink and ordered a third one. "I'm working on that. Watch this."

Alex jumped onstage and grabbed the wireless black microphone from the mic stand in front of Toby Beau. The singer had just finished a synthesized pop version of his one famous hit, "Angel Baby," and had everybody on their feet, clapping and facing him on the stage, when Alex made his move.

"Let's give Mr. Toby Beau a great big round of applause," said Alex to the crowd. "That was just beautiful, and different, I might add. Thank you, Toby."

The crowd started clapping again, but did not know what to make of Alex taking center stage. The bartenders and the waitresses, however, knew that Alex and Mr. Beau had become close friends during the last year. Since Alex lived a minute away, it was not unusual for Alex and Gigi to come out to the Quarter Deck on Wednesday nights, enjoy each other's company, have a few drinks and listen to Toby sing.

"Let's also take a moment and raise our glasses to all of the keynote speakers at this seminar. Let's give them a great big thanks for their contributions and their time. In particular, I'd like to thank Chief Justice Winters, District Judge Phillips and their lovely wives, sitting in the back corner, over there. What great legal minds. We should all strive to be like them: fair, honest, impartial, never bending the rules for anybody, always doing what's right . . . giving the litigants a fair shot, no matter which side they're on."

Grunts, giggles and whistles were heard in the lounge. Everyone knew Alex's comments were far from the truth. Someone in the crowd hollered, "those are not their wives!"

"Ooops," said Alex, grinning, "my mistake. Anyway, here's to you Chief Justice and Judge Phillips." Alex raised his drink, as did everybody else in the lounge, "To truth, swift justice and the American way."

"Hear ye, hear ye," shouted back the crowd.

As Alex said this, he kept his glass raised and locked eyes with Phillips, as if saying: "Remember me?"

Phillips sprang to his feet, stared back at Alex and bolted out of the room. The girl keeping Phillips company that evening tried to stop the judge, "Hey you, come back here! We still need to settle your debt." The call girl ran after him.

CHAPTER 13

A LEX AND GIGI pulled the cord and the bronze doorbell made three loud clangs as the couple stood outside of grandpa's hacienda-style home in Matamoros, waiting for Santiago, grandpa's lifetime assistant, to come open the gate. Several minutes went by, but Santiago never came, and Alex and Gigi started growing impatient. The pair tried to peek inside the house from where they were standing, but the tall wrought-iron gate did not allow such a thing. Alex looked around and noticed a black Suburban with tinted windows parked two blocks away. Since it was close to dusk, he could not make out if there were any occupants in the vehicle.

"*Qué raro*," said Alex nervously. "We agreed that we'd go to dinner tonight. Today's Saturday, right? This is kind of strange."

"Yes," said Gigi standing on her tiptoes, trying to peek over the gate. She pulled the chord and rang the bell eight more times.

"Huh," continued Alex as he scratched his head. "I might have to jump the gate . . . find a way to get inside, see if grandpa's okay."

"Did he know we were coming?"

"Yes," said Alex as he started climbing the gate. "I talked to him earlier this week."

Down the street, the Suburban started moving, inching slowly as if stalking its prey. Alex noticed this and froze while still straddling the gate, high up in the air.

"What's wrong?" asked Gigi.

"That," nodded Alex toward the vehicle as he quickly dismounted from the gate and proceeded to unlock it from inside the property.

The Suburban was now stopped at the intersection, when suddenly it turned right and sped away, tires screeching.

"I could have sworn they were watching us," said Gigi as Alex locked the gate behind them, and the pair started making their way toward the front of the house. Alex looked under a large flower pot by the door and found what he was looking for.

"Great! Here's the key," he said, quite relieved as he went to open the door.

The pair stepped inside. An eerie silence enveloped the place.

"Grandpa?" shouted Alex from the foyer, while Gigi looked for the light switch.

"Are you home? We're here, Gigi and Alex. Hello? *Soy yo*, Alejandro. *¿Estás bien? ¿Dónde andas?*"

Gigi hit the lights. "You should go look in his room. I'll wait here for you. I'm scared."

Alex looked around. Everything seemed intact, neat, just as he remembered it. "Okay. There's the phone over on that table, by the corner, you see it?"

"Yes."

"Dial 066 if you hear me yell, okay? I don't think our cells work here." Alex started going up the spiral staircase, until he was out of sight. After the longest and most suspenseful forty-five seconds, Gigi heard Alex shout, "I found him, Gisela. He fell . . . in the shower. Quick, he's nonresponsive, call an ambulance!"

The waiting area at the Clínica León y Garza was very cozy. A young man dressed in white scrubs was pushing around a metal cart, passing out Starbucks coffee, juice, even magazines for those waiting for their loved ones inside. Alex and Gigi were sitting on a small sofa, staring at the flat screen on the wall, waiting to hear from the doctor. A dubbed version of "A Time to Kill" was playing. While they watched, the pair held hands and sipped on coffee, exhausted from the night's events.

Alex was looking at the other folks in the room, when Dr. Leo Cavazos, an ER doctor with the family-owned clinic, appeared out of nowhere.

"Del Fuerte?" he called in the couple's direction, "*¿hay un familiar aquí del paciente Del Fuerte?*"

"*Sí, nosotros,*" replied Alex, as he and Gigi sprang up from their seat. "That's my grandfather. . . . Is he going to be okay?"

"He's got major swelling of the brain," the doctor said in a grave tone. "We've done everything we can to relieve the pressure . . . I'm afraid we'll have to keep him in a barbiturate-induced coma. He might not make it."

Alex had to sit down. The room was spinning.

"He might die?" interrupted Gigi. "That serious? He came around when the paramedics picked him up at the house. He was animated, even hungry. He said he still wanted to go out and was joking he still wanted to eat *cabrito!*"

"I'm sorry," replied the doctor. "I know this comes as a surprise. But, with all the swelling . . . there's still a chance he might have brain damage, after all. All we can do is wait and see."

Alex got up as he was digesting the doctor's painful words, trying to make sense of the situation. "Who do we talk to in order to have grandpa transferred to a Brownsville hospital?"

"I'll just sign the release and you can have one of our ambulances deliver your grandfather to any hospital on the other side. The paperwork can be ready in a couple of hours. However, I'd rather move him tomorrow, after we've had a chance to stabilize him."

"What are you thinking?" Gigi asked as they drove away from the clinic toward the Gateway Bridge. Alex was at the wheel of Gigi's red Saab.

"I'm thinking that as soon as they bring grandpa over tomorrow, I'll have the ambulance driver take him to Doctor's Hospital. My friend, Dr. Gaytán, is a pretty famous neurologist," said Alex as he looked in his side mirror. The black Suburban from the previous night was following them, but he kept it to himself, not wanting to alarm his fiancée. They were two blocks from the bridge, almost home, anyway.

"He won't steer me wrong."

"How do you know him?"

"Old buddy of mine from high school . . . ran track together."

"I've never heard you talk about him," remarked Gigi.

"Just an old friend . . . I hope he can see him. The whole thing was very strange, don't you agree? And Santiago's supposed to be with him, twenty-four-seven, I wonder what happened."

"Maybe it was his day off?"

"No, he takes Sundays off. That's his day off. It's always been on Sundays." The Suburban was still trailing them about five cars behind.

"Maybe they switched days . . . since grandpa was going out to dinner with us."

"Grandpa was set in his ways. I don't think that's what happened."

"Maybe you're reading too much into it." Gigi paused as she reached in her purse to find some loose change for the toll. "And grandpa gave him the day off . . . thought he could take a shower on his own?"

Alex turned and looked at Gigi, shrugged his shoulders and said, "You're right, I don't know what I'm saying, Gisela. Right now, I'm worried he won't make it."

As Alex started lowering the driver's side window to get ready to pay the toll, he noticed that the Suburban was no longer following them. It had made a U-turn and disappeared down Álvaro Obregón Boulevard.

Alex took the money from Gigi, finished lowering his window and handed the loose change to the lady in uniform manning the booth. "All I'm saying is that for now, I'd like to, at least, rule out foul play. I'll worry about the rest later."

CHAPTER 14

ROMEO SALDÍVAR POKED his head into Alex's office and announced the call. It was Edmundo Tijerina calling long distance. He needed to speak with Alex. He was holding on line three.

"Thanks, Romeo," said Alex, "I got it."

Alex pressed the button and spoke into the receiver. "Hello, this is Alejandro Del Fuerte."

"Alex," said Edmundo, "it's me, Tijerina from up the Valley. Do you have a minute?"

"Yes, Edmundo. I can talk. What's the word?"

"Listen," muttered Edmundo, "I don't think I'll be able to help. I got your money and the copies and everything, but I'm having second thoughts. Besides, my dad heard from Phillips about your shenanigans during the CLE conference on the Island."

"So?"

"Were you taunting the judge?"

Alex hesitated. "Maybe a little. Why?"

"Because he told my dad that you were being a pompous jerk. That you had another thing coming. To watch your back. That it would be a mistake for you to set foot in his courtroom."

"Really?"

"Yes. I've been thinking, and what you need is to bring someone that Phillips fears. Somebody that can make him sit up and take notice, understand? Since he's a family friend, that's all I'm going to say about that. But I think you know what it is that I'm trying to say. Consider it a piece of advice worth ten thousand dollars. *¿Entiendes?*"

"I think I hear what you're saying. Oh, well. Anyway, I appreciate you coming clean with me."

"We're country folk, Alex. I might be a lawyer, but I do shoot straight and have been known to call a spade a spade."

Alex started to hang up the phone, "Okay, see you around."

"I know what I'll do," Alex mumbled to himself. "I need to get on the next plane to Austin."

Alex Del Fuerte felt like a fish out of water. He was standing in the foyer of the Milagro Creek Country Club in the rolling hills outside of Austin, a glamorous designer golf course with magnificent panoramic views of the hill country. Alex couldn't help but gawk at the group as the most powerful men in the capitol city arrived at the club for a late lunch. He was not at all surprised to see scores of lobbyists trailing politicians, like groupies chasing a rock star's tour bus. The group was made up of senators, the lieutenant governor, the speaker of the house and even some folks from the governor's office. The seventeen men in the group had just finished playing nine holes of golf, and now it was time for lunch, courtesy of the ten or so lobbyists in the group. The lobbyists buying lunch and paying the greens fees were folks that, at one point or another in their careers, had also served in the Texas legislature. But for whatever reason, they had not been reelected, perhaps had paid their dues, or simply had gotten tired of eking out a meager living, earning less than six hundred dollars a month for their service. And now, after having gone into private practice, it was their turn to rake it in.

"Alex!"

He turned and was greeted by a familiar smile on the happiest face in the room, the face of his ex-father-in-law-to-be, a guy he had once admired and loved like a second father, Lieutenant Governor Rene Yarrington. Alex had not seen the lieutenant governor in several weeks, and now was having second thoughts about having let Yarrington convince him to jump into the Santibáñez case.

The case was beginning to show the makings of a terrible nightmare, and Alex had yet to step into the courtroom. He had not even squared off for his first skirmish and he'd already been manhandled, arrested for DWI, framed for a felony drug offense and humiliated beyond repair when his mug shot was splashed on the front page of the local paper.

Yarrington gave Alex a bear hug.

"How are you holding up, son?" asked Yarrington. "Listen, I'm really sorry about your grandfather. I know he means the world to you. I pray he makes a speedy recovery."

"Thank you, I'm still trying to figure out if he fell on his own, or if something else happened . . . it's hard to tell."

"What are you saying?"

"Oh, nothing. I'm just glad we found him when we did. I think he's going to be okay."

"Well, I'm glad you decided to come up for the day. Come, I'd like you to meet some of my very good and closest friends."

Alex bit his lip. He was in no mood for formal introductions. He'd flown to Austin to do what once had been the unthinkable—something that did not sit well with him and that could cost him his license, if it ever came to light. The truth was, he was there to call in a favor. Ask Rene Yarrington, the most powerful politician in the entire State of Texas, to step up to the plate, work his magic and pull some strings.

"Can we talk? In private?" asked Alex.

"You don't want to meet my friends? They've all heard about you, Alex. They remember you from the time you came up to testify in front of the ethics committee. If you recall, Senator Cromwell was the guy carrying your bill to stop case running."

"I remember. But something's come up. And we're running out of time. Besides, I need to make it back to the airport, catch my flight, get home."

Yarrington looked around to see if there was a private area where the two of them could talk before he would have to join the others for lunch in the main dining room. He pointed at a door connecting the clubhouse to the pro shop. "Let's talk in there."

Alex followed Yarrington, and the two of them found themselves looking at the $250.00 designer golf shirts. Behind the counter, next to the cash register but at the opposite side of the room, there sat a young college student eagerly waiting to ring up the lieutenant governor's and his guest's purchases.

"I had a long visit with Tijerina, the guy that I thought could make a great local counsel, even out the playing field with Judge Phillips," started Alex.

"And?" Yarrington asked as he inspected the high-quality stitching on a golf shirt.

"He would not get involved. Nobody wants to touch the Santibáñez case. You follow?"

Yarrington was now checking the price tag on the shirt. "What are you saying?"

Alex started inspecting the fashionable leather belts with the sterling silver accents. "Look. I've never been one to break the law or tiptoe around the rules of professional conduct, including the cannons of legal ethics . . . you know that. But if we want to have a chance to get this case to a jury . . . which, I believe, is what we all want, correct?"

"Correct," said Yarrington as he picked out a few golf shirts. "I'd hate to be left pissing in the wind."

"Well . . . I don't want that either . . . but we need divine intervention, and that is all I'm gonna say about that," suggested Alex. "And I don't mean the Vatican."

"Are you sure you don't want to stay and have lunch with my group?" asked Yarrington, quickly changing topics. "It's seafood buffet Friday. The blue crab cakes are to die for. They're served with a chili chipotle hollandaise."

"Are you hearing what I'm saying?" Alex fired back.

"Yes, I get it. I've been doing this long enough where I've learned how to read between the lines, Alex: how to figure out what the person is trying to say when in fact the person is not saying much. Or the opposite, too: how not to read too much into things, despite the person saying a mouthful."

"Look," said Alex, "I'm going to file, first thing Monday morning, a motion to recuse Judge Phillips."

"Do we even have valid grounds?"

"None. Although people heard him say that the moment I set foot in his courtroom, my clients and I have something coming."

"Is that enough?"

"Probably not. But it's the only chance I have, if I want to get this case to a jury. If Phillips stays on, we're doomed. I've been in his courtroom, Tijerina has also confirmed it and Phillips is too cozy with Salamanca. Why is that? I don't know exactly, I couldn't tell you. But that's how it is."

"So who gets appointed to hear the recusal?" followed Yarrington.

"The Region IV judicial administrator, Judge Powers. It's automatic. The moment I file my motion to recuse, either the administrator judge hears the recusal or the Texas Supreme Court sends another judge to hear the matter."

"Hey, I confirmed Judge Powers as the Region IV administrator," Yarrington suddenly remembered. "That was four or five years ago."

The pair had now moved over to the display area for pricey leather golf bags and exotic golf clubs.

Alex was practicing his swing with a four iron. "Well, good. I'm glad to hear you know the man."

"Should Phillips be recused, will it make a difference who gets appointed next?"

Alex put down the four iron and picked up the Big Bertha. "It may or may not. Frankly, I don't care. Just give me a shot. Leave the door, or window, slightly open, just a crack, for me and my clients to be able to squeeze in. Put me in front of a judge that gives both parties a fair handshake. I'd hate to be in front of a judge, or a jury, that has already made up its mind without having heard a single piece of evidence. If that happens, the rest will take care of itself."

"Lieutenant Governor," interrupted an elderly Hispanic man holding a serving tray with two highballs on it. The man sported a tiny moustache, stylish sideburns and a tag on his vest with the name Horacio. His face was shiny and brown, and in his right ear he was wearing a tiny diamond earring. Even though Horacio looked ridiculous, he fit right in at the capital of "weird," Austin, Texas. He shoved the tray up to Yarrington and said, "Your party sent you this, sir. They'd figured you were getting thirsty."

"Thanks, Chacho," replied Yarrington as he grabbed a drink and took a sip.

"And you, amigo?" asked Horacio. This time, he was addressing Alex. "Are you drinking?"

"No, thanks. Later."

Yarrington dismissed Horacio and barked, "Chacho, tell the others not to wait for me, to go ahead and eat. I'll be there, shortly."

"Yes, *jefe*," came the reply as Horacio scurried away.

"Where were we?" followed Yarrington.

"We were talking recusal, remember?"

"Oh, yes. Forgive me," said Yarrington as he eyed a leather golf bag with all kinds of features. "Have you ever thought of picking up golf, Alex? It could be very good for business, you know."

"We had this conversation before. All those years I dated your daughter, remember? You always tried to get me to play golf. I just could never really get into it. I tried, but it just didn't happen. Just don't see myself chasing a little white ball."

"We all have to chase something, don't you agree? Some of us choose to chase power. Others chase fame. Still others chase peace, prosperity, even love. What are you chasing, Alex?"

Alex thought about this for a while as he inspected a pair of brown golf shoes. "The feeling I used to get when I'd go fishing with my grandfather. . . . I guess I felt happy . . . free, like I belonged. Fishing, at least for me . . . is more about the possibilities, enjoying nature. . . a cold beer in hand. That's why I could never join a big law firm. I've always valued my freedom. Like my firm, we decide which cases to take and we eat what we kill. No one breathing down our necks."

"Nothing wrong with that, I suppose," replied Yarrington while sipping his drink. "I, too, sometimes wish that I had picked a different path, done something else. It's hard being a public official, you know. You owe all these people favors, and they all expect to get repaid, one way or another. It's a lot of pressure, a lot of give and take. And of course, sometimes you have to vote against your own friends, the same people that helped you raise hundreds of thousands of dollars, and they get pissed off or won't let you forget it. Or worse, take it out against you the next time you run. They'll fund-raise for your opponent. The truth is, you just can't make everyone happy. That's just the way it is."

Changing the subject, Alex said, "Hopefully, we'll be finished with the Santibáñez case by the time I get married next year."

"I don't know, Alex. Even if you get a jury verdict, you know the foundation will probably appeal, right? And if you hit a home run, notwithstanding the 13th Court of Appeals affirming the verdict, the Supreme Court will, in all likelihood, take the jury award away. Unfortunately for you, the practice of law has changed tremendously in the last twenty years."

"Then, why the hell did you sucker me into taking this case?"

"Oh, I think we can still win it, make plenty of money . . . just have to be careful, plan our moves carefully."

Alex was intrigued by Yarrington's confidence.

Yarrington sipped his cocktail. "Look, I know it's not good enough that you bust your ass, invest tons of money in a case, work it up just right and fight the good fight to get your client a favorable verdict. Nowadays, you also have to worry about getting the right kind of verdict. Why do I say that? Because the verdict you get in a case cannot offend any of the Texas Supreme Court justices' sensibilities. In other words, if you hit a slam-dunk and blow the defendant out of the water, and you get a mega verdict, then the Supreme Court might just say, It's too much money. You don't get to keep all that cash, and we can't let some freakin' Mexicans down in South Texas keep any of it. It would also rub the white Republican leadership in Austin completely the wrong way."

"Excuse me," said Horacio as he returned with two more drinks on his tray. "You said later, so here I am. Care for a drink?"

Yarrington placed the empty drink on the waiter's tray and grabbed another one.

"No, thanks. Later . . . much later," indicated Alex.

"Okay," replied Horacio, who turned around and quickly left the pro shop.

"It's got to be a verdict that comes in under the radar, just right, nonreversible, error-free, fail-proof, so that you and your clients can keep it."

"See what I mean?!" exclaimed Alex. "This is turning into a nightmare. Now I also have to worry about getting the 'right' kind of verdict? What else is there? When does it stop? The right kind of judge, the right set of facts, the right set of clients, the right kind of case, the right courtroom, the right county, with the right kind of jury, the right experts . . . the right-sized verdict. Whatever happened to the simple concept of getting justice for the client?"

"Calm down, let's think of the alternative. What if the foundation decides to throw in the towel and reach some sort of settlement with you and your clients," speculated Yarrington. "That could also be very good, don't you think?

"I guess," muttered Alex, "but I doubt that'll happen."

"Salamanca could pay some cash to get out of the lawsuit, give up some land, some minerals, maybe even some royalties. I can see a scenario where the foundation decides to fund some annuities, make the plaintiffs a ton of money—more money than they'd know what to do with."

"That sounds great," interrupted Alex, "but none of that is going to matter when, a few days from now, Phillips signs the order granting the foundation's motion for summary judgment, and we find our sorry asses out on the street."

"Think positive, Alex. A lot of things can happen between now and then."

"Right now, the only thing that's happening is the case losing value. As a matter of fact, I'm losing money on this deal. We're in the red, as we speak."

"Nah, the case is worth more than that," countered Yarrington, "and I'm not talking just money, Alex."

"Oh, yeah? How would you like to receive 40% of a big fat zero?" asked Alex. "Because that's what we all are going to make, unless we survive the pending motions for summary judgment."

"Look, file the recusal, okay? Let me worry about the rest."

"I'm going to . . . but I'm just saying . . . This case is a dog infested with fleas. No, scratch that! Infested with *garrapatas*. Big-ass ticks, the size of peanuts."

"Then walk away, Alex," advised Yarrington.

"I can't. You know me, once I'm in, I'm in. Besides, I had to beg, negotiate, kiss ass and do all kinds of things to have my partners approve. Hell, I even took a beating at the hands of Salamanca."

"Speaking of, what's going on with the criminal cases filed against you?"

"Gigi's going to talk to her old boss, see if he'll consider dismissing the charges. You know, she's pretty smart. The day after I was released from jail, she rushed me to several labs in town to do a toxicology screen and urine testing."

"And?" asked Yarrington, "what were the results?"

"All of them negative. Three different labs, same results. No traces of marijuana, no coke, nothing. Because that shit was planted . . . "

"Well, that's good, right?"

"I think so. Gigi also had me take a polygraph. The interviewer asked me if the coke was mine. I answered truthfully, said no, and in his opinion, the guy—who happens to work for the Texas Department of Public Safety—concluded that there was no deception. He also asked me if I had been drinking. If I had resisted and struggled with the arresting officer. I answered the truth. I admitted that I had been drinking, should not have gotten behind the wheel of my car. That I never resisted. Again, no deception . . . because I was telling the truth."

"What if you get popped for the DWI? End up with a conviction?"

"I'll take it like a man. If I have to be on probation, pay a fine . . . so be it. I'll chalk it up to experience," explained Alex. "Gigi seems to think that once we show the DA the lab work and the polygraph . . . that'll go a long way to get the felony possession and the resisting thrown out."

"I guess it helps having a fiancée who used to work on the inside, huh?"

"Yep, but when it comes to Salamanca . . . she would not get involved. She had mixed feelings about the firm suing whom she considered a family friend . . . the guy was supposed to marry us."

Yarrington was now trying on some golf caps. "Well, you're not suing Salamanca. You're suing a foundation that was established decades ago, way before Salamanca even showed up. The guy doesn't own the foundation. It's the diocese that owns 90% of the shares. So, tell me, Alex, how do you feel about suing Salamanca's employer?"

"Doesn't bother me. Besides, I think it's been long overdue . . . time to redistribute the wealth. The Monterreals owned those lands at one point in time, then the McKnights lined their pockets. Lately it's been the church. Now it's time to give it back, let somebody else make some money."

"It's going to be a fight. Like trying to take a month-old cub from momma bear."

"Well, I can't wait to get in the ring. Besides, I didn't get my ass thrown in jail for nothing."

"What a way to start things off, huh?" observed Yarrington.

The pair started chuckling.

CHAPTER 15

Wherefore, the Santibáñez heirs, plaintiffs herein, pray this Honorable Court DENY in all things the Agnus Dei Foundation's motion for summary judgment, and allow this case to proceed to trial, consistent with traditional notions of fairness, equity and justice.

Signed, Del Fuerte, Fetzer & Montemayor, PLLC, Attorneys at Law, By: Alejandro Del Fuerte, Lead Counsel.

Gigi was in pajamas sitting in the open living area watching her favorite show, "The Practice," eating a bowl of Cheerios, while Alex was in the home office reviewing his reply brief to the foundation's summary judgment and preparing his motion for the judge's recusal. He was hoping the combination would deliver a one-two knockout punch.

In his reply brief, Alex had argued that there were several fact issues that needed to be resolved by the jury. He reminded the court that the judge was there to resolve the issues of law, but the jury was to decide the fact issues. The principal issue was whether or not the mineral rights still belonged to the Santibáñez clan, given that Ulysses McKnight had only conveyed to his son, Austin McKnight what he wrongfully stole from the Santibáñez heirs, the surface estate. Thus, there remained a real fact issue that under summary judgment analysis had to be decided by the jury, not the judge, as to who rightfully owned the mineral estate. The key evidence was to be found in the exhibits Alex had attached to the brief.

What did the title documents—the deeds and conveyances going back hundreds of years—actually show? The expert, Alex consulted and hired for the limited purpose of fighting the summary judgment motion and preparing a title opinion, had opined in affidavit form that the instruments recorded in the clerk's offices of Cameron, Willacy, Kleberg and Nueces County still showed that Don Arturo Monterreal and his descendants still held title to the mineral estate.

The recusal motion was another story. Unable to raise some valid, solid grounds to justify the filing of his recusal motion (the judge is related to one of the parties, owns stock in the defendant's corporation, cannot be fair, suffers from a disability), Alex had to argue that Judge Phillips had sent a message to destroy Alejandro Del Fuerte if he'd dare touch the Santibáñez litigation or set foot in his courtroom. Attached to his motion was the affidavit of a cocktail waitress from the Quarter Deck that had overheard Judge Phillips say that he "was going to kick Del Fuerte's ass!" the threat stemmed from Alex having embarrassed him and Chief Justice Winters that day during the CLE conference. Alex also included portions of the Texas Code of Judicial Ethics and the Texas Rules of Professional Conduct. In his motion, Alex argued that Phillips was probably biased, which, in effect, would compromise the judge's ability to be fair and impartial.

The sliding doors to Alex's penthouse terrace were open to let in the cool, soft breeze from the gulf. On top of Alex's desk, along with the voluminous response to the summary judgment and his motion to recuse, sat two large manila envelopes. One envelope contained Grandpa César's latest medical records. Romeo had recently delivered them, straight from Dr. Gaytán's office.

The other envelope, also still unopened, had a return address for Naiví García and had been mailed from the campus of Texas Southern University in Houston. Years earlier, Naiví had been the clerk working in Judge Macallan's chambers who turned Alex onto a box of clandestine tape recordings in the Medina case. The recordings had ended up costing Macallan the bench, and a subsequent investigation had also resulted in the indictment of several high-profile lawyers and politicians.

Alex reached for Naiví's envelope. He cracked a smile when he realized the envelope contained a letter addressed to the Honorable Alejandro Del Fuerte, along with a copy of Naiví's most recent curriculum vitae. In the letter, Naiví explained that she had just finished her second year of law school and wanted to come home for the summer, do an internship. She was hoping that the firm of Del Fuerte, Fetzer & Montemayor, PLLC would offer her a summer clerkship position. While enrolled at the Thurgood Marshall School of Law, Naiví had participated in the moot court program, the civil trial advocacy program, the criminal mock trial program and had been her school's law review's first assistant editor. All the while, she had maintained an "A" average. And despite the fact that several firms in Houston had offered her summer clerkship positions, in addition to firms from Austin and El Paso, she wanted to clerk for none other than the Honorable Alejandro Del Fuerte, even if it meant making less money.

Alex toyed with the idea of hiring her for the summer to help on the Santibáñez file. Assuming he could find a way to delay the case and get it to a jury by summer time, could she be part of the team? Was he willing to let a baby lawyer touch this tar pit of a case? Break her spirit with a paper-intensive case that, ultimately, might go nowhere? What if she turned on Alex, or his firm? After all, she had gone after Macallan with a vengeance, the man she'd suspected had been her mother's killer, and had cracked open the window into South Texas' dirty politics.

Maybe it was not such a hot idea.

Alex put down Naiví's resume.

"I'm turning in, are you coming to bed?" called out Gigi.

Alex shouted back. "Yes . . . in a minute. I just need to go over Dr. Gaytán's report."

"Okay. I'll be in bed, sugar. Good night."

"Good night, *mamita*," answered Alex.

Alex reached for the letter opener and slowly inserted one end into the manila envelope. He stopped, couldn't get himself to do it. He played with the envelope and the letter opener. Finally, he tore it open and pulled out its contents. He started reading the report digesting its meaning, the latest MRI findings, from top to bottom, until he found the section he was looking for.

"What? Permanent vegetative state? No freakin' way!" Alex yelled.

CHAPTER 16

ISTRICT JUDGE PHILLIPS was already on the bench by the time Alex and Michael walked in with Romeo in tow. The judge was calling the last of the nine o'clock docket, taking announcements from the lawyers present in the courtroom. Alex and Fetzer found a place to sit among the folks in the audience, while Romeo went back to their car to get the boxes containing materials for the summary judgment and recusal hearings. He had reluctantly scheduled both proceedings for ten o'clock that morning.

"Okay, that was the last of the nine o'clock docket," announced Phillips. "Is there anybody we didn't call?"

There was silence.

"Okay, the court will now call the ten o'clock docket for this morning," continued Phillips. "The court now calls Oscar Santibáñez et al v. The Catholic Diocese of the Southern Coastal Counties d/b/a The Agnus Dei Foundation. Please announce your name for the record."

A group of ten lawyers sitting scattered throughout the courtroom sprang to their feet and started making various announcements. Michael and Alex remained seated, and did not flinch.

"Mike Nicholas, representing intervenor, Shell Oil Corporation. I'm with the law firm of Findley, Flint & Franz, Houston. And this here," said Nicholas, pointing to the redheaded attorney next to him, "is local counsel, Andrew Becker."

Andrew Becker was a local oil and gas attorney who represented landowners in Willacy, Nueces, Kleberg and Webb County

in lease negotiations with the producing companies. He had contributed hundreds of thousands of dollars to Judge Phillips' campaign coffers over the years.

This is getting interesting, Alex thought, everyone bringing in
their local superstars, their hired guns. Good, they'll need all the
help they can get.

"James Hanmore, for intervenor Orion Wind Farm Enterprises, along with co-counsel Robert Ramsey. We're from Cook &
Mellow, Laredo, Texas."

Alex had heard many colorful stories about Hanmore. The
wildest story had to do with James when he was a young rising star
at a Houston mega law firm. After having graduated from the University of Houston Law Center, cum laude, he'd been recruited by
Sheksnuff, Lipp & Frank to form a part of their litigation group. A
few years of racking up defense verdicts for his clients resulted in
his being picked to first chair and defend a lawsuit filed against a
fraternity brother and his fraternity from Rice University. The girl
suing the boy, and the fraternity, claimed that the boy—her
boyfriend at the time—had tape-recorded the couple while making
love and then had viewing sessions with all of his fraternity brothers. In time, copies were made of the tape and were circulated to all
the other fraternity houses on campus. After the girl found out
what had happened, she sued the boy and his fraternity for inva-
sion of privacy, slander, intentional infliction of emotional distress
and defamation. She sued for tens of millions of dollars.

What the victim did not know nor could foresee was that
James Hanmore, the lead defense attorney in the case, was also
having the same viewing parties of her tape in the company of all
the young male associates at his firm, while throwing back drinks
in the large conference room. The private viewings went on most
Fridays after work for a couple of months. Law firms being what
they are, soon everybody at Sheksnuff, Lipp & Frank had heard of
the private showings. In time, the plaintiff's attorney also heard of
the events and had no choice but to also sue James and his firm.

Needless to say, Hanmore was expelled from the firm, was run
out of Houston and told not to ever come back. After several years

of bouncing from job to job, place to place, he'd finally settled in a job in a small boutique firm in Laredo, Texas.

"Mr. Ramsey is coming fresh into the case," explained Hanmore. "He just started with our firm, Judge."

"Good morning, sir," said Ramsey with the utmost respect.

"Very well," nodded Phillips, "anybody else?"

"Tim O'Quinn, on behalf of British Petroleum. The law firm of Tim O'Quinn, New York, New York. This is Carlos Ramírez, our local counsel."

Carlos Ramírez's dad was the mayor of the city of Kingsville. His old man had the ability to deliver thousands of votes to the right political candidate. The attorney and his old man wielded great influence in the community, and the reason Ramírez was brought into the case was not to let Judge Phillips forget it, in case he decided to run for reelection.

"Judge, if I may . . . " continued O'Quinn.

"Go ahead," indicated Judge Phillips, with a pleasant smile.

"Mr. Casey Uhels will be representing intervenors Chevron, Valero and Exxon. He's asked me to announce on their behalf that they're all available by phone, in case you need their input this morning, Your Honor."

"Very well, it will be so noted," replied the judge. "Who else is here in this case?"

A tall, slender, female attorney, with hair down to her waist, in her early fifties, chimed in as she pointed to the two young associates next to her. "Dana McDermott, along with co-counsel, Frank Mosley and Savannah Lee, representing the Catholic Diocese of the Southern Coastal Counties d/b/a The Agnus Dei Foundation. We're from the Kennedy-Gallagher Law Group, Corpus Christi, Your Honor."

Alex's eyes focused on the barbiesque Savannah Lee. She smiled back. He was amazed and delighted at how young she looked, compared to Dana McDermott. With dirty-blond hair parted down the middle and curls flowing freely about her shoulders, she looked more like a Victoria's Secret model than an accomplished litigator. The combination of freckles and large hazel-brown eyes, and the apparent curves rounding out her red business suit, probably had something to do with the images now floating around in Alex's head, images that had nothing to do with courthouses, trials or contested hearings.

McDermott's voice brought Alex back to earth. "These two attorneys over here, Your Honor, are our local counsel. I'm going to let them announce for themselves."

"Good morning," said the first attorney, a tall cowboy in his mid-fifties. "Jeremy Hidalgo, Your Honor. I'm here as local counsel on behalf of the diocese, defendant." Jeremy Hidalgo was a legendary trial lawyer from Nueces County. His great-grandparents once owned land all the way up and down Nueces and Kleberg Counties. They had been cotton farmers. Unfortunately, there was very little gas or oil underneath their lands, so once King Cotton died, the younger generations of Hidalgos had to leave the farm to pursue an education and professional careers. Jeremy had made a name for himself defending maritime claims in federal and state courts throughout the country for all kinds of off-shore work-related injuries.

The other well-known local attorney defending the foundation was none other than Bobby Fonseca. He was from Willacy County, but was very well known in Kleberg and Nueces Counties. He was known for snatching 90% of all highway accidents and rollover fatalities on Highway 77, from Corpus Christi down to Raymondville. Fonseca had made so much money as a personal injury trial lawyer that he had even switched party affiliations and became a Nuveaux Republican, hoping to squeeze a juicy cabinet appointment from the Republican governor or the White House. Despite all his money, and his newfound love for the Republican Party, everyone liked Bobby. With a flashy smile, warm personality and great sense of humor, Bobby always held center court.

"Morning, Your Honor," announced Bobby Fonseca with a great big smile, "good to see you again, sir. I'm also local counsel for the foundation. This here, to my side, Judge, is Teddy Galindo, who'll also be assisting me in defending this lawsuit. He now works for me, Your Honor."

The young attorney, about the same age as Alex, sprang to his feet and introduced himself, right away.

"For the record, Teddy Galindo, is also helping me represent the foundation," explained Fonseca.

Alex suddenly remembered that the last time he'd visited Phillips' courtroom, Galindo had been the assistant DA assigned to his court. *So, Galindo has gone into private practice, and now they're also trying to use that to their advantage, huh? Milk it for all it's worth?*

In Texas, as in the majority of the states, assistant prosecutors usually get assigned to work in one courtroom. In time, the prosecutor and the judge's staff, the bailiff, even the court reporter, became cozy with one another. As the judges grow fond of these young attorneys embarking on new careers, right in front of their very own eyes, the judges also befriend them. For a defendant trying desperately to even out the playing field, it is not unusual to hire the old ex-assistant DA from a particular courtroom to come and lend a hand. The joke among Texas attorneys was that if you have an important case, a bet-the-company-type of case, you not only need a good trial attorney and "local counsel," but you also need "extreme local counsel," like an ex-DA from the court where the case happens to land.

Professor Michael Fetzer was enjoying the spectacle. No wonder the foundation had spent millions of dollars defending this lawsuit. It was obvious that the defendant was worried; otherwise it would not be hiring the best lawyers money could buy.

"Anybody else?" continued Phillips.

Michael and Alex got up slowly, looked around and then looked at each other, as if waiting for the other to make the announcement.

"Good morning," started Michael after clearing his throat and trying to appear calm, cool and collected. "Michael Fetzer for the plaintiffs, Your Honor."

"Alejandro Del Fuerte," added Alex, "also for the plaintiffs, Your Honor, with the firm of Del Fuerte, Fetzer & Montemayor, Brownsville. We filed our appearance recently along with a reply and some other motions."

"Are you prepared to argue the Agnus Dei Foundation's motion for summary judgment?" barked Phillips.

"If push comes to shove, we are, Your Honor," replied Alex, looking around at all the other attorneys in the courtroom.

Michael jumped in. "There's a pending motion to recuse we filed recently, Your Honor. It might be appropriate to discuss it at this time."

"I saw that this morning," huffed the judge. "I don't think you've raised any valid grounds to be entitled to relief. And I'm inclined to deny it, counsel. Get the show on the road."

Alex followed up. "We respectfully disagree, Your Honor. The motion is self-explanatory, the grounds are set out in the first paragraph." Alex was now holding up the motion. "If you'd like, we can get into the meat and potatoes as alleged therein, but I think under the rules, whether the motion lacks merit or not, it's up to the chief administrative judge, what's his name?"

"Powers," added Michael.

"Oh, yes. Judge Powers. He must decide if, with all due respect, Your Honor needs to recuse or disqualify himself from hearing this case."

"What says the defense?" asked Phillips.

All the lawyers started shouting their objections, barely intelligible, as they tried to scream over each other, and things got louder and louder.

The court reporter was signaling with his head from a spot next to the bench that he was having a hard time writing everything down, because he could not understand what they were saying. Judge Phillips noticed this.

"Quiet!" screamed Phillips, banging his gavel on the bench. "One at a time. The court reporter can't take everything down with everyone talking at once." He pointed at Dana McDermott. "You go first."

"Your Honor," blurted McDermott, "we oppose any further delays. Our client's motion for summary judgment has been pending for almost half a year, and we're ready to have it heard this morning. This case was filed almost six years ago."

Judge Phillips had heard of McDermott's exploits. She was the go-to trial lawyer that business organizations called on when in hot water. Even though she was in her early fifties, had been married twice and had children and grandchildren, she still competed in triathlons, raised cattle on her working ranch in South Texas and had a reputation as the "ball buster" in legal circles. She had been the past president of the State Bar of Texas and the American College of Defense Attorneys, including the Corpus Christi Bar Association. Almost everyone agreed that McDermott had the touch when it came to the men and women in the jury box. She could connect with them while commanding a tremendous amount of respect.

Now, how she was perceived by those on the other side of her cases, well, that was another story. She had a great number of detractors that had dealt with McDermott and considered her nothing more than an aggravating, sorry excuse for a lawyer, akin to a large, protruding hemorrhoid. These anti-McDermott attorneys had even created blogs dedicated exclusively to singling out these kinds of lawyers. It was these kinds of lawyers, they argued, that gave the profession a bad name. These lawyers turned every little issue into a federal case. They'd run to the judge for anything and everything in order to pad the bill and bleed the client to death. They even squabbled over misspellings on documents, filed all kinds of unnecessary motions, took thousands and thousands of useless depositions.

"Three or four years ago," corrected Michael.

"Do not interrupt," Phillips reminded Michael.

"No, it wasn't three years ago," continued McDermott. "I'm sure it was longer than that. I'll go ahead and order a complete copy of the file and all of the court reporter's transcripts from all the previous hearings, and we can then get to the bottom of this, Your Honor. We'll see who's telling the truth. We'll have to have a hearing, right away, figure out if it was four, five or six years."

All the lawyers in the courtroom were nodding their heads, while a few spectators and reporters in the crowd were shaking their heads.

"The point is," added Hanmore, coming to her rescue, "our clients have spent a considerable amount of money defending this frivolous lawsuit. This is the third law firm that has touched this case. When is it going to stop? Truth be told, this case should have been dismissed for want of prosecution a long, long time ago, Your Honor."

"Anyone else?" asked Phillips.

Tim O'Quinn spoke next. "Judge, we stand hand-in-hand with the Agnus Dei Foundation. True, this is not our motion for summary judgment, but we join the defendant's objection to delay this case any longer. We think the foundation's motion for summary judgment is ripe for the court to entertain, and these lawyers . . . " He paused and looked at Alex and Michael with a measurable amount of contempt. "This is their way of buying more time. That's all this is . . . a ploy to delay the inevitable: getting thrown out of court and sent home packing."

One by one the attorneys lodged their objections. One by one, the attorneys made offers of proof and found ways to bill their respective clients. After about two hours of useless arguments, Phillips was ready to make a ruling.

"Okay, here's what the court will do, ladies and gentlemen," interjected Phillips. "We're going to take a ten-minute recess. I will call Judge Powers and get from him a date and time when he can be here to entertain Mr. Del Fuerte's motion to recuse. Despite the fact that this court feels the motion has no merit, it's better to let Judge Powers decide that issue. Any further comments or objections?"

The lawyers all replied a "No" at once.

"Okay, we'll be in recess," said Phillips.

"We're back on the record," shouted Judge Phillips after the ten-minute break.

All the attorneys in the courtroom dropped whatever it was they were doing and paid close attention.

"I just got off the phone with Judge Powers. He'll be here tomorrow at nine in the morning to entertain plaintiff's recusal motion. So make arrangements to be back in the morning."

"Judge," interrupted Alex, "can you hang around for a few seconds. Please don't leave the bench?"

"What do you want?" growled Phillips.

"We have a subpoena for you, Your Honor. You're a witness in the hearing, and I need to call you to the stand, make sure you'll be available. My process server, Romeo Saldívar . . . " Alex looked around the courtroom to see if Romeo was ready with the documents to serve the judge.

The twenty or so attorneys present in the courtroom let out a collective gasp.

"Oh, here he is," followed Alex. He nodded to Romeo to approach the bench and deliver the subpoena to Judge Phillips.

Romeo looked nervous, probably because he'd never had to serve a judge in front of twenty-plus enemy lawyers and a spectator-packed courtroom.

"You can't do that!" shouted McDermott, trying to block Romeo with her body and prevent him from subpoenaing the judge. "There's a special procedure to serve judges and public officials."

"Stand back," admonished Alex, "unless you want me to press charges for obstruction of justice and witness tampering."

McDermott backed off, and Romeo delivered the document to the judge, along with the mandatory ten-dollar witness check, as required by the rules. He then scurried back to his seat behind Michael and Alex.

"Off the record," shouted Judge Phillips. "Is that it, Mr. Del Fuerte? I sure hope you know what the hell you're doing?!"

"On the record!" Alex fired back without a hint of remorse. "Was that a threat, Judge Phillips? What was it that you just said?"

Michael turned to look at his disciple, surprised to see such a reaction from Alex.

Judge Phillips stared intently at Alex. He was turning several shades of red, but was biting his tongue. Those present in the courtroom were waiting for the fireworks to continue. They were not disappointed.

"FYI, sir," continued Alex, "all these attorneys just became witnesses at the hearing tomorrow."

He turned around and signaled Romeo to stand up. "Romeo, please prepare handwritten subpoenas for all these attorneys. Serve their asses! I want them all to testify at the hearing in the morning."

"Done," shot back Romeo, the firm's ultimate multitasker.

CHAPTER 17

THE KLEBERG COUNTY courthouse was the place for the showdown, according to the headlines and the media that by now had gotten wind of the story. Consequently, by the time Alex, Michael and Romeo arrived that morning, the place was a veritable zoo teeming with reporters, transmission vans, equipment trucks, portable studios and everything in between.

The trio arrived at the courthouse to find out that word of the heated exchange between Alejandro Del Fuerte, a young gutsy lawyer representing the Santibáñez clan, and Judge Phillips had spread like wildfire. Adding oil to the flames was Michael's posting of a video of the entire hearing on YouTube. While Alex and the others had been duking it out, the sage old professor had been busy with his cell phone, shooting video in a very discreet and unnoticeable manner. So far, the video was up to 3,000 views.

Alex was pushing his way through the crowd, like a boxer on his way to the ring, when someone called out his name.

"Alex!" yelled April Wingate from the courthouse steps as the trio worked their way through the crowd.

Alex recognized the reporter from two years earlier, when he had slipped her a couple of incriminating tape recordings involving Macallan, his cronies, all caught *in flagrante delicto.*

"Do you care to make a comment? We understand you have subpoenaed just about everybody involved in the case, including the presiding judge. Is that true?" she asked.

"Oh, hi, April," said Alex, "good to see you again. Listen, I can't comment on the specifics of the case, but I can tell you this.

We did issue subpoenas for key witnesses. Their testimony will be needed at the recusal hearing."

"Is it true that you subpoenaed Bishop Salamanca also?"

"I wouldn't know anything about that," replied Alex.

"Do you know why he's here, then?"

"No," said Alex, "I had no idea he would attend. Listen, I gotta get inside."

"Alex, wait! What about your own legal troubles? Can you tell us about that?!" shouted the reporter.

"They're trumped-up charges!" Alex shouted back as he ran to rescue Romeo and Michael from the claws of the media and quickly herded the pair into the safety of the courthouse.

Judge Powers was a portly and charming sixty-year-old, with pudgy nose, puffy eyelids and big cheeks. He looked more like a chef from the Food Network than a judge. However, those who knew him could attest to his keen mind and above-reproach reputation for no nonsense and fairness. Early that morning, Judge Powers had instructed the bailiff from the 666th District Court to post a note out on the doors, prohibiting cameras in the courtroom and designating the last two pews in the back of the courtroom for those reporters that could score a seat. It was "first come, first served" to the best show in town.

When Alex, Michael and Romeo walked into the 666th, Dana McDermott, with Mosley and Lee in tow, came up to the trio and announced that Judge Powers wanted to see all the attorneys in chambers.

"What for?" blurted Alex.

"I don't know," replied McDermott. "My guess is he wants to prevent more bloodshed . . . maybe narrow the issues for the hearing this morning, streamline the process, get on with it."

"Get to the heart of the matter," said Mosley, trying to help.

"Tell Judge Powers that there's nothing to discuss. I want a hearing. I need to put things on the record, and my witnesses have all been subpoenaed. They're all out in the hallway, waiting. And we're ready to go."

"Why are you being such an asshole?" spewed McDermott.

"I'm the asshole?" followed Alex, eyes wide open and surprised by the foul language. "Because I filed a motion I'm entitled to file? Because all I'm trying to do is get my case heard by a disinterested judge that will give me, and all of you included, in case you've forgotten, a fair shot?"

"I don't worry about a fair shot," replied McDermott. "I don't need to."

"Of course, you don't," countered Alex, "with a judge in your client's p . . . " Alex paused. "Anyway, why would you?"

Michael jumped in. "Mrs. McDermott, you're not upset because you can't get a ruling on your motion for summary judgment, are you?"

"You stay out of this, you old fart!" hissed McDermott.

"Forget her!" yelled Alex. "They're upset because they're not going to mop the floor with us, like they did with the previous attorneys . . . all thanks to a judge that . . . " He stopped mid-sentence.

"The judge what?" followed McDermott.

"Get out of my way, Dana," insisted Alex. "We need to set up. We're ready to go. I'm in no mood for an in-chambers-pre-trial conference. For what? To hold hands, sing kumbaya? Smoke a peace pipe? C'mon, move out of my way."

McDermott, Mosley and Lee stepped aside, and the attorneys from Del Fuerte, Fetzer & Montemayor grabbed one of the counsel tables and started setting up for the hearing. The rest of the attorneys, including McDermott and her cronies, ran to chambers to tattle on Alex because he refused to play nice.

Chief Administrative Judge Buford Powers was sitting in Judge Phillips' desk, talking to Phillips when all the lawyers came rushing in. Powers looked at the clock on the wall. It was nine-thirty, but there was no sign of Alex Del Fuerte or his partners.

"Where are the lawyers for the plaintiffs?" asked Powers.

McDermott took the lead and answered for the group. "They're setting up outside, Your Honor."

"Why? I said I wanted to see all the lawyers in chambers."

"I don't know what got into Mr. Del Fuerte, Judge. But he says he's ready to go, he doesn't want to meet in chambers . . . thinks it's a waste of time, that there's nothing to discuss, and he does not want to compromise. He wants a full-blown hearing."

"That's right, Judge, I also heard him. He even suggested wanting to go into next week, ruin your weekend, Your Honor," added Fonseca, fanning the flames.

Those had not been Alex's exact words, but Judge Powers did not need to know that. Besides, wasn't that what lawyers did . . . twist things around, embellish and fabricate? And Dana McDermott and Bobby Fonseca were some of the best lawyers in Texas for that very same reason—and to the tune of five hundred dollars an hour.

Buford Powers turned various shades of red. Initially, he thought of having the bailiff go out there, seize Alejandro Del Fuerte by the shirt collar and drag his cocky ass back to chambers. Next, he thought the better thing to do was to take the bench, and, once on the record, ask Alex why he had chosen to disobey the judge's orders. If Alex gave an answer that Powers disliked, then he simply would find him in contempt, fine him five hundred dollars and make him spend a couple of hours in the holding tank until the young attorney purged himself of the contempt. What was happening to the legal profession? Hadn't he learned anything in law school?

At that precise moment, Powers decided to do neither.

Truth be told, there were no rules regarding a lawyer's decorum when paged to chambers. If Alejandro Del Fuerte did not want to meet in chambers, no one could force him to do so. Usually, attorneys agreed to meet in chambers, as a courtesy to one another, and as a courtesy to the judge. They usually tried to work things out with a little guidance from the court if need be, all in good faith, in an effort to avoid a trial or a hearing. Sometimes it was a matter of helping the court out—maybe the judge wanted to cut out early, fly out of town, take the spouse or girlfriend to a show on Broadway, have the litigants work it out, or reschedule the trial to a time more convenient. Likewise, the rules of civil procedure required a full-blown hearing in connection with recusal motions. So, the plaintiffs' lawyers were within their right to push for a hearing.

Powers had Phillips call the court coordinator into chambers and had Phillips instruct her to page Alex and Fetzer to chambers. He was going to get to the bottom of this. Besides, Powers and Phillips had talked on the phone the night before, and Phillips had briefed the chief administrative judge on the allegations in the motion.

A short while later, Alex and Fetzer showed their faces in the doorway of the cramped room. The lawyers were hovering over Judges Powers and Phillips. Judge Powers waved Phillips to give up his chair and let Alex sit in front of him, at the desk.

"Mr. Del Fuerte, is there a problem?" asked Powers.

"No, sir. Why?" replied Alex.

Michael tried to downplay the incident. "Judge, we were just setting up. We were on our way."

"Well, we've been waiting for Mr. Del Fuerte in chambers. Last I heard was that you didn't think it was necessary to meet in chambers. Is that true?"

Alex looked at McDermott. She was grinning from ear to ear. "The rules say I get to have a hearing, Judge. We came prepared for it."

"But Judge Phillips has agreed, I believe, to recuse himself, without the necessity of a hearing. I wanted your input, see if there was a judge out there that you and the defendants wanted me to appoint? That's why you were needed in chambers, young man." Judge Powers then addressed the lawyers. "Do you all have a preference?" Powers looked around the room, trying to gauge everyone's reaction.

"But, I don't understand, just yesterday, Judge Phillips wanted my head on a platter. And now, he's stepping aside, just like that?" said Alex.

"Why call the judge himself to testify, even the attorneys and the courtroom personnel? Make a spectacle, Mr. Del Fuerte? Why make a mockery of those involved in the administration of justice?" offered Powers.

"Why waste everybody's time?" asked Teddy Galindo, the snot-nosed attorney that, in Alex's opinion, was nothing more than a warm body.

Judge Phillips spoke up, but wouldn't look Alex straight in the eyes. "Mr. Del Fuerte, I was out of place. I let my personal feelings toward you and your clients cloud my judgment and, for that, I apologize. I shouldn't have said the things I said. I should have known better."

Alex was caught by surprise by Phillips' apology.

"Okay, with all due respect," replied Alex, "apology accepted. Now, Judge Powers, who do you propose we get in here to take over the case?"

Tim O'Quinn was the first to speak, "I'd say we get retired Judge Don Whistler. He's got a lot of experience in complex, commercial matters."

"No," interrupted Hidalgo. "If I could put in my two-cents worth, I'd say we ask Judge Paula Beck. She's an expert in the area of real property and has dealt with Spanish land grant disputes."

"What we need," argued Hanmore, "is a judge that has a background in oil and gas. That's what we need. The legal issues in the case are quite complex, and we need someone that can steer the vessel straight."

In a matter of seconds, everybody was tossing in ideas, names, and suggestions.

"Hold it!" shouted McDermott. She already knew Salamanca's political action committee had forked over 100 thousand dollars in campaign contributions to Phillips. "I need to check with my client. Again, let me be abundantly clear, I think that Judge Phillips should hear this case. And, although I respect the gesture and the fact that Judge Phillips apologized to Mr. Del Fuerte, the plaintiffs have not raised a single valid ground to recuse Judge Phillips."

"Why the stubborn insistence, Dana?" snapped Alex, seemingly fed up. "We all know the diocese has contributed hundreds of thousands of dollars to many of his reelection campaigns."

"Stop!" demanded Powers, "all of you, settle down. What are you saying? Do you now want to have a hearing on the recusal?"

Alex and Michael jumped in, but Michael went first: "Wait, I think Judge Phillips said he was recusing himself, wasn't that correct, Dana?"

"Well?" followed Powers, as he eyed Phillips.

"Sure, I guess," replied Phillips.

"Well, we object!" cried McDermott.

"You can't object," replied Powers. "It's his call. End of story. Now, it looks to me like you will never be able to agree as to who should hear this case, am I correct?"

Alex and Michael looked around the room as some attorneys looked at each other and at the judges. Powers waited for a response, but the answer was obvious. They would never agree.

"Okay, ladies and gentlemen. This is what I'll do. Tomorrow, like it or not, I will issue an order appointing the replacement judge on this case," said Powers. "In the order I will also include the date for the oral hearing on the pending motion for summary judgment."

"Can we have a real hearing, Judge? Skip doing it by submission?" asked Alex with a great big smile.

"Sure," replied Powers. "In the meantime, let's go outside and put on the record what we've just discussed in here this morning. Any questions?"

Everyone nodded in agreement with Judge Powers.

"Fine," moaned McDermott, disgusted at the prospect of having to explain to her client that the tide, suddenly and without explanation, now appeared to be turning.

Dana McDermott was back in her office, located on the twentieth floor of the Bank of America tower on Seaside Boulevard. She was contemplating the cargo ships in the distance as they made their way in and out of Corpus Christi Bay. Sitting at her desk, nursing the remnants of an earlier migraine headache, she thought about the hearing earlier in the day.

Alejandro Del Fuerte was apparently not easily intimidated. Michael Fetzer, ex-law school professor, former Marine and U.S. attorney, expert on white-collar prosecutions was quite comfortable in the courtroom. Bishop Ricardo Salamanca was powerful, dangerous, connected and probably angry as hell.

Savannah Lee and Frank Mosley stuck their heads in the door. "Is everything all right, Mrs. McDermott?"

"Yes, it's just a headache."

"Bishop Salamanca called," said Mosley. "He said he left the courtroom after we went into chambers this morning. He didn't wait around, went back to Corpus Christi. So he's been calling you, wants to find out what happened."

"What did you tell him?" asked McDermott as she took out a bottle of Extra Strength Excedrin and popped another pill. She reached for the Evian water bottle on her desk and chased down the medicine.

Mosley shrugged his shoulders. "Nothing, I haven't spoken with him."

"I'll call him, later. He's gonna have a fit . . . "

Savannah was still standing at the door, but Mosley was now in McDermott's office, making himself comfortable as he sat down on a leather chair across from the boss.

"Why?" asked Savannah from the doorway, sounding disingenuous.

"Because Phillips was on our side. There was no way the plaintiffs were going to win with Phillips on the bench," explained McDermott. "All his rulings . . . these past few years, had gone our way. You wouldn't know . . . you weren't around when this thing started."

"But the firm can still appeal, right? Should you lose . . . worst case scenario?"

"Sure, we can appeal all the way to the Supreme Court and back, but . . . "

Savannah's eyes lit up. "I've never met a Supreme Court Justice that I didn't like. That would be terrific."

"Yes, it would be, especially the hefty tab. Our firm could make a ton of money." McDermott threw the bottle of Excedrin back into her desk's top drawer. "But that's not the message we want to send. And that's not what our client wants. We want to win all these cases at trial. Once the plaintiffs start winning in the trial court that just encourages others to try their luck."

McDermott sat up straight. "The good thing is that we got to bill the client for the paralegals and Mosley's time, plus mine. That's what . . . another ten thousand dollars, for two days? Not bad. Once our summary judgment is granted, Mosley will be reassigned to the mold docket, and you . . . "

"Yes?" asked Savannah.

"Well," continued McDermott, "let's just say you won't be going back to the complex commercial litigation files. So, enjoy it while you can."

Mosley interjected, "Not all clients are happy to pay premium attorneys' fees, nor can they afford them, you know. It's not every day that a law firm gets a major client like the foundation that can pay its bills . . . big bills."

"That's right," added McDermott, "if you look around, insurance companies have gotten so cheap, they don't even want to pay one-forty an hour."

"The sign of the times," said Savannah as she got up and headed out the door. "It's like that everywhere."

"I guess," replied McDermott in a contemplative mood as she studied young Ms. Lee sashaying down the hallway.

CHAPTER 18

"**B**ELIEVE IT OR NOT, Powers was okay."

"He'd better be."

It was noon time, and Alex and Yarrington were standing over a large fire pit on the ground, used for making Sunday *barbacoa*. The pair was holding ice-cold Bohemia beers in hand, admiring Romeo and Pancho, one of the workers from Alex's El Caudillo ranch, as they gracefully worked around the pit and cleared away ash and coals to slowly reveal two large cow heads wrapped in large *maguey* leaves.

"And Salamanca?" asked Yarrington.

"He was there, but didn't say anything," Alex replied, "did not stay for long."

"If I'd known better, I'd bet that sum'bitch was there to make his presence known, try to remind Phillips who's boss." Yarrington took a swig of beer. "Nothing would please me more than to see you and the Santibáñez clan sock it to Salamanca and his foundation."

"Why do you hate him so much?"

"It's a long story. How much beer do we have?"

Alex pointed to the small built-in refrigerator in the outdoor kitchen near the large swimming pool, next to the pavilion covered by an enormous arbor.

"Come," pointed Alex, "let's get a couple more."

The pair walked over and around the pool and sat down in the Equipal chairs, under the arbor.

"You were saying?" prodded Alex.

"That's a lot of food," Yarrington said, switching topics and looking over to the spot where Romeo and Pancho were standing. "Who else is coming?"

"Gigi, her parents, her brothers, their wives and children, Michael and the staff from my office."

"What are you celebrating?"

"Nothing. This is something we started doing ever since Gigi and I got engaged. She and I talked about starting some sort of family tradition. Kind of like Sunday night dinner at grandma's or Saturday breakfast at Las Brasas, like I used to have with my family. Care to join us? Dinner's at six."

Yarrington finished his first beer and started on his second one. "No, I don't think Gigi will like that. Besides, I gotta get going . . . I've got to pay my respects to the widow of a fallen U.S. Marine, latest casualty of the Iraq conflict. The guy was from Port Isabel . . . the religious services are at six."

"So, you were saying about Salamanca?"

"Well, ten or fifteen years ago when I made a run for the U.S. Congress, Salamanca supported my opponent. Of course, with unlimited cash reserves, I was obliterated. The most expensive campaign I've run. Afterwards, I even had to file for bankruptcy. We were wiped clean. I'll never forget it."

"Did you piss him off?"

"A little. At the time, I was Speaker of the House, and there was legislation pending that would affect the way church property got taxed. Salamanca wanted me to find a way to sweep the bill under the rug, not bring it up for discussion. I went the other way. He never forgot. Next time I ran, he came out swinging. And there you have it."

"Ah."

"You could say there's some history between us."

"That makes sense." Alex finished his beer and opened the next one. He took a swig. "Now that Phillips is out of the way, we're not out of the woods yet. We could still get poured out, you know. We're still in a very weak position."

"I wouldn't worry too much about it, Alex. You're going to be fine."

Yarrington turned around and stared at Alex, then looked away to check on Romeo and Pancho playing *vaquero* chefs and finally said, "You know what your outdoor kitchen's missing?"

"What?"

"A wood-burning brick oven, for pizza. With all the mesquite trees on your ranch, you would have an endless supply of firewood. Best tasting pizza, believe me, especially on a chilly winter night, with a bottle of *tinto*. I think I can even get you the pizza recipes from the folks that own Gio's on the Avenue."

Alex suddenly remembered those happier days spent at Gio's. "Those were some great pizza pies . . . Paloma and I would always go there on Fridays after the football game."

"The Giordellis sure knew their food," replied Yarrington, "best marinara sauce north of the Rio Grande."

"So, how do I get one? Who makes them?"

"I know a guy . . . I'll set it all up, you don't worry about a thing. He made one for my *compadre*, Judge Emiliano Cienfuegos, from San Antonio. You have to get someone that knows how to build them, you know. It's a lost art form. Otherwise, you'll get cracks, and the thing won't work . . . it's got to be just right."

"Okay, sounds good, I guess I could use one."

"Yes, this brick oven guy, you'll like him, luckiest sum'bitch I've ever known."

"How's that?"

"It's a funny story. Guy gets divorced and ordered to pay child support, for three kids, right?"

"Okay."

"Around the same time, he loses his wallet and his social security number and driver's license . . . gets stolen . . . probably by some wetback."

"Doesn't sound like a very lucky bastard to me," Alex said.

"Wait, wait . . . it gets better. So the wetback starts working and uses the guy's social security number. Before you know it, the attorney general issues an order withholding child support, and the illegal alien's employer, up in Chicago, starts deducting child support from the illegal alien's paycheck. So, pizza-oven guy keeps quiet and it's the illegal alien, working the social security number, who ends up paying the oven maker's child support for three children. The alien can't complain or make waves, and the oven guy is laughing all the way to the bank. Oven guy gets paid in cash . . . keeps every penny of it. You see the irony of the whole thing?"

"Another poor bastard left pissing in the wind," said Alex, "as you like to say."

"That could be you, Alex . . . the oven guy. Sometimes, we win by losing. And sometimes we lose when we win. You just never know. For some, fortune comes in an odd disguise. Remember that," finished Yarrington with a wink.

Yarrington got up, threw his empty beer bottles into a metal wastebasket next to the outdoor kitchen sink. "How about throwing a big pizza party after we kick Salamanca's ass?"

"Sure, if that ever happens . . . "

"It's not *if*, it's *when* it happens," Yarrington countered in a serious tone, looking up to the sky as a group of vultures circled above. He cracked a wicked smile.

"Okay, then, *when* it happens. And *when* it happens . . . we'll skip the pizza party and instead slaughter a couple of cows and pigs and have us a real party. *Chicharrones, carnitas, fajitas, moronga, chorizo, filetes, sesitos, lengua.* How's that?"

"I'd like that. I'd say that's better, much, much better."

It was three o'clock when Dana McDermott took the call.

"What are we going to do about Alejandro Del Fuerte?" Salamanca demanded to know.

"Uhm, I . . . Oh, hi, Your Holiness. You know, I was thinking exactly the same thing."

"*Ab actu ad posse valet illatio*," Salamanca blurted.

"I don't understand, Your Reverence?"

"By looking at the past, we can infer the future," explained Salamanca. "Rather strange, don't you think? As if someone else is now pulling the strings?"

"I'd have to agree with you, Your Holiness," said McDermott while reaching for the bottle of Prilosec pills. "Phillips stepped down without so much as a squeak."

"I saw that. The minute Powers said he wanted to see everyone in chambers, I knew something was up."

"What are you saying?"

"I don't know. Intuition, I guess. Maybe they got to Phillips, or Powers."

"Or both?"

"You think?"

"Maybe, I don't know," snapped Salamanca. "*Abeunt studia in mores.*"

"How could Alejandro Del Fuerte do such a thing? He's an unknown, a nobody. No one outside of Beanerville, Texas, has even heard of him. The guy didn't even show up with local counsel! We had everyone lined up. We were ready to go. The summary judgment hearing date had been set for months. Heck, there wasn't even going to be a hearing! It was going to be by submission. We knew what Phillips was going to do. You had already talked to him, right?"

"Yep, he promised he would throw them out," said Salamanca.

"You know what worries me, Your Holiness?"

"What?"

"The next judge assigned to hear the case. I have no idea who that might be."

"I know. I'm gonna have my people keep a close eye on Alex . . . see who he's talking to. Maybe that'll explain things."

McDermott got ready to pop a Prilosec pill. "What else should I do from my end, Your Holiness?"

"What we talked about. Let's see how committed Alejandro Del Fuerte is to the cause."

"Gotcha. She's been working real hard, learning the ropes. She's ready to go."

"*A Deo et Rege,*" Salamanca muttered before hanging up. "God bless."

Still sitting under the arbor and working on his fifth Bohemia, Alex said to himself, "Pizza oven, pizza oven! I'm the one whose ass is gonna get baked in the freakin' pizza oven."

Alex was reviewing the events of the last few days. What was he doing? When did his moral compass get all screwed up? Had his millions in the bank and the lure of more money changed him? And what the hell was he doing talking and associating with Yarrington, consulting him on a case? Years earlier, that had been the cause of his breakup with Paloma. He'd wanted nothing to do with the lieutenant governor! And now they were drinking beers together? What had changed? The fucker was just a little less corrupt than an old Sicilian mob boss.

"I need to talk to Worley, see if this shit is even worth it," mumbled Alex under his breath as he downed the last of his beer and headed over to the pit to taste the moist and tender *barbacoa*.

Gigi and Alex were waiting outside the Cameron County DA's office in a small reception area next to the four-story building's two elevators. Gigi had talked to her old boss and had made an appointment to meet in person, along with Alex, and discuss a way to dispose of the three criminal charges now pending against Alejandro Del Fuerte. The county DA had been gracious enough to allow the defendant to join the discussion. This was something that never, ever happened, in Cameron County nor anywhere else, for that matter.

"Mr. Padilla will see you now," announced the receptionist from behind the glass. "Let me buzz you in. You know your way around the office, right, Ms. Montemayor?"

"Yes. Thank you, Martha," said Gigi as she got up and nodded to Alex to follow her.

The pair walked past the reception area, the door buzzed open, and Gigi and Alex disappeared into the labyrinth of justice.

"Here, take a seat," indicated Jason Padilla, a lanky, forty-five-year old with long sideburns, goatee and bushy eyebrows after welcoming the couple into his office. The guy looked more like a rock star plucked from the seventies than a district attorney. He waited until Gigi and Alex were sitting down and then took his place behind his large, heavy wooden desk.

"What can I do for you, Gigi?" asked Padilla.

Alex remained silent. He let Gigi speak.

Gigi turned to Alex, and said, "I'm going to get straight to the point, boss. We need help. My fiancé, Alejandro . . . "

"Oh, I didn't know you two were getting married," confessed Padilla. "When did this happen?"

"The wedding is next year, in Greece. You and the entire office will be invited . . . of course. We got engaged last summer."

"Thanks. I hope I can take the wife. I guess we better start saving our pennies. So, you were saying?"

"Ah, yes . . . where was I?" continued Gigi. "Alex got arrested for DWI, possession and resisting. It happened three months ago, *más o menos*. I checked and the files are already in your office, in the intake section." Gigi pulled a manila envelope from her purse and set it on Padilla's desk.

Alex shifted uncomfortably in his chair and cleared his throat.

"We'd like to plea to the DWI. Hopefully you will also consider some sort of pretrial diversion . . . that would be even better."

"What about the resisting and the felony possession?" asked Padilla. "Those are some serious charges. He could even lose his license, Gigi. We may have to upgrade the resisting to an assault on a peace officer, make it another felony . . . you know that."

"I know. I think Alex knows that. We're not here to play hardball, boss. We just want to make these things go away, quietly," explained Gigi.

"Okay," said Padilla, "keep talking. I'm listening."

Gigi turned to look at Alex, who by now looked like a high school senior in the principal's office getting an ass chewing. She then faced Padilla and pointed at the envelope on the desk.

"The coke was planted by the trooper," said Gigi. "Alex drinks, but doesn't do drugs. I should know. The day after the arrest, I took him to all the labs in town and had them do toxicology screens. They all came back clean, no dope, no coke, no ecstasy, no meth, opiates, nothing. It's all there in the envelope."

Padilla reached for the envelope and played with it in his hands. He did not open it. He now remembered that when Gigi prosecuted a case, she was the type of assistant DA that left no stone unturned. Now, she was doing to his DA's office what she'd done to the defense bar all those years.

"I also had Alex do two polygraph tests. One with your own guy from the DPS, McAllen office, Sgt. Capuchino. . . . I didn't want you to say we should have used him. The other with a private service. Both times, the same questions were asked. There was no deception and he answered truthfully. It's all in there for your review."

"The polygraph results are inadmissible in a courtroom, Gigi. You know that," replied Padilla while giving Alex the look over. "Besides, even psychopaths and liars can teach themselves to pass these tests."

"I know that, boss. I just want you to know that I'm not pulling any punches. This case, it is what it is. Sure, Alex may have had one too many drinks that night, but he did not have coke with him and he did not resist arrest. What I just told you was confirmed by the responses and questions in both polygraph examinations."

"How so?"

"When asked if he'd been drinking the night he got arrested," pointed out Gigi, "he told the truth. He answered, yes. No deception noted. When asked if he had lost his mental faculties while behind the wheel that night, he answered, yes. No deception noted. When asked if the cocaine found in the car was his, he answered, no. No deception noted."

"Let me guess," interjected Padilla, while chuckling, "when asked if he'd resisted arrest, he answered, no."

"No deception, noted," finished Gigi, "that's right."

"Also," Gigi continued, "state troopers, nowadays, videotape all the traffic stops. If Alex resisted being arrested, then it should all come out in the cruiser's video."

"I can tell you there's no video, in this instance," said Padilla. "I don't know why, but that's what the intake officer noted."

"Probably because it would show Martínez kicking the crap out of me," interjected Alex.

Gigi reached over to Alex and grabbed his arm, trying to get him to remain quiet and sit still. There was no need to escalate things.

Padilla spoke slowly as he glared at the accused. "So, what do you want me to do, Gisela María?"

"Let him have pretrial diversion on the DWI, dismiss the other two charges."

Padilla looked rather uncomfortable to be placed in such a position. He kept playing with the manila envelope. "I can't do that, sorry."

"Why?"

"Because . . . "

"Boss," uttered Gigi, "with all due respect, I've seen you give your close friends better deals than this. Even to rapists and murderers! I've seen you put felons back on the street."

"Just hold on! Are you accusing me of something, Ms. Montemayor?" asked Padilla, now obviously angry. "You have some nerve to barge in here and level such callous and reckless accusations!"

"Well . . . no, but c'mon, you do give your friends and supporters, many from the defense bar, better deals. I've seen it with my own eyes. Like the Akbar Malik case. It's no mystery."

Padilla shifted uncomfortably in his chair and cleared his throat. "Ms. Montemayor . . . Malik has not been the only defendant that my office has allowed to remain out on bail after conviction!"

"But this guy had been convicted of murder! The judge went along with the defendant's request to remain free . . . because your office did not object to defense counsel's request. Why was that? How come nobody objected!? You guys always object . . . even to a $500-bond reduction."

Padilla pounded on his desk. "Enough!"

Gigi continued, now a few decibels louder. "Or was it because the guy defending Malik was your biggest campaign donor?"

Alex reached over and squeezed hard on Gigi's arm, trying to get her to calm down. He was getting worried, his heartbeat was jumping. Things were taking a turn for the worse.

Gigi got hold of her emotions. "I'm sorry. I don't know what came over me. I just feel that Alex was framed by the trooper . . . that's all. You know how I feel about rogue cops."

"I know," Padilla countered, "I know . . . but don't ever bring up the Malik case again, got it? Ever."

"Yes, boss. Got it. I'm sorry we've started on the wrong foot. Can you work with us, is there some room to wiggle here?" Gigi asked in a different tone.

"I might go for the pretrial diversion on the DWI, with a very significant donation to the battered women's shelter."

"We'll give you a donation so big you'll be able to have the Jason Padilla wing, how's that?" Alex blurted out.

Padilla gave them the go-to-hell look.

"He's just kidding, boss," Gigi said, trying to cool things down. "You were saying?"

"He would have to plea to the possession with five years deferred, and I'll reduce the resisting to a class 'C' disorderly conduct . . . he'll just pay a fine. He can plead guilty or no contest to the coke, I don't care. There won't be a finding of guilt, since he's getting deferred adjudication. Mr. Del Fuerte should be able to keep his law license."

"Boss," fidgeted Gigi in her seat, "but to plea to something he didn't do?"

Padilla stared at Gigi. Both knew that in a perfect world, this sort of thing was not supposed to happen, but the reality was that it happened all the time in courtrooms throughout Texas and the rest of the American Union. Innocent folks tired of wrangling with the criminal justice system or disillusioned at the prospect of getting their day in court and proving their innocence, decided it was cheaper to cop a plea to something, anything, and get on with life. It was better than to waste months going back and forth to court, stressing, blowing money on this attorney or that attorney, and maybe get somewhere, or maybe not.

"The system's not perfect . . . we all know that. Maybe your fiancé . . . " he turned and faced Alex, " . . . would like to take his chances at trial. Or maybe . . . we could talk . . . about . . . repaying a favor . . . "

Alex felt like a caged animal heading to a stench-filled slaughterhouse. He locked eyes with Padilla and, after a few seconds, turned away toward the large window facing east, toward the Gulf of Mexico. As his eyes adjusted, he saw on the file cabinet next to the window, sitting on top, a framed photo of Padilla's family surrounding Bishop Salamanca as Padilla's baby daughter was baptized. Salamanca had even signed the darned photo: To Jason Padilla, my *compadre*, congratulations on little Yessenia's baptism. Bishop Rick Salamanca.

"Come on, let's go," ordered Alex, disgusted at the way he was about to be shaken down. He sprang to his feet.

"Alex, wait. No . . . " mumbled Gigi, "he's not finished."

"But I am!" shouted Alex as he tugged on Gigi and pushed her out of Padilla's office.

Alex turned around, stopped at the doorway and announced, "Thanks, we'll be in touch."

"I'm sure we will," yelled Jason Padilla across the room. "And there's always option C, Gisela. Think about it!"

"What was that all about?" Gigi demanded to know, visibly perturbed.

The pair was now in Alex's Shelby Cobra, zooming in and out of traffic, traveling down Highway 48, heading home to South Padre Island. Alex was puffing on a cigarette.

"Salamanca baptized his daughter."

"Of course, Salamanca's a priest," replied Gigi, "that's what priests do."

"No, you don't get it. Salamanca's the actual godfather to Padilla's daughter. ¡Son compadres! I saw the picture. Salamanca was in plain clothes. Father Luke performed the baptism . . . he was also in the picture, for goodness sakes!" shouted Alex over the roar of the engine.

"What? Are you sure?"

"Yes, didn't you see the picture in his office?"

"No."

"He wants me to dismiss the Santibáñez lawsuit. That's where the conversation was going, didn't you notice?"

"Ah," Gigi finally realized, "that's why he was saying that . . . "

"Exactly!"

"Well, then. It's clear. Dismiss the damned suit, and I think he'll reciprocate. You'll be a free man. End of story. *Colorín, colorado . . . "*

"*Qué* end of story *ni qué nada,*" Alex shifted gears, hit the gas and went flying past an old pickup truck towing a fishing boat. "*¿Estás loca?*"

"No, I'm not crazy. I never wanted the firm to touch that lawsuit to begin with. It's brought us nothing but misery. But you're a *cabezón*! You never listen. I think you should start now. Listen to what Padilla was saying."

Alex knew Gigi was probably right, but could not swallow the idea that Padilla could make criminal cases go away if Alex dropped his lawsuit against Salamanca. He punched the accelerator. "And what the heck was that stuff about plan C?"

"C is for *cama,*" explained Gigi, "it's code for getting me between the sheets . . . then he'll get us a deal."

"What the . . . !?" screamed Alex.

"Trust me, I wouldn't touch that pig . . . even if he begged all day. Many desperate attorneys have gone the distance to get the right deal. However, it's very hush, hush."

"Really?"

"Yes, really! Why do you think Megan Willis gets all her cases dismissed?"

Alex's head was spinning. He hit the steering wheel with his fists. "How long are Salamanca's tentacles? That's what I want to know?"

"Who knows? Who cares!" snapped Gigi, seeing that she was not getting through to Alex.

"Well, we'll soon find out . . . won't we?"

Gigi reached over and yanked the cigarette from Alex's lips, threw it out of the car. "Speak for yourself. What's this 'we' business? You're the lunatic trying to bite off more than you can chew."

CHAPTER 19

THE AUSTIN STATE HOSPITAL is located on Forty-Fifth Street, between Guadalupe Street and North Lamar Boulevard. The first mental institution built west of the Mississippi, it was originally called the Texas State Lunatic Asylum. After construction was started in 1857, the first "lunatics" were admitted in the early 1860s. By 1925, the mental institution had been renamed the Austin State Hospital.

Alex and Romeo were sitting in the large waiting area, next to the facility's main information booth. They had arrived in Austin the night before and planned to make contact with Brad Worley, the second attorney in the Santibáñez case. Romeo had tracked Worley's whereabouts and had discovered that, despite having been institutionalized after his involvement in the Santibáñez suit, he'd become a volunteer in the facility. Apparently, he had regained most of his senses and given up the practice of law. He was now lending a hand in the Adult Services Specialty Wing.

"Hi," said a man in his mid-fifties, short, with white hair and a moustache, slightly disheveled and wearing a wrinkled white doctor's coat with a "volunteer" tag on it. "Were you looking for me?"

Alex and Romeo, caught by surprise, jumped to their feet, like grunts at boot camp.

"Hi," followed Alex, "I'm Alex and this is Romeo, a friend of mine. We were wondering if you have a minute? Maybe go get a cup of coffee somewhere?"

131

"Sure," said Worley in a friendly tone. "We could grab a cup at the Central Market H-E-B around the corner."

"I know where that's at," confirmed Alex. "Meet you there in five minutes?"

"Okay," said Worley, "see you there."

"So, what did you all want to talk about?" asked Worley as he sipped his cup of chai tea.

The trio was sitting on a brick bench outside the Bistro area of the upscale supermarket.

"I'm an attorney, down in South Texas," started Alex, stirring his double latte. "My firm got involved in the Santibáñez suit against the Agnus Dei Foundation."

Worley immediately appeared uncomfortable; his entire demeanor changed at the simple mention of Agnus Dei. He fixed his bifocals, started pulling at his moustache and his right foot started tapping the sidewalk, nervously. "Don't get involved. With-draw, get out while you can."

"Can you tell me why?"

"Have you been arrested, yet?" asked Worley.

Alex was taken aback. "Now that you mention it, yes . . . I'm currently facing some criminal charges."

"See! It's starting already. It begins like that . . . they're hoping you get the message. Then things escalate."

"Look, I know Salamanca's powerful, and there are millions at stake. But, how bad can it get?"

By now, Worley was in panic mode, checking out the sur-roundings as if waiting for assassins to jump out of the bushes or a bomber to appear out of the blue and hit the detonator button. "It's not Salamanca, understand? You're trying to take a baby chick from momma eagle . . . the Vatican. Not to mention the alien and drug smugglers using the hidden trails in La Minita . . . they won't be too happy, either. And don't forget all the Border Patrol agents on the take that get paid to look the other way when the loads are moved through the foundation's lands. They'll be angry as hell. You'll be stepping on some sensitive toes . . . They don't like for folks like you to come by and stir things up."

"How can you be so sure?"

"Look, chances are things are already happening to you, but you're in denial. You don't want to believe it. I went through the same thing. I'd sweep little incidents, here and there, under the rug, as just a coincidence. Until one day you wake up and realize you're paranoid, you don't even want to step out of the house, much less set foot in that courtroom. Because that day, when that happens, you realize you're next or it's already too late and you have a gun barrel aimed at your head."

"Well," interjected Romeo, pointing at Alex, "now that you mention it. Alex's Grandpa fell in the shower recently, under highly suspicious circumstances. The old man's still in a coma. They had to put a stent . . . "

"The church is everywhere, Alex. They got ears and eyes in every corner of the world. Listen to me, get out while you can," said Worley.

An SUV drove by slowly, and Worley froze in fear. It was a black Escalade with tinted windows. It parked a few feet away from the trio, on the other side of the hedge separating the bistro's brick terrace and the parking lot. A hushed silence fell over Alex and Romeo as they, too, joined Worley in staring at the SUV. After about thirty highly suspenseful seconds, a young soccer mom got out, opened the rear door and removed her daughter from the car seat. Worley finally relaxed as the woman and her daughter entered the supermarket.

"Sorry, I wish I could help," Worley added. "I have to go. Listen to what I'm telling you. Find a way to get out, cut a deal if you have to, and go ask for forgiveness. Repent before it's too late!"

On the way back from Austin, Romeo suggested they stop at Joe Cotten's BBQ restaurant, in nearby Robstown, for some of the best barbecue this side of Corpus Christi. They were sitting in the back of the restaurant, savoring healthy servings of pork ribs, sausage, brisket, along with the restaurant's famous "family secret recipe" potato salad. Alex was busy, spreading a little creamy cheddar cheese on a cracker, when Romeo, who was facing the door, pointed toward the cash register.

"Isn't that Bishop Salamanca by the front entrance?"

Alex turned around slowly, caught a glimpse of the man, and quickly turned away. "I'll be damned," whispered Alex, trying to lighten the mood. "No wonder the jerk is obese. He probably chows Joe Cotten's every night."

Salamanca was paying the tab, while Tony, the seminary student and faithful assistant to the spiritual leader, was picking up large take-out bags. The cashier quickly gave Salamanca his change, and the pair was gone.

"Is he gone?" asked Alex, not wanting to turn around.

"Yep."

"That guy's everywhere. Maybe I'm becoming paranoid, like Worley said. What do you think?"

"I'm sure it's just a coincidence, boss. Corpus Christi is just five minutes away. Everyone I know from Corpus comes to Joe Cotten's. To them, it's like going to the Stripes down at the corner."

"Speaking of Worley," continued Alex as he worked on a tender pork rib, "do you really think the Vatican is involved?"

Romeo put down his iced tea mug and shrugged his shoulders. "Who knows? Are you getting worried?"

"I don't care if something happens to me, but my grandpa or friends . . . Gigi, you, Michael? That's a different story. You guys are the only family I have. And I'd hate for something to happen to any of you because of my involvement in the case."

"What are you saying? Are you taking Worley's advice?"

"I don't know. I don't know what to think. I just don't want anybody getting hurt."

"Maybe what you need is to get away for a couple of days. Go fishing, clear your head. I heard the reds are running."

"Sounds like a good idea. Let me see if I can get my gear ready. Maybe we can get away this weekend."

"In any event, the foundation's summary judgment is still pending, right? Whatever judge gets appointed, he or she can still kick us out and we haven't gotten over the initial hurdle."

"Still on very shaky ground," conceded Alex, suddenly his attitude changing. "You're right. Why get ahead of ourselves when we haven't even survived their motion. They can still cut our legs from underneath us."

"*Exacto*," Romeo chimed in as he raised his saucy rib in the air and pretended he was toasting as if holding a beer. "First things, first. Then we'll worry about the rest."

CHAPTER 20

A LEX WAS WATCHING Gigi sleep as he got ready to get in bed after coming home late from his trip to Austin. She was wearing his favorite South Texas College of Law T-shirt that Gigi claimed smelled like him and drove her mad with desire. She'd always wear it to sleep when Alex went out of town.

Alex slid into bed, and Gigi shifted her body and pressed against him. He put his arm around her and got comfortable, getting his pillows just so.

"How was Austin?" Gigi asked almost in a whisper.

"I'm sorry I woke you up."

"I heard you come in . . . I couldn't sleep, really. Someone kept calling and hanging up. I disconnected the phone. Probably a prankster."

"How often did it happen?"

"Three times," said Gigi.

"Did they say anything?"

"No. They just hung up. So, how did it go?"

Alex shifted positions and stared up at the ceiling. He was worried. "Austin was fine, baby. We couldn't find the guy we went looking for. He was no longer working at the state hospital."

"Did they have an address for him, a phone number?"

"No, nothing," lied Alex, "the guy fell off the face of the earth."

"Maybe he'll show his face later. Anyway, I'm tired. I'm glad you're home. Good night."

"Good night, honey."

Unable to sleep, Alex slipped out of bed, got dressed and took the elevator to the lobby area of the Contessa di Mare building. He walked next door, to the Radisson Hotel. It was barely 12:45 A.M.

The revelations by Worley, plus running into Salamanca at Joe Cotten's earlier in the evening and now the calls on the penthouse's private land line were playing with his nerves. He needed a drink. When he walked in, the place was practically deserted. There were Jesse and Andy, two local celebrities famous for breaking all kinds of records for sales of timeshares on the Island. They were nursing beers as they waved to Alex. He said hi and proceeded to take a seat at a cocktail table, away in a far corner, and ordered a double Cuba Libre with Bacardi Añejo. He unwrapped a new pack of cigarettes, but waited for his drink to arrive before lighting one up.

The lounge's band started a new set with the Eagle's "Life in the Fast Lane," and two couples in their forties or fifties took to the floor and started dancing. The waitress came by and dropped off Alex's drink.

"Do you want me to run a tab, Alex?" asked Desiree, the waitress. She was a twenty-something, with red, pouty lips and an East Coast accent.

"Sure," said Alex as he stirred his drink. He took a sip. "It's pretty quiet tonight, huh?"

"Yep. Although there's another CLE course starting tomorrow, Friday. I'm glad. We should be busy this weekend. I've got to pay rent next week."

"How long is it supposed to last?"

"Friday and Saturday," explained Desiree, "attorneys from all over the state have started trickling in already."

"Do you have a light?"

Desiree reached into her short's pocket and pulled out a blue Bic lighter. She lit Alex's cigarette. "Here you go." She then put the lighter away. "Where's Gigi?"

"At home, sleeping. She's tired, been working long hours."

"Haven't seen her in a while."

"She's got her hands full right now," explained Alex, "planning the wedding and all . . . "

"Call if you need anything," said Desiree as she started to walk away. "Last call is in an hour."

Alex was checking his messages in his voice mail, nursing his fifth Cuba Libre, not paying any attention to his surroundings, feeling somewhat tipsy, when Desiree delivered another drink.

"What's this?" he asked, totally surprised.

"A Sex on the Beach," said Desiree.

"I didn't order this."

Desiree did not flinch. She just stood there. "The girl at the bar sent it. Do you want me to take it back?"

"Who?"

"That girl," pointed Desiree, "the one wearing a sun dress and sandals."

Alex's jaw came unglued, and the cigarette fell from his lips into his drink. From the bar, all the way across the lounge, Savannah Lee raised her wine glass and flashed a beautiful smile at Alex, but he was unable to move. All he could mumble was a wimpy "*Virgen Santa de Dios*. Holy Mother of Jesus."

Alex awoke to find himself alone in bed, naked, in one of the resort's cabana rooms facing the pool at the Isla Grand. He had a splitting headache and was confused. It took him a couple of minutes to realize what had happened. His clothes were on the floor, next to the king-sized bed, along with Savannah's sun dress, panties and sandals. When he saw the clothes on the floor and Savannah's suitcase by the corner, including her make-up bag on the nightstand, next to his cell phone, his heart jumped out of his chest.

"*¡En la madre!* What have I done?!" Alex yelled. "Gigi's going to kill me! *Dios Santo*. Oh, my God! This can't be happening!"

He shot out of bed, grabbed his clothes and rushed to get dressed, when he noticed Savannah's business card next to his cell. She had left him a handwritten message:

"Alex, sorry I didn't get a chance to say
good-bye. CLE classes started at 8:00 A.M. BTW,
you were amazing! Come by tonight, Savannah."

The whole room started spinning, and Alex started feeling sick. He struggled to focus and read the time on his phone while the throbbing in his head became louder and more painful. It was nine-thirty. He saw several missed calls. One had been from Romeo, another from Yarrington and the last five from Gigi.

He ran into the restroom and started throwing up.

CHAPTER 21

"**I**T'S THIS WEEKEND?"

"Yes, I thought I'd told you already," screamed Gigi. "Anyway, where the hell did you go last night?"

Alex had poked his head into Gigi's office, trying to pretend nothing was out of the ordinary while at the same time trying to piece together the sketchy "episode." As much as he'd tried, he was having a hard time remembering the details of what he surmised had been an "all-out" one-nighter. The last clear memory was Desiree delivering a drink, and then Savannah coming over to say hi. After that, the night was a big blur.

"Huh, I couldn't sleep. So I took a walk on the beach, *mi amor.*"

"And why didn't you answer my calls?"

"Because my cell was dead."

"So, you walked all night, or what? Where the hell were you?"

"After I walked down to the jetties, I went across the street to the Sea Ranch Marina, and I crashed in my sailboat. I'm sorry, I should have called. My fault. I would have tried, but my cell was dead."

"I don't think you're telling me everything, Alex. I don't know what it is, but there's something going on, and I don't like it."

"Nothing's going on." He looked up to the ceiling, then he looked away from Gigi, as if getting ready to come clean. "Okay, there is . . . a little something, I admit. You got me."

"What is it? You better not be jerking me around, Alex. I mean it."

"All right, here's the truth. The reason I went to my sailboat was because I wanted to book the villa in Greece for the wedding. I wanted it to be a surprise. So, because of the time difference, our time zone and their time zone, I had to do it in the wee hours of the morning. I couldn't do it from home. You would have found out. There. Now you know. *Es la meritita verdad.*"

"Really? You booked the villa, the one on top of Santorini Island, overlooking the Mediterranean? The one I wanted?"

"Yep, I exchanged emails with a girl named Mina Dukakis . . . Patakis, something like that. You want to check my emails?" Alex offered, knowing full well the whole idea could backfire at any minute. Especially if Gigi decided to look at his phone. "She's sending confirmation later on in the day."

Gigi's demeanor changed, instantly. "No, baby, I believe you. It's not necessary. I trust you," responded Gigi. "I'm sorry I over-reacted. Come here."

Alex went around Gigi's desk. She got up from her chair, and they embraced. He looked into her eyes. She reached over and kissed him, pulled back and stared into his green eyes.

"Promise me, Alex, that we will always be truthful with one another. That's all I ask."

"I promise," answered Alex, feeling like the biggest charlatan.

"Oh, before I forget," said Gigi, "I promised my nephew Max that we would take him to the movies this weekend. Hopefully we can do it on Sunday? My brother and his wife are coming into town for the couple's shower this Saturday. I hope you don't mind."

"I wanted to go check on grandpa, but for you, *preciosa* . . . anything, my sweet princess. Sure, we'll take little Max to the movies. What are we going to go see?"

"He's been wanting to see 'Over the Hedge.'"

"Sounds good. And the shower? Are we ready? Who else is coming, do we know?" asked Alex, happy that they were no longer talking about the hours when he was probably engaged in the most intense, the most naughty and pleasurable sex he'd ever had, and yet he did not remember any of it. *Qué desgracia.*

"Most of my old friends from the DA's office, and my best friend from college. And you? Did your college roommate reply?" she asked.

"Who, Neto?"

"Yes, Ernesto. Did he confirm? I'd love to meet him and his wife. Find out what you were like in college."

"I was an angel."

Michael poked his head into the office. "Alex, come take a look at this. The order appointing the new judge in the Santibáñez case just came in."

"Who is it?"

"Judge Emiliano Cienfuegos. Do you know him?"

"No, I don't know him. But I've heard of him."

Gigi went back to her chair and continued working on her computer, not really wanting to know, or hear, or have anything to do with the Santibáñez case.

"Well, looks like he's ready to get going. Here's Cienfuegos's order setting the foundation's summary judgment for hearing, first thing on Monday at 10:00 A.M. I guess we'll be working all weekend."

"But the couple's shower . . . and Max . . . the movies?" Alex muttered as he turned to face Gigi.

"Don't look at me," she declared, "you figure it out. You're the one that wanted to get involved in the case."

Alex turned around and faced Michael. "I'll figure something out. Don't worry."

"Good," said Michael as he walked away and down the hall-way to his office.

CHAPTER 22

J UDGE EMILIANO CIENFUEGOS was the spitting image of the world-famous Mexican revolutionary Pancho Villa. The only difference between Villa and Cienfuegos was the fact that Judge Cienfuegos wore horn-rimmed glasses, appeared to have attained a certain level of social refinement and spoke in a calm, soothing voice. In other words, his voice and manners did not go with the Mexican *pistolero* look.

When he took the bench that morning, he wasted no time in kick-starting the hearing on the foundation's summary judgment. Without looking up at any of the parties present in the courtroom, the judge picked up the court's file and read from it.

"Good morning. Please be seated. The court now calls cause no. 2002-12-111-C: Santibáñez et al. v. The Catholic Diocese of the Southern Coastal Counties d/b/a The Agnus Dei Foundation. Are we ready to proceed?"

"Yes, Your Honor," announced Dana McDermott, "this is our motion."

Before making his announcement, Alex looked over at opposing counsel's table and saw that Savannah Lee was not in the courtroom. Frank Mosley was present, apparently ready to play second fiddle to McDermott, but there was no sign of Savannah, anywhere. Alex was miffed. Had she quit the firm? Had she been fired? Had McDermott found out she had slept with the enemy?

Behind McDermott's table, all the other attorneys representing the intervenors in the case were standing, ready to announce that they were aligned with the foundation and that they were also adopting the foundation's summary judgment, but would let Mrs. McDermott handle the arguments.

Before Alex could announce, Tim O'Quinn, who loved to hear himself talk, chimed in, "Your Honor, I'm Tim O'Quinn with the law firm of Tim O'Quinn, from New York."

The judge cut him off, "I've seen the intervenors' motion to adopt the Agnus Dei Foundation's summary judgment, Mr. O'Quinn. Will you or any of the attorneys representing the intervenors be arguing here this morning?"

"Ah, well, no, Your Honor," said O'Quinn, "it's just that . . . "

"Okay, then," said Cienfuegos, "the record will reflect that all the lawyers representing all the intervenors are present in the courtroom. Let me hear from the plaintiffs."

"Yes, Your Honor," said Alex as he got up slowly from counsel's table. "Good morning, Alejandro Del Fuerte for the plaintiffs, along with my partner and co-counsel . . . "

Michael joined in. "Michael Fetzer, Your Honor, I also represent the plaintiffs. We're from the Brownsville firm of Del Fuerte, Fetzer & Montemayor. We're ready."

"Very well," acknowledged Cienfuegos, in a calm manner, putting everyone at ease, "let me do this. The court has read the five-hundred-page motion filed by the Agnus Dei Foundation, along with the volumes and volumes of exhibits. The court has also read all of the intervenors' briefs in support of the foundation's motion. I have also read the plaintiff's response to the summary judgment and the foundation's three-hundred-page response to the plaintiff's response. Everybody with me, so far?"

"Yes," came the collective response.

"Okay, since it is the defendant's motion, I will give the defendant and the intervenors ten minutes each to argue, then the plaintiffs will have forty-five minutes to reply, and then there will be a final five minutes—total—for any rebuttal. Now, go Mrs. McDermott . . . the clock is ticking."

Alex thought about the argument he'd prepared over the weekend, his overall knowledge of the case, the law, and suddenly the reality and the enormity of his predicament hit him dead smack between the eyes, like a 2 X 4. Here he was about to make his first argument in a courtroom full of lawyers and spectators, in a case that had landed in his lap less than seven weeks ago. He'd barely scratched the surface while the lawyers on the other side— many of them board-certified in real estate and oil and gas—had kicked around the same case with two other plaintiffs' lawyers for now close to four years. Alex knew he was about to get a spanking, plain and simple. He should have let this dog lie . . . should have listened to Gigi and should have walked away while he still had a chance. When was he going to learn?

Dana McDermott's raspy voice brought Alex back to reality. "Judge, could you give me five minutes to go, at least, into the background of the case, and not count those against me or my client? Let me keep my ten, intact, plus the five for rebuttal."

"Mr. Del Fuerte, what do you think?" asked Judge Cienfuegos.

Alex looked at Michael, and Michael shrugged his shoulders. "We don't care, Your Honor. Mrs. McDermott can have five minutes to go into the background, no objection."

Tim O'Quinn interjected again, "We know the court is familiar with the background of the case, but in the event of an appeal, the court of appeals will benefit by reading and learning of the background from the record. It makes sense."

Judge Cienfuegos gave O'Quinn a look, as if saying "zip it."

"Very well. Mrs. McDermott, please continue," added the judge.

Still surprised that strict time limits had been imposed on her and that Alex appeared overly confident, the seasoned attorney gathered her papers, found her reading glasses and reached for a yellow pad with some notes on it.

"Don Arturo de Monterreal," she said, rolling her double r's, "was a Spanish settler who received the land grant or a *porción* directly from the King, Charles III of Spain, in 1767. Don Arturo had one son, Bernardo de Monterreal. Bernardo had four descendants, but three of them died without issue, or descendants, and left no spouses. The lone surviving descendant, Nicolás de Monterreal, had four daughters. Three of those daughters never married, died of old age and had no issue. The last remaining daughter, Isabel de Monterreal married Joaquín de Santibáñez, and they had seven children, sons and daughters. By 1820, Mexico recognized that these seven children and their heirs, including Candelario Santibáñez, were the rightful owners of La Minita land grant, a tract comprising almost a million acres. It's important to remember that the U.S.-Mexico War did not occur until 1846, so in the 1820s Texas still belonged to Mexico, along with Arizona, New Mexico, California and Colorado. In any event, by the early 1900s, for various reasons, the Santibáñez interests in this enormous tract, either by conveyances or by reason of unfavorable judgments, including many bad business deals, had largely evaporated. Candelario's siblings sold or abandoned their portions, but not Candelario. By 1937, there was still one sizeable piece of land, close to half a million acres, still held together by Candelario Santibáñez and his heirs.

"Enter Ulysses McKnight, a prospector and opportunist, who came through South Texas after the Great Depression. He first married Candelario's oldest daughter, Teresa, and together they had a son. The son died after getting kicked in the head by a horse named 'Chiflado,' at the tender age of ten. After Teresa died, heartbroken because of her loss, Papá Candelario followed. Needing a shoulder to cry on, soon Ulysses McKnight found himself crying on Amelia's shoulder, Candelario's other, younger daughter. Eventually, these two married—see, I told you McKnight was an opportunist—and when Amelia died after giving birth to a boy, little Austin, the only comfort Ulysses McKnight could find was at the bottom of the bottle."

McDermott paused and pointed at a timeline being projected onto one of the walls in the courtroom in support of the motion. She then had Mosley, who was in charge of the laptop and the PowerPoint presentation, click on the next slide.

"These right here, Your Honor, are also exhibits that have been attached to our motion," said McDermott, and she then proceeded to explain what each piece portrayed and how they established certain key facts that the court needed to consider. On the wall, there were now maps and surveys being projected of the disputed area, along with Austin McKnight's last will and testament, witness affidavits, old warranty deeds, quit claim deeds, judgments, old photos of Candelario, Doña Berta and their daughters, Teresa and Amelia, along with photos of Ulysses McKnight, and many other historical documents, even *actas* and *escrituras* from the *registro* civil in Tamaulipas, Mexico. McDermott took great pains to explain the legal significance of each one of these pieces of evidence and how it all buttressed the Foundation's position."

"You've got three minutes left," interrupted the judge.

McDermott resumed her argument. "Austin McKnight also died heartbroken, childless, in 1969, but left a valid will where he gave everything to the Agnus Dei Foundation. That will was admitted to probate in a Texas court. The executor of the will properly provided the requisite inventory and accounting and distributed the corpus to the devisees as per the will. Since then the Agnus Dei Foundation has owned whatever remains of La Minita.

"If the Santibáñez descendants had an issue with La Minita or thought they were the heirs, they had time to fight and file a will contest. They had time to show up to court and contest the validity of the proceedings. They had time to file a claim, get in line to get something going. Do something. Anything. But, instead, they did nothing. They chose to sit around, twiddle their thumbs and let time slip away. The law requires that you act reasonably under the circumstances and to be diligent, not show up forty-some years after the fact, demanding that the possessor return what 'may have very well been' rightfully yours, at one time.

"Now, Judge," McDermott pressed on, "my client is entitled to summary judgment, as a matter of law, because of the following reasons. First, it is undisputed that Ulysses McKnight gave everything he had to his son, Austin, back in the 1950s. The fact remains that Austin had adversely possessed the land for many years, and his family had been living on it for even longer. Since fifty years ago, the McKnights have been receiving gas and oil royalties from these same lands. Which means that if the plaintiffs wanted to fight over the lands, they should have filed their lawsuit a long, long time ago. The Santibáñez descendants could have discovered through the exercise of due diligence that they had a claim as Arturo's heirs . . . "

Judge Cienfuegos suddenly interrupted, "Which Arturo is this?"

"I'll get to that in a minute, Judge," said McDermott, "but it's not the same Arturo that took straight from the King of Spain, way back when. It's another Arturo. So the heirs could have taken action forty some years ago. Now, some forty years later, it is too late to do something about it. Clearly, the statute of limitations bars all of the plaintiffs' claims. They only had four years to act from when they knew they had a claim or should have known they had a claim . . . and that was back in the fifties because Arturo told of tales of how he was dispossessed of his lands. And those tales were passed down from generation to generation. So, at a minimum, they all knew as far back as 1950 or 1960 that they could have had a claim to the lands.

"In conclusion, Your Honor, the rationale behind a four-year statute of limitations is to prevent the litigation of outdated claims. If a plaintiff wants to pursue a lawsuit, they only have so much time, so that evidence is preserved, documents can still be produced and witnesses may still testify while their recollections are not impaired, while their testimony is still fresh in their minds.

"Moreover, even if the argument that the statute of limitations fails, the fact remains that the McKnights have occupied that piece of land since the 1930s, and said occupation has been open, notorious, continuous and hostile to the Santibáñez interests. And yet, the plaintiffs waited more than sixty years to do something about it? We don't let people wait around sixty-plus years to then decide to sue. It just doesn't work that way, I'm sorry. But even if they could, the McKnights adversely possessed the land longer than the ten-year period under the law, more like sixty-plus years, and they came to own, by adverse possession, both the surface and mineral estates to all of La Minita. Which, ultimately, Austin McKnight had the right to bequeath or give away to whomever he pleased, pursuant to his last will and testament.

"For these reasons," concluded McDermott, "we're asking this honorable court to grant summary judgment for the Agnus Dei Foundation and award attorney's fees in the amount of $500,000.00, which are customary and reasonable, when it takes these many lawyers to defend a lawsuit for well over three years, and such lawsuit should have never been filed in the first place. Thank you."

Judge Cienfuegos noticed right away that McDermott had never fully answered his question regarding Arturo. He was now intrigued.

Tim O'Quinn wanted to interrupt, and so did Uhels, Nichols, Fonseca and the others. They were all chomping at the bit.

Judge Cienfuegos spoke, restoring order in his courtroom, "Thank you, Mrs. McDermott, that was very interesting and informative." He then looked at the other lawyers in the court-room. "What say the intervenors?"

Jim Hanmore went first. He was brief and effective, arguing that it would be manifestly unfair to allow a bunch of welfare mis-creants to take the reins of an empire, when in fact they could not even run a two-bit *tortillería*. Giving them back their lands would not only cause havoc in the energy sector, but it would also spell doom to financial markets all around the world.

Tim O'Quinn followed next and argued that by denying the foundation's motion for summary judgment and allowing the case to get to trial, a dangerous legal precedent was being established. That many other Hispanic families all along the entire U.S.-Mexico border would follow suit and clog the courts with frivolous and expensive lawsuits that would ultimately destroy the integrity of the entire American judicial system. Why not just give Mexico all of their lands back and call the United States of America the Unit-ed States of Mexico?

Casey Uhels picked up where O'Quinn left off and argued that if the case went to trial and a jury found that the Santibáñez con-tinued to be the rightful owners of La Minita, then it would be impossible to calculate the staggering back-due royalties owed to the heirs. In all likelihood, the billions and billions owed would bankrupt his clients. Even if the companies were lucky enough to survive bankruptcy, the experts still predicted that, once the pro-ducers were ordered to repay these monies, the price of gas would probably hit the eighty-dollar-a-gallon mark. The whole thing spelled gloom and doom!

Even Parker McFarland, an assistant attorney general representing the Texas Land Office, was allowed to speak. He reminded the court that even though there existed the separation
between Church and State, the State of Texas stood shoulder-to-
shoulder with the foundation in this instance. The Texas Attorney
General had filed amicus briefs supporting the foundation's position, and an adverse court ruling would ultimately result in political, social, legal and economic upheaval.

Finally, after hearing more rambling from the defendants, the
court addressed the plaintiffs. "Mr. Del Fuerte? Your turn."

Without even looking at his notes, Alex picked up where
defense counsel had left off. "Thank you, Your Honor. What Mrs.
McDermott and all these lawyers representing the intervenors and
the State of Texas forgot to tell you, Your Honor, or conveniently
left out, is a little known fact that dramatically changes the entire
analysis in these proceedings. That is, Candelario wanted to have
a son very much. Everybody knew so: the *vaqueros* at his ranch,
the help inside the house, the cook, his business associates and
other third parties. In fact, he wanted a son so much that he found
a way to have himself one, out of wedlock. His name was . . . "

Dana McDermott sprang to her feet and objected. "Hearsay,
Your Honor. This is all hearsay, there's no reliable evidence that
Arturo was the biological son of Candelario Santibáñez."

Alex did not wait for Cienfuegos to rule the objection. "This
is argument . . . my argument, Your Honor?"

"Keep going," said Cienfuegos, "I want to hear this."

"Candelario's illegitimate son was Arturo Santibáñez aka Arturito. The same person you asked Ms. McDermott about, remember?" Alex paused for effect. "Anyway, Arturito's mother was the
wife of one of the *vaqueros* at the ranch. And it was a well-guarded
secret. Candelario was married to Doña Berta Santibáñez, and she
would have killed him had she found out. Fortunately, the unsuspecting cowboy never found out, and neither did Doña Berta . . .
or maybe they didn't want to find out. Who knows? Doña Berta
eventually died, but she died thinking that Candelario would give
everything to their daughters. Well, that never happened. Candelario willed everything to Arturito, the entire tract, including the

mineral interests and everything else. Candelario had figured that since his daughters had married or would marry, their husbands would take care of them and support them, like any self-respecting man would do. One interesting fact, Your Honor, Doña Berta would not have had any claim to the tract because this was all Candelario's separate property. He already owned La Minita before he married Doña Berta. It was not community property. I just want to make sure we all are on the same page.

"Are you with me, so far, Your Honor?" asked Alex.

"Yes. You've got seven minutes, counsel," replied Judge Cienfuegos.

"So, the land is actually bequeathed to Arturo in Candelario's will. Of course, just because you have a will in hand saying something is yours doesn't necessarily make it yours. We all know that. You must do something with the will. Record it, take it to court, get it admitted to probate.

"Now," continued Alex, "before I continue talking about wills and the probate of wills, and about Arturo, and his heirs—my clients—and Candelario and his daughters, I'd like to remind this honorable court and everyone else present in this courtroom of the legal principles applied in summary judgment hearings. It's not rocket science. In other words, let's say you dared to sue the president and there's a federal law that says no one can sue the president of the United States of America, EVER, for whatever reason. The president would be entitled to summary judgment as a 'matter of law,' period, no ifs, ands or buts. Whoever sued the president would be thrown out of court, along with his or her lawsuit. Because the law says so, end of story, that's the way it is. And the other way a party is entitled to win is if an element is missing from the plaintiff's prima facie case or the defendant is missing an element of his or her defense. The best example is when a shopper sues Sam's Club because he bought a soft drink in the store, gets home and finds a severed thumb inside the drink. In that instance, Sam's would not owe a duty to the shopper and should be let out of the lawsuit, via a summary judgment motion. The shopper might have a claim against the Coca-Cola Bottling Company, but not Sam's. Sam's did nothing wrong. We say Sam's owed no duty to the shopper because of the method involved in bottling the Coca-Cola product.

"With that said, a motion for summary judgment is easily defeated if there's a single fact issue that a jury must first decide. In this instance, it won't matter that the Agnus Dei Foundation papered the court to death and decimated a rainforest in the process of assembling its summary judgment motion. It will not matter that the foundation generated a five-hundred-page motion. It doesn't matter that the foundation cited a million cases in that same motion. Or that along with their motion, they filed boxes and boxes of exhibits and that all together they filled an entire room with mountains of documents or that there are thirty briefs from the intervenors also supporting the foundation's position. None of that is important, not even the fact that the Texas attorney general joined in support of the foundation. In the end, the size of the motion has no relevance and carries no weight."

While Alex continued arguing, Bobby Fonseca, Jeremy Hidalgo, Teddy Galindo and the others paced back and forth, making facial gestures and shaking their heads, hoping to send the message to Judge Cienfuegos to ignore Alex.

Alex paid no attention.

"Because if the evidence presented with the Santibáñez' response," Alex paused for effect, "raises a single, meager, tiny, infinitesimal fact issue . . . that fact issue must be decided by the jury, along with the rest of the case. In other words, the granting of a summary judgment is not proper when the party opposing the summary judgment attacks what the foundation is saying and raises a genuine issue of fact by way of affidavits, exhibits, documents, other types of evidence, which must, first, be decided on by the trier of fact . . . a good, abled jury from Kleberg County."

"Two minutes," indicated the judge.

"In the case at hand, Your Honor, the granting of the foundation's motion would be improper because there is one fact issue that defeats what they're saying regarding the statute of limitations argument and the adverse possession argument. Arturo, the illegitimate son, did do something with his daddy's will."

There was a collective gasp in the courtroom. The horror on intervenors' faces and McDermott's was immediately apparent. They started objecting, shouting over one another.

"Order, order!" yelled Cienfuegos, "all of you . . . settle down!"

Alex forged ahead, "He recorded the will in Cameron County in the property records. The will, however, was in Spanish, written in Candelario's own hand, witnessed by several *vaqueros* and very hard to read. Remember, this tract of land extends over four counties: Nueces, Kleberg, Willacy and Cameron. Arturo recorded the will as muniment of title, because in the old days that was the norm and you could record the will anywhere the property was situated. So it is presumed that the whole world had notice that Arturo now owned the disputed tract. By the way, all my clients are descendants of Arturo—we're claiming through him.

"The will is attached to our response, is not translated, quite hard to read, written in old Spanish, and if you don't know what you're looking for, or if you don't read Spanish, *español castellano*, you will miss it. It is Exhibit I(A)(ii), attached to the Mexican *Actas* and *Escrituras* in our response. Also, the parties' names are backwards in that in Mexico people carry both the paternal and maternal last names, even a middle name. And sometimes those get mixed up, and people don't pick up on it. That's probably what happened here. An American title examiner could never have picked up on it. But guess what?"

Everyone in the courtroom sat up straight, waiting to see if Judge Cienfuegos would ask the obvious question.

"What?" asked the learned judge.

Before Alex could respond, McDermott was already signaling Foley to dig for the Santibáñez response and find the page Alex was alluding to, fast. All the other attorneys in the audience started scrambling, trying to find the document referenced. Alex and Michael appeared to be enjoying the spectacle immensely. It was like a scene out of a movie.

McDermott raised her hand in victory. "It's here, Your Honor. I would object to the court considering this exhibit, since it was not translated, and we were not given notice of its existence. Also, any argument related to this exhibit would be nothing more than hearsay."

Judge Cienfuegos looked over at Alex. "Mr. Del Fuerte, do you care to respond?"

"This document was produced in discovery years ago, Your Honor. The defendants never objected. Also, it's been part of the court's file for well over three years. The defendants never objected. And it is an official public record. It has been an official public record since it was filed, decades ago. It is self-authenticating, it's reliable, clearly an exception to the hearsay rule—some would argue it could be a dying declaration. It's admissible and it comes in. And any objection these lawyers may have had was waived long ago."

"Judge," cried O'Quinn, "we would join Mrs. McDermott in her objection . . . we were never told of its existence."

Judge Cienfuegos shook his head. "The objection is overruled. Besides, it's been on file these many years, and I don't see a written objection, anywhere. Continue, Mr. Del Fuerte. "

"Thank you," interjected Alex. "The point is, Your Honor, now we have a fact issue. Was the land really McKnight's or was it Arturo's? And here's another fact issue. If Arturito received everything from Candelario, then what was there for McKnight to receive? Everything had already been willed away, right? How could McKnight give away something he did not have? Does a probate proceeding trump the filing of the will as muniment of title, or vice versa? Can Arturo's will be considered a will contest to McKnight's? Since it is in Spanish, what does the will really mean? How much property does it dispose of? Is there a residuary clause? Does the residuary clause come into play? What was the legal significance of the will's language? Since Arturo filed it in Cameron County and he and his heirs maintained a house on a portion of the tract, in southern Cameron County, does that defeat the McKnight's adverse possession claim? Would it affect only the claim as to the surface estate, or the mineral estate, or both? And if the muniment of title affects Austin McKnight's will, does it also affect the gift to the foundation?

"I can go on and on, Your Honor. There are more facts here than you, or I, would care to count . . . facts that, procedurally, must first be decided by a jury. There are enough fact issues to prevent the granting of the foundation's motion. Would you like me to keep going, Your Honor?" Alex turned and winked at McDermott. She was fit to be tied.

"I think you've made your point," replied Cienfuegos.

"Rebuttal, Your Honor?" asked McDermott, not wanting to pass the opportunity to bill her deep-pocket client some more.

"I've heard enough, Mrs. McDermott. I would have to agree with Mr. Del Fuerte. There appear to be key issues that need to be addressed first by a jury. The defendant's motion for summary judgment is denied."

"Judge, Judge!" cried McDermott, "wait . . . "

"The final pretrial will be on December 5th, with jury selection scheduled for December 12th, and we will promptly commence trial on December 15. How long will it take to try the case?"

"Three weeks, at the most," said Alex.

"Ha! Wishful thinking," interjected Uhels. "With all the intervenors and the sheer size of the case, I doubt we'll be finished in two months, Judge."

"I'd say about twelve weeks, at least, Judge. Three months, for sure," added O'Quinn.

"Three months just for my client to put on its case," added McDermott as she crunched numbers in her head. She could easily find a way to bill the foundation $200,000 for a three-month trial. "That's how much time the foundation will need to put on its case-in-chief and present all of its experts, Your Honor."

"Well, I guess we'll work straight through the holidays, then," answered Judge Cienfuegos. "We'll be in recess!"

"All rise for the Honorable Emiliano Cienfuegos," shouted the bailiff. "This court is now in recess."

Judge Cienfuegos left the bench, and Romeo, Michael and Alex started collecting their things. McDermott, O'Quinn and Uhels came over to their table.

"This is not over, Del Fuerte," admonished McDermott. "It's gonna get ugly. Don't say I didn't warn you."

"Hey," Alex shouted back as he shoved papers and his yellow pad into his leather briefcase, "you know what they say . . . sometimes the very thing you're looking for is right in front of you . . . staring you straight in the face, but you just can't see it."

McDermott also faced Alex. "Oh, before I forget, this is for you." She handed Alex a folded, sealed envelope. "I suggest you open it while you're alone, in private."

"What is it?"

"You don't know?" she asked.

"No," answered Alex.

"Really? You have no clue?"

"No," repeated Alex, totally oblivious, still reeling from having handed the foundation its first defeat.

"My goodness," she said with a wicked smile, "it's a DVD."

Alex stashed it in his coat pocket, not knowing what else to make of it. Maybe it was a courtesy copy with exhibits that McDermott wanted Alex to have. He turned around to see if Michael or Romeo had witnessed the exchange. Michael was off to one side, holding the dolly, while Romeo loaded the boxes full of exhibits onto it.

CHAPTER 23

ALEX TORE OPEN the envelope and pulled out the DVD, along with a handwritten Post-It note. The bright-yellow sticky read: "Walk away or end up on YouTube." He turned on his desk computer, waited a minute for the computer to boot up and plopped the DVD in one of the drives. After a few more seconds, the computer's RealPlayer opened the DVD, and Alex hit play. As the DVD started playing, a sudden realization came over him: there would be no destination wedding, no European honeymoon and no happily ever after.

The images on the DVD had Alex and Savannah standing up next to the king-sized bed inside Savannah's pool-side cabana, kissing, undressing and tumbling onto bed. What was now very clear to Alex was that the foundation was capable of anything in order to hang on to its most valuable possession, La Minita. Whatever the cost, whatever the tactic, whatever the price, it was all fair game.

Panic, sheer unadulterated panic, invaded Alex. Bishop Ricardo Salamanca had just kicked him, full force, in the privates. His firm had just survived the first of many legal obstacles still to come, and Salamanca was already waterboarding Alex with obvious gusto. Horrified, he hit the eject button on his computer, yanked the DVD and quickly tossed it into the compact, heavy-duty shredder under his desk.

He then clicked on the Explorer icon and got on the Internet. He pulled up YouTube and started doing a search for the video. Nothing. He then Googled his name, Savannah's name and the

157

words "sex," "affair," "one-night stand," but his search came up empty.

In a frenzy, he went to the State Bar of Texas Website and clicked on the "attorney search" link and typed the words Savannah Lee in the box. Nothing. There was a Wayne Lee of Houston, and a Donald Lee from El Paso, including a Jennifer Lee from Beaumont, and a Darby Lee, even a Rose Lee, and a Morgan Lee, but no trace of Savannah Lee. Obviously, she was not an attorney.

Alex continued doing frantic Google searches, trying to track down an address or phone number for the girl, but he was coming up empty-handed. He then went to the Website for the Kennedy-Gallagher Group to see if Savannah Lee worked with McDermott. He clicked on the "firm's attorneys" link. *Nada*. No Savannah Lee. He then clicked on the "staff" link, with the identical result. He was growing desperate. Who was Savannah Lee?

Finally, a link popped up directing him to Wikipedia. He clicked on it.

Savannah Lee, f.k.a. Sue St. James was born in New Orleans, Louisiana, on August 18, 1975.

"She's a former porn actress who has been dubbed 'the chameleon' for her uncanny ability to change looks. She started acting in erotic films and soft porn in 1999, after having worked as a Victoria's Secret model. By 2003, she'd earned a cross-over role in a horror film directed by Quentin Fratelli, where her performance earned her praise from the critics."

Alex cursed his luck. He was in this mess because he'd refused to listen to Gigi, and he'd been so stubborn and blind that he'd decided to fight the church, God and Salamanca. And now he was paying the price.

"Mr. Del Fuerte?" came Astrid's voice over the intercom. "You have a call on line one."

"Who is it?"

"Bishop Salamanca," replied Astrid, "says he needs to talk to you."

Alex picked up the line to Astrid. "I can't talk to him. He's being represented by counsel. Does he want to get me in trouble?"

"He says it won't take but a minute," Astrid explained. "He insists on talking to you."

"Have him leave a number where I can reach him. I just can't talk to him, not right now."

Alex hung up the phone and continued to stare at Savannah Lee's seductive photo splashed all over the screen. He thought about Salamanca calling for a moment. Was he calling for a settlement? Work out a truce? Sure, Salamanca had Alex bent over a barrel, but Alex had also given the foundation its first black eye. The fact remained, the Santibáñez lawsuit was going to trial, finally.

"Can you put me through to Dana McDermott, please?" ordered Alex.

"I'm sorry," said the receptionist at the other end of the line, "She's on a call."

"I'll wait," replied Alex. "It's important."

"Okay, please hold."

Alex waited for Dana McDermott to pick up the line as a feeling of helplessness came over him. He was way in over his head, and he couldn't even confide in his partners. The minute Michael or Gigi found out what had transpired, they would put brakes on the Santibáñez litigation. Things were getting out of hand. First the arrests, then Savannah and now Bishop Salamanca calling. What could possibly happen next?

McDermott picked up the phone and, in her usual raspy voice, greeted Alex. "Dana McDermott speaking. How can I help you, Mr. Del Fuerte?"

"Listen, you piece of shit!" screamed Alex. "Who the hell do you think you are?! Do you think you can scare me because you got me on video with a porn star? Do you think I'm going to concede and just walk away? Is that what you and your goddamn client think?"

"Wait just a minute! Watch your tone, Mr. Del Fuerte," snapped McDermott, "or I'll hang up, right this instant. What do you want?"

"Bishop Salamanca has been calling me," explained Alex. "You need to tell him to stop calling, stop harassing me and leave me the hell alone."

"Salamanca calling you should be the least of your worries, Alex. We tried to warn you, but you wouldn't listen. Now it's too late . . . I'm afraid."

"Too late, huh?! Now, you listen to me, you don't know who you're messing with!" screamed Alex, completely out of control. "The both of you are going to wish you were never born by the time I'm finished with you and your stupid, worthless client!"

McDermott started chuckling on the other end of the line. "You and what army?"

"I don't need an army."

"Well, then, if you don't want the video to be posted all over the Internet . . . I think you know what you need to do. Why don't you just bow out, gracefully? Walk away? Pack your 'Dora the Explorer' backpack and go home?"

"Never, you hear?! Never!"

"We're going to be asking for our attorney's fees, once this is all over, Alex. Have you taken the time to explain to all your clients what will happen if they lose the case? How much in attorneys' fees they will have to pay, reimburse the foundation, the intervenors?"

"You'll never collect! These folks don't have a dime to their names."

"That may or may not be the case. But it's your job to inform them. And I bet you haven't done it because you know what'll happen. Most of your clients, if not all, will want to walk away, put an end to this silly, unrealistic dream. It's attorneys like you that clog the system with all kinds of ridiculous clients and ridiculous claims. It's attorneys like you that over-promise results to the clients and then find themselves unable to deliver."

Alex thought about that for a moment. McDermott was right. Since the last wave of tort reform, the Texas legislature had created the "offer of settlement" statute that said that if a defendant offered to settle a case for X amount of dollars, but the plaintiff did not accept the offer, or lost at trial, or maybe even won, but the jury award was substantially less than the defendant's offer to get the case settled, then the losing party reimbursed the victor all its attorneys' fees and court costs. It was another blatant attempt at clipping the country's trial lawyers' wings.

It was a provision in the Texas Rules of Civil Procedure to make the trial lawyers and their clients think twice before suing. In this case, the foundation had tendered an offer of settlement early on in the piddly amount of $10,000 for close to five hundred heirs. If the plaintiffs accepted the offer, once the attorneys deducted their fees and costs back, the plaintiffs could expect to go home with less than ten bucks a piece.

"My clients want justice," screamed Alex. "That's why they're in it. They're not going to walk away because of the danger of having to reimburse attorneys' fees or court costs. The plaintiffs have nothing to lose . . . and everything to gain, in case you forgot!"

"I'll tell you what," said McDermott, "I'll make you a deal. If you walk away peacefully, I'll recommend to my client to spare your clients the attorney's fees and for your firm to be reimbursed any costs incurred thus far. What do you say?"

The comment pushed Alex over the top. "Screw you, Dana! And screw Salamanca, and Mosley, Savannah Lee, your firm and the horse you all rode in. *Me van a hacer los mandados. ¡Tú y todos tus pinches abogaditos de mierda! Vas a ver, no sabes con quién te estás metiendo.*"

McDermott replied in perfect Spanish, a move that totally surprised Alex. "*Y tú me vas a pedir perdón de rodillas, cabrón, cuando me entregues tu licencia.*"

Alex was so upset, so blinded with rage that McDermott's last comment went over his head. Had he caught himself, cooled down a bit, he would have realized that McDermott was now threatening to yank his law license.

"You haven't been reading the *Texas Lawyer*, have you?" asked McDermott, still chuckling, while trying to drive the stake deeper into Alex's heart. "There's a little-known case out there where the plaintiff's attorneys lost a med mal case against a doctor, and it was the plaintiff's attorneys that had to pay the defense counsel's fees and costs, not the clients. The Texas Supreme Court ruled that the lawyers knew or should have known the case was a dog and should have never been filed. Doesn't that worry you?"

"You and Salamanca can kiss my ass!" yelled Alex as he slammed the phone down.

"Nice!" Romeo couldn't help but break into a wide grin. "You mean to tell me that Salamanca actually has you on video with Savannah Lee, the porn star?"

Not knowing who else to turn to, Alex decided that he needed a drink to calm his nerves and invited Romeo to get a beer. Gigi had called that she and her mom were up the Valley setting up the wedding registries at various department stores, so Alex had time for a drink before going home. The pair was sitting inside the Vermillion Restaurant, in a booth tucked away in the back of the lounge area.

"The worst part is that I don't remember any of it," said Alex, picking at a platter of fajita nachos, with sour cream, jalapeños and mounds of guacamole.

"Are you sure?"

"Nada, *compadre*. Zilch."

"You had a wild night with a porn star, and you're telling me that you don't remember absolutely anything? C'mon, I don't believe you," said Romeo as he finished his beer and reached for another Michelob Ultra from the ice bucket at the center of the table.

"Sad, but true."

"Do you still have the DVD?" Romeo asked as he reached for a nacho.

Alex shook his head. "I destroyed it in my shredder."

"Too bad."

Alex finished his beer, reached for another Shiner Bock and shrugged his shoulders in disappointment as he took a swig.

"You know what this means, don't you?" asked Romeo.

"What?"

"She probably slipped a clonazepam pill in your drink."

"The date rape drug?"

"Sure," said Romeo, "for you not to remember anything at all, I'd have to say that's what happened. Think about it. You've had one too many drinks before, and that's never happened before."

"I guess that would explain it."

"I bet that's what happened."

"How do I prove it?"

"You're the lawyer, *¿qué no?*"

Alejandro Del Fuerte grabbed a five-dollar bill sitting on the table and gave Romeo an angry stare. He then got up and headed for the digital jukebox by the door leading to the restrooms.

He put the money in the jukebox and started making his selections. He felt angry at himself, angry at the entire situation and afraid of what was still to come. The trial was less than three months away, and Salamanca had already sucker-punched him twice and had gotten him arrested. Alex and his firm had barely touched the case.

Alex finished making his selections at the jukebox and stood there waiting for the first song to start playing. He thought about the hell he was about to pay when word hit the streets that he had been videotaped in the buff with a porn star. He had failed Gigi, betrayed her trust and, in the process, started losing himself.

Bowie's "Changes" came blaring from the jukebox and Alex rejoined Romeo at their booth.

CHAPTER 24

THAT EVENING, after leaving the Vermillion in a cab driven by an old friend of Romeo's, Alex went to spend the night on his sailboat. He'd left Gigi a text message disclosing his whereabouts so she wouldn't worry. He'd stayed up looking at the stars, drinking coffee, chain smoking and thinking of his next move.

Alex grabbed his cigarettes, a lighter and decided to cross South Padre Island Boulevard and go for a walk on the beach. It was time to head home. He thought about patching things up and walking away from the lawsuit. Perhaps it was best to simply marry Gigi and settle into married life. Things would work themselves out; they always did, anyway.

Besides, what could be more important than family? Especially now that Grandpa César was not getting better. Since the last stent was put in place, the old man had had a series of small strokes. Things were not looking up. Maybe it was time to throw in the towel.

All the dreams were contingent on him being able to put a lid on things, though. As long as the DVD remained hidden away and was never published, Alex could probably still have a very nice life. He still had plenty of money in the bank, had an enormous ranch with producing oil and gas wells. A successful law practice, a beautiful penthouse on the beach. And in a few weeks he would also have a gorgeous wife. He just needed to find a way to walk away from the Santibáñez lawsuit, quietly. He needed to figure out an exit strategy.

The good news, so far, despite all the trouble brewing and now weighing heavily on his shoulders, was that his clients were still standing. They were still in the lawsuit. No matter what crazy scheme McDermott, Phillips or Salamanca conjured.

After a forty-five minute walk, he tagged the door sensor with his magnetic key to one of the Contessa di Mare's gates down by the beach. He pushed it open and let himself in. He stopped by the shower stall nearby to rinse his sandy feet and then walked past the tennis courts, the deep pool with the cascade feature, the shallow pool, the margarita shack and made it into the lobby area of the building. He walked up to the security desk, near the elevators.

"Morning, John," Alex said. "How are things?"

John, the security officer, looked up from the monitor in front of him. "That was you, by the beach?"

"Yep, just out for a walk."

"But it's five in the morning?"

"Couldn't sleep," replied Alex as he hit the elevator button. The elevator doors opened, and he jumped in. "See you."

"See you, Mr. Del Fuerte," said John.

Alex hit the button to the twentieth floor and waited for the eight-second ride to end. By the time the elevator doors opened to the penthouse floor, Alex knew exactly what he needed to do.

Gigi was awake when Alex walked in. She was sitting out in the wrap-around travertine balcony to the penthouse, looking out to sea. She was holding a half-full glass of wine in her left hand. Alex noticed the empty bottle of chardonnay on the floor, along with the folded "Lifestyle" section of the local newspaper.

"What's wrong, honey? Is everything all right?" asked Alex.

Gigi did not answer. She just kept staring at the ocean, the first rays of sunshine barely emerging over on the horizon.

"You know," she started, holding back a bit, "our engagement announcement came out in the local paper, today. Did you see it?"

"Yes, I saw it. You look amazing." He came and sat by her side, but she did not turn to see him. She kept staring out over the ocean.

"Does it really matter?"

"What do you mean?" swallowed Alex.

"There's not going to be a wedding, right, Alex? You know what I'm talking about."

"Huh, ahem . . . no, I don't know what you're talking about. Why don't you fill me in, princess?" asked Alex, seriously worried.

Alex's mind was racing at the speed of light, and he had no clue if he'd been busted because of the DVD, or if Gigi had called the Island of Santorini looking to confirm the booking of the villa. He did not know what to say, so he just sat there, expecting the worst. Thank God Gigi was looking out toward the ocean because otherwise she would have picked up on the "guilty as charged" look Alex was now sporting.

"No, I think you know what I'm talking about. Hell, I'm not even supposed to be drinking because I'm supposed to be on meds, except I really, really needed a drink. I'll start on the pills tomorrow."

"What are you saying?"

"You mean you don't know?"

"Um, no . . . I don't," Alex replied. "Sorry."

"You mean you have no idea what you did? Is that what you want me to believe?"

"C'mon! Stop playing games, just come out and tell me, once and for all. What did I do?"

There was silence. Gigi kept staring out into the distance. After about a minute, she spoke. "I'm pregnant, Alejandro! There won't be a wedding in Greece. We need to get married, now. Otherwise, my folks will kill me."

Alex started pacing back and forth, massaging his temples. This was worse than expected. Sure, he was excited about becoming a father, but the fact remained that he would soon be exposed. Salamanca was coming after him, like a runaway locomotive about to T-bone a stranded motorist in the middle of the railroad crossing.

"Wait!" Alex responded, pretending to be ecstatic about the news. "Shouldn't we be celebrating, instead? Are you sure? Besides, why would your parents care? You've been living with me, now, close to a year. What do they think we've been doing? Sleeping in separate beds?"

"I wanted to do everything by the book. You don't understand," she said as tears ran down her cheeks. "I've let them down, Alex. Their little girl, let them down. In the end, I was no different than many of the other girls I grew up with. I ended up pregnant before getting married."

"Come here," said Alex as he sat down next to Gigi. "Things are going to work out, *mami*, don't worry about it. We'll have the baby, we'll get married. Even if your folks get upset, what are they going to do?"

"I don't know . . . what if, maybe they . . . "

"Disown you? No. Banish you from their circle of trust? That's never going to happen. Once the baby comes, they'll forget about all that. The baby is a blessing, they're going to be happy and excited for you, us, and everything is going to be okay. We'll be married, we'll have our own family. Things will be great."

"You think?" Gigi said, her spirits improving a bit.

"I know it," said Alex. "Come here."

They hugged and kissed, and Alex felt okay, if for a moment. Gigi cracked a slight smile, trying to compose herself.

"I shouldn't be drinking."

"How much did you have?"

"Not even a glass, that's all that was left. I just couldn't. I wanted to, but I just couldn't. Besides, tomorrow I've got to pick up some prenatal vitamins . . . and who knows what else the doctor is going to put me on."

Alex smiled. "How far along are we?"

"Nine weeks. I was due for my pap smear . . . so I went in . . . and there you have it."

"Do we know if it's a girl or a boy yet?"

"No, it's too early to tell."

"This is the best news ever, Gigi. Thank you."

Alex hugged her and kissed her, while deep in the recesses of his mind he caught flashes and glimpses of his life spiraling out of control.

CHAPTER 25

THE MOMENT ALEJANDRO Del Fuerte set foot in the lobby area of his office building, he was surrounded by hordes of reporters and cameramen. The herd stampeded toward him, shouting questions.

"Alex, is it true that you have been excommunicated from the Catholic Church?"

"Why would Bishop Salamanca do that? Do you know?"

"Does it have anything to do with the fact that your firm defeated the foundation's summary judgment and you'll be squaring off in less than three months?"

"Can you beat the foundation, Alex?"

"Will the heirs get their lands back?"

"How will you spend your share of the pie, Alex?"

Alex was surrounded and was unable to reach the elevators. He took off his sunglasses and addressed the crowd. "I don't know why the bishop would excommunicate me from the Church. He must have his reasons. You'll have to ask him."

April Wingate shoved her microphone in Alex's face. "But, Alex, is it true that Arturo having filed Candelario's will changes everything. That his muniment of title could, in fact, be enough to defeat the Agnus Dei Foundation and for all the heirs to get their lands back?"

"It's quite possible," Alex answered, "and that's why we've asked for a jury. They'll have to decide that."

"But aren't you afraid to get a jury that can't vote against the foundation? The Church?" continued Wingate. "Most of the jurors will be Catholic, don't you think?"

Before Alex could answer, a Spanish-speaking reporter butted in, "*¿Señor Del Fuerte, qué pasaría si perdiera el caso?*"

"*El caso ya está ganado.*" Alex indicated, suddenly savoring all the attention.

Wingate came back with a vengeance, "Wait, wait, wait! You've won the case?"

"All I'm saying is that I believe Arturo's will is the lynchpin. It's game over," explained Alex. "Now, whether or not the Texas Supreme Court—should there be an appeal—will bow to outside interests and politics and choose to overlook that indisputable fact . . . well, it wouldn't be the first time that happened."

Alex squeezed his way through the crowd, got to the elevators and pushed the button. "Sorry, folks, I got clients waiting . . . "

"Have you heard?" asked Romeo as he poked his head into Alex's office.

"Now what?" asked Alex, obviously annoyed at the thought of a group of reporters hanging out in the building, waiting for an interview. He pulled a pack of stale Marlboros from his top drawer and proceeded to light one up.

"Worley's dead."

"What?" asked Alex, eyes wide open as he choked on a cloud of smoke.

"I read it on the Internet. It was in *The Austin American-Statesman's* webpage, just this morning."

"How did he die?"

"They found him floating, face down, in his apartment's swimming pool. He'd been there a couple of hours. Papers said several sources confirmed the guy didn't know how to swim. Killers probably threw his body in there, make it look like a drowning," surmised Romeo. "What do you think?"

"It has Salamanca written all over it." Alex said. "Here, close the door behind you and take a seat."

"What is it, boss? Is everything all right?"

"No, everything's not all right," huffed Alex, belching out a puff of smoke. "Look, I need to tell you something, but no one can know."

"Okay."

"I was planning to meet with Salamanca, see if we could smooth things out . . . see about getting out of the case."

"¿Qué? But why walk away, not like that . . . "

"This case is different," Alex conceded. "We're fighting more people than Salamanca . . . there's others involved, watching our every move. This case is too important for them."

"Who is 'them'?"

"The Church, the Vatican . . . the Pope . . . it's not just Salamanca. It's an entire organization, capable of just about anything."

"So? Since when has that mattered to you? You've never backed down. Did not back down for Yarrington or Chordelli, or Harrow, or even Slick Stevens. What's the matter with you, boss? I've never seen you like this."

"Before, I had nothing to lose."

Romeo gave him a confused stare. "I don't get it."

Alex put out his cigarette, got up from his desk and went to the window. He was looking at the bottlenecked traffic, now blocking the intersection in front of his office building. Hungry motorists waiting to turn into the Luby's across the street, the Vermillion or El TacoDepot next door and the Oyster Bar in back.

"Gigi's pregnant."

"Really?"

"Yep, I'm going to be a dad."

"That's fantastic! Congratulations!"

"There's a major problem, though . . . "

"What? You're worried about the DVD? Is that it?"

"Yep, and I'd like to live long enough to see my child." Alex returned to his seat behind the desk. "It's just a matter of days before that darn video gets uploaded to the Internet, don't you think?"

"Why don't you come clean with Gigi? Explain what happened, and ask her to forgive you. Preempt McDermott and Salamanca before they leak it. At least it won't be a shock to Gigi and her family."

"I might very well end up having to do that. But first, I'm going to talk to Salamanca, see what he wants," explained Alex, reaching for the slip of paper with Salamanca's direct number. He waved it in front of Romeo. "I never thought it would get this ugly."

"I'll go with you if he wants to meet face-to-face. Let me know, whatever we need to do, okay, boss? Anything. *Lo que sea,*" said Romeo as he started getting up and headed for the door.

"Thanks. I'll let you know, see how it goes," Alex added as he picked up the phone and started placing the call.

"Hey," said Romeo, before making his exit, "*dando y dando, pajarito volando,* I'd always say."

Alex smiled. Romeo was absolutely right. The expression meant *quid pro quo,* tit for tat. I give you X, you give me Y in return, and everyone goes home happy. Would Salamanca turn over the master copy of the DVD, forgive Alex's insolence—perhaps even spare his life—if Alex walked away from the lawsuit? There was only one way to find out.

CHAPTER 26

THE END OF AUGUST marks the beginning of the migration of red fish from the North Carolinas down to Florida, into the Gulf of Mexico, down the Texas coast and into Northern Mexico. As September begins, the bull reds run in big schools along South Padre Island's beachfront, providing excellent fishing for jetty and surf fishermen alike. Alex loved this time of year because he could also chase the schools of fish in his boat, since they were easy to spot in the crystalline waters off South Padre Island.

Most of the young redfish caught in the early days in September, Alex knew, would measure between nineteen and twenty-six inches. The bigger adults, those weighing more than thirty-five pounds, would start showing up during the month of October as the water temperature dropped a few more degrees.

Alex was sitting at the helm of his boat, a twenty-six-foot Monza with twin Yamaha engines, while Romeo was putting away the fishing gear. It was a boat that had come Alex's way via a client who could no longer afford to pay his fees. Alex had gotten the UPS driver's pending possession of marijuana and DWI charges dismissed so that the driver could remain employed—making thirty-five dollars an hour, plus overtime—and that way continue paying child support to three former wives. Jobs paying that kind of money in the Valley were hard to come by, and the driver desperately needed to hang on to that job. In the end, Alex had delivered a miracle, and the guy had finished paying the attorney's fees with his boat.

Romeo was drinking an ice-cold Tecate Light, studying the horizon with a pair of Bushnell binoculars. They had been fishing the tip of the jetties since four in the afternoon and had already caught their limit for redfish, including one cobia, two snook and several speckled trout. Now, all they had to do was wait.

"Did he say he was coming?" asked Romeo as he continued to scrutinize the horizon.

"Yep. He said he's coming in the diocese's yacht. Said he would be leaving Corpus Christi before noon, should be getting close."

"Where's the rendezvous?"

"Two miles due east off the Bridgepoint tower," explained Alex. "Salamanca said he knew the building. The foundation owns several condos in the tower, including one of the penthouses."

Romeo turned around to visualize the Bridgepoint tower, the second tallest building on South Padre Island, and then looked out to sea again. "Hey, I see something, out there. Straight ahead . . . two o'clock."

"Is it a large yacht?" Alex asked.

"It's a large boat." He paused to adjust the binoculars. "Yep, a forty-foot yacht, at least. Still a couple of miles out . . . heading this way."

"It should have a command bridge, way up high. Do you see one?"

"Yep. It's got to be a $600,000 boat, at least. What do you want to do?"

Alex started his boat's outboard engines, turned her around and headed out to sea. "Let's go greet her highness."

By any measure, the *Santa Magdalena* was opulent and projected power, wealth and influence. Romeo had stayed behind in Alex's boat, while Alex boarded the *Santa Magdalena* and met privately with Bishop Salamanca. The pair had decided to keep the rendezvous to themselves. Had Michael and McDermott found out, they would have hit the roof because the rules of ethics prohibited attorneys from talking directly to a party that was represented

by counsel. Alex hoped to be back in an hour. If he took longer
than that, Romeo had been instructed to get help.

Alex was met by the yacht's captain and was cordially invited
to join Bishop Salamanca in the main cabin. When he entered,
Alex could not help but notice the spacious area and the expensive teak wood finishes and tasteful décor. There was an "L"
shaped leather sofa and two small leather chairs. Bishop Salamanca was sitting down in one of the chairs, petting a Siamese cat cud-
dled up on his lap, while Tony, his loyal assistant, refilled his
snifter with Canticle.

The bishop motioned to Alex to come sit down across from
him and gave Tony a signal to get Alex something to drink and
then leave the pair alone. When Tony asked Alex if he cared for a
drink, Alex politely declined. He explained that he still needed to
sail his own boat back home, and he never drank when he went
out to sea. The lie did not go unnoticed by Salamanca's watchful
eye.

"Thanks for returning my call the other day," started Salamanca, "and making the effort to meet me out here, where nobody
can see us, Alex. Before we begin, let us pray . . . *bene orasse est
bene studuisse.*"

Alex did not know what to say, so he just bowed his head, pretended to be praying, but out of the corner of one eye he was
watching Salamanca.

"Oh, heavenly father," whispered the Bishop, "please send
your holy spirit to enlighten us both, your humble servants. Let
us see the error of our ways as we prepare to discuss important
matters regarding your church, lawyers, clients, life, faith, death,
sacrifice, justice and all those other things that might come up
during our discussion. Please let cooler heads prevail and let both
sides see the truth in your teachings. We pray all these things in
your name. Amen."

"Amen," mumbled Alex, the fervent pretender.

Bishop Salamanca took a sip from his snifter and then twirled
the brandy around, straining to see its beautiful legs develop.
"Hey," said Salamanca, "the captain remarked that you were on a
Monza, is that right?"

"Sure enough," replied Alex, "it's a great fishing boat."

"Do you do a lot of fishing?"

"Any chance I get."

"I could never do it," indicated Salamanca, "the whole thing is so barbaric and sad. To see the poor little fishes just flap around, gasping for air . . . too much horror. Entirely too cruel, in my opinion. So tell me, how long have you been fishing?"

Alex thought about it for a second. "My whole life. I never had a boat, though. It was always wade fishing in the bay or surf fishing the gulf. I got the Monza a year ago."

"And what kind of fish puts up the best fight?" asked Salamanca inquisitively.

"I hear tarpons don't go down easy . . . I've never caught one, though."

"Interesting. Listen, Alex let's talk about why we're here. When people negotiate or entertain settlement discussions—and you've probably heard this, you're a lawyer—they have to know what they want, so that they can try to find a way to get there. From point A to point B, you follow what I'm saying?"

"That's not necessarily true," disagreed Alex. "Sometimes a party can attend a negotiation to see what the other party's bottom line is."

"True, a party may want to attend and have no intention of resolving the dispute . . . I can see that happening, like a scouting mission."

"Like a recon mission," agreed Alex, "sure, it happens . . . see how strong or committed one party is to one position, or not."

"What are one's weak points or strong points . . . as the case may be."

"And what is negotiable and what isn't," Alex countered.

"Today's negotiation is a little different, I suppose," continued Salamanca as he sipped on his drink. "As I see it, you're already in a weak position. Some would even say I've got you by the short hairs, don't you agree?"

"I would respectfully disagree. Judge Cienfuegos is letting this case get to a jury, but certainly you're entitled to your own opinions, Your Most Reverend and Holy Excellency."

Salamanca chortled, "No, that's incorrect. I think you might want to play dumb, but the truth is, Alex, I got you by the balls. *De los huevos, aquí en mis manos.*" Salamanca clenched a fist.

"You forget that a party can also show up at a settlement conference, or a mediation, even an arbitration, just to tell the other side to go to hell, too. Have you heard of that happening, Your Holiness?" Alex said, preparing to draw a line in the sand. He paused and glared at Salamanca. "Why don't you get to the point and tell me what it is that you want, Bishop? Once and for all, stop wasting my time. You called me, remember?"

"You're right, you're right. I digress, excuse me. It must be old age. I'm just going to come right out and say it, okay?"

Alex got up, as if getting ready to make his exit. "Well, say it, then."

"You need to take a fall at trial, Alex. That's it. Either you dismiss the lawsuit and go your merry way, or take a fall."

"Why should I?" snapped Alex. "McDermott seems to think she and her cronies are going to kick my ass. If it's true, why would you need my help? Just get in there and do it."

"That scenario carries with it a certain degree of risk. What if you get a jury that rules for your clients? Things go your way, and you get an exorbitant verdict. Then there will be one or two more appeals, maybe three. More expenses for all involved. Maybe there will be other lawsuits from other brave unknown heirs that come forward, who had never before considered suing. Others that now decide they want their share of the pie. It will never end."

Alex sat back down again. "And what makes you think that I would even consider doing such a thing?"

Salamanca raised his snifter and twirled its contents. "I don't think you have any choice in the matter, Alex."

"I thought we were going to negotiate? This sure as hell doesn't sound like a negotiation to me . . . sounds like bribery, or black mail, even extortion."

Salamanca scowled. "Don't be so naïve, Del Fuerte. You are going to do what I say. Might as well get used to it. Get it? You're now . . . how do they say in French . . . ah, yes, I remember now . . . *ma pute* . . . so get used to it."

"I don't have to do shit, Your Holiness. And certainly I ain't your whore!"

"Do you really want to see your face splashed all over the Internet? Or end up being convicted of felony assault on a peace officer? How about a cocaine conviction? Does it scare you. . . to never practice law again, for the rest of your life? Or worse yet, end up like Dugger? Worley? Have you been reading the news? The cartels south of the border are killing each other as they fight over territorial control, the alien traffickers have lucrative smuggling routes in place . . . and you want to come stick your nose in their business?"

Alex was taken aback, unable to utter a single word. What had he gotten himself into?

Several minutes went by, and Alex finally managed to mutter, "So what exactly am I supposed to do?"

"Find a way to get the case dismissed with prejudice, or let us get a solid defense verdict."

"Well, I guess I could still try the damned thing. Just do it half speed, on auto pilot, without really trying," said Alex, reconsidering the unfair and one-sided proposal.

Salamanca smiled, glad to see Alex was coming around. "Maybe leave out Arturo's will . . . don't even introduce it."

"If I do it, what's in it for me?"

Salamanca reached for the Canticle and poured himself another two fingers. "No DVD. Guaranteed to disappear, forever. No scandal. I'll make the criminal cases go away, too. You'll marry Gigi, live happily ever after, enjoy being a daddy."

"What?" asked Alex in shock. "Her family doesn't even know. How do you know?"

"Well, it helps to have friends, everywhere . . . I suppose. Certainly, it doesn't hurt. And the Valley is a small place . . . everybody knows everybody else's business."

Alex was shaking his head, disgusted at the fact that Salamanca had his number and nothing was going according to plan. "I don't know . . . the whole thing . . . "

"What else do you want?" asked Salamanca. "You get to live to fight another day."

"I'm not convinced I should be the one doing the devil's work . . . Your Holiness."

"Consider it charity," replied Salamanca with a smirk.

Alex appeared to be struggling with the proposed arrangement. "Let me ask you this, Bishop, what happens if I do my part, but McDermott doesn't deliver and the jury still finds against you? Just because I'm willing to throw in the towel, doesn't mean the jury's going to like the defendant. I don't care what you say, the foundation is not getting a jury of 'its' peers. I doubt you'll find a single priest on the panel."

"Sure, that may or may not be," conceded Salamanca. "But is it likely? No, I don't think so. Is it possible? Sure, anything's possible. But that scenario is not likely, Alex. I'm sorry. If I was a betting man, with your assistance and with the firepower we're bringing to the table, I'm sure we'll get the defense verdict we want."

"Well . . . " huffed Alex.

"Are you in or not?" interrupted Salamanca. "I'm not going to sit here with you and waste the entire afternoon 'second-guessing' each other to death."

"I have to think about it."

"C'mon, Alex. You'd rather have your video with Savannah on the Internet? For all the world to see? What do you think Gigi is going to say? Aren't you two getting married soon?"

"There's not going to be a wedding."

"Why?"

"It's none of your business," snapped Alex.

"You're breaking up? Does she know of the DVD already? Is that why?"

Alex had to admit it was useless to continue pretending he could still come out on top. No matter how hard he tried to whisle Dixie, Salamanca had him on the ropes. No two ways about it.

"We're just going to elope," blurted Alex, "because of the baby. No need to have a wedding."

Salamanca chuckled, "Lovers, when will they learn?" He waited to get a reaction from Alex, but there was none. "See why this is important, Alex? This way we can bury the nasty DVD, once and for all. Bury the hatchet. Put this uncomfortable episode behind us, forever. Now's the time to decide, son. Are you in or out?"

"Can I have a few days to think about it?" asked Alex, popping his knuckles, " . . . at least?"

Salamanca stared at Alex. "Sure, think about it . . . You know, this whole thing . . . it reminds me of when I was a young man, maybe a bit younger than you. I was very much like you, Alex. Impulsive, reckless . . . would never consider the resulting consequences of anything I did. I'm sure, when you decided to jump in and help the plaintiffs you had good intentions, son. Nothing wrong with that, I suppose. Your heart was in the right place. You meant well. Except we all need to grow up, sometime. Wouldn't you agree?"

"I suppose," mumbled Alex, as he contemplated his predicament.

"And it has been my experience that the only way we, humans, can change, grow . . . mature, is to make mistakes. Learn from them . . . you follow?"

Alex let out a big sigh. "I suppose."

"We'll need a very visible win," Salamanca ordered as if the deal had been consummated and Alex had already signed along the dotted line. "*Bella horrida bella.*"

"Everything will disappear? The video, the trumped-up charges, everything?" asked Alex, sounding irritated.

"Everything. One call. Done. Like that," Salamanca said, snapping his stubby little fingers.

Out of nowhere, Tony, the seminary student, appeared. "You called, Your Excellency?"

"No, son. I'm sorry. We're still talking," Salamanca said, dismissing him.

Alex looked at his watch. "I gotta go."

"So, are you gonna play ball or not?" asked Salamanca, again, pointblank. "I need an answer."

Alex did not reply, but continued thinking of Oscar Santibáñez, the other heirs, Yarrington, Michael, Gigi, the State Bar of Texas, McDermott, O'Quinn, Judge Cienfuegos and the other thirty or so lawyers and paralegals breathing down his neck, wanting to eat his lunch, bust his kneecaps and toss his body into a pauper's grave.

"I can't say. I told you, I need more time," complained Alex, "but let me ask you . . . Did you really have something to do with Dugger and Worley meeting their maker?"

Salamanca sipped his Canticle and finished savoring the delicate bouquet and aroma. He paused and put the snifter up against the light. "Look," started Salamanca, "there are things that I can control. And there are other things that are outside of my control, Alex."

"I'm afraid I don't understand."

Salamanca cleared his throat. "I report everything to the higher ups, okay?"

"You mean, the Vatican?"

"Yes. Sometimes, things happen . . . let's say . . . without my knowing. Certainly, they don't consult me, understand?"

"So, you mean it's possible . . . "

"Nothing's impossible to God, my son. You know that."

"Savannah Lee? Was that you? Or them?"

"I've known Savannah for quite some time. Isn't she great?"

"Okay, let me ask you. Worley? Was that you or them?"

"*Celari vult sua furta Venus*," repeated Salamanca in Latin.

"What the hell is that . . . speak English."

"Venus does not want her secrets to be revealed, Alex." Salamanca then pointed toward the ceiling.

"Dugger?"

Again, the bishop replicated the same hand gesture and chuckled again. "Alex, I'm small-time, son. I don't get involved in those ministerial tasks . . . nor am I consulted on anything. All I know is that things like that do happen. Just like God, you can't see him, but he does exist, he's all around us. That's why I want to know now if you're in or not. I have to report this. We're losing valuable time."

Alex's heart was pounding louder, and louder. He glanced at his watch. He'd been in the presence of Bishop Salamanca close to forty minutes. He now wished he'd never picked up the phone that day when Paloma called seeking a divorce lawyer.

"What would you do, Alex, if you were in my shoes? If you had crazies shooting your priests, and it was these same crazies that were also suing you? When, in fact, all you want to do is spread the gospel. What if someone wanted to take your license away? Your ability to make a great living? Would you just take it lying down?"

"Huh, no, yes . . . I mean, I don't know," stuttered Alex.

"The only way for me to provide sanctuary for you and your friends is for me to know of your intentions, Alex. I need to know . . . and we don't have much time. The trial is less than two months away."

"And you guarantee that you can protect me, Gigi, my friends and colleagues?" asked Alex.

"I'll see to it."

"Okay, but let me ask you," said Alex in a serious tone as his demeanor changed. "Let me see if I got this straight. Are you saying there are others out there that have a vested interest in La Minita?"

"*Nolo contendere*," pled Salamanca with a solemn face. "That's an area protected by the confessor-clergy privilege. I'd rather not go there."

Salamanca stared at his snifter, then looked up at Alex. There was a long, uncomfortable silence. And right there and then, Alex knew the answer. This was no longer a simple legal dispute over who claimed title to some lands. There were other things going on that he had never considered. Things that, certainly, could cost him his life.

Salamanca finally broke the silence. "These lands are so vast that there's no way to keep tabs on everything . . . I don't think anybody knows, really."

Alex felt a pit in his stomach. He ran his fingers through his hair as he tried to contain himself. He finally understood. He took a deep breath. "Okay, listen. Romeo's waiting for me. He's got instructions to call the Coast Guard if I'm not back in an hour. Can I think about this?"

"Sure," said Salamanca, "take a week, but that's all. I need to know."

"All right, I'll be in touch," Alex said as he got up and let himself out.

"How did the meeting go?" asked Romeo as he reached for a beer from the cooler and tried to relax, let his guard down. Alex was now at the helm, looking severely preoccupied and steering the boat in a westward direction, toward Padre Island.

"Fine," grumbled Alex, "we cleared the air. He wanted me to desist, get out of the case. I put my foot down, said I couldn't do it."

"How did he take it?"

"He was pissed," lied Alex, "threatened all kinds of shit. Which, of course, got me more mad. I told him to go to hell, that we're ready to go to trial."

"Really?"

"Sure, then he changed his tune, tried another tactic and offered us tons of money to lose the case on purpose."

"How much money?" Romeo pressed on.

How much is a life worth? thought Alex before giving Romeo an answer. "Ten million, all hush money."

Romeo's eyes grew wide open. "We could do a lot of things with that money, don't you think, boss?"

"I agree. But could we live with ourselves? That's the question."

Romeo also thought about it, long and hard. He finished his beer and opened another one. He took a couple of swigs. "So, what happened in the end?"

"Nothing. I put my foot down, I said no. We're going to trial. My clients deserve their day in court."

"Man! You got some big *cojones*, boss," Romeo blurted out, "to turn down money like that. I don't know if I could do it, honestly."

"We're gonna kick his ass," lied Alex, who at that precise moment was more concerned with finding a way to please Salamanca, get in His Holiness' good graces and have him run interference with his superiors.

He needed to find a way out of this mess, and quickly.

CHAPTER 27

WITH GIGI OUT of commission due to severe morning sickness, Alex was forced to pick up the slack at the office. Since his meeting with Salamanca, he'd been neck-deep in depositions, contested hearings, client interviews, meetings with experts and several pretrial conferences in different courtrooms throughout South Texas. His time had also been spent organizing an impromptu wedding in Vegas, which had to happen before the news of Gigi's pregnancy was announced to her parents.

As a result, Salamanca's proposal was on the back burner. He was already ten days late and still did not have an answer. The pressure was getting to him. He was staring at a grenade launcher aimed straight at the large bull's-eye painted on his chest.

Alex had just hung up the phone with Gigi, when Romeo walked into his office. He was holding a large manila envelope addressed to Alejandro Del Fuerte.

"This came in for you, boss."

"What is it?"

"It's from the State Bar of Texas, Office of the Chief Disciplinary Counsel."

Alex frowned and snatched the envelope from Romeo and played with it in his hands. "Fuck, fuck, fuck! Now what?"

"What is it? Is it bad?"

Alex looked as if he was about to pass out. "*Pinche* McDermott. I bet she filed a grievance against me." Alex tossed the envelope back to Romeo. "Open it and read it, tell me what it says."

In law school, Alex had heard about lawyers like that. Lawyers who threatened to report the opponents to the State Bar for any lit-

tle thing, including not putting the right amount of postage on a
letter. These lawyers were the equivalent of a schoolyard bully.
Eventually, the State Bar would get involved. The grievanced attorney had no choice but to waste time, effort and more money
defending the frivolous complaints.

"Okay," Romeo replied as he started tearing into the envelope.
He pulled out its contents. "Let's see. Okay, it says right here:

Dear Mr. Del Fuerte:

A grievance has been filed against you by the
Honorable Dana McDermott. In particular, the
complainant alleges that you engaged in conduct
unbecoming a lawyer and that you are not fit to
practice law in the State of Texas, or any
other state. Mrs. McDermott alleges that you
have engaged in behavior that has violated the
Texas Rules of Professional Conduct. Section
8.04 states that a lawyer shall not (1) violate
the rules, knowingly assist or induce another
to do so, or do so through the acts of another, whether or not such violation occurred in
the course of a client-lawyer relationship; (2)
commit a serious crime or commit any other
criminal act that reflects adversely on the
lawyer's honesty, trustworthiness or fitness as
a lawyer in other respects; (3) state or imply
an ability to influence improperly a government
agency or official.

The complainant alleges that recently, during the course of a telephonic conversation,
you threatened to do harm against the complainant and her client; you threatened to
engage in criminal acts; said acts could be
construed as constituting conduct rising to
the level of a misdemeanor offense: a) harass-
ment by phone, and b) verbal assault. The complainant further alleges that she became seriously worried about her safety and the safety
of others, namely her client and coworkers, and
that in the course of the exchange you also
boasted that you had the ability to sway the
judge or influence the judge involved in the

matter pending between you and the complainant. The complainant also alleges that
you used vulgar, offensive and coarse language
during the exchange and that you alluded that
you had powerful connections to see that the
complainant, the client and her entire law firm
be destroyed.

WARNING: You have thirty days from the date of
this letter to provide a reply to the allegations
and to demand a hearing in front of your local
disciplinary committee. If you fail to respond,
action may be taken against you that may result
in sanctions, suspension and/or disbarment. If
you have any questions, please consult the website for the State Bar of Texas or call toll free
1-555-MY-TXBAR.

Alex's heart skipped a beat as Astrid came on the intercom and
announced that he had a call from Bishop Salamanca. He was
waiting on two.

Alex saw the red light blinking, but kept hesitating. Pick up.
Don't pick up. Pick up. Don't pick up.

He picked up the phone, grudgingly, "Alex speaking."

"Alex," said Salamanca, "did you get the grievance filed by
McDermott?"

"I got it. It's a bunch of bullshit, though. And you know it."

"I know, I know. But you'll have to defend it, waste time on it,
hire counsel, stress over it and deal with one more fire that needs
to be put out. A fire that you just don't need right now. Don't you
agree?"

"True," groaned Alex. "So, what do you want?"

"You know what I want. Do we have a deal?"

There was silence at the other end of the line.

"Look, Alex, stop screwing around," demanded Salamanca.
"You know what's gonna happen, right? If you don't play ball, it'll
be years before you get in front of a jury."

"What are you going to do, whack me, too?"

"I have very little control over that," continued Salamanca. "But what I can control is this. The trial is due to start the second week of December. With the holidays getting in the way, you'll still be in trial well into January. And you know what that means, don't you?"

"It means I'm still alive?" theorized Alex.

"No," snapped Salamanca, "it means that the legislature will be in session. Which means, I will hire, and bring on board, State Senator Gustavo Hightower, as additional counsel. Cienfuegos will have to grant our mandatory legislative continuance. The case will be delayed for another six months . . . at a minimum."

"You wouldn't dare," said Alex as if taunting the bishop.

"Watch me."

"Bastard," mumbled Alex under his breath.

"And if that's not enough, I'll make damn sure that the Vatican's political action committee pitches the governor a juicy reelection campaign contribution. And watch him repay the favor by calling a couple of extra, special legislative sessions . . . which will delay the case even more . . . especially if Hightower has to keep requesting more continuances. You don't think I can do that? The governor doesn't care. It happens all the time. The leech will make something up . . . school funding, school vouchers, property taxes, voter ID, illegal immigration enforcement, border security, you name it. We can come up with a crisis, a myriad of new issues, it's no problem."

"You're sick, you know that. Screwing with people's lives like that, just because . . . "

"Because I can?" yelled Salamanca. "You of all people should know. You're Yarrington's *compadre*. Or must I remind you that in Austin money talks . . . bullshit walks."

"Yarrington's not my *compadre*," cried Alex.

"Well . . . if you don't pull the plug on this misadventure, you'll leave me no choice but . . . "

"But, what? C'mon, say it!"

"Just give me a God-forsaken answer, son! Let me hear a 'yes' and I'll call off the hounds. Make the grievance and everything else go away. I need to know right now. No more games, Alex. No more delays. I'm trying to help you . . . I've been too, too patient," insisted Salamanca. "If you force me to file the legislative continuance, then I'll pay any of the intervenors to file bankruptcy. The case will be delayed an additional three years."

¡*Hijo de puta!* thought Alex, his mind racing at a hundred miles an hour. *Leave me alone. Go away. Stop screwing with my life for the love of God.*

There was a prolonged silence at the other end of the line. Salamanca could hear Alex's heavy breathing.

"One condition, though," Alex finally uttered. "Before I get in the ring, I'd like to see the dismissals of all the charges pending, the grievance included and confirmation that the DVD has been destroyed."

"To the first two, yes. However, I can't destroy the DVD, at least not yet, son. I'll take care of the dismissals and speak to McDermott about dismissing her complaint. I'll have to hang on to the DVD until after the trial. I need insurance. That's the best I can do. If we don't do the deal, the DVD gets uploaded to YouTube this evening."

"Fine! Okay, you got my word. I'm all in!" screamed Alex, pounding his desk, while at the same time slamming the receiver down.

CHAPTER 28

"DO YOU WANT TO see the face?" asked Gigi's OB-Gyn, Dr. Rose Kingsbury, as she applied ultrasound gel to Gigi's tummy and glided the transducer all around, trying to show the baby up on the screen.

"Can you?" asked Alex, faking excitement. He was worried sick for Gigi, the baby and his life, too.

"Let's see," replied the doctor, "here it is. Do you see the eyes, the outline of the forehead?"

Gigi and Alex both strained to try and see what it was that the doctor was seeing. "Oh, yeah," both replied, not really sure, but somewhat excited, nonetheless.

"You hear that?" followed Dr. Kingsbury. "The sound of an old washing machine on the wash cycle?"

"Is that?" asked Gigi, all giddy and full of smiles.

"That's it. Your baby's heart."

Gigi squeezed Alex's hand. Alex, on the other hand, was thinking of an old Paul Anka song he'd heard his daddy sing in and around the house, way back when his parents asked him to help them pick a name for his new baby sister. Alex had come up with a name. She was going to be María Fernanda.

Of course, Alex never had a chance to meet his baby sister. Mom had been eight months pregnant that fateful day, outside Mexico City, when daddy's Ford Pinto was rear-ended by a speeding eighteen-wheeler, and the car's exposed gas tank burst into flames, charring everybody inside.

"Oh, my God," the doctor suddenly shouted, "Wow!"

Alex snapped back to reality.

"What is it?" asked Gigi.

"What do you see?" followed Alex.

"You're having twins. See? There it is. The other baby was hiding behind the first one, until it moved."

Again, Gigi and Alex strained to see, but this time they could make out the outline of the second head. Dr. Kingsbury proceeded to pinpoint, mark and measure the heads' circumferences and printed pictures for the happy couple to see. Gigi was better able to see things, where Alex thought there was nothing. She was able to make out a leg, a tiny hand, the heads, but all Alex saw was his life slowly beginning to change before his very own eyes.

Alex's head was spinning from the whirlwind of emotions. He was feeling ecstatic, scared, worried, happy, afraid, blessed, but most of all, he was confused. Blessed by the same loving God—which in a strange twist of fate—some would say he was now battling.

Dr. Kingsbury wiped Gigi's tummy, helped her sit up and then went to turn on the lights in the small examination room. Alex excused himself while Gigi and the doctor continued to discuss scheduling future follow-up visits.

With the trial date less than three weeks away, Alex and Michael had started working on their opening arguments, direct and cross-examination sample questions, motions in limine, responses to defendants and intervenors' motions to bifurcate, which meant that no punitive damages could be discussed, until the jury found some fraud was committed by the foundation. And Romeo was busy delivering subpoenas to all the witnesses needed for the case.

As it sometimes happens in high-profile cases where smoking guns or anonymous envelopes with key evidence surface *sua sponte*, a mysterious attachment showed up with an email for the Honorable Alejandro Del Fuerte. The subject line in the email read: *Documentos: Registro Público*. The attachment was in PDF format. The return email address was server@biblio.archivos.gob.mx. This meant that anybody in Mexico could have sent Alex the document, and it would be impossible to trace the sender.

Alex clicked on the attachment, and, within a matter of seconds, the Adobe Reader opened a ten-page file. It was a copy of a yellowed, old, hand-written document. The purported author was Don Candelario Santibáñez. The document appeared to be hundred-plus years old and it looked to have been inscribed in the Registro Público de la Propiedad in Mexico City. In the document, which was quite difficult to read due to the bad penmanship of the author and its condition, there was mention of the *porción* called La Minita. After a careful reading of the entire document, two things were clear. One, the fact that Arturo's will had been filed as a muniment of title was no longer of any consequence to the upcoming trial. Secondly, this document was the *escritura* by which Candelario deeded the entire tract to his bastard son, Arturo. This meant that Candelario had prepared the will, just in case, but before he died had made sure he'd transferred the property to Arturo, *en vida*. This was what was commonly known as an inter vivos transfer.

This would have required Candelario to travel to Mexico City, the capital, and employ a *notario público*, as Mexican lawyers were called back then, to prepare the documents for his signature, and then have the same *notario* file them in the property records. This part of Texas was still considered part of Mexico, even though the areas north of the Nueces River had become the Republic of Texas. It would not have been unusual for a landowner of that time to attempt to handle all of his or her legal affairs in what was still his capital city, such transactions being commonplace.

From an evidentiary standpoint, this new discovery helped Alex and his clients in a very significant manner. McKnight could not have received anything from his spouses because his father-in-law, years back, had given everything away to somebody else. Since McKnight's father-in-law had given away the inheritance to Arturito, his bastard son, then McKnight could not have received anything from his own wives. Looking at it another way, how could McKnight give something away that wasn't his to begin with? How could the foundation receive something from McKnight, when McKnight had nothing to give the foundation?

It made perfect sense, and a jury would have no problem understanding that. It wouldn't be difficult to prove that a person cannot give something away if the person doesn't own it in the first place. This new discovery certainly clouded the foundation's claim that it had clear title. This would also make it easier for the foundation to want to settle the case and pitch the Santibáñez clan some money, because the foundation's position was no longer as solid as it once looked.

The problem was that Alex had given his word to Bishop Salamanca that he would go along and play opossum. And if he broke his promise, all kinds of horrible things were in store for him. He did not even want to think about it.

The biggest problem now, as far as Alex was concerned, was the fact that he had an obligation to disclose the discovery of this new evidence to McDermott, O'Quinn, Uhels and all the rest. Especially if he intended to use it at trial. With less than three weeks to trial, chances were that Judge Cienfuegos would not let him use this key piece of evidence, anyway. Moreover, he only had a PDF copy of the document. He needed to fly down to Mexico City and obtain a certified copy of the handwritten note, get it officially translated and then get the apostille certification so that it could be used in a legal proceeding in Texas. And there was not enough time to do that.

The other problem was that he also had a duty to use it at trial in order to help his clients win. Ultimately, his duty should be to his clients and not Bishop Salamanca. But that was the dilemma: to use it and reveal its existence or pretend he did not know it existed and simply do nothing.

The other legal issue that had Alex worried was that when Texas was annexed to the United States in 1845, it subsequently fell under a new set of American real property laws. How would that affect the inter vivos transfer that took place in Mexico City earlier? Could it be argued that the United States should recognize the inter vivos transfer as valid under the full faith and credit clause of the U.S. Constitution? Could the United States give such credit to a transaction that happened in another country, under a different set of laws, years earlier? And what about the fact that the laws of

Mexico, initially based on Roman law, had also applied to Texas before Mexico lost its territories to the United States? It was a mess!

Alex called Lieutenant Governor Rene Yarrington on his cell and broached the subject of the anonymous email. They were on the phone for more than an hour, speculating who may have wanted Alex to have that key document, and why? For his part, Alex explained the ethical dilemma he found himself in, without revealing that he and Bishop Salamanca had secretly met and that he had already agreed to "throw in the towel." Never once did Alex mention that deep down inside, he hated Yarrington for duping him into taking the Santibáñez case. Nor that he felt like a complete and utter fool because he should have known better than to listen to the lieutenant governor, a *político* full of hot air . . . just like all the other politicians he'd met in his lifetime.

In any event, Alex wanted to bring up the topic because he needed to discuss it with somebody else, but couldn't do it with Michael. The professor would have immediately instructed Alex to come forward with this new discovery and request an emergency hearing in front of Judge Cienfuegos. That way, everybody would be put on notice about this new key evidence. There would be no unfair surprise. When things like that happened, normally judges would allow the parties sufficient time to learn more about the new discovery. Especially if the discovery of the new evidence would increase the chances of the case settling without a trial, or the plaintiffs' dismissing their claims.

The discussion and production of this new evidence clearly meant to Alex that the trial could be postponed. It also meant that since everyone now knew of the discovery, Alex would be expected to use it at trial. And if he had to use it at trial, then there was a real possibility that the Santibáñez clan might win. And that would throw a wrench in the gearbox and bust the deal with Salamanca.

Another serious concern was that if Alex divulged the existence of this new discovery and he failed to present it at trial, he and his firm could end up being sued by his clients. Once the Santibáñez clan started asking questions and ended up with other lawyers who did an instant replay of what had transpired in the case, the lawyers would start asking questions as to why Alex and Michael had failed to present the inter vivos transfer evidence. They might even ask why the attorneys had not presented the muniment of title evidence. Alex and his firm would instantly become targets, and the problem with becoming targets was that Alex and Michael, indeed, had deep pockets. Sure, the firm had malpractice insurance and the insurance company could defend and maybe pay on a judgment. But if the lawyers were aggressive, they could come after Alex and Michael and their assets as well.

Yarrington recognized some of the ethical dilemmas now being kicked around by Alex. In fact, Yarrington had never considered all the possibilities and negative outcomes now being speculated upon. His advice—he had never in his lifetime tried a case, but wanted nothing more than a share of the pie—was for Alex to stop worrying and just spring the evidence on everyone the day of trial. Of course, that move would automatically put Alex's head on Salamanca's chopping block.

"Alex," Yarrington said, "when the trial starts, you'll be in front of a really good judge, son. Plus you never know what a jury may or may not do. And if I were you, I would not worry about anything. Trust me on this one. You're going to be fine."

"I wish it was that simple."

"Look," snapped Yarrington, "don't waste your time doing all these mental gymnastics, Alex. I mean it. Get in there and try that damned case. Worst case scenario, think what trying the case will do for your reputation, 'the kid lawyer that took on the foundation!' Either way, you'll make your mark as a trial lawyer. A true maverick!"

"Oh, I'm going to try it, all right, I promise you that much."

Now comes the Cameron County District Attorney by and thru its Assistant DA Honorable Gabriela Ortegón, and, in the interest of justice, hereby dismisses the following charges against the defendant, Alejandro Del Fuerte:

> Driving While Intoxicated. Resisting Arrest.
> Possession of Controlled Substance.
> Signed, Asst. DA Gabriela Ortegón

Alex was sitting behind his desk, reviewing the dismissal and another fax from the State Bar of Texas, Office of the Chief of the Disciplinary Counsel. Along with the fax cover sheet from the state bar, there was a letter addressed to the Honorable Alejandro Del Fuerte. In it, the Office of the Chief of the Disciplinary Counsel explained that the complainant, Honorable Dana McDermott, had wished to drop her complaint and no longer wished to pursue any action against the target attorney.

Alex crumpled the letter from the State Bar and threw it in the wastebasket. Sure, he was happy to see that Salamanca had kept his word, but was not entirely satisfied with the language in the dismissal from the DA's office. Particularly because under Texas law, it would be almost impossible to expunge the three arrests from his criminal record, since the dismissals had been carried out "in the interest of justice." Had the dismissal contained language that said that the state "lacked probable cause" to charge the defendant or if the language read "insufficient evidence," then Alex would have had no problem expunging the arrests from his record and that would be that. He had dropped the ball, and it was no one's fault but his.

He punched the intercom button and summoned Romeo into his office. He needed to do one last thing before selling out to the devil.

"What is it, boss?" asked Romeo as he poked his head into the office.

"You got your passport ready?"

"Yes, why?"

"There's a Continental flight leaving Brownsville for Houston in an hour. If you hurry, you'll make the connecting flight to Mexico City. It arrives in Mexico at eleven P.M. this evening."

Romeo was scratching his head. "*¿Y luego?* What am I supposed to do in Mexico City?"

"Research," said Alex, "valuable research."

"For the trial?"

"Yes. Go on and get on Priceline, book your flight and hotel. Ask Betty to put it on the firm's credit card. Call me tomorrow, as soon as you wake up, and I'll tell you where to go."

"You know me, I love to travel," said Romeo with a wide grin, as he started walking away while singing an old familiar tune, "*La cucaracha, la cucaracha, ya no puede caminar. . . .*"

CHAPTER 29

HE ALARM WAS set to go off at 6:00 A.M., but Alex had been awake since four that morning. As the trial date grew closer, the butterflies had reappeared and now were becoming a constant in his life again. Gigi had remained sleeping when he stumbled out of bed and turned off the alarm. He shuffled into the kitchen and started a pot of coffee. As soon as the coffee finished brewing, Alex grabbed a cup and went outside to the terrace. He sat there listening to the waves in complete darkness. Today was the final pretrial, and he needed to clear his head. He wondered if Salamanca had let McDermott in on their little secret.

Upon his return from Mexico City, Romeo had scrambled up to Kingsville and had taken with him the boxes of exhibits and trial materials and equipment. He'd rented a couple of hotel rooms and turned one of them into a war room. Alex and Michael would drive up together, leaving South Padre Island by seven in the morning. It would take them two hours to get from Padre to Kingsville. The final pretrial hearing was scheduled at ten that morning.

Romeo had already called the clients and started lining them up for the trial. His job was to make sure the equipment was working, the witnesses were all available and ready to testify when needed.

Alex's job at the pretrial, at least in principle, would be to act the part of a seasoned lawyer, figure out if he needed to mention the discovery of the new evidence and try to get through the pretrial without making Cienfuegos too upset.

He would go through the exercise and try not to worry about the inter vivos transfer finding. Besides, he and Michael had their hands full with other last-minute details. Over the weekend, the faxes had been coming in nonstop, and all the defendants and the intervenors had been papering Alex's firm with all kinds of last-minute motions.

For starters, everyone had filed competing motions in limine, along with motions to bifurcate and motions to enlarge the time for voir dire and opening statements, including Alex's motion to equalize juror strikes. O'Quinn had even filed a motion asking that, of all the intervenors, he'd be allowed to go right after the plaintiffs and defendants. And Uhels had filed a motion asking that all potential jurors be given questionnaires and that all the attorneys be allowed to get copies of the responses prior to trial. Likewise, Fonseca had filed a motion to increase the size of the jury panel from fifty to three hundred. The rationale for increasing the size of the panel was that everybody in Kleberg County knew the plaintiffs and the defendant or was related to the attorneys, witnesses, plaintiffs, and it was going to be extremely difficult to find a fair and impartial jury of twelve from a miniscule jury panel of fifty. Finally, McDermott had filed a motion to quash Alex's subpoena that directed Bishop Salamanca and Pope John Michael IX to appear and give testimony during the trial.

Both Michael and Alex would handle the pretrial conference and then stick around the courtroom to pre-mark all their exhibits for Monday. The idea was that after the Thursday pretrial conference, Michael and Alex would return home, go into the office and work the weekend, tweak their openings and cross-examinations, and make lists of the exhibits needed to prove their case and that needed to be introduced at trial. Likewise, Alex made a list of all the key points he needed to cover with certain witnesses.

Prior to jumping in the shower and getting dressed, Alex thought one last time about how to handle the thirty lawyers on the other side. Would he even get a chance to speak? And could Judge Cienfuegos reign in all the lawyers, despite their huge egos?

As he adjusted the water temperature, Alex thought about Uhels' untimely request to have all the jurors also fill out questionnaires, especially if Cienfuegos granted the motion to enlarge the panel. This meant that if two or three hundred prospective jurors were asked to answer a simple ten- or fifteen-page questionnaire (personal information, religious background, education, work history, etc.), then the clerk would have to photocopy each questionnaire ten times, so that the lead attorneys in the case could each have a copy. By the end of the exercise, three thousand plus questionnaires would have been distributed, and jury selection would no longer be a one-hour affair, but would turn into a two- or three-week elimination ordeal.

Was that McDermott's strategy? For the jury selection to take the entire month of December, so that January would come and Senator Hightower could be hired? Drag things out? And then have the politician file a mandatory motion seeking his legislative continuance and delay the case another seven to nine months?

After worrying about the case, and his future with Gigi under threat, Alex got out of the shower and set his mind to the task at hand.

By 8:30 a.m., Alex and Michael were at the Whataburger off the main highway on the outskirts of Kingsville, Kleberg's county seat, enjoying cups of freshly brewed black coffee. Michael was spreading a little strawberry jelly on his biscuit, while Alex was pouring the restaurant's picante sauce on his egg-sausage-and-cheese breakfast *taquito*.

"Are we ready to do this?" asked Michael before taking a bite, looking ready for battle.

"I think so," said Alex.

"Tell you the truth. I never thought we'd get this far," confessed Michael. "For starters, I didn't even think we could survive the foundation's summary judgment. But you found the will giving everything to Arturo—if you could even call that yellow old thing a will—and managed to survive."

"Pretty wild stuff . . . "

"And then, just when I think there's no way in hell Judge Phillips will be recused . . . you go and get it done. Hell, we didn't even have valid grounds. Yet, something miraculous happened, and we get a new judge . . . who, so far, has been pretty decent."

"*La mano de Dios.*"

"What's that?" Michael asked, then took a bite of his flaky biscuit.

"God's hand. God has chosen to stop helping the bad guy and now he has switched sides and decided to give the good guys a push . . . that's all."

Michael stared at Alex, his pupil, his good friend, and now law partner. And Alex stared back in silence.

"Well, whatever you call it, I hope it keeps working." He paused. "You know, I'd like to win this case, not because I have anything against the foundation, but because it's important to show that the little guy can still get his day in court in America, Alex. People have lost faith in the legal system. Everyone knows that if you're just a guy with little or no money, you don't have a shot. That only those with lots of money, expensive lawyers and sway with the judges can get justice. That's what our system has become, unfortunately."

"I agree."

"So, I want people to know that in this day and age, the average Joe can still sock it to the big guys. That all the money in the world can't and won't save you. That a courtroom can be a leveled playing field, where the facts and the evidence can be splashed on a canvass of sound legal principles, and truth and justice can still prevail. That it's not about who's got the better-dressed lawyer or the most lawyers, or the best PowerPoint presentation, or the most expensive testifying experts, or who is closest to the judge. I'd like to think that, for once, 'what's right' can triumph over money, power, even, corruption."

"That's what I also want to believe," declared Alex. "However, to me, it's more than just right over wrong. Honestly, to me it's more about playing Robin Hood . . . and spreading the wealth around, among us, *nuestra gente*, our people. Why should the foundation get to keep it all? Why send all this money to the Vatican? That money should stay here, in Texas. Put it to good use.

Let it trickle down here, at home. Unfortunately, the more things change, the more things stay the same."

"What do you mean?"

"What's happening is no different than the conquistadores sending all the gold and silver back to the crown. Now, the only difference is that the wealth is being transferred to the Vatican. So, five hundred years later, we're still in the same position: foreigners pillaging our resources. How's it possible that the Valley is so rich in oil and gas, but we have the poorest counties in the nation?"

"Yes, but the folks who had it before never did anything with it, Alex. That's why they lost it in the first place."

"They didn't lose it. It was stolen from under their noses. Land speculators, the Texas Rangers and others snatched the lands from them."

"Yes, but it's all the same. They got it from the king, who stole it from the natives. It's the same thing . . . only a different version."

Alex swallowed the last of his breakfast, cleared his throat and said, "I hate having to agree with you, but I get what you're saying." He finished wiping his lips and his hands with the napkin. "Truth be told, I've also struggled with the idea that just because the king gave it to the Monterreals, now it's all theirs. I see the logic behind your thinking . . . the king stole it, too! What I'd really like to know is where does the sense of entitlement come from, you know?"

"Bingo! I guess it's not difficult to give away what's not yours to begin with. His majesty felt entitled, took the land and gave *porciones* to others. In essence, playing Robin Hood, too, don't you agree? Isn't that the same thing we're trying to do here?"

"Yes, I guess," muttered Alex.

"And it has been going on and on, forever and ever. Someday, maybe the United States will no longer be the greatest democracy in the world. When that day comes, a dictator or a military junta might take over. And then the new government will declare that those lands no longer belong to the foundation. And in order to feed the masses and keep them from uprising, there might be land reform, and everyone gets a chunk. And at least for a while, everyone will be happy, if for a short while."

"Like it happened in Mexico, in the forties, fifties and sixties."

"Exactly," said Michael, "just another form of redistributing the wealth and the land among the many. That's all."

Alex started picking up around the table, placing the wrappers and empty coffee cups on the tray. "Well, let's go see if we can take it from the foundation, give some of it back to our clients."

"Bring it on," Michael said with a flashy grin. "Hopefully, we'll get to keep a chunk of it. Then, I'll retire for good. Maybe even go do some real charity work."

CHAPTER 30

THE KLEBERG COUNTY courthouse was a media fest by the time Alex and Michael pulled into the parking lot. Even though Judge Cienfuegos had no standing order against cameras in the courtroom, he had ordered the bailiff to hand-pick ten reporters to sit in the courtroom during the trial. The bailiff, being a heavy-set bachelor, quickly scanned the crowd and selected nine of the best-looking female reporters in the State of Texas and a lone, scruffy-looking male reporter. As per the judge's rules, this once, the cameras would have to stay out in the hallway or report from the steps and sidewalks in front of the courthouse.

The streets surrounding the courthouse had become a tent city, with satellite dishes, miles and miles of cable, lights, transmission vans, and cameras and microphones designed to capture even the smallest details connected to the case.

Mexico's Network Televisa had sent an army of reporters to cover the trial because some of the Santibáñez heirs claimed dual citizenship—they were U.S. citizens and Mexican nationals—and as such, Mexico wanted nothing less than for its citizens to get a fair and just trial. CNN had sent Nancy Grace to give a play-by-play analysis of the trial.

Romeo had arrived first that morning, having been instructed to snatch the counsel table closer to the jury box and not to move until either Michael or Alex had arrived to reinforce their claim. In law schools across the nation, all the trial skill classes taught students to start thinking of ways to gain every conceivable advantage over an opponent. Rule number one was to always claim the table closest to the jury box so that those attorneys could start building a rapport with the jurors sitting nearby. They were advised to make plenty of eye contact, flash a warm smile here, a greeting there, and show them plenty of consideration.

After Romeo had arrived, attorney Uhels showed up with his entourage in tow. Uhels' group drove up in three black Hummers, transporting no less than six associate lawyers, three paralegals and two investigators. All were color-coordinated, sporting grey wool suits. The two investigators, left behind to unload the boxes of exhibits, were wearing gray roper boots, gray Wrangler jeans, gray blazers and cowboy hats.

Despite the fact that the Texas Rules of Professional Conduct prohibited discussing aspects of a case that would have a substantial material impact on a trial or its outcome, Uhels stopped to answer a few questions from the mob of reporters.

"Will the court grant your request to have all jurors fill lengthy questionnaires?"

Uhels cleared his throat. "I think we're entitled to know everything and anything about the potential jurors. This is a very important case for our clients and for the State of Texas. Therefore, it is extremely important that the lawyers get to select just the right kind of jury to hear this case."

Another reporter shoved her microphone in Uhels' face. "By 'right kind of jury,' do you mean the kind of jury that would favor you? A jury that will help you win?"

Uhels seemed bothered by the question and was about to come up with an answer when another reporter asked, "But isn't your request nothing more than a delay tactic, Mr. Uhels?"

"Absolutely not!" cried the seasoned attorney. "The rules allow for questionnaires."

"Some would say you're doing it only to bill your client, that in civil cases folks usually don't fill questionnaires, only in criminal cases involving the death penalty. What do you say to that?"

The questions kept coming.

"What about the rumor that the defense will hire Senator Hightower to delay the case even more?"

"Is it true Senator Gustavo Hightower is charging half a million to use the legislative continuance in order to help the foundation?"

"Wouldn't that be considered a bribe?"

"Isn't using the legislative continuance a way to delay justice?"

"What do you think of Alejandro Del Fuerte?"

"Will there be an appeal, in case the plaintiffs win?"

"Is it true that Orion Wind Farms is considering filing for bankruptcy?"

Uhels took a step back. "Please, one at a time. Listen, I am not about to comment on Mr. Del Fuerte. He's trying his best to fight for his clients. He's doing a commendable job. Unfortunately, in this instance, he's outgunned, and he's going to go home wishing he'd never picked this fight. Mr. Del Fuerte should have realized long ago that this is not a mock trial competition down at the law school."

"What about the judge?"

Somebody else picked up on the question. "Are you worried about Judge Cienfuegos?"

"Is it true that Judge Phillips was bought and paid for by big oil and gas?"

"And that Phillips had been receiving illegal campaign contributions from a PAC linked to the Church?"

"And that's why the previous attorneys were 'railroaded' from the get-go?"

Uhels hesitated at the tone of the questioning. The reporters were getting downright mean and vicious. "Both Judge Phillips and Judge Cienfuegos have served with honor, distinction and decorum. I can't say anything bad of either judge. Now, if you'll excuse me, I have a case to try."

"Wait," shouted someone in the mob, "is it true that Judge Phillips had a private audience with the Pope?"

Next, Dana McDermott, Mosley and four others showed up in a shiny new suburban, followed by a U-Haul truck driven by her firm's investigator and errand boy. McDermott was dressed in a low-cut, navy-blue business suit, and Mosley was wearing a dark-blue, Brooks Brothers pin-striped suit. While the rest of their team unloaded the truck, McDermott began answering the reporters' questions.

"Mrs. McDermott, are you worried your client will lose La Minita?"

"That'll never happen," answered McDermott. "We're prepared to take this case to the U.S. Supreme Court, if need be."

"But if the Agnus Dei Foundation wanted to settle, would you advise Bishop Salamanca to throw in the towel?"

"I would never push for a settlement, unless that's what the client really wanted. I'm a trial lawyer."

"Were you surprised to see the plaintiffs move to recuse Judge Phillips? Call it quits?"

"I've been trying cases for well over thirty years, and nothing surprises me anymore. Stranger things have happened."

"Will you prevail?"

"I believe the plaintiffs are not ready to try this case. They won't be able to prove what they're claiming to the jury. It's as simple as that. Remember, Alejandro Del Fuerte jumped into this case less than five months ago. And this is only the second major case he's tried. Thank you. Gotta run."

"Wait! Is it true that jury selection will last the entire month of December?"

Other reporters shouted more questions at her, but she had turned her back to the mob and marched on.

Alex and Michael were standing at counsel's table, looking over their notes, when the bailiff announced the arrival of the Honorable Judge Emiliano Cienfuegos.

"Good morning," said Judge Cienfuegos, "please be seated. What do we have?"

Alex sprang up to his feet like a rocket. "Judge, good morning," said Alex, "this is the final pretrial. I believe there are more than fifty motions pending, most filed by the defense over the weekend. Most of them are frivolous and without any merit, if you ask me."

O'Quinn bolted from his seat. "Judge, I object to the sidebar."

Uhels followed, "Same objection."

Then McDermott, "Same objection."

One by one, everyone objected, including the amateur Teddy Galindo.

"Ladies, gentlemen," waved the judge, "hold your horses. Can somebody please tell me what's pending before the court this morning?" He looked over at Michael, "How about you, Mr. Fetzer? What do we have?"

"Good morning, Your Honor," said Michael, "in a nutshell, there are several motions in limine, and various defense and intervenor motions having to do with jury selection."

"Like?"

Uhels interrupted, "Like our motion to order all prospective jurors to fill out questionnaires. This is an important case, and . . . we've also filed a motion for jury shuffle . . . "

"Wait," said Cienfuegos, again waving his hand in the air, "you mean to tell me that with all these lawyers set to ask questions of all the prospective jurors, we still need to dig deeper and do questionnaires?"

"Well, uh, sure . . . Your Honor," stammered Uhels, "questionnaires would be appropriate in this case."

"Did you bring a copy machine with you this morning, Mr. Uhels?" asked Judge Cienfuegos.

There were chuckles in the courtroom.

"Eh, well, no, Your Honor," Uhels explained, "the deputy clerk can run copies . . . and pass them around . . . to all the lawyers."

"This county's close to bankrupt, Mr. Uhels, and I find it difficult to believe that we need to waste time on questionnaires when the thirty or so of you in this courtroom can figure out what to ask or what not to ask."

McDermott jumped in, "Judge, even if you're thinking of denying Mr. Uhels' request, which I think has some merit, we have a motion pending to enlarge the size of the jury panel from the usual forty-five in district court to three hundred."

"You want me to summon a panel of three hundred? And spend the Christmas holiday reviewing questionnaires to come up with twelve good people to hear this case?"

"Well . . . yes," McDermott replied, "I don't see anything wrong with working through Christmas."

"Both motions will be denied," said Cienfuegos, banging his gavel on the bench, "including the request for jury shuffle. The court, however, will order the district clerk to send us a panel of seventy-five . . . to make room, just in case, see if we don't bust the panel."

In his two years of trying cases, Alex had never had the pleasure of participating in a case where the attorneys ended up busting the panel. Busting the panel meant that after jury selection was conducted, most panel members had been stricken or excused from serving—for whatever reason—and there were not enough members left to even assemble a meager group of twelve jurors.

"Bust the panel?" asked Bobby Fonseca in a somewhat incredulous tone. "You really think so, Your Honor?"

Uhels, McDermott, O'Quinn and all the others acting as local counsel turned to look at each other. Judge Cienfuegos now appeared intent on derailing the defense and intervenors' best laid plans.

"Well, then," interjected Michael, "it appears as if only the motions to bifurcate damages and limine motions remain. Jury selection should be a breeze."

"Wait, wait," cried McDermott, "this morning we filed several other motions on behalf of our client, Your Honor. Here are copies for everybody."

McDermott's staff quickly handed out the newly filed motions.

"What kind of motions?" asked Cienfuegos, somewhat angry. "This late in the game? The day of trial?"

McDermott replied, "We're asking the court to seal the proceedings, Your Honor. Particularly when evidence is presented in connection with our motion to bifurcate."

"You mean discussions about the wealth of your client?" asked the judge.

"Yes," said McDermott.

In many high-stakes trials throughout the country, the defense always filed motions to bifurcate the trial. It meant that before the net worth of a defendant could be discussed in front of a jury, the plaintiffs had to prevail and prove that the defendants had either committed fraud or had acted with gross negligence and wanton recklessness. The motion to bifurcate in essence split the trial in two parts: the liability part and then the damages part. This meant that the plaintiffs had to win round one, so that they could then begin discussing money in round two. The reasoning always advanced by the defense was that juries were so incredibly ignorant and stupid that if a defendant's net worth was discussed from the beginning of the trial, the jury would no longer pay attention to the evidence and would simply want to start spreading the defendant's money around.

"What about the first amendment?" asked Judge Cienfuegos. "You want me to kick out the reporters when the net worth of the defendant is discussed for purposes of the motion to bifurcate?"

"Yes, Judge," said McDermott, "we don't need to discuss the net worth of my client until, and only if, there's a finding by the jury that the Agnus Dei Foundation engaged in fraudulent conduct."

"Why shouldn't we be able to discuss your client's net worth, among us?" cried Alex, as he pushed for Judge Cienfuegos to allow him to bring the issue of the foundation's net worth up for discussion, during the trial, "certainly that same question was asked of the defendant in discovery years ago, and the defendant played hooky and has never fully answered, Your Honor."

"Is that so?" asked Judge Cienfuegos.

"Yes," said Alex, waving his hand and snapping his fingers at Romeo to dig up the foundation's discovery responses so he could show the judge. He appeared to be enjoying himself, "I'll show you. FYI, Judge Phillips never entertained the previous attorney's motions for sanctions, and we never raised the issue, although it has been pending all this time."

"You mean," Cienfuegos stared, eyes wide open, "Judge Phillips denied the previous attorneys a hearing on their motion to sanction the foundation for discovery abuses? For failing to fully answer and provide appropriate responses?"

"It would appear so, Your Honor," Alex said, flashing a grin.

Romeo finally handed the discovery file to Alex and pointed at the portion in the file that had been tabbed.

"Do you have a copy of the motion for sanctions that was never taken up by Judge Phillips?"

Alex approached the bench to show the judge the inadequate discovery responses the foundation had provided Dugger and Worley, the previous attorneys. In the meantime, Uhels, O'Quinn, McDermott and all the others huddled nervously over to one side and appeared to be discussing a way to get out of this mess. No one even remembered that the old sanctions motion had never been resolved. Things appeared to be heading downhill quickly for the defendant and the intervenors.

"Judge," cried McDermott, "we're going to withdraw our motion to seal the proceedings."

"Not so fast," replied Cienfuegos. "I want to know more about this discovery abuse issue."

Uhels tried to come to the rescue. "Judge, can we visit in chambers?"

"Nope," said Cienfuegos, "I want to know what's been going on. Why has the defense been allowed all this time to toy with the plaintiffs?" He then turned to Alex. "Counsel, did you find the previous motions for sanctions and to compel discovery?"

Alex waved the two motions high up in the air. "They're here, Your Honor. I've got 'em."

"You mean to tell me," started Cienfuegos, "that those motions have been sitting there, gathering dust and Judge Phillips never ruled on them?"

"Never even set them for hearing," finished Alex, "I guess we know why."

Cienfuegos started flipping through the thick court file in front of him. He found the originals of the motions in question. "Here we go. Let's see. Mr. Del Fuerte, I see here that the defendants objected on grounds that this information could not be provided until the time of trial, but only if the plaintiffs proved they were entitled to exemplary damages or if the plaintiffs proved the alleged fraud. What do you think?"

"I think it's called hiding the ball, Your Honor," Alex said with sheer delight.

Alex immediately panicked after his last comment. He remembered that, on the one hand, he was supposed to be fighting for his clients, but on the other, he and Salamanca had an understanding. Suddenly, albeit inadvertently, he appeared to be socking it to the foundation. And Judge Cienfuegos was ready to throw McDermott and all the others into the meat grinder and sanction them to oblivion and back. What if the sanction was what the lawyers called "death penalty sanctions," and the defendants were not even allowed to put on a defense? What if the Santibáñez clan won without Alex really meaning to?! Who had ever heard of such a thing? How could he keep things straight.

Michael, who was clueless as to Alex's predicament, added, "It's not even a proper objection, Judge."

"I agree," replied Cienfuegos, "and not only do I agree, but it is the court that decides if the requested discovery should be produced, when it should be produced and if such a production should be done in chambers, under seal or out in open court."

"Judge," Alex said, "maybe we can revisit the sanctions issue at a later time. Can we start jury selection?"

All the lawyers in the room did a double-take. Even Michael and Romeo glared at Alex in apparent confusion. As a lawyer, if the judge threw you a soft ball, you made sure you hit a home run. And here, Judge Cienfuegos was doing just that. What the hell was wrong with Alejandro Del Fuerte?

"I'll do no such thing, Mr. Del Fuerte," Cienfuegos said. "The Texas rules of civil procedure exist for a reason. Now, I know there are judges out there that don't give a hoot about them. Rogue judges that do whatever the hell they want or bend over backwards and disregard the rules in order to help their friends and political allies. Then, there are attorneys like Mrs. McDermott and you, and everyone else in here, that think that the rules should be used, sometimes, but only if they will help their position. Otherwise, they should be disregarded. I will do no such thing. Those rules were created for a reason."

Judge Cienfuegos then turned and faced McDermott. "Counsel, are you going to answer the discovery and provide the information requested? Or will the court be required to entertain a hearing on the kinds of sanctions we need to apply in this case?"

McDermott was at a loss for words. She turned to Mosley and whispered something in his ear, then bent over and whispered something in O'Quinn's ear, and then Uhels', and then Fonseca's. After about a minute of this, she turned to face Cienfuegos.

"I have to call my client, Your Honor," she stuttered.

"I take it that's a no?" Cienfuegos asked.

Michael seized the opportunity and also jumped in. "Judge, we would ask that you make all of the intervenors provide similar responses. The same discovery was propounded to all the adverse parties, and they never answered, either."

Alex wanted to die. He did a one-eighty and looked at Cienfuegos, then Michael, then Cienfuegos, then Michael again, then the floor and finally at McDermott. She looked lost. And he was no longer in control. His strategy had completely backfired. Was there a chapter on this in law textbooks? What happens when a judge takes over a case? Talk about complete extremes. Phillips had been the foundation's whore, bending over backwards to help Salamanca and his cronies, and now Cienfuegos wanted—single-handedly—to crush Salamanca and his pals.

"With all due respect, Your Honor," McDermott began speaking, slowly, trying to regain control, getting a hold of her nerves, "if you give me thirty minutes, I should be able to get you that information."

"Okay," Cienfuegos said, "then you'll provide that information and we'll be in recess. Depending on what happens in thirty minutes, then we might get to the motions in limine or not. We'll see. Otherwise, we might have ourselves a little "sanctions fest" first. Because, depending on the sanctions, we'll see how the trial is going to play out. We'll need to know if the foundation, and the intervenors, deserve to present any evidence, during the trial, on their affirmative defenses, if at all. Got it?"

What Cienfuegos was saying was that if he found that the defense lawyers, along with the intervenors, had purposefully withheld evidence that the plaintiffs were entitled to see, then he would find a way to make things right. Sometimes a judge could prevent a party from mounting a defense—by not allowing the party to present any witnesses—and in this manner sanction the offending attorney. It was all very clear, Cienfuegos had no qualms being judge and executioner.

"Judge," cried O'Quinn, "does that mean my client also has to provide evidence of its net worth?"

"What about mine?" cried Uhels.

"And mine?" asked the other defense attorneys in the group.

"You all have thirty minutes to comply," shouted Cienfuegos. "All of you have had more than two years to provide this information to opposing counsel. And I know you all can make one call and get that information from your clients. One call . . . that's all it'll take . . . to get your clients' net worth."

"Your Honor," cried Uhels, "that information is all available online. The plaintiff can just go to my client's website and see it. We're a publicly traded company, Judge."

"That might be so, but I'm ordering YOU to provide it," huffed Cienfuegos as he turned to face Alex. "Mr. Del Fuerte, is there anything else that the defense has failed to provide or has failed to answer in discovery?"

Alex's mouth felt dry like the Sahara desert. "Huh, I . . . don't know, Your Honor, I guess I could . . . check."

"Okay, do me a favor, go ahead and look into it. I don't want to start this trial unless you have everything you need and everything you're entitled to, under the rules, in order to try the case the way you want to do it."

"Will do, Your Honor," said Michael, beaming with joy and relishing the fact that they appeared to have landed in front of a plaintiff-friendly judge.

"Thirty minutes. We're in recess," shouted Cienfuegos.

Alex noticed that Romeo and Michael were smiling and giggling like two little girls as Judge Cienfuegos took the bench after the thirty-minute recess. Unfortunately, Alex could not share in their joy, although he was pretending to relish the fact that Cienfuegos was making McDermott and her cronies squirm. In fact, he wished he could simply announce that he'd had a sudden change of heart and that he no longer wished to be involved in the case and now just wanted to go home, get in bed, pull the sheets over his head and disconnect the phone.

"Please, be seated," ordered Cienfuegos in an impatient tone. "Mrs. McDermott, do you have the information I asked for? What about the intervenors?"

The nine female reporters and the lone male reporter in the back of the courtroom were all scribbling furiously on their notepads, barely coming up for air, all waiting to hear McDermott's response.

"It's all right here," said McDermott as she waved a three-ring binder in the air.

"Well, turn it over to the plaintiffs, Mrs. McDermott."

McDermott gave it to Mosley, who then walked over to Alex's counsel table to hand it over. Alex took the binder and then gave it to Michael to hold. He wanted no part of it. Michael immediately started pouring through it.

"Now, can we address our motion to bifurcate, Your Honor?" asked McDermott.

Michael was shaking his head. "Judge, we're still waiting on the intervenors' financials. Do they have them?"

"We have them," said O'Quinn as he turned over a packet to Mosley to turn over to the plaintiffs.

"Can we have a minute to inspect them, Your Honor?" asked Michael.

"Sure," Cienfuegos agreed. "Now, Mrs. McDermott, let me ask you . . ."

"Yes, Judge?"

"Why would you think of filing a motion to bifurcate, prevent the plaintiffs from talking about net worth, when you never provided them with the information requested? How were they supposed to even attempt to discuss punitive damages in front of a jury—assuming they got there—when they had nothing to discuss? Did you not think that discussing one would necessarily mean not discussing the other?"

"May we approach the bench?" asked McDermott.

"You may," said Cienfuegos.

All the lawyers approached the bench. Alex, Michael and McDermott were in Cienfuegos's face, while the others were inching closer, trying to hear McDermott's explanation.

"Judge," McDermott began, "this is off the record."

Cienfuegos signaled the court reporter to stop transcribing. The court reporter took advantage of the break and proceeded to insert a fresh tape into her recorder and change the paper in her transcription machine.

"Judge," whispered McDermott, "I have a very difficult client, who also has to follow orders from above. This, in turn, makes things complicated because there are aspects of our legal system that the Europeans just don't get or even care to understand. Do you understand what I'm saying?"

"I think I do," Cienfuegos answered.

"So, I might explain to them that this or that needs to happen or this or that needs to be produced, but the client may have other ideas. Now, I had to raise the issue of the bifurcation because it was going to be an issue in the trial, sooner or later."

"The white elephant in the room, huh?" Cienfuegos asked.

"Exactly, and I'm the trial lawyer. I'm the one in the trenches, and I'm the one that's going to be blamed if this trial goes south for us. So, I had to file my CYA motion and protect myself, just in case . . . because, ultimately, I'll be the one who gets scrutinized, and they'll want to know why I didn't do this or failed to do that or the other. And someone, invariably, will ask why I didn't think of filing a motion to bifurcate prior to trial."

Alex felt somewhat sorry for McDermott. Her explanation made total sense. An attorney's obligation always ran to the client, and, if the client wanted the attorney to handle the case in a certain way, or defend it this way or that way—as long as it was legal and ethical—the attorney had a duty to obey the client. When push came to shove, 99% of the time it came down to money. And clients with money called the shots.

Judge Cienfuegos had heard enough. "Okay, back on the record. Counsel, you may all go back to your seats. Let's move the case along."

The lawyers dispersed and took their seats. Michael continued to go through the packets of financials now sitting in front of him. He was beaming with delight.

Cienfuegos retook control of the proceedings. "Let the record reflect that the defendants and intervenors have complied with the court's earlier instructions to provide the plaintiffs with the financials as to net worth, previously requested in discovery."

Cienfuegos paused, looked up from the bench, and locked in on Alex. "Mr. Del Fuerte, do you still want the court to entertain a hearing on the sanctions? Find out why it took two years for the plaintiffs to get those discovery responses? Or do you want me to take up the matter of defendant's motion to bifurcate?"

"Huh, ahem, yes, Judge . . . I see," he mumbled, then looked at Michael as if asking for help.

"It's not a trick question, Mr. Del Fuerte," Cienfuegos pushed further.

Michael took over, "Judge, as long as the record reflects that the foundation's estimated net worth is fifty billion dollars and the intervenors' collective net worth exceeds three trillion dollars . . . "

There was a collective gasp from the crowd and the reporters in the audience.

"Quiet!" announced Cienfuegos as he pounded his gavel on the bench. "Go on, Mr. Fetzer. Since it appears your co-counsel is unable to think right now and answer a simple question."

"We can carry the sanctions motion along until the end of trial and agree not to talk about the defendant's unmeasured wealth, but until the plaintiffs have prevailed on the liability part of the trial, first."

"So, you're asking me to grant Mrs. McDermott's motion to bifurcate?"

"That would be the right thing to do . . . so, yes, Judge. That's it," Michael said as he looked at Alex, his co-counsel trying to double-check and confirm that, indeed, that was the plan. Alex was fumbling with his yellow pads, pretending to be reading some notes in front of him.

"Don't you think that the sanctions are important because they will affect the defendant's ability to put on a defense?" asked Judge Cienfuegos. Obviously upset, the judge added, "I mean, if I ever saw a case where death-penalty sanctions were more than appropriate, it's this case, Mr. Fetzer. Shouldn't we discuss that first?"

Michael elbowed Alex in the ribs. "Judge, let me confer with my co-counsel. Give me just a second."

Michael, Romeo and Alex huddled together. Michael spoke first. "Alex, did you just hear that? This guy is ready to hand us the foundation on a silver platter. What do you want to do?"

"I guess . . . we have to, ah . . . go through the hearing, right?" Alex asked, not knowing what else to say. *What a mess. Remind me to surrender my license after this trial is over . . . that is . . . if I'm still alive. Holy freakin' shit! Where did they find this crazy judge?!*

"Okay," interrupted Cienfuegos, looking at the clock on the wall. It was 11:45 A.M. "I'll tell you what. We're gonna break for lunch, and, at one-thirty, we'll begin the hearing on sanctions. Then, after that, we'll entertain motions in limine. We're in recess."

"All rise," shouted the bailiff.

The lawyers, spectators and reporters all stood up to show respect for Judge Emiliano Cienfuegos as he left the courtroom through the side door.

"Back at one-thirty," announced the bailiff.

CHAPTER 31

ALEX, MICHAEL AND ROMEO were sitting in Chili's outside of Kingsville, waiting to order lunch. Across the restaurant, in the bar area, McDermott sat with her legal team, while nearby, Uhels, Nicholas, O'Quinn and some of the other intervenors sat at large tables with local counsel and their staff.

Alex's cell phone started vibrating, and he reached for it in his shirt pocket. The ID showed the words Private Call.

Alex looked at the call and excused himself from the table. "It's Gigi calling. Let me take it outside." He looked at Romeo and said, "Just order me a cup of enchilada soup and a grilled chicken salad, no dressing. I'll be right back, okay?"

"Got it," Romeo confirmed.

Alex walked out of the restaurant and stood in the parking lot. He answered the call. "Hello?"

"Alex, what the hell is going on?" barked Bishop Salamanca. "I thought we had a deal. Now, I come to find out you're pushing Cienfuegos' buttons, and I hear the guy's ready to knock our teeth out. What did you do to him?!"

Alex looked around nervously, making sure no one was within earshot. "I had no idea, I swear . . . "

"You better fix this absolute mess, Alex. Or else," snarled Salamanca, "*age quod agis.*"

There was a long pause.

"Okay. I'll figure something out," Alex whispered, looking around, making sure he was still alone. He could feel the beads of perspiration forming on his forehead and dripping down his side-burns.

"You better not screw this up. Or I won't be able to run inter-ference, anymore . . . understand?"

Alex looked down. "Cienfuegos is out of control . . . I don't know if anyone can control him, really. He's intent on doing what-ever the hell he damn well pleases. This is very obvious . . . just by the way things are going in the courtroom."

"Should I be worried?" asked Salamanca.

Alex's voice quivered, "I don't know . . . "

"Well, then?"

Alex cleared his throat. "It's just that he's the kind of judge that runs his court the way he wants to. He's not one of those that lets the lawyers run the show."

"Well, you better figure something out," repeated Salamanca, angry as hell.

"All right," said Alex, trying to muster a new resolve, "I'll find a way to make things work."

"We're counting on you, Alex. Don't let us down. I'd hate to have to renege on our deal."

"Got to go," replied Alex as he pushed the end-call button.

Judge Cienfuegos was on the bench already by the time the liti-gants started trickling back into the courtroom. He and the bailiff were discussing going down to Port Mansfield over the weekend to do some fishing. Anytime Judge Cienfuegos got an assignment to preside over a trial down in South Texas, he brought his fly-fishing rod and his waders with him just in case the opportunity to go fishing presented itself. The judge loved fly-fishing, espe-cially making his own lures.

"Ladies and gentlemen," Cienfuegos said to the crowd now taking their seats at counsel table and elsewhere. "A couple of housekeeping matters before we start the trial."

Alex looked up from counsel's table. "Yes, Judge?"

"What is it, Your Honor?" McDermott followed.

"First, there will be no hanky-panky in my courtroom," explained Cienfuegos.

All the lawyers did a double-take. Alex and Michael were looking at each other, trying to figure out what Cienfuegos was talking about.

The judge continued, "Don't invite me to go to lunch with any of you. Don't show up with breakfast tacos for me or my staff, or *pan dulce*, tamales or whatever. I'm not like the judge from Laredo that got invited to the NBA finals. Got it? It simply amazes me the things lawyers sometimes do."

"Yes, Judge," came everyone's reply.

"Okay, as far as the sanctions are concerned, I've decided what I'm going to do. I will issue my ruling after jury selection. And when I'm finished, I will let you all make an offer of proof, so that you can object or not, and put whatever you want to put on the record, in case you all are interested in preserving any points for appeal. But, we're not going to have a hearing, per se. Everyone with me, so far?"

O'Quinn raised his hand. "Judge, do I understand you correctly in that you will not require a full-blown hearing on the plaintiff's stale motion for discovery sanctions?"

"That's correct. The truth of the matter is that you all just complied with the plaintiffs' request. Two years after it'd been made, of course. The way this case has been handled was not fair to the plaintiffs. They've been asking for that evidence, and they should have gotten their hands on it sooner."

"So, what are you proposing, Judge?" asked Uhels. "The plaintiffs never filed a proper motion to compel seeking any type of relief."

"That's debatable," chimed Fetzer.

"This is what I'm thinking. I'm inclined to strike one expert witness per intervenor and defendant. Or maybe, the Court will not allow the defendant and intervenors to put on any evidence on the statute of limitations defense, nor will they be allowed to offer impeachment evidence on that point."

"But, Judge," cried Fonseca, "my clients can't be without their experts. We need them."

"Mr. Fonseca," said Cienfuegos as he flipped open the file. "I see here that the Agnus Dei Foundation has listed at least five testifying expert witnesses, and each intervenor has also designated at least six or seven expert witnesses. That's a total of forty-plus experts that are expected to testify at this trial. With that many experts, we will be here until doomsday. I suggest you all talk among yourselves and figure out how to cut the fat. If you can't do it, then maybe I'll do it for you. I'm thinking of allowing only one expert per party, on the defense and intervenors' sides."

Michael turned to Alex just as Alex turned to face his mentor. Things were getting pretty interesting. Michael and Alex both knew that many a case was won or lost on the strength of expert witnesses. These expensive hired guns gave expert opinions on just about any topic imaginable. You want an expert to say the doctor-defendant had breached the standard of care? You got it. How about one to say that the quadriplegic-plaintiff was going to need round-the-clock nursing care for the rest of his life to the tune of $30,000,000? Doable. Or one to say that to a reasonable degree of scientific certainty, the town's water supply had been contaminated by the defendant's chemical plant seeping hazardous materials into the ground? Presto. Any party with the right expert by his or her side could easily tip the scales in his or her favor. "Judge," cried O'Quinn, "that's not fair, Your Honor. We have gone through a tremendous amount of expense and effort to line up these experts who come from all over the country to testify. And now you want to clip our wings?"

"Is that an objection?" asked Cienfuegos.

"I'm just saying . . . " replied O'Quinn.

"When the time comes for me to make my decision about the expert issue or the affirmative defense issue, then you will all be allowed to make your objections and your offers of proof," instructed Cienfuegos. "In the meantime, let's discuss the motions in limine and figure out how large of a panel we'll need for Monday. Understood?"

Alex, Romeo and Michael were nodding in agreement with Judge Cienfuegos' proposal, while McDermott, Uhels, Nicholas, O'Quinn and all the others were shaking their heads in disgust.

An offer of proof was a commonly used procedure wherein if a lawyer was not allowed to present evidence during the trial or the lawyer was prevented from asking certain questions, then he could make an offer of proof. Usually, offers of proof were made during a break or at the end of the day and always outside the presence of the jury. The exercise requires the attorney to dictate to the court reporter why he was not allowed to present certain evidence explaining why he thought the evidence would have been relevant to the case.

This way, the attorney can preserve his objections on the record for a possible future appeal, depending on the outcome of the case. An attorney makes the offer of proof, just in case things don't turn out the way he'd planned, because he feels the evidence was improperly excluded. However, if at the end of the day, the attorney prevails, then the offer of proof is meaningless and of no consequence. It becomes an important aspect of the trial when the losing party wants to appeal and complains of being denied the opportunity to present evidence through a witness or otherwise.

If the foundation or the intervenors lost the case and later on decided to complain that the elimination of experts had severely limited their ability to put on a defense, then the court of appeals could go back, look at the record and decide whether or not having presented those experts' testimony would have made a difference to the jury. The justices on the appellate court would ask themselves if the exclusion of such evidence or testimony constituted either harmless or harmful error.

"All right," Cienfuegos said as he pounded his gavel on the bench, "let's first take up the plaintiff's motion in limine. Then we'll address the foundation's, then the intervenors', in that order. Is everyone with me?"

"Yes, Your Honor," the lawyers replied, grudgingly.

The motions in limine are designed to keep the jury from hearing certain things that could be harmful or inflammatory and have no relevance to the actual case. It is a procedure by which a party brings to the court's attention certain evidentiary issues that should be addressed, first to the judge, before the jury gets to hear or see the evidence. These are usually things that could make the jury dislike or favor one party over the other. Lawyers are trained to keep highly prejudicial evidence from reaching the jury, especially if that evidence has zero probative value and could sink their case. For instance, Alex's motion in limine also covered the shooting by Cousin Mago. Why talk about Cousin Mago killing Father Benito, when that had nothing to do with the issues in the Santibáñez' lawsuit?

After items like this are brought to the court's attention and the court issues a ruling, normally the attorneys discuss with the witnesses the scope of the motion in limine and remind them not to get into any matters addressed in the motion. The witnesses must always be warned that certain topics are off limits, and no one should discuss them, much less bring them up.

"Let me hear from the plaintiffs first," ordered Cienfuegos. "What do you want, Mr. Del Fuerte?"

"Judge," said Alex as he cleared his throat, "our motion in limine is very simple and basic. One, we would like to prevent the defense from discussing any arrests, for whatever reason, of any of our clients or witnesses, including mine. Unless there's a showing the person was convicted of a felony or a crime of moral turpitude, and said conviction happened within the last ten years, then neither the defense nor the intervenors should be allowed to get into those matters."

"What says the defense and intervenors?" asked Judge Cienfuegos.

"Not a problem," answered O'Quinn, "unless counsel opens the door, Your Honor."

"That's right," said McDermott, jumping into the fray. "I'd hate to rain on the plaintiffs' parade, but if their witnesses open the door, then we should be allowed to ram a fire truck through it."

"I understand," replied Alex. "I'd like the record to reflect that opening the door cuts both ways. If the witnesses for the defense also open the door, then we should be allowed to ram a jumbo 777 through it."

Cienfuegos rolled his eyes. "It will so be noted."

"Also, Judge," continued Alex, "the defense should not be allowed to bring up any evidence of prior bad acts committed by any of the plaintiffs, for any reason whatsoever."

"That will be granted," said Cienfuegos, "unless the defense can show that such evidence is necessary to rebut or explain certain evidence or to show some bias, scheme, pattern or relevant motive of the plaintiffs."

"That's fine, Judge," replied Alex. "Also, any mention by the defense or intervenors that the lawyers are trying to hit the Texas Lotto or the Texas Mega Millions or some such comment, Judge. Or anything having to do with my firm's fee arrangement with the clients."

"That'll be granted," Cienfuegos said.

"Or that the plaintiffs' lawyers and the clients concocted a scheme to extort the foundation or blackmail the foundation by trying to force some sort of settlement. Or even that this is just another attempt by a bunch of money-hungry plaintiffs to line their pockets."

"Granted," Cienfuegos said.

"Any personal attacks, on me or Professor Fetzer," Alex said.

"Granted."

"Or that one of the Santibáñez family members murdered Father Benito del Angel and is awaiting trial."

"Granted."

"Or that legal documents from Mexico have no validity here in the United States. As the court knows, all of the documents that we intend to use at trial have been on file more than thirty days with the court. Additionally, we filed affidavits of business records proving the origin of those documents. Finally, the time to have objected to any of those documents has come and gone. Any objections that could have been made have been waived."

"Granted. What else?"

"We're almost done, Your Honor," said Alex. "Let me see."

He leaned over to Michael to discuss a few more items scribbled on a yellow pad. Alex finally looked up. "Finally, Your Honor, we would ask that the defendants or intervenors refrain from any sidebar remarks that the plaintiffs or witnesses have had a juvenile record or that they must be incompetent or not credible because some of them aren't fluent in the English language."

"That will be granted. Anything else?" asked Cienfuegos.

"That's it, Your Honor," Alex concluded.

Cienfuegos looked at McDermott. "Mrs. McDermott, what do we have?"

"Your Honor," started McDermott as she glanced at her yellow pad, "any mention of insurance or that any party to these proceedings has insurance coverage should not be brought up."

"Mr. Del Fuerte?" Cienfuegos asked.

"No problem, Judge. We won't bring it up," said Alex.

"What else?" Cienfuegos asked.

"Any mention of the number of lawyers and assistants defending this lawsuit, Your Honor. Or any comparisons of David versus Goliath."

"That's fine, Judge," answered Alex. "I think the jury will figure it out, anyway. It is David versus Goliath."

"Any mention by Mr. Del Fuerte that the defendant must be really worried or must have done something wrong by the sheer number of lawyers defending the foundation, Your Honor," announced McDermott.

"That'll be granted," replied Cienfuegos.

"Also, Judge," continued McDermott, "any mention of the defendant's net worth during the liability portion of the trial."

"That will be granted," said Cienfuegos.

"Any mention that the foundation has dragged things out and that that's the reason this case has taken years to come to trial."

"Fine."

"Or that the plaintiffs have had to wait years and years and years to have their day in court," said McDermott.

"Mr. Del Fuerte?" asked Cienfuegos.

"What's the harm, Your Honor?" asked Alex. "It's the truth. My clients have waited almost four years to get to trial."

Cienfuegos glanced over at McDermott. "Mrs. McDermott, what do you say?"

"Judge, the implication is that we're the bad guys, and we dragged our feet, and we're the ones that have prevented these poor souls from having their day in court. That is not true. Which reminds me, Your Honor, we don't want the plaintiffs to mention that Attorney Dugger died in a highway crash or that Attorney Worley committed suicide."

"Who are those folks?" asked Cienfuegos.

"The two previous attorneys that worked on the case," continued McDermott. "They're no longer with us."

"First things first," interjected Alex. "On the four years of waiting to get to trial, what's your ruling, Your Honor?"

"That will be denied," answered Cienfuegos. "It is what it is."

"Fine," growled McDermott, "but Dugger and Worley, what's the relevance?"

Cienfuegos raised his eyebrows. "Mr. Del Fuerte, what do you say?"

Alex and Michael were in conference and did not realize Cienfuegos wanted an answer.

"Counsel, do you have a problem with keeping out the previous attorneys' names?" Cienfuegos asked again.

Alex turned to face the judge. "Since the court has allowed us to bring up the fact that it has taken the plaintiffs four years to get to trial, I think the prudent thing to do, Your Honor, would be to mention Dugger and Worley if that comes up. However, I agree that we don't have to say how they died. No one is suggesting the foundation had anything to do with their demise."

"I object to the sidebar!" cried McDermott, "and my client resents any suggestion, innuendo or remote speculation by Mr. Del Fuerte to that effect."

"You're reading too much into things," responded Alex. "Calm down."

"Counsel!" shouted Cienfuegos, "let's move on. Or we'll be here all day. It's already three o'clock and we haven't even discussed the intervenors' motions in limine. How much more do you have, Mrs. McDermott?"

McDermott proudly waved a bound notebook. "Our limine motion is fifty pages long, Your Honor."

"Jesus!" grumbled Cienfuegos. "What could you possibly have in there? What? You don't want the plaintiffs to mention that the sun rises in the east and sets in the west? C'mon! Let's wrap this up. Dugger and Worley can be mentioned as long as no one discusses that they're dead or how they died. Now, let's move on!"

McDermott picked up where she'd left off. "Any mention by the plaintiffs that the defense attorneys have been milking the file by dragging their feet for well over four years, Your Honor. That, we believe, would tend to upset the jury and turn them against the lawyers. They could then take it out on our client."

"Granted," said Cienfuegos.

"Or that our experts' opinions are not founded on solid scientific research, unless, of course, we first have hearings outside the presence of the jury to determine whether or not their opinions survive a Robinson-Daubert challenge," McDermott said.

"Fine," Cienfuegos said, throwing his arms up in the air. "Hurry up, let's wrap it up, Mrs. McDermott."

"Is that one granted, Your Honor?" asked McDermott.

"Yes, it is. Let's go," Cienfuegos said.

McDermott continued discussing point after legal point of her lengthy motion in limine, while Alex tried to figure out a way out of the mess.

And so the discussion and arguments surrounding the litigants' motions in limine would carry into the evening. Of course, as often happens, just because the overly cautious attorneys have filed motions in limine, that doesn't mean the potential jury, or the public for that matter, won't get to hear all the lurid details related to a case. With a courtroom full of journalists taking down every little exchange between Alex, McDermott, Cienfuegos and all the others, all this legal wrangling would be reported in the six o'clock news, discussed in blogs and become headlines in the morning paper.

It is one thing to avoid discussing certain topics in front of a jury in the middle of trial; it is another to stop the media from reporting to the nation everything that happens at the courthouse. This sudden but cruel realization hit Alex like a bolt of lightning as he realized that Salamanca was not going to be a happy camper with the way things were playing out in the courtroom.

CHAPTER 32

THERE'S NOTHING WORSE for a trial lawyer than to suffer a panic attack the weekend before a big trial. Alex, Michael and Romeo were back in Brownsville, going over some last-minute details and getting ready for jury selection on Monday, when Alex realized that he was not ready to try this monster of a case. And not only was he not ready to deal with the enormous complexity of the case and the piles of evidence and documents, but he had no idea if Salamanca's plan would work.

How could he lose a case when the judge appeared poised to take over the trial and try the damn thing himself? How could he throw in the towel, when the majority of the potential jurors probably hated the foundation, anyway? They were distant relatives, acquaintances or friends of the folks that once owned La Minita before it was snatched away by McKnight. True, the foundation had come into it via a bequest in a will, and one could argue it had clean hands—that it had no knowledge that McKnight never held title—but why should the Church get to keep all the money? Why send it all back to the Vatican? Why not keep it here, in the Rio Grande Valley, with all the folks that so desperately needed it?

For Alex, the anxiety attack came as he was trying to figure out the key pieces of evidence to use in order to prove his case to the jury. And he'd realized that he had never had time to prepare the witnesses or reviewed any depositions previously given in the case and had never sufficiently analyzed the supporting documents that were now sitting scattered on the floor in his conference room.

The more he thought about it, the more frazzled he became. From the beginning, Michael had agreed to let Alex take the case; to first-chair the litigation. This meant that Michael, as second chair, would do whatever Alex asked him to do, but before that could happen, Alex needed to get intimately familiar with the case to assign specific tasks to Michael and Romeo. He needed to know where everything was in order to pull any document at a moment's notice. The desperation and sheer terror pushed Alex, forty-eight hours before the trial was due to start, to frantically rummage through his desk in search of Naiví García's curriculum vitae.

He dialed the number on the CV and waited for an answer.

"Hello?" answered a female.

"Naiví? Is this you?"

"Yes, who's this?" she replied.

"It's Alejandro Del Fuerte, Naiví. Are you in town?"

"Yes, sir," explained Naiví, "my last final was on December 2nd. I've been home on break for a little bit over a week."

"What were you planning on doing during the break? Do you want to make a little extra holiday cash?"

"Why? Do you have some work for me?" Naiví replied, sounding eager to work. "Classes don't resume until January 17. I have more than a month. I'd love to work."

Alex cleared his throat. "I could sure use some help. I'm in over my head in a case that starts on Monday, but there's a catch."

"I'm listening."

"You'd have to start this morning. Can you do it?"

"Yes, Mr. Del Fuerte. Let me just take a shower and I'll be right there, okay? Are you still inside the Boca Chica Tower?"

"Yes, we are."

"Will I be helping you on a case? Or working around the office?"

"You'll be helping on the case. I'm the lead attorney, but to be honest with you, I don't think I'm ready . . . it's a very bizarre case that landed on my lap . . . but . . . I'll explain more when you get here."

"Okay."

"By the way, what's the going rate for a first-year summer law clerk in Austin? Do you know?" asked Alex.

"My friends are making between twenty and twenty-five dollars an hour."

"How would you like to make fifty an hour, Naiví?"

"That's a lot of money, Mr. Del Fuerte."

"That's how desperate I am. I really need help, here. I'm going down with the ship."

"Make it seventy-five," countered Naiví, "and I'm yours for the entire holiday break."

"Are you kidding me?" complained Alex. "Okay, fine. Hurry."

"Where's Ms. Montemayor? Professor Fetzer? Aren't they helping?"

"That's another story. I'll tell you all about it when you get here. Hurry!"

After the call, Alex felt somewhat relieved. He made a mental outline and figured he'd start working on the jury charge, while Naiví went through the boxes of documents. Once his jury charge was finished, he would go over the key pieces of evidence and make a list of the witnesses he would use in order to introduce the key documents. He would then turn over his trial exhibits to Romeo and have him scan them and put together a PowerPoint presentation to show the jury. Meanwhile, he would ask Michael to work on jury selection questions and tailor a juror profile. On Monday night, or whenever the jury selection process was concluded, Alex would then prepare his opening argument, and he and Michael would alternate calling witnesses to the stand. Alex now felt a little better. At least now he had a plan.

The jury charge or court's charge is a compilation of questions, instructions and definitions, written on letter-sized paper that the judge hands to the jury at the end of trial. The jury is then asked to answer the questions contained in the document. It is designed to resolve the factual issues in the case and, depending on the jury's answers, one party or the other is declared the winner. Normally, each side prepares a proposed charge, and the judge determines which questions the jury will answer at the conclusion of the trial. This is done, again, outside the presence of the jury.

For example, in a lawsuit against a tire maker for manufacturing defective and unsafe tires, one of the questions the jury might have to answer might be: Was there a manufacturing defect in the tire at the time the tire left the possession of tire maker X that resulted in the rollover accident in question? Answer Yes or No.

Depending on the answers provided in response to the questions, the jury might get to move on and decide the damages questions. A jury might get the following question: What sum of money, if paid now in cash, would fairly and reasonably compensate Jane Doe for the unnecessary amputation of both her legs and arms as a result of the rollover accident? Answer in dollars and cents.

These kinds of questions are always used at the end of the trial in order to sort out the proportionate responsibility of the parties. Each case can have a multitude of different questions that the jury must answer. For example, a jury charge might also ask about exemplary damages or punitive damages. So, if medical expenses should be awarded to the plaintiff, what kind of expenses? Past? Present? Future? And pain and suffering? In short, the jury can be asked to answer all kinds of questions regarding responsibility and damages.

One thing is certain, though, a good lawyer always prepares a draft jury charge at the outset of each case. This is so because the jury charge provides a blueprint, or a road map, of the pieces of evidence that are going to be necessary to prove the plaintiff's or defendant's case.

Alex figured that the only way he would get a grip of the case was to quickly put together the jury charge and pull the relevant pieces of evidence. All he needed to do was make a decent showing while presenting his case. That way, the Santibáñez clan wouldn't complain that he was incompetent and turn around and sue him, too. It was a fine line he was toeing. On the one hand, he needed to look like a well-prepared, thoroughly competent trial attorney. On the other, there was the "back room" deal with Salamanca that he needed to honor. He was about to commit hari-kari.

He could not go for the foundation's jugular but more important-
ly, he needed to let the foundation's attorneys make sushi out of
him. Of course, his partners could never find out the shenanigans
he was neck deep in.

"Mr. Del Fuerte," Naiví said as she poked her head into the conference room where Alex was working diligently at a computer.

"Hey!" said a surprised Alex, "I didn't expect you this early."

"I let myself in. I noticed the door was open and I waited up
at the front . . . but didn't see anybody. I hope you don't mind."

Naiví looked radiant. She exuded confidence and was smiling
from ear to ear.

Alex got up from the conference table. "No, not at all. Professor Fetzer is due back here in a couple of hours, and I sent Romeo
to get breakfast."

"Where's Ms. Montemayor?" asked Naiví as she looked
around the conference room.

Alex hesitated, but finally answered. "She's not working on
this case. She didn't want to touch it."

"Why?"

"The defendant."

"Who's the defendant?"

"Ever heard of the Agnus Dei Foundation."

"I don't think so."

"How about its leader, Bishop Salamanca?"

"Of course. Everyone knows Bishop Salamanca." She paused,
and then the light bulb went off. "Don't tell me you're defending
him in a sexual assault case?"

"I should be so lucky. No, of course not. We're suing the foundation to see if we can get back the lands being held by the
Church. Return them to the original owners. It's basically a land
grant case," Alex said, pointing at the boxes. "It's the mother of all
land disputes, if there ever was such a thing."

"*¿De veras?*"

"Really," Alex assured her.

"You know, I aced both of my real property classes, Mr. Del Fuerte."

"No kidding. Really?"

"Yes, sir. Highest grade in both classes, Real Property I and II. I have to confess, I felt like a nerd . . . I loved the subject . . . Professor Moore, she was excellent. Of course, when we start dealing with people's lands and mineral interests and inheritances . . . it can, and usually does, get nasty and messy. People do all kinds of weird stuff to hang onto their land."

"Tell me about it," complained Alex. "This here is one of those animals."

"Are you afraid?"

"No," lied Alex, "but, between you and me, I wished I had declined taking on such a case."

"Why?"

"Let's get some coffee," Alex said as he signaled Naiví to follow him. "I'll tell you more in a minute."

Naiví followed Alex out of the conference room, down a hallway and into the firm's community kitchen. Alex reached into one of the cabinets, pulled out a coffee filter and proceeded to get the coffeemaker ready. He then found a can of Folgers Colombian Roast and reached for two cups from the cupboard as he tinkered with the coffee can.

Once the coffeemaker started brewing, Alex continued his explanation. "I took the case because I knew that we wouldn't even get to trial. I knew that it was a long shot, and I seriously doubted we would even survive the defendants' motions for summary judgment. But, I wanted to do a favor for a friend, and I promised I would take it and help the plaintiffs. Now, remember what I'm about to tell you."

"What?"

"In the law business . . . no good deed ever goes unpunished. Drill that into your head."

"Why do you say that?"

"Well, I'm just helping out a friend. No one thinks the case has a chance of getting to a jury. That's the reason I agreed to jump in. Doing it to help out . . . I'm thinking . . . just one hearing, the defendant's summary judgment gets granted . . . I'm gone. My friend looks good, I look good. Hey, at least we tried to help the plaintiffs, right?"

"Right," followed Naiví.

"Next thing I know, we survive the motions for summary judgment, a new judge takes over the case, and now here we are less than forty-eight hours before trial. And I'm about to have a meltdown. Never in a million years did I think we'd get this far."

Alex reached for the coffeepot and poured himself and Naiví a cup each. "How do you take it?"

"Two creams, one sugar, please."

Alex pointed to the fridge behind Naiví. "Reach behind you. The creamers are in the fridge. It's the box on the bottom shelf."

Naiví spun around and grabbed a couple of creamers and quickly came up again.

"So, why did Ms. Montemayor refuse to help with the case? You never told me."

"Because she didn't want me to sue Salamanca's foundation when we were contemplating asking him to come marry us. She said she didn't want any part in it . . . and she thought the whole thing was stupid."

"How so?"

"Because these kinds of cases are very difficult to win. And even if you win, the Texas Supreme Court will find a way—make some shit up—and take the verdict away."

Alex felt Naiví was asking too many questions, which of course could be attributed to the training she was receiving in law school, all thanks to the "so-called" Socratic method. The only topics Alex was not prepared to discuss were anything related to Gigi, her pregnancy or the wedding. He was hoping she wouldn't bring it up.

"So, then," asked Naiví as she sipped her cup of coffee, "why did you take it?"

Alex thought about this for a minute. He drank from his cup of black coffee as he tried to come up with an answer. "Honestly?"

"Honestly."

He shrugged his shoulders. "I don't know what the hell got into me. Maybe I was blinded with greed, or maybe I jumped the gun. I guess I thought we could change the law, if we won. I'm hoping there's an underlying reason that, hopefully, someday, will become clear to me. To tell you the truth, I kind of wish maybe I had listened to Gigi. Now, I'm up to my neck in this mess, and I can't get out. I'm afraid I'm going to be the one left holding the bag."

"Why can't you just withdraw?"

"Other reasons . . . personal reasons I can't discuss."

The pair walked back to the conference room and glanced at the piles of boxes waiting to be opened.

Naiví broke the silence. "Do you think you can win?"

"I don't want to win," blurted Alex.

Naiví's honey-colored eyes grew wide open. "What do you mean? Let me guess. Another long story, right?"

Alex motioned Naiví to close the door to the conference room and then to sit down at the conference table across from him. He looked around, trying to choose his words carefully and not really knowing where to start.

"Look," Alex started after clearing his throat, "there are things about me that nobody knows."

Naiví looked intrigued. "What things?"

"Things that I've never told anyone. And the reason no one knows is because I don't want my partners to freak out and force the firm to withdraw from the case. I want to finish the case, no matter what."

"Is your life in danger?"

"Of course not," Alex lied. "I'm talking principles here. To me, this case is a matter of righting a wrong. Standing up for what you believe, and if need be, to not back down. My partners would probably say that it'd be real stupid to take a case simply on principle. They'd argue that one should take a case because it'll make money for the client, the firm, all involved."

"I get it," said Naiví, "it's like winning a case where you can't collect, right?"

"Exactly," Alex answered with a nervous laugh, "some would even say it's moronic."

Alex could not bring himself to disclose to Naiví the exact situation and the predicament he was in. He wanted to, and he felt he needed someone to talk to, and he really, really tried, but just couldn't do it. Could he trust her?

"Is that it?" she asked, sounding less concerned.

"Something like that, anyway, I'd rather not get on my soapbox," Alex flashed a fake smile. "Let's get ready for trial. We have some big fish to fry."

"Okay, did you pull the survey?" Alex asked.

"Yep, I've got it right here," said Naiví. She was holding an ancient survey of La Minita.

It was eight o'clock at night and the pair was still hard at work. Michael had worked most of the afternoon, and Romeo had gone home to change, grab a bite and was expected to be back Sunday morning. Once again, he would be in charge of packing all the boxes and moving them up the valley, to Kingsville.

"What does it say there?" Alex asked pointing at a stamp on the survey.

"It says legal description of 667,258.40 acres carved out of the original *porción* known as La Minita tract and owned by the Catholic Diocese of the Southern Coastal Counties, a.k.a. the Agnus Dei Foundation, together with an affidavit of the surveyor, Thomas N. Williams. The affidavit is dated and executed on November 29, 2003," explained Naiví.

"And the property description? Is there one?"

"Yes, it's here as an exhibit. It's attached to the affidavit and a map of the surveyed area." She pointed at the map. "I guess this big rectangle inside this larger square is the portion in dispute?"

"Yes, that's it. Can you read the legal description?"

"Yes," Naiví started, "property description, 667,258.40 acres (grid area), more or less, of land in the eastern portion of the La Minita Grant, Abstract L-5, Willacy County, Texas; the patent (No. 312, Vol. 25) from the State of Texas of the said La Minita Grant being dated February 20, 1901, and recorded in the General Land Office File San Patricio 1-987, and also being of record in Vol. 3, P. 359 and 360, of the Deed Records of Cameron County; and the said 667,258.40 acres (grid area), more or less, being more particularly described as follows." She paused. "Do you also want me to read the metes and bounds descriptions?"

Alex shook his head. "No, that's okay. Are those documents all certified?"

"Yes, right here."

"Okay, let's go to the next one. Do we have the family tree for our clients?"

Naiví pulled out the next document. It looked like an Excel spreadsheet. "Here it is. All the heirs, beginning with the plaintiffs, then the names of their parents, then the grandparents, great-grandparents, great-great-grandparents, great-great-great grandparents, great-great-great-great-grandparents."

"Who prepared that document? Does it say?"

"Doesn't say, but there's a notation, right here on the back, that Amelia Santibáñez-McKnight also claimed in a court action in Cause No. 71-G-012-C that she was the heir of Candelario Santibáñez, who was a descendant of the original owner of *la porción* entitled La Minita and that she had an interest in said land . . . that said ownership was confirmed in a lease dating back to July 1939 . . . and that said lease . . . shows that some of the Santibáñez heirs entered into a contract to lease portions of the lands, years later, to Austin McKnight."

"That appears to be important. Put a yellow sticky on that page with the description. When we were going through the boxes . . . do you recall seeing the July 1939 lease?"

Naiví thought about it. "No, nothing like that. But I'll check again."

"No," answered Alex, "let's keep going, otherwise we'll never finish. What's next?"

"I have a copy here of what appears to be the original land grant, from King Charles III of Spain to the first settler . . . Don Arturo de Monterreal."

"What's the date on that?"

"Let me see . . . it's kind of hard to read . . . and then the year 1767 or 1761? I can't really make out the numbers. Does that sound right?"

"Yes," Alex said. "Let's put that exhibit over here, on the table."

Naiví pulled the ancient document and carefully placed it on the conference table.

"Have you located birth certificates?"

She reached for a rubber-banded stack of documents from another box. "Yes, I have some right here. Let me see . . . here's a notification of birth registration for Austin McKnight, from 1929. There's another *fe de bautismo* for Arturo Santibáñez, and then for Teresita and Amelia . . . alongside Arturo's other unknown heirs, and so on. There's some affidavits attached to the birth certificates as well."

"Okay, pull those out and set them over here, too," said Alex. "Do you see any other certificates of baptism?"

"Got some right here," she said, waving another stack. "And some birth certificates from Mexico."

"What about death certificates?"

She looked around in another box, then another. "Here's some . . . for Ulysses McKnight and his wives and a little boy . . . says here his name was Samuel McKnight Santibáñez."

"That's the little boy that got kicked in the head by a horse and died," explained Alex. "Teresa's son."

"Do you want me to pull those?"

"Yes," said Alex as he pointed to the table. "What about reports from experts regarding the signatures on Candelario's will to Arturo, and Arturo's will to his children? Any *actas* from Mexico City? Anything that says their signatures are authentic?"

"I remember seeing those reports over here in this box," said Naiví as she reached for a box at the bottom of a pile. "Here's one from Hans Ulrich, a forensic chemist. He conducted thin-layer chromatography with the use of an infrared image converter . . . he was asked by Dugger to take samples of the wills and the birth certificates and determine if the age of the signatures matched the age of the paper."

"I guess he wanted to know if the document was written in the old days."

"Exactly," replied Naiví, "but look how he hedges his bets . . . The guy concludes that there's no other clear and convincing evidence, which suggests the document was written at any time other than the purported date of the signature."

"Interesting. I guess he's not saying yes, it was signed and executed on that date. All he's saying is that there's nothing to indicate on the document that it could have been produced in any other time period, right?"

"I suppose," said Naiví.

Before Alex could say another word, his cell phone started ringing. He checked the caller ID: Gigi.

"It's the boss. I'll be right back," said Alex.

CHAPTER 33

"Hi, baby," said Gigi, "are you still at the office?"

"Yes," answered Alex. "Naiví and I are pulling then trial exhibits. We're almost done."

"Who's Naiví? Is that a new file clerk?"

Alex scratched his head. "Uh, no, not exactly . . . she's a first-year law student who came home and wanted to work during the holiday break. I told you about her a while back. Do you remember? She's pretty great."

"I bet," griped Gigi. "Anyway, how long are you going to stay at the office?"

"Another hour. Why?"

"I'm craving some tacos. Can you bring me some?"

"Sure, honey. I'll pick up some crispy *taquitos* from the Dairy Queen on Boca Chica Boulevard. What do you want on them?"

"No, *chiquito*," she protested, "that's cheating . . . That's not what I want. I want some real tacos . . . real greasy and delicious."

"How's that cheating?" chuckled Alex.

"It is. Anyway, I'm craving *taquitos* from El Gordolele, from across, in Matamoros . . . but the ones from the original location on Cuauhtémoc Avenue."

"You're kidding, right?"

"No, I'm not. I want thirteen *taquitos*, with all the trimmings, but no onions. Also, please bring me a bottle of Joya de Manzana

and a bottle of Coke. You know I don't like American soft drinks
. . . they're made with fructose, and I'd rather have drinks made with
cane sugar, like the drinks in Mexico . . . they just taste better."

"Sure, *mi amor*, anything else?" Alex asked, deep down cursing the untimely interruption.

All the literature Alex had read spoke of pregnant women having cravings for stuff like ice cream, pickles, rare steak, even mud
and talc—stuff one could find at the local supermarket or convenience store. But tacos from Gordolele? From Mexico? And not
just from Mexico, but from Matamoros, where recently the narco-
violence had escalated to such a degree that the newspapers were
full of stories about drug-related killings, kidnappings and gun-
fights between Mexican soldiers and drug cartels now fighting for
territorial control.

"No, that's it, but hurry. Your babies and momma are very, very
hungry."

"Should I bring you some *charro* beans?"

"No, the beans from there give me indigestion. Just the
taquitos . . . unless you want to stop and bring me some from Las
Parrillitas, the place by the soccer stadium. Those are great."

"*¿Algo más?*"

"No, oh, and don't forget to take Veterans Bridge with your
sentry pass. You won't have to wait in line to get back."

The sentry program allowed people cleared by U.S. Customs
and Homeland Security to use a pre-designated bridge lane to
travel back and forth between the United States and Mexico without any delay. Cleared people had their cars outfitted with a special transmitter to monitor their comings and goings.

"Fine," snapped Alex, "I gotta go."

"Okay, baby. Will Romeo go with you?" asked Gigi.

"No, he already went home. He had visitation with his kids,
and he promised to take them to the movies."

"Fine," blurted Gigi, "Don't go alone, it's dangerous. Does
Naiví have a sentry pass?"

"Don't know, I'll ask her," Alex replied.

Only individuals cleared by U.S. Customs and Homeland Security could ride in the cars with the special tags. Gigi blew Alex a kiss over the line. "Just be careful, okay? I love you."

Just what I need right now, mumbled Alex under his breath, *to go on a stupid taco run.*

Alex and Naiví were stopped at a traffic light at the corner of Sixth and Cuauhtémoc Avenue. They were in the firm's beige Cadillac Escalade, discussing the last exhibits and evidence they still needed to pull from the boxes. Their plan was to deliver the food to Gigi, then return to the office and work late into the night. Alex was explaining to Naiví how the evidentiary puzzle would fit together and how it would match up with the jury charge, when a black, double-cab pickup truck slammed into them from behind. Gigi's tacos went flying everywhere.

Alex managed to yelp, "What the . . . "

And before either he or Naiví could comprehend what was happening, three armed individuals surrounded their vehicle and a fourth one rushed to the driver's side, banged on the window and yelled at Alex to unlock the door. Alex fumbled with the door and somehow managed to unlock it.

The driver's side door flew open, and the man yanked Alex out of the Escalade onto the asphalt.

"Don't hurt the girl!" Alex shouted as he struggled to get back on his feet. "Don't touch her!"

"You're coming with us," said a heavyset guy with a goatee, flat-top haircut, bulky gold chain and a Dallas Cowboys T-shirt. He looked to be about thirty-five and had two small tattoos in the shape of teardrops under his right eye. With his right hand, the size of a *jícama*, he made a handgun gesture, pointed it at Naiví, then pulled the trigger. He stared her down and proceeded to blow the imaginary gun's smoke from his fingertips, smirking.

Naiví was then ordered out of the Escalade, told to get behind the wheel and drive away. She was crying, so completely terrified that her hands were trembling. The heavyset guy addressed Naiví. as he stuck a gun in her ribcage, "*Ni una palabra, ¿entiendes, mi reina? O también a ti te carga la chingada. A este culero nos lo vamos a llevar un ratito, ¿okay?* We're gonna show him a good time. And if I come to find out that you called the cops, then you won't see him again, *te lo juro.*" He pressed the gun hard against her ribs and whispered in her left ear, "*Yo aquí mando, y aquí se hace lo que yo digo, ¿está claro?*"

Naiví looked straight ahead and nodded her head in total agreement.

The thug slammed the door shut and tapped the vehicle's roof as if slapping a mare in her hindquarters to get her to scram. She drove away, but not before glancing in the rearview mirror and noticing Alex struggling to free himself, kicking and screaming as he was being shoved into a black Dodge Ram pickup truck.

The safe house was two blocks away from Matamoros' busiest police precinct, near the intersection of Twentieth and González Street. If somebody had ever suggested to the kidnappers that they should keep a safe distance between their operation and the police, obviously they had not gotten the message. As a matter of fact, after they threw Alex into the car, they didn't even blindfold him, much less handcuff him. Nor did they appear overly concerned with being identified by Alex at some future police lineup. Their behavior clearly indicated that these guys had the protection of either the police, the *federales* or another very powerful force.

The thug in charge of keeping his weapon pointed to Alex's head—a man in his twenties sporting a bulletproof vest, Wrangler jeans and a western long-sleeve shirt—got off the truck and went to open the gate to the carport leading into a house. Once he'd managed to open the lock and undo the heavy chains, his heavy-set partner drove the truck up the driveway and into the compound. The other two men jumped out of the truck and dragged Alex into the empty, white-washed cinder-block house, while the driver went to lock the gate behind them.

Alex sat down on the floor of the empty living room and quickly noticed a heavy, foul stench floating in the stale air. Two of the assailants removed their vests and placed their weapons on the lone wooden table in the room. They walked out of the house. In one of the corners of the room, Alex noticed a black, two-hundred-gallon steel drum full of a brown gel-like substance.

Alex demanded an explanation. "*¿Qué chingados quieren conmigo, cabrones?*" He wanted to know what the hell was going on.

"El Tiny will be with you, Señor Abogado," replied another in a very polite manner. "You'll have to wait to talk to him."

Fifteen minutes passed, and just as Alex was about to speak again, a group of twenty undocumented Central Americans came marching through the front door, escorted by Tiny and two other machine-gun-toting criminals.

The heavyset guy, known as Tiny to the thugs, started barking commands. "Put the *pollos* in the back rooms and go get them some food," he said as he pointed to two of his helpers. He pulled out a wad of cash and handed over a couple of bills for the food run.

"You," he continued, pointing to the polite one, "stay with me. Go get the instruments."

The quiet one went down the empty hallway, and Alex could hear the bedroom doors at the end of the narrow hallway slamming shut. He now remembered that the alien traffickers usually called the illegal aliens *pollos* or chickens. It was a way to dehumanize the poor souls and to think of them as commodities. And it was not uncommon for federal agents, when dismantling these organizations, to find sheets of paper among the pieces of evidence, along with the word *pollos* scribbled at the top of the lists that detailed the amounts of money paid or balances owed for their smuggling, transportation and food.

Tiny pulled out a chair and sat in front of Alex. "Do you know why you're here?" he asked as he pulled out a baggie of coke and used the truck keys to shovel some of it up his nose.

"I can only guess," said Alex shrugging his shoulder. "Salamanca put you up to it."

He licked the tip of the ignition key and cracked a wide smile. "Wrong. Try again."

"Why don't you enlighten me?" replied Alex sharply.

Tiny put away his stash in his shirt pocket and tossed the keys on the table. "Oh, I will enlighten you, you piece of shit. But let me say this: you're either too fucking stupid or you think you're too smart. So, which one is it?"

Alex spat down on the floor. "I don't have to answer shit!"

Tiny ignored the gesture. "I guess you're fucking stupid, then. Why would you even consider taking a case that can't be won and will only bring the wrong kind of attention to the entire area? Didn't you figure you'd be stepping on someone's toes?"

"If you're talking about Salamanca, I'm not afraid of him, and I'm not afraid of you," lied Alex as his pulse raced like never before.

"I'd say my suspicions have been confirmed then. You're just plain stupid . . . maybe crazy, *un pendejete.*"

Tiny turned around to see the polite one walking back into the room carrying a thick phone directory, a bottle of Topo-Chico soda water, another bottle of habanero chile hot sauce and a nylon sack full of oranges.

The sight of the phone directory, the soda water and the sack of oranges did not register in Alex's head. He was more concerned with getting out of the mess he was presently involved in.

"I tell you what, why don't you tell me how a *pendejo* like you crossed paths with the Santibáñez wackos? I'm always interested in a good story. Who put you up to this?"

Alex did not answer. He just kept glaring at Tiny and over at the polite one, who by now had popped open the bottle of Topo-Chico and was doing something with it and the bottle of habanero sauce.

"All right, then," Tiny volunteered, "I'll go first . . . I'll tell you how I know about you. A decade ago, our organization negotiated a pact to use some remote, uncharted and inaccessible routes inside La Minita. We've been using these routes to conduct our business . . . you follow?"

"So?" said Alex smugly.

"So? Is that all you can say, so?! So, now you come play big *chingón* lawyer. Now you want to come and screw up a good thing, huh?"

Tiny paused and signaled to the quiet one to bring over the bottle of soda water spiked with the chili sauce. The quiet one obliged and handed over the bottle to Tiny. Tiny placed his thumb over the bottle's mouth as if getting ready to give it a good shake. The quiet one produced a pair of handcuffs and quickly proceeded to cuff Alex's hands behind his back.

Alex struggled to break free. "Hey, what are you doing!? Leave me the fuck, alone . . . *cabrones, hijos de puta. ¡Suéltenme, culeros!*" He fought and screamed at the pair, even kicked furiously, sending his UT Longhorn crocks flying, but it was no use. "*¡Hijos de su chingada madre!*"

As Alex caught his breath, Tiny suddenly yanked Alex by the hair and forcefully squirted the spiced soda water up his nose.

Alex's brain exploded in pain. He screamed in agony. "Aagghh, stop, stop! Let me go, *cabrones!*" He screamed and shrieked for about five minutes. Then after the pain from the soda water's bubbles subsided, a second wave of intense burning pain took over his sinus cavity and the entire frontal lobe of his head. His head felt on fire, and he was breathing heavily, delirious with pain. "Aaaagh, make it stop! Make it stop! *¡Me muero, aayyy!* You won't get away with this, I swear, motherfuckers!"

"I'd say," continued Tiny, calmly, while disregarding Alex's empty threats, "we've been using those routes, what? Close to ten years?"

"At least," the quiet one chimed in.

"During which time my bosses have paid off the Border Patrol and others to let us work in peace, look the other way . . . and my *pollitos* have paid handsomely. How much is that?" Tiny asked the quiet one again.

"A thousand a head," replied the quiet one, now working over at the wooden table. He was doing something with the sack of oranges.

"You figure," Tiny added as he shook the bottle of Topo-Chico and placed his thumb over the top, preventing the pressure from escaping, "we move over one hundred aliens a week, fifty-two weeks a year . . . What's that in a year?"

"Five million," replied the quiet one.

Tiny reached for Alex's hair and again yanked his head back. He shoved the Topo-Chico bottle up his nose and released another painful spray of soda water.

Alex collapsed on the floor, and he convulsed around, kicking, crying and screaming in pain.

"So, you see . . . I've made a lot of people a lot of money . . . all in the span of what?"

"Ten years," finished the quiet one.

"Everyone is happy . . . everyone is making money . . . we take care of each other." Tiny was grinning, brimming with pride, but then his demeanor changed. "Unlike you, you ungrateful, miserable fuck. All you care about is yourself."

He pulled Alex up from the floor by the hair and emptied the remaining Topo-Chico in his nose.

Alex squealed in agony and started gagging, coughing. He couldn't breathe. "What . . . what . . . what do you want from me? Please, for the love of God, no . . . no . . . no more, pl . . . please, God, no more, *te lo suplico, diosito santo.*"

"Ah," exclaimed Tiny, sounding indignant, "now you're asking God for mercy, huh? Now you want the good Lord to descend from the heavens and save your sorry little ass, no? Well, you should have thought about that before suing my friends, you worthless *mamón*. Who the hell do you think you are? You think you can just come in here, strut your stuff, get everybody riled up and we're going to bow down to you? We're going to let you mess everything up?"

Alex managed to mumble, "I never imagined . . . "

"I can't believe you're this fucking stupid," Tiny yelled. "And you went to law school? If the land changes hands, a lot of people, important people, from here to the *presidente*'s residence in Mexico City will not be happy."

"I had no clue," cried Alex as he coughed up blood.

Tiny picked up Alex like a wet noodle and held him up while the quiet one came over, carrying the Yellow Pages like a mallet. He smashed the thick book over Alex's head, careful not to hit another part of the body where larger, visible bruising could occur.

Alex fell to the ground, close to passing out, his head throbbing. "Please, what do you want? For the love of God, please. No more. No more. I'll do whatever you guys say. I beg you, please."

"*Ahora sí pides piedad, ¿eh? Pinche joto . . .* " Tiny stood over Alex, shaking his head. "You've had lots of chances, *maricón.* On Monday morning, you'll walk in court and announce the plaintiffs no longer want to pursue their claims and dismiss everything. If you screw this up and don't deliver . . . we will find you. We know where you live, we know about your ranch, your sailboat, your office, Gisela Montemayor, the twins, your grandpa, your cars, your shopping habits. We know everything."

"Okay, I get it," Alex muttered, "I'll . . . do it . . . I'll . . . get . . . out of the case."

Tiny spat on Alex. "I didn't say you could get out of the case. Aren't you listening?"

He kicked him again. Alex squirmed with agonizing pain.

"You will do no such thing. You are going to dismiss the case . . . in front of the entire world, *¿entiendes?* That's what we want."

Alex was now confused. "But I thought I was supposed to get in there and try the damned thing . . . but if you want me to dismiss it . . . I will, I swear . . . *de veras, lo juro por Dios.*"

Tiny kicked Alex in the rib cage. "There you go again, using the name of the Lord in vain."

Alex curled up in pain, still trying to digest what was happening. Hadn't Salamanca ordered him to pretend to try the case, but lose it on purpose? And now these guys wanted him to dismiss it. "I'm sorry, please . . . no more. I'll do as you say . . . whatever it takes."

"And how the hell do you plan on controlling Cienfuegos?" asked Tiny. "What if he refuses to let you dismiss the case?"

"I'll just nonsuit it . . . Cienfuegos can't stop me . . . It's within my right," mumbled Alex. At this point in time, he would say anything to stop the torture. "I'll figure something out . . . please, let me go," begged Alex.

Tiny stepped away, went to the window next to the door, peeked outside, then looked over at the quiet one and said, "It's time."

"*¿Naranjas?*" asked the quiet one.

"No, let's make *pozole*," replied Tiny, "*pa' que este payaso entienda.*"

"*¿De qué?*" the quiet one asked as he eyed Alex on the floor.

Tiny did not immediately answer. He was now looking out the window again toward the police station down the street. After a few seconds, he turned around, took out the baggie with coke, and reached for the keys on the table. He stabbed the cocaine with the ignition key again and quickly shoved two bumps up each nostril. "*De pollo.*"

The words *pozole* or chicken soup did not make sense to Alex, who was still handcuffed, curled up on the floor, squirming and praying for the suffering to end.

The quiet one went outside the house and whistled for the other two to come in and help. The trio then headed to one of the bedrooms in the back of the house, and Alex could hear the shuffling and scuffing as the henchmen yelled commands to the undocumented. After about five minutes, the trio returned with two of the aliens in tow. One seemed to be a twelve-year-old boy. He was wearing a tattered sweater, brown polyester pants and torn tennis shoes. The other was a middle-aged man with a thin moustache, wearing worn work boots, jeans and a denim jacket. Both looked hungry and terrified.

Tiny picked Alex up from the floor and made him watch as one of the thugs restrained the older man, and then the quiet one and the others proceeded to blindfold, gag and bind the boy with duct tape. Then they stripped him naked. The older man and Alex watched in horror as the quiet one and his assistants picked up the naked boy and proceeded to drop him in the drum full of brown liquid, head first. The boy tossed about for about a minute until his legs slowly stopped moving. It was the most horrific and cruel thing Alex had ever witnessed in his life. Had he known that the practice of law could get him tortured and killed from daring to lock horns with the wrong party, he would have remained a bartender on Austin's Sixth Street for the rest of his life. What could be better than tending bar, getting cash tips, meeting cute women down at Barton Springs and not having a care in the world?

"Don't worry," said Tiny as he turned to look at Alex, who was looking down at the floor, trying to avoid having to witness the horror. "The caustic acid will eat all his flesh and bones. The only thing that will be left will be the teeth."

Then Tiny turned to face the older man, who by now was violently throwing up all over his jeans and boots. "Let that be a lesson, *culero. Si tú y los otros me dan cualquier problema, o tus familiares no pagan . . . éstas son las consecuencias.*" Tiny picked up the boy's clothes from the floor and shoved them in the older alien's hands. "Show the others, tell them we don't want any problems from them or the families, to pay . . . or else. We don't fuck around."

Again, Tiny pulled his coke baggie from his shirt pocket and did two more bumps. He then lit a cigarette and took a drag. He addressed the older man again. *"En media hora van a usar el teléfono para llamar a sus familiares pa' que empiecen a mandar dinero. ¿Entiendes?"*

The spooked man vigorously nodded his head, signaling that he understood that he needed to have his family come up with money, ready to do whatever Tiny wanted.

"Max," barked Tiny at his partner who was holding the man, "in thirty minutes . . . after they find out what just happened and are scared shitless, let the *pollos* start using the phones so they can call their relatives in the States, and they can start hitting them up for the cash." He then ordered, "Take him back to the others."

Tiny pointed at Alex and barked to his lieutenants in the next room, "Put this one back in the truck."

The quiet one and the other two carried Alex outside and tossed him into the back of the pickup truck. After a few minutes, Alex heard Tiny come out of the house, talking on his cell in Spanish, discussing payment arrangements with the person at the other end of the line. Tiny and the quiet one got in the truck, while another one opened the gate so the truck could exit the property.

Alex fervently prayed to the same God that Bishop Salamanca dutifully served. "Help! *¡Auxilio! ¡Auxilio!*" he tried to scream over the sock stuffed in his mouth, while black and white scenes of his entire life flashed before his blindfolded eyes.

CHAPTER 34

ALEX LIMPED SHOELESS across the Veterans Bridge by 8:00 A.M. on Sunday morning, but not before being detained, humiliated, strip-searched and interrogated for about an hour. Since he did not have his wallet, he had a hard time convincing the customs agents he was a U.S. citizen. Violated and terrified, he staggered another mile to the nearest Stripes convenience store to use the pay phone. He borrowed fifty cents from a stranger and dialed Gigi's cell number. After one ring, she promptly answered.

"Alex? Where are you? Are you okay?"

"Yes . . . " Alex replied and then broke down sobbing. "They . . . let me go . . . finally. I thought I was going to die . . . I needed you so much . . . Gisela."

"I'm coming to get you, baby. Where are you?"

"Don't call the cops, please," cried Alex into the receiver, "no one can know what happened . . . these guys are dangerous."

"I know, I know. Naiví called me from your cell as soon as she could. Apparently your cell and your wallet landed on the floor of the Escalade. She's been with me since then. Anyway, don't move an inch. Be right there."

"So you have no idea who these thugs were?" Gigi asked as she gave Alex the look-over. Her once-charming and dashing fiancé now looked as if he'd been in a boxing match, losing most rounds. "No idea what they wanted?"

"No," lied Alex as he rubbed his temples. "They saw the fancy car and wanted to shake me down for money. You know . . . like they've been doing to people on the other side."

Alex, Gigi and Naiví were back at the office, sitting around the conference room. Gigi was grilling Alex, wanting to know exactly what happened, ready to call her old friends over at Brownsville PD to make an incident report and prosecute whoever was responsible for hurting her future husband.

"But they usually keep the victims until the ransom is paid, Alex. Why did they let you go right away? It doesn't make sense," Gigi reminded him. "We should go to the police."

Alex threw his arms in the air, his demeanor suddenly changing. "Whoa! What are you saying? You wanted them to keep me longer?"

"I'm just saying . . . this is not the way these guys operate. The whole thing's very unusual. They let Naiví go with your car, and they didn't even steal your wallet . . . I don't know . . ."

Gigi was absolutely right. Since Mexican President Rogelio De León had ordered his country's army to start patrolling the entire U.S.-Mexico border, the drug cartels had found it increasingly difficult to do business. Under constant watch by the military and without the ability to move about freely and operate at full speed, their cash flow had been diminished tenfold. In desperation, the cartels had started shaking down local, millionaire businessmen for money in order to survive. And more recently, the drug organizations were resorting to kidnapping anyone who appeared to have the means to pay a quick forty-, twenty-, even a ten-thousand dollar ransom.

"I had to talk my way out of it," Alex lied some more. Why alarm Gigi and reveal to her that Tiny and his men had both their numbers? They knew where he and Gigi ate, worked, lived, who drove which car, when, how, where, why . . . everything. "I told them I knew El Dandy . . . they checked it out and they let me go. Dandy vouched for me."

It was rumored that a gangster called El Dandy ran operations for the Gulf Cartel. He supposedly had been authorized by the higher-ups in the cartel to control the drug trade in Matamoros.

He also charged a tariff to other lesser drug smugglers and illegal alien traffickers to be allowed to operate out of the same city. Whoever ran La Plaza, the franchise, called the shots.

"How the hell would you know that guy?" asked Gigi, eyes wide open.

Naiví was watching the exchange, looking ragged after having spent the entire night waiting for news of Alex. She looked ready to quit.

"Remember the guy I represented in federal court last year? The truck driver that had the cocaine inside the Roman columns made out of Mexican limestone," Alex said as he continued to fabricate another lie, taking care to coat it with some elements of truth. "The guy was facing fifteen years, but I got his sentence down to sixty months? I want to say his name was Omar Reyes . . . Don't you remember?

"Anyway, who do you think Reyes worked for? They let me go because I begged my kidnappers to call El Dandy. Dandy finally remembered that it had been me who made sure his boy Reyes didn't spill the beans . . . that I'd worked real hard to get Reyes a hell of a deal. Sure, the guy debriefed to get the deal . . . but he didn't give up anybody from his organization. He gave up his rivals, folks that worked for the competition. The feds were happy."

Gigi sized Alex up, not totally convinced. "So, are you going to postpone the trial tomorrow?"

Alex knew whatever answer he gave, he was screwed. If he said no, Gigi would jump all over him because she was still mad at him for getting involved in the first place. If he said yes, and he tried to get a continuance, he was a dead man. Not that he had valid grounds for a continuance, anyway. What was he going to say? That he needed more time because he'd been kidnapped by Salamanca's minions? Cienfuegos would probably die laughing.

"I'm going to finish what I started, Gigi. I'm going to try this damned case. Hopefully, it'll be over quickly. Honestly, I wish I'd listened to you. But now, I'm neck deep into it . . . and the clients need me. I can't walk out on them!"

"Alex, you're hiding something from me. I don't know what it is . . . "

Alex sprang to his feet. "That's the truth, Gisela María!"

"Look, I don't know what kind of mess you've gotten yourself into, but you need to understand that whatever you do . . . not only will it affect you, but it will also affect me and our babies. You're a few months away from becoming a dad, Alejandro. Don't you get it? The rules have changed, baby." She looked at him tenderly. "Please, tell me, what's going on? You can come clean with me . . . "

Alex sat down again; he was quietly squirming in his chair, looking defeated.

Gigi looked at him, then at Naiví. "Do you want Naiví to leave the room? C'mon, baby, we've always been honest with one another. We've never kept secrets from each other. What is it?"

Alex shrugged his shoulders, then let out a sigh. "Nothing's going on, all right? *Nada.* I was just at the wrong place at the wrong time. What matters is they let me go, that nothing happened. I'm okay. I just need to go home, shower and sleep for a couple of hours. Then I'll be pumped to come back and finish getting ready for trial."

Alex turned to face Naiví. "We could work for a couple of hours this evening, huh? Then try this thing in the morning."

Naiví looked at Gigi, obviously nervous, not really knowing what to say. She hesitated. "Sure, I guess."

Gigi threw her hands up in the air. "How can you be thinking of going to trial? You need to go to the police. File a report. Bring in the FBI."

"I will do no such thing. You want me to piss off El Dandy? The guy did me a favor . . . because of him, I was let go. Don't you get it? Now you want me to go and start an international scandal? I don't think so."

"Are you serious?!"

Alex lashed out, "I am serious, Gisela. Besides, what are the city cops gonna do? All the politicians have promised to do something about the violence but not one, not a single one, has done shit! The only one with real balls has been President De León. But on the U.S. side, nothing has been done and nothing will be done. The FBI and DEA don't give a shit. Those thugs are better armed than our own agents. And this is our fault. We allowed it to happen with the second amendment and the right to bear arms. We condemn violence but we are responsible for arming those criminals. We won't look in the mirror and admit that we're the addicts, the drug dealers and the users, we're the real problem."

Naiví did not know if she should stay, run, quit, talk or to tell them to take it elsewhere.

"*Mira*, Alejandro Francisco Del Fuerte. First of all, you're preaching to the choir. I was a prosecutor, remember? I'm well aware of the drug war. I fought in the trenches putting away the bad guys. Don't insult my friends."

"C'mon! What are your friends down at the police station going to do?"

"They could open an investigation, call their colleagues in Mexico, ask for help in apprehending your assailants."

"Please, the stash house these guys took me to was two blocks from police headquarters. Those guys are in bed with the police. It'll be a waste of time. I don't have time. I've got better things to do."

Gigi stormed out of the conference room and could be heard yelling as she walked down the hallway. "Fine, you always do whatever the hell you want, anyway! Just don't come crying to me when you go down in flames . . . you hear? You're simply amazing, and, on top of that, you're a liar!"

CHAPTER 35

THE SKY WAS overcast, and the air was a chilly fifty-five degrees on that windy December morning that welcomed the start of the trial. A cold front had arrived in South Texas on Sunday night, bringing with it half an inch of rain, cooler temperatures and howling winds that had chased away the sunny clear skies of the previous month.

The media had already set up camp around the county courthouse and were gathered by the main entrance to the historical building, waiting for the lawyers to arrive. Across the street from the courthouse, long lines of cars waited to get into the main parking lot. It was the residents of Kleberg County coming out in droves to participate in what was known across the state as Jury Mondays. From these groups of eager Texans, twelve fair-minded jurors and two alternates, would be plucked to sit in judgment of the Agnus Dei Foundation.

Alex, Michael, Romeo and Naiví arrived at seven-thirty and pushed their way through the crowd until they made it to the top of the courthouse steps.

As Michael held the door open for Romeo, who was reloading boxes onto the dolly after having carried them up the steps, a reporter placed a microphone in front of Alex.

"So, Mr. Del Fuerte . . . are you ready to roll the dice?"

"Sure. We're ready to try this thing, if that's what you're asking," Alex replied with what appeared to be renewed confidence. The truth was, he had no idea how to begin to get out of the mess he was in.

"Can you tell our audience watching at home who you expect to call as your first witness?"

"I can't comment on any specifics of our trial strategy," stuttered Alex as he started inching closer to the building's main entrance, "but later on, after jury selection is complete and we have our twelve in the box, I promise to give you something . . . will that work?"

"Okay, sure . . . I'll be waiting," winked the cutie from *The Austin American-Statesman*. Her name tag read Erin Mijares.

In district court, all potential jurors must be at least eighteen years of age, citizens of the State of Texas, registered to vote in that county, be of sound mind and good moral character, be able to read and write, to not have been convicted or under indictment for any misdemeanor or felony, and not have served as juror in the preceding three months in county court or six months in district court. For a lawyer wanting to win a case, these qualifications mean nothing. The trick during jury selection is to eliminate the jurors that appear poised to side with the opponent and to select those that will favor one's client.

The Foundation's defense team had brought in three high-dollar juror consultants: one from New York, one from Houston and one from San Francisco. Confused beyond words and not knowing what to do anymore—lose the case, win the case, get out of the case or dismiss the case—Alejandro Del Fuerte's strategy for jury selection was all his own. He was going to use the tried-and-true South Texas Method of Jury Selection: *Eeny, meeny, miney, moe, all the Gringos have to go!*

Weeks before the real exercise, Alex had worked out the details to come up with a profile for the perfect juror.

The large landowners in the area? Gringos. Gone.

The owners of local oil and gas production companies? Rednecks. Gone.

The owners of local banks, car and farm equipment dealerships? White and ardent supporters of TLR (Texans for Lawsuit Reform). Gone.

Owners of nearby refineries? White. Gone.

All healthcare providers? Mostly white. Tort reformers. Gone.

Alex's strategy had been to end up with a jury made up of modest, blue-collar workers, hopefully mostly Hispanic or from some other minority group, and who, for the most part, would be disillusioned with the Catholic Church and felt the gas and oil companies made too much money. Jurors that felt that these companies always stuck it to the little guy. To tip the scales in his favor, Alex would need jurors that could relate to his clients.

The problem with attempting to get rid of all the *güeros*, Alex knew, was getting around the due process clause and the Sixth and Seventh amendments of the U.S. Constitution. The minute Alex started striking all the Anglo jurors, the defense would object and argue that their client was not getting a jury of its peers. So the trick, Alex had figured, was to find something other than race to explain why Mrs. Judy Juror had to be removed.

For example, if Mrs. Judy Juror answered that she thought there were too many frivolous lawsuits, then that would be the reason that Alex would give as to why he removed her. Alex would have argued that it was obvious she was biased against plaintiffs in general because of her comments on lawsuit abuse. Forget the fact that she was as white as a ghost, he would never admit that she had been removed because of the color of her skin. He'd figured all he would need would be a little nail to hang his hat on.

Of course, all those plans appeared to be out the window now. Alex understood, regrettably, that if he was "too chicken" to walk the plank and could not bring himself to dismiss the case, then he would at least try to select jurors that could, and would, rule against his own clients.

Alex and Michael were sitting at counsel's table, watching McDermott, Uhels, O'Quinn and their posse of associates, legal assistants, techies and other lesser minions, get ready for kick off. Alex was feeling butterflies, this was the case that was supposed to define the rest of his career as a trial lawyer. Was he going to throw in the towel, as he'd promised Salamanca? Or come out swinging, kick Salamanca's sanctimonious little ass and send the foundation home packing? Or was the lawsuit that was supposed to put Alex and his firm on the world map, end up being the case that destroyed him and everything else around him?

"Counsel, are we ready to proceed?" asked Judge Cienfuegos, looking around at all the lawyers scattered about the courtroom.

"Plaintiffs are ready," responded Alex.

"The defense is ready," announced McDermott.

"Casey Uhels for intervenors, Your Honor. We're ready."

One by one, everyone made their announcements.

Cienfuegos glanced over to where the bailiff was standing. "Please help my coordinator bring in the jury panel. Make sure they sit where they're supposed to."

"Right away, Judge," replied the bailiff, nodding to the court coordinator to come help. The pair quickly went out to the hallway to collect and organize the jury panel.

"May it please the court, ladies and gentlemen of the jury," Alex said from counsel's table, as he nodded at the twelve sitting in the box and the two alternates sitting nearby, "Good morning." He walked over to the jury, cleared his throat and looked at his watch. He then waited for a response.

"Good morning," replied the bunch.

The jury appeared eager and ready to decide the case. It was made up of eight men and four women. The two alternates were also men. Among the white men sitting in the jury, two were rednecks, one black, four Hispanics. Among them were a farmer, a fireman, a cop, a used-car salesman, a P.E. coach from the local high school, two students from Texas A&M-Kingsville and a retired school principal. The Hispanic females in the group were a nurse, a school bus driver, a housewife and one small business owner who happened to own the only Wing Stop franchise in town. The alternate jurors were a UPS delivery driver and a very young shift manager from the nearby Whataburger, both were also Hispanic.

Alex paused, nodded to the jurors one last time, and then turned to acknowledge Judge Cienfuegos, Michael and McDermott and the others. He took a deep breath and, with new resolve, proceeded with his opening argument in a firm and confident tone: "I am the Lord your God, you shall have no other false Gods before me. Do not take God's name in vain. Keep holy the Lord's day. Honor your father and mother. Do not bear false witness. Do not kill. Do not commit adultery. Do not steal. Do not lie. Honor your neighbor's goods."

He then looked over at Bishop Salamanca, hiding behind McDermott's counsel table. "*Los diez mandamientos*. Those are the ten commandments. This case deals with the seventh commandment. You shall not steal."

Alex then paused and looked at every single one of the jurors, making sure they were getting his message. "That's what this case is about. Plain and simple. Nothing complicated. Thou shall not steal. *No robarás*," Alex said pointing and looking at Officer Martin Arriaga, the young cop sitting in the first row of the jury box.

"Objection!" cried McDermott as she sprang to her feet. "Would the court instruct Mr. Del Fuerte to speak English, Your Honor? I don't think all the jurors are fluent in Spanish. What does no *roubaharas* mean?"

"Did the jury understand the phrase?" asked Cienfuegos of the jury.

The fourteen of them nodded their heads.

"Your objection will be noted," continued Cienfuegos and then addressed Alex: "Try to keep the Spanish at a minimum, Mr. Del Fuerte. You know we need to conduct these proceedings in English. That way the court reporter can take everything down."

"Yes, Your Honor," replied Alex. "May I continue?"

"Go on," Cienfuegos said.

Alex turned to face the jury and continued to deliver his opening argument.

"I could stand here and tell you that the evidence is going to show this or that, that the defendants did this or the other and that the oil and gas companies raped the land and stole billions of dollars from the oil and gas deposits underneath La Minita, but I'd hate to waste your time. And you probably already knew that. So, remember those words 'Thou shall not steal.' Those all too important words . . . thou shall not steal.

"I could also go on and on and on and tell you that the defendant in this case," said Alex as he pointed to Bishop Salamanca on the other side of the courtroom, "the Catholic Diocese of the Southern Coastal Counties, along with the Agnus Dei Foundation, has been guilty of breaking the seventh commandment . . . thou shall not steal. But, instead, I will show you the evidence that will prove what I'm saying. We will bring you the evidence, and the witnesses, and the documents. We have that burden and we will meet that burden.

"At the end of the case, when you find that, indeed, this is what happened in this case, I will ask you to order that the plaintiffs have their lands returned to them and also award them damages to make them whole again, for being without the fruits of their lands for all these years. Thank you." Alex then scurried away and took his place at counsel's table.

Michael was in total shock, and looking quite disappointed, he leaned over and whispered into Alex's ear, "that was a lame opening argument."

"I know," Alex whispered back, shaking his head, "I'm so sorry. I got so nervous my opening argument went up in smoke."

"Ms. McDermott," snapped Cienfuegos, "you're up."

"Thank you, Your Honor," said McDermott. Her retained local counsel—Jeremy Hidalgo and Bobby Fonseca also stood up and smiled at the jurors as she opened, "Ladies and gentlemen of the jury, the defense has prepared an opening argument. However, we will reserve our opening until after the plaintiffs' case is presented."

Cienfuegos interrupted her, "Are you then reserving your opening argument until such time, counsel?"

"Yes, Your Honor. We are."

"What about the intervenors?" asked Cienfuegos.

Mike Nicholas, standing shoulder-to-shoulder with Andrew Becker, added, "We're counsel for Shell Oil Company, intervenor, ladies and gentlemen of the jury. We're also reserving our opening, Your Honor."

"James Hanmore, for intervenor Orion Wind Farm Enterprises, along with co-counsel Robert Ramsey. We'll reserve our opening argument, as well."

"Fine," huffed Cienfuegos, "anybody else?"

Tim O'Quinn spoke next, "I, along with co-counsel, Carlos Ramírez, have the honor of representing British Petroleum. We'd like to reserve."

Three suits representing Chevron, Valero and Exxon also got up and made a quick announcement that they would also be reserving their opening until after the plaintiffs had finished presenting their evidence.

"Very well, the record will so reflect," replied Cienfuegos. "Who else are we missing, anybody?"

In 99% of all jury trials, the defense also gives an opening argument, immediately after the plaintiff has delivered his. Likewise, in a criminal case, after the prosecution has delivered its opening argument, the defense attorney follows suit. This is done to steal the wind from plaintiff's sails as quickly as possible. The thinking is that if a plaintiff's opening argument made an impression on the jury, then somebody needs to come in right away and counter it. No use letting the plaintiff be the only one to make the first impression.

Occasionally, the defense might decide to wait to deliver its opening argument until after the plaintiff has presented all of its evidence. The logic is that by waiting to deliver the opening argument until after the plaintiff finishes or "rests," the defense does not signal or telegraph to the plaintiff what its evidence and intended trial strategy will be. The advantage lies in that there is no blueprint advanced by the defense of what the evidence will show. In other words, the defense is playing its cards close to the vest. "Well?" asked Cienfuegos, "anybody else?"

Casey Uhels got up slowly from the other cramped counsel's table. "Your Honor," he said, "I have a small opening statement . . . if I may."

Judge Cienfuegos nodded in approval, and Uhels proceeded to address the jurors from his place at counsel's table. "Ladies and gentlemen of the jury, good morning. You have not seen or heard a single piece of evidence or testimony this morning. All I ask is that you keep an open mind. Even though you've heard plaintiffs' counsel give his opening statement, I ask that you wait to hear all of the evidence in this case. Once you hear both sides . . . then . . . "

"Judge," interrupted Alex, "we object to Mr. Uhels' opening. He sounds like he's already delivering his summation, his closing argument. This is totally improper."

"I agree," said Cienfuegos, then turned to face Uhels. "Counsel, are you prepared to discuss what you believe the evidence is going to show?"

"Well," muttered Uhels, "I just wanted to remind the jury to refrain from forming an opinion . . . since no evidence has been presented. . . . I'm not ready to get into my opening."

Judge Cienfuegos frowned. "Then sit down."

Alex was totally surprised. *Jesus . . . I wish I'd known they were reserving. I could have gone on for another twenty minutes . . . really steal their thunder. I had no idea. Very well, then . . . it's game on, jerks! Wait, what am I saying? It's not game on. I've got to throw in the towel.*

Cienfuegos turned to Alex. "Call your first witness."

Alex did not answer. He was deep in thought, hoping no one noticed he was in a real pickle.

"Mr. Del Fuerte?" repeated the judge, "are we ready?"

Michael kicked him under the table and whispered, "Alex, call our first witness. Let's go."

"Oh, yes, Judge. Sorry," blurted Alex, as he cleared his throat. He then stood up. "We call Oscar Santibáñez to the stand," replied Alex, without missing a beat. "And we invoke the rule, Your Honor. Also, we'd ask that the court take judicial notice of all contents in the court's file. In particular, the plaintiff's expert's title opinion letter . . . that's been on file since May 2004."

A title opinion letter is a report prepared by an independent examiner or a title attorney that digs up the property records and figures out who owns what and in what percentages, in reference to a certain piece of land. An expert had been hired by the first attorney, Dugger, to render an opinion as to who held the title to the tract known as La Minita. Dugger's expert had prepared a fifty-page document covering approximately 690,000 acres of land situated in the Counties of Kleberg, Raymondville and northern Cameron County, Texas. The letter described the legal expert's findings, starting with the original conveyance to Don Arturo Monterreal through a Royal Spanish Grant and then later confirmed by the Mexican State of Tamaulipas in 1825, and subsequently by the Texas legislature.

"In particular," Alex reminded the judge, as he looked over at the jurors, "we ask the court to take judicial notice that this land grant, and its ownership, was confirmed to Monterreal, his heirs and assigns, by an act of the Legislature of Texas, approved on April 18, 1852, being Confirmation No. 15 for Cameron County. The title opinion letter confirmed the existence of 690,000 acres of land, contiguous to the north end of Padre Island, and being more particularly described in a certain claim filed of record by an A. Santibáñez, dated December 12, 1947, as same appears of record in the office of the Cameron County Clerk, in Book 11, Page 245 of said county, bounded on the north by the Nueces County boundary line, on the east by the meander line of the Gulf of Mexico and on the south by a line drawn parallel to the common boundary line of Cameron and Willacy Counties, and at a sufficient distance from there to include within such boundaries a large portion of said 690,000 acres of land."

"It will be so noted," ruled Cienfuegos.

"Judge," replied Alex, "we'd like the record to reflect that this opinion letter covers the period from 1767 to the year 2004."

"Any objection?" asked Cienfuegos.

"No objection," the defendant and intervenors announced in unison.

Cienfuegos then turned and instructed the bailiff, "Please swear in the witness."

The bailiff obliged, and Oscar Santibáñez took his place on the witness stand.

Oscar Santibáñez spent most of the morning attempting to testify about his family's genealogical history. He then spoke of Don Arturo Monterreal and what he knew of his most famous ancestor.

Of course, it did not take long for McDermott and all the others to start objecting on the grounds that Mr. Santibáñez's testimony constituted nothing more than hearsay, upon hearsay, upon hearsay. That the witness lacked personal knowledge, and that there had been no proper foundation established to elicit such testimony from Mr. Oscar Santibáñez. To Alex's dismay, Cienfuegos started sustaining all of their objections, and afterwards the legal proceedings came pretty much to a grinding halt.

Alex, all cotton-mouthed as he peeked at the spectators in the courtroom, lodged a complaint, "Judge, can the defense and the others stop objecting?"

There was a collective chuckle from the spectators in the courtroom.

Judge Cienfuegos turned to McDermott, "Counsel, do you care to just make a running objection? At the rate Mr. del Fuerte's going we'll be here till Charro Days."

"We can't, Your Honor. If we just allowed a running objection . . . the jury still gets to hear all this hearsay, and by then, the jury might believe that everything that was said about Mr. Candelario Santibáñez, the McKnights and the Monterreals is true. Mr. Del Fuerte should have thought about how he was going to get into those very ancient matters without violating the Texas rules of evidence."

With over two hundred pairs of eyes bearing down on him, Alex felt like a complete idiot and by now was so nervous that his mind drew a blank. Small sweat beads started forming on his forehead. So, in an attempt to save face, he managed to utter a feeble, "I'll move along, Judge. I'll ask him something else."

Cienfuegos rolled his eyes. "We're waiting."

More chuckles could be heard in the courtroom. This time, the snickering came from McDermott's camp. The defense attorneys were watching Alex squirm . . . and loving every minute of it.

CHAPTER 36

"ARE YOU OKAY, princess? I saw that you called. What's up?"

Alex was outside the courthouse, calling Gigi on his cell phone. Judge Cienfuegos had called a twenty-minute recess to allow the jurors to stretch their legs, get a drink or use the restrooms. Meanwhile, Michael, Naiví and Romeo were in the courtroom trying to find a way around the Texas rules of evidence that would allow them to use Oscar Santibáñez's testimony.

"Everything's fine," answered Gigi. "I just wanted to tell you that Dr. Gaytán called. He said grandpa's now breathing on his own. I thought you'd want to know."

"That's great news!" exclaimed Alex, "finally, something goes right."

"Why do you say that? Isn't the trial going well?" asked Gigi.

"Nope," confessed Alex. "McDermott and the others keep objecting, and I can't get into all the family histories or the history behind La Minita. The judge sustained every single one of their hearsay objections."

"What did you think was going to happen?"

"I don't know . . . I guess I thought Oscar and the other family members could just start talking about what they knew . . . stories passed down from generation to generation, you know?"

"*Ay, papi,*" Gigi replied, "but that's all hearsay. You know that. There's a big difference between telling old tales around the campfire and what actually gets admitted as evidence in a courtroom."

"I know. I feel like a complete idiot. When the objections started flying, I just froze. The whole courtroom was staring at me, waiting for me to come up with some kind of reply, an exception to the hearsay rule, and I just couldn't. I don't know what I'm going to do. I guess we're screwed."

"I'm sorry to hear that, Alex."

"No, I'm sorry . . . I should have listened to you. I should have never taken this case. What the hell do I know about Spanish land grants, anyway?"

"Are you throwing in the towel, then?" asked Gigi.

"Yes, I mean, no. Listen, I gotta go . . . I'll explain later, okay?"

"Okay," said Gigi and hung up.

After the short break, Alex passed the witness and one by one the enemy attorneys took their shots at Oscar. It was not a pretty sight. First, McDermott got him to concede that the heirs knew, as far back as 1960, that they needed to do something about La Minita and that his parents and uncles had even consulted and talked to attorneys about a potential lawsuit.

Alex knew that this one piece of evidence would probably not make much of an impression on the jurors listening to the case, but for purposes of an appeal, this little fact was probably the nail in the coffin. He didn't think the appellate court would let the plaintiffs keep any portion of their verdict, since it now appeared that for forty years the Santibáñez clan knew they needed to do something to recover their lands, and instead chose to do absolutely nothing. Even if the jury sided with the plaintiffs, the verdict would be overturned because at the end of the day, the heirs had taken too long to sue. The appellate courts would rule that they had blown the statute of limitations.

Tim O'Quinn followed up. "Sir, is it then your testimony that as a young child, you accompanied your parents and other relatives to consult attorneys about the lands in question?"

"Yes," said Santibáñez.

"Did you come to learn if your parents and relatives ever hired an attorney?"

"I believe they did," replied the witness.

"And do you remember a name? Who was this attorney?" O'Quinn followed up.

"A Mr. Tony Guerra, or Juan Antonio Guerra . . . something like that."

"How would you know that? Did you see them hire the lawyer?"

"I went with my daddy a couple of times to deliver money to the attorney. His office was in Raymondville . . . we'd all pile up in daddy's truck and go see him."

"Are you sure?" asked O'Quinn.

"I'm pretty sure," continued Santibáñez. "My aunts and uncles would come by the house and drop off money . . . they were all pitching in . . . trying to get something going. When my dad put together twenty or thirty bucks, we'd go deliver our payments."

"Did Mr. Guerra ever file a lawsuit, if you know?"

"No, the guy just took our money and sat on his ass. To the best of my knowledge . . . he just strung my parents and uncles along, and never filed anything."

"So, he stole the money?"

"I'm pretty sure," Santibáñez agreed. "The guy would tell us that he'd gone to Austin to talk to some legislators . . . try to get everything fixed . . . you know . . . on the side."

"Well," O'Quinn said, "do you remember your parents or your uncles ever going to court?"

"No, Mr. Guerra would just talk about Austin . . . that he'd met with some people and that was it. He would always come back and ask for more money."

O'Quinn looked at the jury to see if they were paying attention. "But to the best of your recollection then, nothing was ever filed in a courtroom . . . like this, huh?"

"That's right."

"One last question. As far as you know, about forty years ago, your parents and relatives tried once to do something about these lands, correct?"

"Yes."

"Pass the witness," announced O'Quinn.

Judge Cienfuegos took over. "Let's break for lunch. Ladies and gentlemen of the jury, be back at 1:30, and remember, no talking about the case. We'll be in recess."

Alex, Michael, Romeo, and Naiví were all sitting around a table inside a little Mexican restaurant, a few blocks from the courthouse.

"Alex," said Michael, trying to break the uncomfortable silence around the table, "what's the plan? We're getting slaughtered in there."

"I don't know," said Alex as he played with his plate full of *calabacita con pollo* while pretending to be mad at himself. He continued to show remorse, looking the part, while counting silently all the different ways he could use to lose on purpose. The good news, however, was that Oscar Santibáñez had, single-handedly, torpedoed the plaintiff's lawsuit, and now the whole case was listing dangerously on its side. At least this way, it would look as if he was keeping his promise to Salamanca.

"Do you think we can rehabilitate Oscar? Fix some of the things he said about his family having knowledge almost fifty years ago?" Michael asked after swallowing a spoonful of beef *caldo*.

"I guess I could try," muttered Alex. *Let him screw things up. Who cares? I just want to put an end to this. Maybe go check on Grandpa.*

Michael looked at Naiví. "What do you think, Naiví? Is there a way out of this mess? You have a fresh view on this thing?"

She stopped playing with her lemonade and put the glass down. "Would it look too bad if we impeach our own witness?"

"What do you mean?" asked Michael.

"I took a class in law school that dealt with Spanish land grants. There's even a treatise we studied on the subject. It's called *Fowler on Royal Land Grants.*"

"And how would that help?" asked Alex, still pretending to care.

"It would help to get in all that background information that we couldn't get into with our own witness, Oscar," said Michael.

"Yeah, but that information has nothing to do with our case," replied Alex.

Naiví elaborated some more. "True, but there's mention of La Minita and Don Arturo Monterreal . . . and his son Arturito Santibáñez, from there you introduce and connect all the names of all the descendants with the birth certificates and the *actas*. You can also show who married who with the marriage certificates."

"And how do I do that?" asked Alex, acting as if he was not familiar with the concept of impeaching one's own witness.

"You ask him if he's heard of the treatise and the contents in the book. As you ask him if he's heard of Don Arturo Monterreal, Candelario or McKnight and the others . . . you then ask him if he agrees or disagrees with what's been written . . . on the pages in the treatise."

Alex went along. "And?"

"Whether he agrees or disagrees does not matter. The jury gets to hear the background . . . all the relevant stuff to your case. If he agrees, then it just reaffirms what we're saying. The jury gets to hear the history behind the case because it all comes from the treatise. And the treatise will carry weight with the judge, since such books are always used in law schools. We don't need to worry about the rules of procedure. Even Professor Fetzer, if need be, could take the stand and set the legal foundation. He could tell the jury that these treatises are reliable and trustworthy. They're the maximum authority!"

"Bingo! There you go," said Michael, totally impressed with Naiví's legal abilities, "that's how you do it. Except, I'd rather not take the stand. Just have Cienfuegos take judicial notice that *Fowler's* treatise is used in law schools throughout the Southwest."

Romeo put down his taco and started paying attention.

Likewise, Michael was finally showing signs of life. "It's just a big puzzle, Alex. That's all."

"But we can't still change the fact that our clients have a statute of limitations problem. Forty years ago, they already knew they needed to do something about their lands, and they never followed through," Alex exclaimed.

"True," countered Michael, "but there might be a way to make that little problem go away. Let me think about it."

"So, what do you all want me to do?" Alex asked.

Naiví jumped in. "You excuse the witness and ask the judge to allow you to recall him, if need be, later on in the trial. That gives you time to read the treatise and prepare your questions to impeach Mr. Santibáñez."

"And where is this treatise, anyway?" inquired Alex.

"I have it at home. I brought it from school, along with my other books I didn't get to sell back," explained Naiví. "I can drive home, get it, and you'll have it for when you need it."

"And in the meantime?"

"Call Salamanca to testify," Michael interjected. "Let's have some fun. I'd like to cross-examine the guy."

Alex gulped hard. "Are you sure?"

"Can't hurt," smiled Michael, "we have nothing to lose, anyway."

"Fine, but if somebody is going to cross-examine that bastard, it's me," Alex demanded, still pretending that his head was in the game.

CHAPTER 37

"**A**RE WE DONE with this witness?" asked Judge Cienfuegos as he pointed at Oscar Santibáñez still sitting on the witness stand.

"Yes," replied all the defense attorneys and the intervenors.

"Judge," Alex interrupted, "we'd like to reserve our right to recall Mr. Santibáñez, if need be."

Oscar did a double-take, eyes wide open, as if saying, "You mean it's not over?"

"Very well," said the judge, and then addressing the witness said, "Mr. Santibáñez, don't go anywhere. Your counsel might recall you to the witness stand. You need to be on standby."

The judge then turned to face Alex, "call your next witness."

"We call Bishop Ricardo Salamanca," announced Alex, fed up with his situation, "as a hostile witness, Your Honor."

"Very well," said Cienfuegos.

The entire courtroom became quiet as the portly bishop got up slowly from his place on the first pew behind his team's table and proceeded to walk toward the witness stand. Tony, the seminary student, helped Salamanca make his way to the witness stand and adjusted the microphone in front of him.

"Let's proceed," instructed Judge Cienfuegos. "Please swear in the witness."

The court reporter administered the oath. Then it was Alex's turn to take a crack at the witness.

"Good afternoon, monsignor," said Alex, still not knowing if his next move was the right one. To the world and everybody else in that courtroom, he needed to appear in control, as if he was really fighting for his clients. He'd decided to be aggressive with Salamanca, which, of course, made him even more nervous.

Salamanca corrected him: "It's *Bishop* Salamanca."

"I'm sorry," said Alex, blushing, keeping up the charade, "my apologies, Bishop. Can you tell us your full name?"

"Ricardo Emmanuelle Salamanca."

"And how old are you?"

"Sixty-six."

"Where were you born?"

"Guadalajara, Mexico," replied Salamanca. "That should help explain the slight accent."

"Are you a U.S. citizen?"

"For forty years, at least."

"When was it that you came to the States?"

Salamanca looked over at the jury as if to say, I'm one of you. "After I finished the seminary in Mexico, I came to do a masters in theology at Notre Dame. Eventually, I was recruited to stay here in the United States and lend a hand along the border. My first assignment was in Piedras Negras, over in West Texas."

"How long have you been at the helm of the Catholic Diocese of the Southern Coastal Counties?"

"You mean, how long I've been a bishop?"

"Yes, sure," said Alex.

"Twenty years, thereabouts."

"Since eighty-six?"

Salamanca smiled and turned to the judge, "That's about right, yes."

Alex was watching the jurors' reaction to Salamanca, but couldn't really tell if the spiritual leader was making a connection or not. "Let's switch gears, Bishop, and talk about the Agnus Dei Foundation."

McDermott and the others sat up straight and started paying close attention.

Alex pressed on. "You sit on the board of the Agnus Dei Foundation, correct?"

"Yes, I'm the president."

"And it is this foundation that owns La Minita, is that correct?"

"Yes, the entire tract of land is titled under the Agnus Dei Foundation," explained Salamanca. "So, yes, the lands are owned by the foundation."

"Let me ask you, Bishop, what does Agnus Dei mean?"

Salamanca now turned to the jury. "It means 'Lamb of God.' A sacrificial lamb, of course, as when Jesus died on the cross."

"Now," Alex continued, "these lands stretch how far?"

"The tract we're talking about stretches from northern Cameron County, through Willacy, Kleberg, all the way to Nueces County, just south of Corpus Christi."

"Is there oil and gas on these lands?"

Salamanca paused and looked at McDermott. She stopped scribbling on her yellow pad, looked up and put her pen down, probably a signal that it was okay to answer the question. Alex and Michael picked up on this.

"Yes," mumbled Salamanca, "there are deposits, yes."

"And wind farms, too, correct?"

"Yes," answered Salamanca, glancing over at McDermott. McDermott was now twirling her Montblanc pen in her hand. Probably another signal telling Salamanca to be cautious.

"What else do those lands produce, Bishop? Please tell us."

The portly bishop shifted uncomfortably on the witness chair as McDermott continued twirling her pen with her fingers. "Well, there's cattle, farming, transmission towers, railroads, even a shrimp farm, and there's even talk about building an alternate landing strip for the space shuttle."

"How many oil and gas companies have leases with your foundation to explore and produce the oil and gas under the surface?"

"I couldn't tell you," responded Salamanca smugly.

"Why is that?"

Salamanca turned to face the judge and said, "Because the accountants have that information. I wouldn't want to mislead the jury and not be accurate with my answers."

"Well, then," recoiled Alex, "let's do it this way. As the president of the board, is it you who signs and approves all the leases on those lands?"

"Yes," grumbled Salamanca.

"Do you recall ever signing a lease with Exxon?"

McDermott sprang to her feet. "Objection, Your Honor. The question as phrased is vague and overly broad."

"Sustained," said Cienfuegos.

"In the last five years, Bishop," clarified Alex, "have you signed and approved oil and gas leases with Exxon? Do you recall?"

"Ah, yes," answered Salamanca, "there's been a couple."

"What about Chevron? In the last five years, have you renewed leases with Chevron?"

"I believe so."

"And Shell?"

"I'm sure they hold some leases on our lands, yes."

"Judge," cried McDermott, "I object. Where is Mr. Del Fuerte going with this? Why are we talking about leases and oil companies? That's why we filed our motion to bifurcate the trial. Discussing these matters is not appropriate at this time."

Cienfuegos glanced over at Alex. "Do you care to respond, Counsel?"

"Judge," said Alex, "we're just showing the range of business partners the foundation has. No one is trying to discuss net worth, or revenue, or sources of income . . . nothing like that. Bishop Salamanca is the president of the board and as such he knows who his foundation does business with. The jury is entitled to know those simple housekeeping matters."

"The objection is denied," said Cienfuegos. "Mr. Del Fuerte, make sure you steer clear from those other subjects."

"Will do, Judge."

"Carry on," ordered Cienfuegos.

"Bishop," Alex continued, "would you agree with me that your foundation does business with many oil and gas companies?"

"Yes."

"Anybody else?"

"What do you mean?"

"Does the foundation do business with anybody else, besides the oil and gas companies and the wind farms and all those other folks we mentioned before? Do you know?"

"Just the railroads and the folks that keep transmission towers on the land . . . like the phone companies. I've already answered that."

"Anybody else?"

"No, that's it," snapped Salamanca, "Oh, the wind farms, too."

Alex pressed on, "Anybody else?"

Salamanca rolled his eyes, "That's it."

"Are you sure?"

McDermott sprang to her feet again. "I object," she shouted. "Asked and answered. Bishop Salamanca has already answered, Your Honor. Can we move on, for the love of God? The jury's half asleep."

Cienfuegos gave a stern look to Alex. "Mr. Del Fuerte, the witness has already answered. He said no. What else do you want?"

"I want to find out," started Alex, not knowing what came over him, "if you, the Vatican, or the Agnus Dei Foundation get money to allow alien or drug traffickers to use portions of La Minita to conduct business and get their product up north? That's what I'm interested in, Judge."

All the spectators suddenly perked up and started paying attention.

"What?!" cried McDermott, her eyes about to pop out of their sockets. "That's ridiculous. And that line of questioning has no relevance to these proceedings, Judge. We object."

Cienfuegos replied, "I'll allow it. The question relates to the foundation's income."

Salamanca was now staring Alex down, visibly upset, and about to lose his composure. Clearly, Alex had pushed a hot button?

"You heard the judge," said Alex with a smirk as he stared back at Salamanca. "Do smuggling organizations pay your foundation money for access?"

"No," Salamanca snapped back, "that's the craziest thing I've ever heard!"

"Isn't it true, Bishop, that you have knowledge that smuggling organizations use your lands and yet you choose to turn a blind eye?"

McDermott and the intervenors were looking at Alex as if he had lost his mind. Finally, McDermott decided to put a stop to the spectacle. "Objection! Relevance?"

"I don't know where you got that," Salamanca chortled as if mocking Alex.

"Excuse me, Bishop," interrupted McDermott, "there's an objection on the floor. Judge, can we have a ruling?"

But before Cienfuegos could rule, Alex plowed right ahead. "That your smuggling associates are responsible for the deaths of several aliens that have perished in La Minita?"

All the other attorneys now joined McDermott in making objections.

"Objection, Your Honor!!!"

"Relevance!"

"Highly inflammatory!"

"Order! Order!" yelled Cienfuegos.

"Prejudicial!"

"Improper, outside of the scope of these proceedings!"

"No probative value!"

Cienfuegos banged his gavel on the bench. "Settle down! Order in the court, quiet! Settle down!"

All the attorneys continued yelling objections over each other.

"No foundation!"

"Inadmissible! Calls for self-incrimination."

"Calls for speculation . . . what can the Bishop possibly know about the deaths of aliens on La Minita?"

"May we approach the bench?" McDermott begged the judge.

"Quiet! Let's take a break," announced the judge, the veins on his neck about to pop. "I want to see all the attorneys in chambers."

"This court's now in recess," announced the bailiff.

As the attorneys met in chambers, the media frenzy started. The first day of the trial wasn't even over and already there were fireworks in the courtroom. To the media, the serious allegations raised by Alejandro Del Fuerte against the Agnus Dei Foundation meant higher ratings for the six o'clock evening news. For someone in Bishop Salamanca's situation, all this new attention would probably mean increased scrutiny and perhaps even a federal investigation.

Back in the courtroom, Bishop Salamanca had stepped down from the witness stand and was now sitting next to Tony, his assistant, while trying to dismiss and brush aside Alejandro Del Fuerte's insolence and belligerence. Tony was texting messages on his cell phone. Salamanca and the spectators were all waiting for the trial to resume.

After all the attorneys had met in chambers, Judge Cienfuegos ordered the bailiff to send the jurors home for the day. The trial would resume the next day, early in the morning. However, all the lawyers were ordered to come back to court.

Judge Cienfuegos had decided to have an afternoon hearing in order to determine whether the plaintiffs should be allowed to elicit testimony of Bishop Salamanca regarding the alien trafficking organizations using La Minita to conduct business.

According to Cienfuegos he was going to allow Alejandro Del Fuerte the opportunity to show the court why the plaintiffs considered said testimony relevant and whether or not said testimony carried with it any probative value. Likewise, the defense would also be allowed to show why the fact that alien traffickers may or may not use said lands had no relevance to the case. After hearing arguments, he would then issue a ruling.

"Alex, I sure hope you have evidence to back up your claims," Michael said, sounding worried as he chewed on a double cheeseburger with grilled onions. The pair was having dinner at the Dairy Queen, down the street from their hotel. "I can't believe Judge Cienfuegos is going to let you ask Salamanca about a smuggling ring."

Alex had just popped an onion ring in his mouth. "Well, you said we should have some fun with him . . . so that's what I plan to do."

"Did you see McDermott's face? And the others?" asked Michael with a grin. "They were beside themselves . . . I can't wait to see what happens when you resume Salamanca's examination tomorrow. If I was the judge, I wouldn't let you get into those matters."

Alex chewed on his burger as he thought about Michael's last comment. He managed to swallow his food and finally said, "Professor, I gotta be honest, come clean with you."

"What's the matter? Is something wrong?"

"This case might be the end of me," said Alex, point-blank.

"What?"

"Salamanca wants me to take a dive . . . lose the case on purpose. I told him I'd do it. What you saw in the courtroom was just a dog-and-pony show."

Michael almost choked on his burger. "What?!"

Alex put down his burger. "I'm supposed to pretend and go through with the case . . . let the others walk all over us, except there's a problem . . . "

Michael looked like he'd seen a ghost. "Wait, wait, what are you saying?"

"Even if I lose the case, and give Salamanca what he wants, I could very well end up six feet under. Others out there also warned me to keep my distance . . . to walk away . . . I didn't listen. Now, I'm afraid it might be too late."

"Is this a joke?" mumbled Michael. "Slow down. What are you talking about?"

"This past Saturday, Naiví and I were working late at the office. Gigi called me and asked if I could bring her some tacos from Matamoros. She had a craving . . . being pregnant and all."

"And?"

Alex sipped on his Coke. "Well, Naiví and I go to Matamoros to fetch the tacos and on the way back, we're carjacked. They let Naiví go, but they held me the entire night, until they let me go the next morning, but not before roughing me up pretty good."

Visibly troubled, Michael asked, "Why didn't you tell me?"

"Because I was really scared, and even if I told you, there's nothing you or I could do."

"That's a load of crap! We're partners, Alex! We depend on each other."

Alex shot back, "I thought I could handle it . . . I was just going to walk away . . . just drop it."

"Well, then? What's the problem?"

Alex ignored the question and kept rambling on. "I'm stuck. Salamanca's forcing me to try the case . . . he's got the goods on me. On the other hand, these bad dudes from across . . . they want me to dismiss it, walk away. Not bring attention to La Minita. They think I'm stepping on their toes. Either way, I'm dead."

Michael had put down his burger, and his jaw was on the floor. "Wait a minute, who? Why? How can you be so sure they want you dead?"

"Trust me . . . they're the real thing . . . they killed a little boy in front of my very own eyes . . . barbaric . . . the only way to describe it. I never told anyone the story because it sounds unbelievable, but . . ." Alex paused, he pushed his tray away. He'd lost his appetite.

Michael continued to struggle with the new information. "I still don't understand . . . "

"These guys move undocumented people through Salamanca's lands. They feel threatened by what's going on in the courtroom . . . all the attention, the media and the headlines . . . the spotlight potentially being shined on them . . . I messed with the wrong dudes."

"*You* screwed with the wrong dudes?! What about us, the firm, me, Gigi, Romeo . . . ? Did you ever stop to think about us? You know what your problem is?" asked Michael, throwing his hands up in the air.

"What?"

"You're too damned self-absorbed . . . you're a selfish ingrate. It's all about you! How could you put us in this predicament? Drag the entire firm through something like this and no tell us? What the hell were you thinking?"

"I had no idea!" said Alex, feeling like a wimp. "These people want me to dismiss the case . . . shut down the litigation."

"And?"

"I couldn't . . . I can't leave the clients hanging."

Michael started feeling sick to his stomach. "So, what are you saying?"

"Look, I've decided . . . I took the case . . . I'm gonna finish it. If it'd been up to me, I would have just filed my motion to withdraw and gotten us out of the case a long time ago. Even though that's not what these people want. They want me to dismiss it, kill it, put an end to it. Salamanca wants me to finish it, go through with it, lose it on purpose. That's the mess I'm in."

Michael had removed his reading glasses and was wiping them clean with his silk tie. He was fuming. "So, that's what's been going on, huh? I knew it. I knew something was not right. You were not yourself. I was starting to wonder . . . "

"I'm sorry, really, I am. As we sit here, I'm a marked man."

Michael was shaking his head, looking dumbfounded and angry as hell, all at the same time. "So, why are you asking about the alien trafficking? Why are you even going there? I just don't get it."

"I don't know what came over me . . . frustration, I guess. Who knows, maybe the jurors will think I'm really trying to win this thing. Oscar, too, will think I'm getting down and dirty, fighting like mad. Don't you see? That's what Salamanca wants. That way no one can say this was just a half-ass attempt, and then they can discount this loss, and somebody out there tries again. This has to be the final nail in the coffin."

"I'm really, really disappointed," conceded Michael.

Alex felt as if the world around him had started collapsing. All he could say was, "I hope you can forgive me."

"How long has this been going on? When were you going to tell me?"

"Things started happening as soon as I got involved with the case, but I threw caution to the wind, and now things are out of control . . . Never did I imagine that the other goons also had a stake in the case."

"No shit, Sherlock."

"I bet you didn't know Salamanca even has me on tape screwing Savannah Lee, the porn actress."

Michael was sipping his coffee when this last revelation caused him to choke and spit most of it out. "What? But you're getting married!"

"I seriously doubt there's going to be a wedding. Gigi and I were planning to go to Vegas and just elope. Of course, that might not even happen if Gigi finds out I've been screwing around. Salamanca will leak the video if I don't come through. He's threatened to post it on the Internet."

"I can't believe you never told me any of this. It just keeps getting worse and worse. It's like a bad dream."

"I was working up the courage to tell Gigi, but seriously, I never wanted to put you guys at risk."

Michael took a deep breath and looked at Alex. "I don't know how you're going to get out of this mess, but if I was you, tomorrow, when you continue examining Salamanca, I'd stay away from all this alien trafficking stuff. That's not going to get you far and, if it's true, I'm sure Salamanca is not going to appreciate you rubbing his nose in it."

"Okay," said Alex, "I get it."

"And when this is all over, you might consider surrendering your bar card."

"My license? Why would you even say that?"

"Because I think you've lost sight of what it means to be a lawyer, Alex." Michael started to get up, "You can't possibly call yourself an attorney."

"I'm sorry," muttered Alex.

"No," Michael snapped back, "I'm sorry I ever partnered up with a liar and a shyster. You're no different than all the lawyers out there, you're truly disgraceful!"

CHAPTER 38

T HE SECOND DAY of the trial started with Alex recalling Bishop Salamanca to the witness stand. He spent the entire morning being extremely nice to Salamanca and asking him about the other members that sat on the board of the foundation. He asked about the monthly meetings the board normally held and whether or not the entire Agnus Dei Foundation was owned by the Catholic Diocese of the Southern Coastal Counties. Alex and the jury were surprised to learn that 90% of the foundation was owned by the Church and that the other 10% was owned by T. Blake Morgan, a reclusive Houston billionaire who owned all the water rights in and around and under La Minita.

After the lunch break, McDermott and all the other attorneys spent the rest of the afternoon asking questions of Salamanca, especially highlighting all the social causes that the foundation supported. Salamanca relished the attention and beamed with pride as he detailed all the charities the foundation spent millions on. But, of course, the jury never got to hear that none of those charities did any work in South Texas. In fact, ten or so of the charities that received funds from the foundation were all in Italy, and their task was to maintain and preserve churches, museums, monasteries, convents, holy sites throughout the world, the Vatican and all the priceless works of art in it.

"What are we doing?" asked Michael as Alex drove the firm's SUV back to the hotel. Romeo and Naiví were following the pair in Romeo's pickup truck.

"Just going through the motions, I guess," said Alex, shrugging his shoulders.

"When do you think you're going to present Candelario's will?"

"Maybe tomorrow, we'll see," replied Alex.

"Well, it's time to make a decision. Either you pull the plug on this thing and we go home or . . . "

"Or?"

"You start representing the clients like they deserve to be represented. Decide. Either you come out swinging, give it your all, and whatever has to happen will have to happen," Michael reasoned. "If we all bite the bullet, so be it. I've lived a good life, I've had more fun than a kid at the Mall's Hobby Town store and my children will inherit more money than they'll know what to do with. So, you need to make up your mind."

"I understand," Alex answered as he thought of his grandfather undergoing rehabilitation, and how Salamanca would react when he caught on and realized that Alex was not going along with the plan. Or was he?

The next morning Alex and Michael's team pushed and shoved their way through the throngs of reporters blocking the entryway into the courthouse.

"Alex," shouted April Wingate, "do you have a comment about the sex video posted on YouTube?"

Alex stopped dead in his tracks. "What sex video?"

"The one where you and a Ms. Savannah Lee can be seen making love. It's on YouTube. As of last night, it had thirty-five thousand hits."

Alex's mind went blank, and for the life of him he could not put together a coherent response. His tongue was in knots. "That's ehm . . . not me on that video . . . I'm sorry. I'm sure somebody doctored it."

"Can you roll back your shirt sleeve?" asked another reporter.

"I will do no such thing," yelled Alex.

"The man in the video has a quarter-sized birthmark on his right forearm," explained a third reporter, "right close to the elbow. Do you have one? Can we see?"

"Look, I have a case to try. We can discuss my sex life at a later date, okay? Please, get out of my way. I've got to get back in that courtroom."

"Alex, Alex!" shouted the mob of reporters. "What does your fiancée say about this? Is the wedding still on? Does she know?"

Salamanca was grinning from ear to ear when he took the witness stand. And Alex felt as if he'd just been smacked across the face by a thug with brass knuckles. The sex video posted on YouTube could only mean one thing. Salamanca was no longer playing nice. The gloves were off.

"Are we ready to proceed?" asked Judge Cienfuegos of the attorneys.

"We are," said McDermott, sporting a smirk on her face as she turned around and winked at Alex.

Cienfuegos spoke again. "What say the intervenors?"

O'Quinn bolted to his feet. "We're present and ready, Judge."

"Same announcement," said Uhels as he proceeded to stand up from his table.

"We're ready," announced Nicholas, and Becker, and everybody else.

Judge Cienfuegos then looked over at Alex's table and waited for a response. Michael had his head buried in some documents and did not notice. Alex was also distracted as he was fumbling with his cell phone, trying to read Gigi's text message before turning it off. It read: "Ur a PIG. The wedding is off! How could you?!"

Finally, Naiví, who was sitting next to Alex, elbowed him in the ribs.

Alex sprang to his feet, "I'm sorry, Your Honor. I'm trying to turn this thing off. We're ready to proceed."

"Then, let's go," indicated the judge. "Your witness."

"Ah, hem, yes," said Alex clearing his throat as he tried to gather his thoughts. The text message had thrown him for a loop.

Sure, the reporters alerting him that morning to the existence of the video was one thing. But for Gigi to know so soon . . . Not twenty minutes after having walked into the courthouse, the whole thing was about to give him a heart attack.

"We're waiting, Mr. Del Fuerte," admonished Cienfuegos.

"Bishop Salamanca," started Alex as he tried to pick a topic to cover during his renewed cross-examination, "Good morning, Sir."

"Good morning to you," answered Salamanca, and then he acknowledged the jurors and nodded to them.

"Sir," said Alex, still thinking about the text message. "Do you have any reason to dispute the validity of Candelario Santibáñez's will giving everything to Arturito?"

"No, sir," said Salamanca politely.

"Do you have reason to dispute the fact that said will was admitted as a muniment of title many, many years ago, by his descendants?"

"No, sir."

"To the best of your knowledge, did the Agnus Dei Foundation, or anybody else for that matter, ever dispute the filing of said will as a muniment of title?"

Salamanca shifted in his chair and said, "No, we never did."

"How about the title opinion prepared by the previous attorney's retained expert, sir? Do you have any reason to dispute the findings in that title opinion?"

"I'm not a surveyor," Salamanca answered as he looked at the jurors, "but the answer is no. I don't have any reason to dispute those findings."

"And Bishop, you don't deny that La Minita covers land from Nueces, down to Kleberg County to Raymondville all the way to northern Cameron County, correct?"

"That's correct," said Bishop Salamanca. "It's a very large tract of land."

"Isn't it true that Don Arturo Monterreal received these lands through a Royal Spanish grant?" asked Alex.

"That's true. Everybody knows that."

"Do you know if said conveyance was later confirmed by the Mexican State of Tamaulipas, in 1825?"

"That I wouldn't know."

"If Attorney Dugger's expert, Mr. Paul Becerra, said that's what happened, do you have any evidence to dispute that?"

Salamanca shrugged his shoulders. "No, I don't have any evidence, but my attorneys might have something . . . an objection of sorts."

"Isn't it true that the grant and ownership to Monterreal and his heirs was confirmed by the legislature of the State of Texas on April 18, 1852?"

"I believe that's what the title opinion letter says," Salamanca agreed.

"Do you understand Mr. Becerra's title opinion letter covers the years 1767 to the year 2006?"

"I understand," said Salamanca, "although the competing title opinion prepared by our experts disproves some of Becerra's flawed findings. If I recall, that expert was hired by Mr. Dugger, the previous attorney, before he passed away."

Alex was going to take issue with the witness' answer, but he let it go. That morning, after receiving the news of the posting of the video, he'd decided it was time to learn to pick his battles. And at that precise moment, there was no battle more important than to try to salvage his relationship with Gigi, the mother-to-be of his twin babies.

"Pass the witness," Alex announced, sounding utterly depressed.

CHAPTER 39

DURING THE MONTH of December, the trial continued, uninterrupted until the four-day holiday break. Cienfuegos could have cared less about the attorneys, but he had a soft spot for the jurors and wanted them to spend the short Christmas break with their families. Hours and hours had already been spent parading engineers, surveyors, handwriting experts, forensic document experts, probate experts, economists, lay witnesses, the Santibáñez heirs, rebuttal witnesses and every other conceivable type of witness. But a long break meant the jurors would probably forget much of the evidence already presented.

Alex spent the Christmas break completely alone, and Gigi had moved out of the Contessa di Mare and relocated back with her parents, as far away from Alejandro Del Fuerte as the local geography would allow. Michael had gone home to Houston to see his kids, since they would be in town visiting their mother, his ex-wife. He'd told Alex that he missed his grandkids and wanted to see about taking them to the downtown Aquarium, the IMAX and to a Texans football game at Reliant Stadium. It was the first time in the history of the football franchise that the Texans were fighting for a berth in the play-offs. And Michael wanted to share that event with his grandkids, at least once in his lifetime, before being shipped to a nursing home.

Alex continued regretting the error of his ways. During the holidays, he'd tried calling, texting and emailing Gigi, but all his communications had gone unanswered. Out of desperation, he'd called Gigi's mom, asking about the pregnancy and Gigi, but his *suegra* had made it abundantly clear that he'd become *persona non grata* in the Montemayor household. At the end of the conversation, his ex-mother-in-law-to-be had driven the stake deeper into Alex's heart when she announced that her daughter would not be going back to work at Del Fuerte, Fetzer & Montemayor.

Despite feeling depressed, two positive events had happened during the holiday. One, grandpa had been released from the hospital and was now in a rehab facility, slowly recovering. Alex had been able to spend time visiting. The other positive note had been the opportunity to spend some time with Naiví and her family after she invited Alex to come over for dinner on Christmas Eve. Alex had been pleasantly surprised to learn that it had been Naiví who'd prepared the exquisite *bacalao*, a Portuguese-style dish made with cod fish, the smoked turkey tamales and even the *rompope*, or eggnog.

"Members of the jury," called out Cienfuegos, "both sides have rested and closed. That means that you've heard all the evidence there is to hear in connection with the case. As I told you earlier, when I read to you the jury charge, after closing arguments you will retire to the jury deliberation room, nominate a foreman, and start answering the charge. Any questions?"

The jurors shook their heads and had no questions. The two alternates, sitting off to the side, said nothing, but looked bored out of their minds.

"Very well," continued Cienfuegos, "Mr. Del Fuerte, are you ready with your closing argument? I'm sure the jurors are dying to hear it."

"I am, Your Honor," said Alex as he got up from the counsel's table and turned to acknowledge the jury. He put down his pen and yellow pad and walked empty-handed toward the jury box. He stuck one hand in his pant pocket, cleared his throat and . . .

"Let me stop you, Mr. Del Fuerte," interrupted Cienfuegos. "Jurors, remember that until you render your verdict, you're still under my instructions not to watch stories on TV about this case or the lawyers involved in it. Same goes for newspapers, and even YouTube."

There were loud giggles in the courtroom, and half of the jurors turned to look at Alex, obviously aware of the video's existence.

Alex turned several shades of red, was shaking his head in disbelief, completely surprised that Cienfuegos would want to inject such humor into the proceedings. "Thank you, Your Honor . . . for that timely reminder."

"You're welcome," replied Cienfuegos with a grin.

Alex managed to compose himself, winked at the nurse juror smiling back at him, and started his final summation. "May it please the court, Mrs. McDermott, Mr. O'Quinn, Mr. Uhels, Mr. Nicholas, Mr. Becker, Mr. Ramírez and everybody else." He then turned to face the man he thought would end up being the jury foreman, the retired high school principal.

"Members of the jury, it is now Friday, January 21, 2007. We have been in this courtroom, together, close to seven weeks. There is no more evidence to present. Everything that was supposed to be considered by you has been talked about, discussed, analyzed and introduced as evidence. All sides—the plaintiffs, the defendant, the intervenors—have rested and closed and that's it. Now it's your turn to decide what happens next.

"Now, I could summarize every single piece of evidence and try to highlight the important points that were raised by each witness or attack the credibility of others." Alex paused, turned and pointed at the empty witness stand.

"Instead, I will tell you a story. When I was a boy, my mother would read to me her favorite passages from the Bible. Every night, after dinner and my bath, she would tuck me in bed and read to me. We enjoyed reading and learning of Jesus' parables. She would also explain to me what it all meant. This went on for a number of years, until both my parents and baby sister were taken away from me when they perished in a car accident. I was seven years of age when they died. After that, my grandfather César—my abuelo—raised me."

Alex paused for effect and looked over at the jury. The fourteen pairs of eyes were glued to him.

"The one parable that always stuck in my mind, and still does to this day, is the parable of the rich man and the beggar, Lazarus. Have you all heard of it?"

All the women in the jury nodded their heads, but only the high school principal and the cop reacted.

"In Luke 16:19–31, there is the story of a very rich man, rich beyond anything imaginable. This rich man wore fine clothes, lived in a beautiful home and enjoyed all of life's luxuries, from exquisite wines and foods all the way to fine furnishings and exotic wild animals, servants and even slaves.

Alex turned around and stared at Salamanca. Salamanca pretended not to notice and continued scribbling on a yellow pad as he sat next to McDermott.

"Well, it just so happened that one day a dying beggar appeared at the gate of this rich man's home. The beggar was Lazarus. Lazarus was sick, full of sores, starving and begging for food, anything, scraps, whatever. The parable tells us that even dogs came and licked Lazarus' sores. Lazarus ended up dying, but the rich man was surprised to see the beggar being carried away by angels and the angels delivering him to Abraham. Months later, the rich man also died and was buried; when he woke up, he found himself in Hades . . . what the folks then called the 'afterlife.'

"There, the rich man opened his eyes and saw that he was really in Hell, but that Lazarus, the beggar, was in a beautiful place, rejoicing and dancing with Abraham. The rich man cried and complained that he was thirsty. He wanted Abraham to have mercy on him and allow Lazarus to bring him some water to cool his throat. Abraham replied, 'Son, remember that you, in your lifetime, received your good things, and Lazarus, in like manner, received bad things. But now he is comforted and you're in anguish. Besides all this, there is a great gulf between us so that those who want to pass from here over to you are not able, and none may cross over from there to us.'"

Alex then walked closer to the jury box. He looked around the courtroom and noticed the crowd hanging on his every word.

"The rich man then begged Abraham to send Lazarus back to life to warn the others, those like him, that there was still time to

THE LAND GRANT

291

repent and change course. To remind those back on earth of Jesus'
teachings, including sharing with those who don't have. With
those who have less than us. Not to horde, but instead to open
your heart, your home, your pocket, spread the wealth . . . So
Abraham told the rich man, 'If no one listened to Moses and the
prophets, what makes you think they'll listen to Lazarus if I send
him back?'

"Today, you the jury, by your verdict, you get to be like
Lazarus. You get to deliver a message. Today, your message will
not only reach South Texas, but the entire world. Believe me . . .
your message will be heard from Kingsville all the way to Washington and even Wall Street and the rest of the world. Because
only you, by your verdict, can change the way the rich man lives.
Only you, by your verdict, can make things right. It has been over
eighty years since the rightful heirs of La Minita have seen a penny
or any benefit from their lands. It has been decades since any of
the fruit, the money and billions and billions of dollars in gas and
oil royalties from these 'lands of ours' have been shared with the
poor among us . . . with you and me and those of us who call
South Texas home. These are the plaintiffs, your neighbors, your
friends and acquaintances . . . maybe even your long-distance relatives. And you have the power to change all that. Today, right
now, right here, from this humble courtroom.

"You'll have an opportunity to send a message, loud and clear.
You'll have the chance to right a wrong when you start answering
the jury charge," said Alex as he held up a packet of documents
and waved them in front of the jury. "These are questions that you
will need to answer based on the evidence you've heard in this
case, in this courtroom during the entire trial. So, let's take a quick
look at the questions in here."

Alex found the page he was looking for.

"I'm asking you to answer question number one with 'Yes, the
will from Candelario Santibáñez to his illegitimate son, Arturo
Santibáñez, was a valid will.' If you answer 'Yes' to question number one, then you move on to question number two. Question
number two reads, 'Did the filing of Candelario's will in the
Cameron County property records serve as muniment of title?'

Again, I'm asking you to answer 'Yes.' Remember by muniment of title . . . all that means is that by filing the will in the county records the world is on notice as to who owns the property described in the will.

"You will continue to remember the evidence, the credible evidence that was presented to you from old documents, witness testimony, the experts, even ancient maps, surveys, old letters, government records and other exhibits, and you will answer the questions in the charge as you find appropriate. Now, this document is seventy-five pages long, and it has over fifty questions to answer. Take your time, deliberate, remember the evidence and use your common sense. There's no rush. Depending on some of your answers, we might see you again . . . after your deliberations."

"Objection!" shouted McDermott. "Counsel knows there's a motion to bifurcate. . . . It's improper to bring up or mention a second phase at this time."

"Sustained," Cienfuegos ruled. "Are you almost done, Mr. Del Fuerte?"

"Yes, Judge. I'm done," said Alex, "thank you."

"Ms. McDermott," called out Judge Cienfuegos, "are you ready to proceed?"

"We are," said McDermott as she walked over to the jury box, yellow pad in hand, while her staff finished bringing up images of what was to be a PowerPoint presentation on one of the walls in the courtroom.

"Very well," snapped Cienfuegos, "let's go."

CHAPTER 40

THE JURY HAD worked diligently for a week already, and still there was no verdict. The courtroom had been emptied out of all the gadgets that lawyers use to put on their case. Even the mountains of boxes hauled into court by all the lawyers had been promptly removed after the jury had heard all the closing arguments and had been handed the jury charge in order to start deliberations.

Dana McDermott had left Mosley in charge, in case a verdict was returned, and she went back to her main office in Corpus Christi to prepare for the next phase of the trial in the event that the foundation took a hit. Worst case scenario, she would rush back and fight head-on any of Alex's attempts at discovering the real net worth of the foundation.

Likewise, Uhels, O'Quinn, Hanmore and Nicholas had all left. They were relying on their local counsels to keep them informed. The thinking was that even if the jury found that for some strange reason the foundation had committed some type of fraud and the plaintiffs were entitled to punitive damages, Judge Cienfuegos would probably give everybody a week break before resuming the punitive damages portion of the trial.

Alex and Romeo stayed behind, and Michael went back to Brownsville. Gigi refused to go to work and was not returning anyone's phone calls, emails or text messages. Before heading back to Brownsville, Michael had mentioned to Alex that it was time to start thinking about winding up the affairs of Del Fuerte, Fetzer & Montemayor.

With Michael gone and Naiví back in law school, the routine for the entire week had been the same. Alex and Romeo would get up early, leave their hotel and head to the courthouse. By 8:15 in the morning, the pair could be found inside the courthouse's small coffee shop having coffee and biscuits. By 8:30, the other attorneys involved in the case would also start showing up to grab cups of coffee before heading to the courtroom to wait for something to happen.

Judge Cienfuegos had instructed the jurors to show up by nine, break for lunch and resume their deliberations by 1:30 in the afternoon. He did not want them working past 5:00 P.M. If they had not reached a verdict by the end of the working day, they could continue to deliberate the next day.

Alex, Romeo and all the other associates, including Ramírez, Becker and Fonseca, were dying of anticipation. During the entire week of deliberations, the jurors had not even sent Judge Cienfuegos a single note or question. In fact, the only communication they had with anyone was on the first day when they asked the bailiff to bring all the boxes with deposition excerpts and exhibits back to the jury room.

Alex and Romeo were finishing the last of their biscuits, when Alex glanced at his watch. "It's 8:50 A.M. on Friday . . . they've been at it since last Thursday. That's seven days since the deliberations started. I wonder what's taking them so long."

"It was a monster of a jury charge," Romeo said. "Even though I work at a law firm and know of these things, I still have a hard time understanding how it all works together. Those poor souls in there . . . I doubt they know what they're doing. We might be here another month."

"Cienfuegos won't let it go that long," Alex countered. "I'm sure that by the end of today, if nothing's happened, he'll want to visit with all the lawyers and discuss giving the jurors the Allen Charge, if need be."

"What do you think is happening in there?" asked Romeo.

"I don't know, and to be honest, I don't know if I care. I should never have taken this case. It's brought nothing but misery to me and Gigi," said Alex as he pounded the table. "I don't know if Gisela will ever forgive me."

"Think positive," Romeo countered, trying to lift Alex's spirits. "What if we win? Wouldn't that be awesome?!"

Alex kept thinking, *Shit, that's the worst thing that can happen. I'll be dead.*

CHAPTER 41

THE PAGE SUMMONING all the attorneys to report to chambers came precisely at eleven o'clock on Monday morning. Alex was outside the courthouse, smoking a cigarette, wishing he could have a double scotch, when Romeo came running out.

"Alex, the jury sent a note. Cienfuegos wants everyone in chambers."

Alex quickly threw the cigarette down on the sidewalk and put it out with his shoe. "Let's go see what it is."

Ramírez, Fonseca, Hidalgo, Becker and the lesser associates were all in chambers when Alex showed up, Romeo in tow. They had their cell phones at the ready, anxiously waiting to relay the content of the jury note to the others. Within seconds, McDermott, Uhels, O'Quinn, Hanmore and the rest would also be on the phone talking to their clients, trying to figure out the significance of the message in the note.

Judge Cienfuegos was sitting behind his desk, holding a folded piece of paper in his right hand while in his left he held a cup of black coffee.

"Mr. Del Fuerte," said the judge as he put his coffee down, "there you are . . . we were waiting for you."

"I'm sorry," said Alex, almost out of breath. "I was out front, smoking a cigarette, Your Honor. Romeo, my assistant, just told me about the note. We ran up the stairs as soon as I got word."

"Sit down," said Cienfuegos with a grin. "Take one of those chairs."

Cienfuegos waved at Fonseca to get up and give his seat to Alex. The other chair across from Cienfuegos was being occupied by Carlos Ramírez.

Ramírez broke the silence, "Have you read the note, Judge? What does it say?"

"I have not," said Cienfuegos, matter-of-factly. "I don't want to be accused of any kind of impropriety. We'll get to see it and read it together, at the same time."

All the other attorneys in the room had already pre-dialed the home office on their cells, and all they needed to do was hit the send button.

Alex gulped hard. The last thing he needed was a jury note that indicated or suggested that the jury would decide for the plaintiffs. He held his breath and started praying.

Cienfuegos opened the note and started reading it to himself. He arched his eyebrows in complete amazement; his jaw dropped to the floor. "Well, I'll be damned," exclaimed Cienfuegos as he tossed the note on the desk. Like piranhas about to devour wounded prey, the attorneys reached for the note.

Ramírez got his hands on it and started reading the contents out loud so that everyone could hear, "We're ready to start awarding damages. What's the minimum, maximum? Would $400,000,000 be too much?"

"What?!" yelled Alex as the room spun faster and faster. "You can't be serious."

"Oh, my God!" screamed Hanmore, seemingly terrified, "this is not good."

"*No puede ser,*" cried Fonseca, followed by Ramírez and all the others standing around. He plopped down on a chair.

"Ouch!" cried Becker.

"Damn you, Del Fuerte!" added some other lowly associate with the firm of Mike Nicholas.

Cienfuegos tried to regain control of the situation. "Gentlemen, before you call your clients . . . tell them I have not accepted the verdict. And even though this is just a note, do tell your clients that it appears they're ready to render a verdict. I suggest you tell your clients to settle this thing, while we still can. Once the court accepts their verdict, then we'll have to go to the punitive phase of the trial . . . it is not going to be pretty. From reading this note, it appears that it could be a blood-bath. You have a couple of hours. I'm going to send the bailiff with a note letting them go to lunch early and instruct them to come back at 2:00 P.M. How's that?"

But before Cienfuegos could get an answer, the attorneys had scurried away like rats on a sinking ship, ready to go and deliver the tragic news.

Alex and Romeo were in the courthouse coffee shop waiting for McDermott to call. In the meantime, Alex had instructed Romeo to send a text message to Michael and let him know what was happening.

Alex picked up his cell and dialed Oscar Santibáñez. After about six rings, a voice answered. "Oscar, is that you? This is Del Fuerte."

"Anything?" asked Santibáñez.

"Yes," answered Alex, "thirty minutes ago, the jury sent out a very telling note. I think they're with us, brother. The judge is trying to avoid starting up the second phase of the trial . . . wants to see if we can settle this thing."

"Alex, we never thought we'd win. We'll do whatever you think is right. You decide."

"Look," said Alex, "I think we can squeeze these bastards for some money. Seriously, even if the jury decides to give us the lands back . . . these guys will fight us tooth and nail . . . all the way to the Supreme Court. And there's no way in hell we'll win there. We'll lose, we'll never see the lands and we won't see a dime . . . we'll all go home empty-handed."

"Can we pop them for five, ten million? That's a lot of money . . . we could all get about fifty thousand a piece . . . it's always been a long shot. Something's better than nothing."

"Okay," Alex replied after testing the waters with the lead plaintiff. "Let me see what I can do. I'll call you in the next thirty minutes."

Alex's cell phone started vibrating. He reached for it and looked at its screen. It said "Private Call." His heart skipped a beat. It had to be Salamanca. He just knew it.

"Hello?" mumbled Alex, "who's this?"

"You shouldn't have to ask," said Salamanca in a stern voice. "I hear we have a runaway jury."

Alex waved at Romeo to go refill his coffee cup. Once Romeo was out of sight, he cleared his throat. "Huh, yes . . . it would appear so. What do you want me to do?"

"You know what you have to do, Alex. Don't screw this up. I've already instructed McDermott not to offer you a dime. We're not settling. We're going through with this, and you better pray to God that it's a defense verdict. Otherwise you're going to wish you were never born. We had a deal, remember?"

"But this is out of my hands," pleaded Alex. "The jury appears to be ready to hand down a plaintiff's verdict. They even want to award damages in the hundreds of millions of dollars. Don't you see?"

"It's not my problem, Alex."

"Are you sure there's no middle ground? Throw the plaintiffs a bone, get your confidential settlement agreement and move on. I could get them to agree to renounce La Minita, mineral interests and all. They just want cash . . . they need cash. You could get out from under this mess really cheap. I just talked to Oscar . . . it wouldn't take much, you know?"

"Even if we take a hit, you know we will appeal, and this case will drag on for another five years, Alex," explained Salamanca. "And we will win, one way or another. I'm not worried about that. Hell, all the justices in the court of appeals are bought-and-paid for with oil and gas money. What really worries me is you being a man of your word, Alex."

"Listen, listen!" begged Alex. "Right now the jurors are close to handing us a plaintiff's verdict . . . which is something you don't want. Such a verdict will only encourage others to sue . . . and this will never end. Can we just try to resolve this thing . . . *por el amor de Dios*?"

"You better find a way to deliver a defense verdict, Alex. That's all I'm interested in. That was our deal. Don't screw things up."

"What about the video? We had a deal too?" screamed Alex. "You went and published it!"

"You've been warned," growled Salamanca. The line went dead.

"But . . . but . . . " stuttered Alex as his neck muscles tensed up. "Wait . . . don't hang up." He stared at the phone and felt like a felon on death row after being told his final stay of execution had just been denied. He was a dead man.

"So," asked Cienfuegos, "have you all had a chance to talk? See if the case can be settled before the jurors come back from lunch?"

All the lawyers were back in chambers, including McDermott. She had driven herself back to Kingsville in record time.

"We're ready to settle," lied Alex, "we'd like to see if the defendants want to put some money on the table."

"We don't have a number for Mr. Del Fuerte or his clients, Your Honor. Sorry. I have instructions to receive the verdict, whatever that might be, and then appeal if needed. My client feels pretty good about our chances on appeal," answered McDermott.

"What about the intervenors?" asked Cienfuegos as he looked over to Becker, Ramírez, Ramsey and Fonseca. "What do your clients say, gentlemen?"

"We stand with the foundation, Your Honor," said Ramírez. The others were nodding their heads in agreement.

"I've called the clients and we're in the same boat, Your Honor. We can't settle if the foundation doesn't settle. So, we will take our chances . . . see what happens when the verdict comes in," said Fonseca.

A look of frustration came over Cienfuegos. "Okay, if that's what you want. Just remember that a verdict for the plaintiffs here today will open the floodgates of litigation, and the Agnus Dei Foundation will continue to spend millions and millions defending these suits."

"It's the same thing if we settle, Your Honor," interjected McDermott. "It sends the wrong message. We're damned if we do and damned if we don't. When other folks find out my client likes to settle cases, then they'll also want to sue and hope to squeeze some quick money out of the diocese as well."

Alex was more confused than ever. On the one hand, he had already told Santibáñez about the note, and his clients were expecting some sort of settlement. On the other hand, despite the note, the defendants were apparently still unwilling to pitch them anything, not even a penny. This of course meant that there would be a verdict, and, if the note was any indication of things to come, then Alex, for all intents and purposes, had already one foot in the grave.

Cienfuegos threw his hands up in the air and got up from behind his desk. "Listen up, everybody. It's now one o'clock in the afternoon, the jury is due to come back at two. The way things are going, it sounds like we'll have a plaintiffs' verdict, soon. You need to get this thing settled . . . Do we understand each other?"

"But, Judge," objected McDermott, "my client is firm in his position. I've tried convincing Bishop Salamanca that it's best to settle, but I can't get anywhere with him."

"Go back to your clients one last time," said Cienfuegos, "before I accept whatever verdict is coming. I have a suggestion. Have you all thought about the bond?"

"What do you mean?" asked McDermott.

"I knew you guys hadn't thought things through," Cienfuegos remarked as he played with his moustache. "It's obvious."

"You mean the supersedes bond?" asked Fonseca.

"Of course," Cienfuegos said, "the supersedes bond, what else? Before anybody can appeal, the appellate bond will have to be posted, and it will have to be cash. Remember? Otherwise, the plaintiffs will be entitled to execute on whatever judgment they get, since no bond was posted . . . and if I was the Agnus Dei Foundation, I'd be worried . . . there are a lot of assets out there."

This last comment caught all the attorneys by surprise. It was true, and it was something they had failed to consider. If there was no bond posted in order to stop Del Fuerte from executing on the judgment, Alex could seize all of La Minita, including the producing oil and gas wells.

"Well, how big can this bond be?" asked McDermott, staring at the judge. She was starting to sweat bullets.

"Let's say the jury awards actual damages of 400 million dollars, as their note discusses," proposed Cienfuegos.

"But they would have to find the foundation committed fraud on them, too," Ramírez interjected, "to really worry about a punitive damage award, right?"

"Right," answered Cienfuegos. "Let's say they do. So, the 400 million would be multiplied 2.5 times."

McDermott almost fell backwards and Mosley had to catch her. "That would be a judgment worth about 1.5 billion dollars."

"That's right," declared Cienfuegos and then, looking intently at McDermott, he added, "And you're telling me your client is adamant about refusing to settle this thing, Counsel?"

Becker was heard mumbling in the background, "Who has . . . money . . . to post a 1.5 billion dollar cash bond?"

"Well, y-y-you know . . . " stuttered McDermott, "I guess . . . "

"I guess, my ass!" snapped Cienfuegos. "You go tell Bishop Salamanca that in case the Agnus Dei Foundation takes a hit, before any appeal can be perfected, the foundation will have to post a 1.5 billion dollar cash bond. See what he says . . . and then get back to me."

Alex gulped again, his eyes now as big as half dollars. He could not believe things were taking a turn for the worse. It looked as if Cienfuegos was intent on making the parties settle. The added pressure coming from the bench would only piss off Salamanca and, in all likelihood, would end up costing Alex his life. Things could not get any uglier.

Fonseca dared to speak up, "But, Judge, what if the award is only the 400 million in the note, and the jury refuses to make a finding of fraud. Then the bond would have to be 400 million, right?"

"What do you think?" asked a seemingly disgusted Cienfuegos. "The bond will be whatever the final judgment adds up to, plus interest and court costs."

Becker was crunching numbers in his head, sweating profusely, biting his nails. "Even if it's a three- or four-hundred-million-dollar judgment . . . it would have to include pre-judgment interest . . . since the time the Foundation received the property from

McKnight many decades ago. And that would be . . . close to . . . oh, my God. Ten billion!"

"Judge," Alex chimed in, "what if we got it wrong? What if the jury's just trying to get a reaction from us, the attorneys."

Cienfuegos looked ready to reach across the desk and slap some sense into Alex. "Son, I've been at this long enough to know that this jury is getting ready to hand you and your clients a mega-million dollar winning ticket, power ball included. Now, I could be wrong . . . but I doubt it." Cienfuegos then looked at all the other attorneys in the room. "I suggest you all go outside, call your clients and remind them of the cash bond they will have to post before any appeal is taken."

"Judge," Ramírez blurted out, "but . . . how do we . . . "

Fonseca interrupted him, "I can't believe this, my client's gonna flip."

Becker stated: "*Caramba*, never in a million years did I imagine it would come to this!"

"Enough!" yelled Cienfuegos. "Go out and get this thing settled." He then turned to McDermott and in a very serious tone said, "remember, if we have to go into the damages portion of the trial . . . these jurors will get to consider the net worth of your client. What do you think they're going to award when the highest income earner only makes fifty thousand dollars a year working long stressful hours as a nurse down at a hospital? What do you think is going to happen when they hear evidence that the Foundation makes that in an hour on days when the price per barrel of crude trades above the fifty dollar mark?"

McDermott was in disbelief. What Cienfuegos was saying, unfortunately, was true, and it made perfect sense. Once the jury considered the fistfuls and fistfuls of money the Foundation made, every month, it would not have any difficulty awarding 400 million and more.

McDermott now had a frown on her face, and so did Fonseca, Ramírez and Becker. The sad, sad reality of their predicament started to sink in. Instead of having the appearance of successful trial lawyers, the group, Alex included, looked like a bunch of sad relatives at Granny's funeral. McDermott and the others could already see in their minds the closing argument Alex would deliver after the second phase of the trial. He would probably get up in front of the jury and ask them to now ask the Church to tithe 10% back to his clients. Not 20%, not 50%, just 10%. It was a simple argument, easy to understand. The jury, made up of Catholics, would understand the concept. With just a 10% tithing from what the foundation made every year, going back to when McKnight wrongfully, and without authority, willed La Minita to the defendant, the number would probably be in excess of two billion dollars. At the end of the day, the plaintiffs were poised to receive a billionaire verdict, and the foundation and the others would have to post an equal bond before even attempting to appeal. The whole thing was sickening.

"Go make some calls, people," suggested Cienfuegos as he looked down at his wristwatch. "It is now 1:15, so be back in thirty minutes . . . I'll be waiting. And don't forget . . . the intervenors might be asked to pitch in and help with the bond . . . if the Foundation doesn't have the cash reserves. Just so you know. Now scram!"

CHAPTER 42

"LADIES AND GENTLEMEN of the jury," announced Judge Cienfuegos, his gold-rimmed bifocals perched on top of his nose. The jurors were now back in the courtroom. "I sent my bailiff to go get you because I've been informed that the parties have reached a settlement and that your services are no longer needed. I want to thank you for your hard work. Due to your diligence, this case is now settled. Because you took the time to listen to the evidence, evaluate the same and work very hard during your deliberations, a compromise was reached. Congratulations!"

The jurors all looked at each other, looking half-surprised, half-confused. Despite their reaction, there was a collective sigh of relief.

Cienfuegos continued talking. "I know you all must be really tired and anxious to get back to your loved ones. It's up to you if you want to stick around the courthouse and talk to the lawyers involved in the case. Likewise, you don't have to talk to anybody if you don't want to. So, you're all excused, and thank you for all your hard work. Go home and get some rest."

"Thank you, Judge," replied the jury, at once, and proceeded to march out of the courtroom, single file, following the bailiff, without making eye contact with any of the lawyers.

Earlier, in an effort to get the jurors home, Judge Cienfuegos had instructed the bailiff to escort them out through a back exit. That way, the jurors would not have to face the throngs of reporters outside.

As it happens quite often—particularly in trials that last several weeks—jurors have no desire to stick around and talk to the attorneys. Most jurors simply want to come up for air, get back to their families, their jobs and daily lives. Once Cienfuegos was informed that the jurors had left the vicinity of the courthouse, he directed his attention to the attorneys in the courtroom. "Who's going to prepare the settlement documents?"

"I will," volunteered McDermott, still trembling, about to go into shock. "That won't be a problem."

"I want the documents signed by all the parties in ten days," instructed Cienfuegos, "and the settlement checks delivered in fifteen days. Don't forget to keep this confidential . . ."

"Judge!" cried Fonseca, "that's not enough time. As the court is aware, not only do we need a confidential settlement and indemnity agreement, but the plaintiffs will have to sign and file quit claim deeds giving up all rights to La Minita. There's over 300 plaintiffs . . . we cannot possibly get it all done in fifteen days."

"Yes, I understand," countered Cienfuegos, "but the joint motion to dismiss, the settlement documents and the checks can be exchanged in fifteen days. You guys can then worry about finalizing the deeds and any other title documents later. I'll give you an additional sixty days to get that portion done. I'm sure Mr. Del Fuerte can help you with that . . . gather all the clients and have them sign those other documents you all want."

"Sure," chirped Alex.

"See?" Cienfuegos banged his gavel on the bench. "Okay, this court is now adjourned."

"All rise!" yelled the bailiff as he waited for the judge to get down from the bench and exit the courtroom through a side door. "We'll be in recess."

"So, how did we do?" asked Romeo as he and Alex drove down Highway 77 on their way home.

"Two-fifty," answered Alex, shrugging his shoulders.

"Two hundred fifty thousand! Wow, that's not bad. That's a lot of cash. The clients are going to be very happy."

Alex turned and looked at Romeo. "Two hundred fifty million. We're talking nine figures here, 250,000,000 . . . a quarter of a billion dollars."

Romeo's jaw dropped to his lap, and he almost lost control of the Escalade. Alex had to reach over, grab the steering wheel and help him under-correct. "Watch it! You're gonna get us killed."

"Are you serious?" asked Romeo, eyes wide open. "That's about $100,000,000 in fees for our firm, right?"

"Something like that."

"Wow, boss. You did it! You socked it to Salamanca and his lawyers . . . that's freaking amazing. Nothing short of a miracle!"

Alex was now working on his third cigarette. "I don't know . . . I'm not so sure."

"What do you mean?" asked Romeo.

"Oh, nothing. It's not gonna matter, anyway. The firm's splitting up."

"What?"

"Look, Gigi doesn't want to be around me. Michael and I had some words the other day. He said he wants to go back home, to Houston. So maybe it's better if we all go our separate ways. I screwed up. I threw it all away because I was too blind to see, or too stupid."

Romeo fumbled with the radio and found a station playing *conjunto* music. He lowered the volume. "But, you and I can still work together, right? I mean you'll have your own office, take your own cases, right?"

Alex looked out the window. Over in the eastern horizon, he could see the entrance to his ranch, El Caudillo. "*No sé*. What's the use of having another fifty or a hundred million in the bank if you can't have the one thing that matters most to you."

It was four o'clock in the afternoon when Alex and Romeo strolled into the office building. Betty and Astrid started clapping and cheering as soon as the boss and Romeo set foot inside the reception area.

"Congratulations, Alex," cheered Astrid from behind the reception desk. She was beaming with pride. "We've heard the news already."

"Yes," added Betty, "there was a newsbreak on channel 5, at three o'clock. The bulletin said that the parties had reached an undisclosed, confidential settlement, that the case was over."

"That's right," Alex said.

Astrid put her index finger to her lips, looked around making sure no one else was watching, and whispered that Gigi was in her office, down the hall. With her hands, she gestured to Alex that she appeared to be packing things up.

Alex seemed surprised by Astrid's revelation, but went ahead and removed his coat, tossed it to Romeo, loosened his tie and rolled up his sleeves. He needed to face the music.

"I didn't expect to see you here," started Alex as he poked his head into Gigi's office.

"Just packing my things," Gigi replied, trying to be polite. "I don't think I'm going to be practicing law for a while." She was emptying her desk drawers, throwing things into a trash can while separating the important papers and placing those on her desk.

"I see. How've you been feeling?" asked Alex. "Are you still throwing up?"

"No," she shrugged her shoulders, "now I'm just hungry all the time."

"You look great," volunteered Alex. "I mean it."

"With this *panza*? You gotta be kidding. I'm at thirty-five weeks and look how big I am. Sleeping is proving to be impossible. I don't know if I'll make it to forty weeks. This is the hardest thing I've ever done."

Alex smiled and said, "Well, you look beautiful. And I completely understand if you don't want to have anything to do with me or this law firm."

"Let's not go there, okay? Let me just pack my things and get out of here. Maybe we can talk some other time, but not now. I have a doctor's appointment in thirty minutes, and I've got to finish packing these boxes. If you don't mind, my brothers will come by later on during the week and move out all my office furniture and these boxes."

"They don't need to do that," remarked Alex. "I can hire an outfit to move the stuff for you . . . deliver it to your home or storage, whatever you want."

"It's okay, they've agreed to help. Thanks."

Alex let out a big sigh. "Okay, then. And where should I send you the $20,000,000 you have coming from the Santibáñez case? We just settled it for 250 this morning . . . It's confidential, just so you know. As a partner, you still get a cut from that."

Gigi finished stuffing and taping the box sitting on top of her desk. "I want no part of it. Thanks. Keep it, spend it, do whatever you want to do with it. Give it back, I don't care. It's not mine. I didn't earn it and don't deserve a penny of it. That case brought us nothing but misery. And you and I have paid the ultimate price."

"Okay, I see. I get it. Anyway, I'll be down the hall," protested Alex as he started walking away, feeling helpless and annoyed. "Holler if you need anything. *De veras, lo que sea.*"

"Good-bye, Alex," replied Gigi, "we're done."

CHAPTER 43

O SCAR SANTIBÁÑEZ WAS all smiles as he sat across from Alex's desk, holding a two-inch stack of settlement checks totaling $150,000,000. It had been fifteen days since the trial ended, and the checks in his right hand had finally been issued from Del Fuerte, Fetzer & Montemayor's trust account, with some being as little as $50,000 and some as large as $5,000,000. Michael and Alex, under the guidance of their trusted CPA, Manny Valdez, had decided to split the loot among the plaintiffs in accordance with whatever percentage of ownership they each had in the mineral estate of La Minita. Thus, each plaintiff's individual recovery would be in proportion to the size of his or her ownership interest.

Oscar, the leader of the clan and the group's organizer, had received a check in the amount of $3,000,000. Mago's kids—the deranged cousin that had blasted Father Benito—would each receive checks for $100,000 for a total of $1,000,000.

"What are you going to do with your money?" asked Alex, pretending to really care as he studied Oscar sitting across from him. Alex peeked at his watch. It was 9:00 A.M. His mind was racing, and it had nothing to do with the $100,000,000 he had made his firm or how he was going to spend it. He was seriously preoccupied, almost obsessed, with finding a way to get Gigi back. What was going to happen with his twins? Would Gigi find another guy, marry him and move out of state, far away from Texas?

"Probably pay for my grandkids' college education. Then, I'll give some to the church and try to save the rest. Maybe even start a little business, who knows. I do need a new fishing boat, though. I think I'll splurge on that."

"The church, really?" asked Alex.

Oscar shrugged his shoulders. "I guess it's part of my upbringing . . . we were taught to give to the church."

Alex's cell phone started vibrating. He looked at the screen. It was Yarrington. "That sounds really good. Listen," he said, looking up, "I've got to take this phone call."

"I'll get going. I've taken a lot of your time," said Oscar as he got up and headed for the door, manila envelope in hand. "I'll let myself out. Again, thanks for everything."

Alex pressed the cell phone to his ear and finished waving good-bye to Oscar while also signaling to close the door behind him.

"This is Alex."

"Alex, son," Yarrington said at the other end of the line, "just wanted to give you a heads-up. There's a trial lawyers' continuing legal education seminar at the Bellagio in Vegas in February. Are you going?"

"I hadn't planned on it," countered Alex.

"Why don't you make plans to attend. It's important."

"Do you have the dates?"

"It starts on Thursday, the 17th, and goes until Saturday, the 20th. It's the Super Trial Lawyer's Boot Camp. It promises to be a lot of fun."

"I don't know if I can make it. Gigi's slated to give birth early part of March, around that date. I'd like to be around for the birth of my twins," explained Alex. "They could come early."

"I'll tell you what," continued Yarrington, "just come up for one day. Any day. We'll take care of business and then you can fly back. What do you say?"

"All right, I'll figure something out. We'll be in touch."

"See you in Vegas," finished Yarrington.

Alex and Michael were having a late lunch at the Macaroni Grill in McAllen. It was almost four o'clock, and they had just left Reagan Denham's office, the Rio Grande Valley's supreme mediator. He had helped them split the partnership, divide the remaining cases and work out a severance package for the employees.

"Well," started Michael, "I'm glad we got this done. I hope Gigi's happy with the arrangement. Too bad she didn't want to participate, although I think we got her a really good result."

Michael and Alex were referring to the trust they had created for Gigi's benefit. It would be funded with her share of the Santibáñez settlement, and it would provide for her and the kids, nicely, for the rest of their lives. She would also have access to an account flush with cash, all of five million dollars.

"You've been talking to her, right?" asked Alex. "The truth."

"How is the truth important now, Alex? Besides, what does it matter, anyway?"

Alex played with his snifter full of Amaretto di Saronno and gave it a couple of twirls. "It's just that I'd like for you to deliver a message."

"And what's that?"

"That I love her and . . . would like a second chance. To see if she could find it in her heart to forgive me," Alex had a hard time uttering the words.

"Alex," said Michael as he played with his *gelato,* "be a man, . . . learn from this experience and move on. I'm embarrassed to see you beg, really. You look pathetic . . . stop it."

"I love her, professor," cried Alex as he ran his fingers through his hair. "I now realize what an idiot I was. If I'd just listened. Don't you see, I'm completely alone. I have no one. My partners and my law firm, gone! Gigi wants nothing to do with me. My grandfather fell down, broke his hip, and is now back in the nursing home. I'm not even twenty-eight-years old and I'm a freakin' mess. I screwed everything up. Even you," continued Alex, "you've threatened to turn me in to the state bar."

"Alex!" snapped Michael, "you're being ridiculous. You're going to bounce back, find another girl and have plenty more children. And you and I know the State Bar of Texas is not going to do anything to you. But it's my obligation. The rules of professional conduct say I have to report you. Anyway, you'll just get a slap on the wrist, if anything. Cheer up, Alex. How many guys your age would kill to be in your shoes?"

"I might as well be dead . . . The settlement was not supposed to happen. I was supposed to lose the case," said Alex.

"But that was not your doing," exclaimed Michael. "That was the jury. And the judge forced you guys to settle."

"I suppose . . . but . . . "

"Come on," indicated Michael as he flagged their waiter to bring the tab. "We had a good run, Alex. We tried some good cases, we made money, you helped me regain my health. If I were you, I'd be packing my bags, getting ready to go travel the world. Meet girls and people from all over . . . and wait a few more years to settle down. Hell, I'd call Naiví up . . . tell her to take the semester off and invite her to Europe. I mean, when she worked at the office, I could see she really liked you. "

"Naiví is too smart to get involved with a *pendejo* like me. Besides, she almost got killed, too."

"You're being too hard on yourself, son. But I guess I understand how you feel. We have to go through some rough patches in life . . . it's a time for introspection . . . see what we want out of life . . . or figure out how we can enrich the lives of others. We need to experience the pain . . . it makes us grow up, change. Without change we're dead."

"I guess I have some growing up to do."

"We all do," said Michael, "sooner or later."

The waiter came around and delivered the tab. Michael pulled a roll of one-hundred-dollar bills from his pant pocket, peeled one away and tossed it on top of the check presenter.

"Keep the change," Michael insisted.

CHAPTER 44

YARRINGTON WAS ON his fourth single malt scotch and was down to his last thousand dollars in poker chips. He had been waiting, by himself, at the five-hundred-dollar-a-chip blackjack tables inside the Venetian for more than an hour. But there was no sign of Alejandro Del Fuerte. It was almost 2:00 A.M. when Alex finally showed up and took a seat next to him.

"What took you so long?" asked a startled Yarrington, his speech somewhat slurred.

Alex pulled out a pack of cigarettes, and before he could find his lighter, the croupier reached out with his. He took a couple of puffs and let out a big cloud of smoke.

"You try turning five million in cash into chips," replied Alex, as he got comfortable around the table. "What are you drinking, anyway?"

Yarrington placed one of his chips on the blackjack table. "Glen rocks, with a twist."

The dealer dealt Yarrington an eight of clubs and a two of diamonds. A cocktail waitress approached and asked Alex if he wanted something to drink. He ordered a scotch on the rocks.

"Hit," called out Yarrington to the dealer while simultaneously finger-tapping the table. Yarrington got a jack of hearts.

"Twenty," said the dealer.

In a matter of seconds the waitress was back with Alex's drink. He thanked her and continued to watch Yarrington play.

"Stay," called Yarrington.

The dealer then flipped her next card. "Twenty-one," announced the dealer.

Yarrington cursed his luck and tossed the dealer his last five-hundred-dollar chip as a tip.

Both Alex and Yarrington got up from the table and headed toward the elevators. The doors opened and Alex pushed the button to the tenth floor.

"So, what did you think of Cienfuegos?" asked Yarrington.

"The guy was a blowhard."

"Sure, but wasn't El Mago amazing? We don't call Cienfuegos 'The Wizard' for nothing, you know."

"Was that your doing?" asked Alex as flashbacks of the trial came gushing.

Yarrington sipped his drink while enjoying the slow ride to the higher floors. "I told Powers what we needed done . . . and he took care of the rest."

"What do you mean 'took care of the rest'?"

The elevator stopped. The doors opened, and Alex and Yarrington got off. They started to walk down the hallway.

"Look," said Yarrington, "the only way you were going to win the case was to have a judge that wanted to play ball, understand?"

"I don't follow," said Alex as he set his empty glass down on a tray from room service, outside one of the rooms. The gold tray was covered in cloth napkins and plates with leftover toast points, lox, capers and purple onions.

"I've known for a long time that Powers wanted to be appointed to the Texas Supreme Court. The only way that was going to happen was for someone to whisper his name in the governor's ear. And that someone would be me. So, in exchange for having him appoint Cienfuegos to hear the case, I had to come through. If you read the papers next week, don't be surprised when you find out who'll be the newest appointee to the Texas Supreme Court."

"You're fucking amazing, you know that," Alex reproached, reaching for another cigarette.

"It's politics, son. People don't realize or don't like to hear it, but that's how the game is played . . . unfortunately that's our system."

"And Cienfuegos?"

"I asked Powers to do me a favor, make sure Cienfuegos got to hear the case. Emilio was glad to do it," explained Yarrington. "That's one judge I can always count on, always reliable, always dependable, always willing to lend a hand. It's hard to find judges that want to get in the ring and fumble-tumble, you know. But those that do . . . go far, career-wise, and become very rich."

Still reeling, Alex pulled the card key to his room from his coat pocket, opened the door and let Yarrington in first. He flipped the lights on and pointed at a duffel bag on top of the coffee table. "It's all there . . . more chips than you'll ever know what to do with."

Yarrington unzipped the bag, reached in and pulled a handful of ten-thousand-dollar chips. "Five million?"

"Yep. Five million."

"Aren't you glad I thought of you, Alex? To bring you in to handle the Santibáñez suit? I knew that with your guts and my connections we could make great things happen."

"Honestly, I wished I'd listened to Gigi . . . and not gotten involved. Things didn't turn out so great."

"Why would you say that? Powers gets what he wants, I make a nice referral fee, Cienfuegos will get the appointment that he wants to the Court of Criminal Appeals and your firm makes another cool one hundred million bucks. Where else can you get that kind of money?"

"This case almost got me killed . . . and I don't think I'm out of danger yet." Alex said as the pair started walking out of the room. "Looking back, I really didn't need another fifty or a hundred million in the bank. What's the use if I don't have anybody to share it with?"

"You don't have to be alone, Alex. Paloma has always loved you. You could give her a call . . . see where that goes."

"Stop," demanded Alex, "don't even go there."

"Anyway, I wouldn't worry about Salamanca. The guy's a pussycat."

"A pussycat?! This is the same guy that never forgot you voted against him. The guy that financed your opponent when you ran for Congress and defeated your ass, so convincingly, to the point you had to file for bankruptcy, remember? Or have you already forgotten?"

The pair started walking out of the room.

"That's water under the bridge, son." Yarrington suddenly annoyed, changed the subject. "Anyway, how long are you staying in Vegas?"

"Friday morning. I've got to get back."

"Too bad. Cienfuegos is one of the preeminent lecturers at the seminar. He comes in Saturday morning. I wish you'd stay. We're going to hit the craps tables . . . maybe play some roulette. Head out to the strip clubs. Should be a lot of fun," added Yarrington as he lifted the duffel bag and tossed it over his shoulder. "Maybe even bring six or seven girls back to our room."

The attorney and the lieutenant governor were now standing in front of the elevators. Alex went to push the down button, but Yarrington reached out and said, "Wait, Alex. There's one more thing."

"What?"

"A new and interesting business proposal," declared Yarrington.

"Are you kidding me?!"

"Let me just put it out there . . . see what you think. If you're interested, we can talk later, okay?"

The elevator suddenly opened. Some people walked out and Alex and Yarrington jumped in.

Alex was shaking his head, looking down at the carpet, waiting for the doors to close. Yarrington started explaining the new venture.

"In case you didn't know, Mexico has over two hundred consular offices throughout the United States. Now, every time an illegal alien, or even a U.S. permanent resident that migrated from Mexico, dies or gets injured, even gets arrested over here, the U.S. authorities have to call the closest consular office. It's all in the Hague Convention. I've had my staffers do the research, it's quite simple, really."

"So?"

"Think about it."

"Think about what?" snapped Alex, waiting for the elevator to stop.

Yarrington was now flashing his trademark toothy grin. "The unlimited stream of referrals, the never-ending supply of wrongful death lawsuits. Maybe even some headline-grabbing criminal cases. Remember the one with the Mexican kids that got shot by U.S. Border Patrol agents? You'd be getting calls for similar cases."

"Those cases are hard to make," answered Alex, "all kinds of governmental immunity issues."

"So what?! Think of the publicity, Alex. You get your name out there and join the big leagues. You could be the next DeGuerin, Scheck, David Boise or Gerry Spence."

"I'm not interested," Alex declared.

"If you don't jump in, some asshole lawyer from Austin or Houston will steal it, run the case, right under our noses . . . don't you see?"

Alex was looking down on the floor, shaking his head. "Listen to you. 'Our noses'?"

"It's all there for the taking, son. All we need to do is get an appointment with the Mexican president, have him order all of Mexico's consular offices to call you . . . the 'well-connected' Alejandro Del Fuerte and presto!"

"What makes you think you or I can get in to see the Mexican president, anyway?"

"An old golfing buddy of mine happens to be one of his closest advisors. All it'll take is a call."

Alex was baffled. On the one hand, having done business with Yarrington had almost cost him his life, had also taken a toll on his relationship with Gigi, not to mention his friendship with Michael. On the other hand—he'd hate to admit it—the lieutenant governor had the golden touch and the friends to make great things happen. It was no different than the U.S. president invading a foreign country to help his *compadres* in the oil business. Or the same thing the Texas governor had done when he suddenly —without rhyme or reason—created the Texas Construction Development Council to insulate all his friends and campaign contributors in the construction industry from lawsuits. *Puro* "scratch my back and I'll scratch yours."

Alex cleared his throat. "I'm not interested. For starters, you're going to want a cut, so will your golfing buddy, and so will the *presidente* and everybody else for that matter. Or are you telling me that you don't want anything out of this deal?" asked Alex, point-blank.

"Hell, no! I'm putting the deal together. . . . I'd like my cut," cried Yarrington as he waved the large duffel bag in front of Alex's face. "We could then approach the presidents of Argentina, Brazil, Guatemala . . . every Tom, Dick and Harry that has consular offices in the U.S. They'll all be sending us their cases. You and I will be billionaires!" Yarrington declared, brimming with excitement.

"What about the state bar of Texas?"

"What about it?"

"They can yank my license for splitting fees with non-attorneys or for paying for cases."

"The state bar will leave us alone, I wouldn't worry about them. I'll handle them. Look, if you're so concerned, we form a foreign corporation that earns consulting fees, and it's that foreign corporation that cuts the checks to the foreign leaders."

"I appreciate the offer, but I'm going to pass, okay?"

"Or, if it makes you feel any better," continued Yarrington, "you set up a nonprofit to be funded with the millions made from the cases referred by the foreign governments, hire my wife and Paloma to run it . . . "

"No," Alex cut him off.

"Well," replied Yarrington, "think about it. Let me know if you change your mind."

"I've made up my mind, and it's no, thanks anyway," Alex said in a polite manner.

Yarrington stood there, silently, observing Alex. The elevator doors finally opened and Alex hurried out.

"Well, I guess I'll see you back in Texas," said Yarrington with a flashy smile. "Have a safe trip."

"Later," replied Alex as he watched the doors slide shut and Yarrington disappear.

Yarrington was waiting for Judge Cienfuegos in a courtesy limo from the Venetian, outside the Las Vegas airport. It was nine in the morning on Saturday and despite having stayed up all night, playing blackjack and losing over $100,000, he'd managed to freshen up and look presentable for the upcoming get-together with his dearest and closest *compadre.*

As he sat there, in the back of the limo, Yarrington noticed Cienfuegos walking out of the airport while being assisted with his bags by the chauffer who would be driving them around that morning. The driver quickly tossed Cienfuegos' bags in the trunk and proceeded to get the door for the judge.

"Well, look at you," said Cienfuegos stepping in and stretching his right hand out. "Looks like you've been having a lot of fun already. I've got some catching up to do."

Yarrington shook hands with the judge. "Don't worry. You'll have plenty of time to catch up." Yarrington put the divider up for additional privacy. "We could stay here an additional week, if you want. We certainly can afford it."

"How did we do?" Cienfuegos asked, grinning from ear to ear. He was wearing linen shorts, a tropical print short sleeve and leather sandals. "A million each," lied Yarrington. "Yours is back at the hotel, all in chips, waiting to be cashed out."

"Not bad for six weeks' worth of work," Cienfuegos mumbled. "Thanks for bringing me in on this deal. It'll pay for my daughter's graduate school. Did I tell you she's pursing a masters in contemporary art at the Sorbonne, in Paris?"

"Josie?"

"Yep, she's the baby, but the one that I worry about the most. My three others are all married, with good jobs, and doing their own thing. But Josie? Ha! That's another story . . . that girl marches to the beat of her own drum."

"Well, she shouldn't have any problems landing herself a good-looking man," remarked Yarrington. "She's a gorgeous little girl. The freckles, the green eyes, the long brown curls."

"She's very picky, though. Really spoiled, if you ask me."

"And whose fault is that?" Yarrington reached for a Budweiser from the mini bar in the limo. "Care for one?"

"Let me knock out my presentation, and then we'll do some serious drinking. How's that?"

"What time do you go on?"

"One o'clock. It's just forty-five minutes long. Then we can go have us some real fun, huh?"

Yarrington opened his beer and took a big swig. "Hey, let me ask you. How did you get the parties to settle? That must have taken some arm-twisting . . . ?"

"It was tough, all right. For a moment there, I thought my house of cards would come tumbling down. Talk about judicial misconduct."

Yarrington finished his beer and proceeded to light up a Cuban cigar. "This sounds like something I want to hear."

"Well," started Cienfuegos, "it had been almost ten days, and the jurors hadn't reached a verdict and hadn't sent out any notes. We were clueless as to what was happening in the deliberations room. They'd given no indication, not even a note, a question, a request for us to send in more material or exhibits . . . I mean nothing. We had no idea what the hell was going on in there. But I kind of knew that some of the jurors would probably want to award something to the plaintiffs."

"Was that because the time it had taken?"

"Yep. Usually, if their minds are made up . . . they come back one way or the other, but fast. And here, they were probably struggling. So I saw a window of opportunity and jumped all over it."

"And what was that?"

"On the tenth day we finally get a jury note." Cienfuegos leaned forward and whispered, "And the bailiff delivers it straight to me, right?"

"Okay."

"And none of the lawyers are around. I guess they're all scattered about the courthouse . . . but no one is back in chambers."

"So then?"

"Well, the bailiff hasn't read it. He's not supposed to. So, he doesn't know how it reads. Or what's in it. So, I read it. It's from the foreman. It says, Judge, we're deadlocked, 7 to 5 for the foundation."

"Oh, my god," cried Yarrington. "And then?"

"I replaced their note with my own note."

"What?" asked Yarrington as he puffed furiously, the hint of rum and spices wafting through the air.

"I wrote a fake note, instead. My note said, 'Judge, we're ready to start awarding damages. What's the minimum, maximum? Would $400,000,000 be too much?'"

Yarrington started laughing hysterically. "You wrote the jury note?"

"Yep," Cienfuegos answered, beaming with emotion. "But I still had to sell it to the parties. So, I sent the bailiff back with a response to the real note. He's not around when I write it, so I just have him deliver it. It says,

> Dear jury, you've been working too hard. Maybe you need a break. Let me send you to a three-hour lunch, be back at 2:00 P.M., and then we'll decide what to do.
>
> Signed, Judge Cienfuegos.

"And then?" Yarrington asked as he reached for another beer.

"I call everybody to chambers. We have a jury note we need to discuss."

"And how did you convince them? That must've been a tough sell, right? What if you'd gotten caught?"

"I had to use the extreme 'appellate bond' argument because McDermott's client did not want to settle. They didn't care. They were going to appeal and run the plaintiffs ragged and into the ground. When they saw the note, the amount of damages being discussed, it finally worked. Once they put pencil to paper and looked at the whole thing from a purely business-decision perspective . . . it made sense to get the case settled."

"Wow! I guess that's why you're worth the big bucks, Emilio. Well, congratulations. Good job." Yarrington stretched his hand out, took the judge's right hand in his, and firmly shook it.

"Now I need to enjoy the fruits of my labor," countered Cienfuegos.

Yarrington raised his can of beer and toasted. "Indeed . . . indeed, you deserve it, all of it!"

As the pair toasted their good fortune, Yarrington secretly hoped that his close friend would never find out he'd yipped him out of his share from the remaining three million dollars.

CHAPTER 45

WEEKS AFTER the trip to Vegas, Alex found himself having breakfast at La Fonda Chiquita. He was sipping his coffee while reading about Papichulo—how one of the Cartel's top lieutenants had been gunned down by Mexican Marines outside Tampico—when his cell phone started vibrating. It was Gigi's mother.

"Hello?"

"Alex," said Mrs. Montemayor, almost out of breath. She sounded extremely upset. "Gisela's missing. She didn't come home last night. Is she with you?"

"What?!" cried Alex. "What do you mean missing?" Immediately, images of Tiny and his henchmen flashed in Alex's mind. "Are you sure, Mrs. Montemayor? When was she supposed to be back?"

Mrs. Montemayor started sobbing at the other end of the line. "She called me from the mall that she felt a painful contraction coming on and she was going to swing by her doctor's office . . . just to get it checked out . . . make sure she wasn't in labor. She never came home."

"Did she make it to the doctor?" asked Alex, now increasingly upset and agitated, his stomach in knots.

"Yes, Dr. Kingsbury saw her. Everything was normal. She sent her home. That was around 5:30 in the afternoon. A nurse leaving work said she saw Gisela walking to her car, there in the parking lot."

Alex got up from his table and headed outside the restaurant to the parking lot, where he could smoke. "Have you called the police?"

"That's why I was calling you. I was hoping you could help us. Tell us what to do."

"You stay by the phone, got it? I'm heading over to see some friends at the FBI, see if they can help. I'll call you in thirty minutes."

Alex snapped the cell shut, walked inside the restaurant and threw a twenty on the table. He picked up his car keys and bolted out the door.

"Is everything all right?" shouted Juan from inside.

"No," yelled Alex, "it's Gigi."

The new FBI headquarters in Brownsville was located inside a residential neighborhood. On the outside, the place looked like a normal home, but inside, the place resembled an emergency command center. When Alex walked in, he went up to a receptionist and asked for Special Agent Schlaeter. Behind the reception area, there was only one door that was secured by a special lock.

The pretty receptionist got on the phone and dialed Schlaeter's extension. "He'll be right with you, Mr. Del Fuerte. Please take a seat."

Alex was pacing back and forth. After about five minutes, Agent Schlaeter popped out from behind the door and waved Alex to follow him to the back.

After walking down a hall, they stopped in Schlaeter's office. The special agent asked Alex to sit down, and Schlaeter took his place behind his desk. "What can I do for you, Mr. Del Fuerte? The receptionist said it was an emergency, are you all right?"

"Remember Gigi Montemayor, my fiancée?"

"Yes."

"She's missing. She's pregnant with twins, apparently went to her OB-Gyn for a quick checkup yesterday, and hasn't been heard from since. Her mother's freaking out. I decided to skip BPD and come straight to you . . . see if you could help."

Schlaeter uttered, "Really?"

"Yes, I've tried calling her cell . . . she's not answering . . . goes straight to voicemail. Can you help us find her?"

The special agent reached for the laptop on his desk. "I'll need some information. For starters, let me have her car's license plate number and the make and model."

Alex gave him the information, including Gigi's full name, date of birth and a general physical description. As he sat there, sitting across from the agent, Alex said he could email Schlaeter some pictures of Gigi he had stored on his cell phone. "These should also help," Alex said as he hit the send button.

"Do you know if the OB-Gyn has video cameras for the parking lot?"

"They should, it's a professional plaza, with different doctors for tenants. But, I'm not exactly sure," confessed Alex.

"Which professional plaza is that?"

"It's the one next to the new CVS, across from the old hospital."

Schlaeter continued typing all the information on his laptop. "I've put out a missing person's bulletin with her information to all the other sister agencies, ICE, Border Patrol, DEA, including our neighbors south of the border. Let me send one of my junior agents to the medical plaza to see if there are any videotapes."

"Thanks, Jim. I owe you. Let me give you my card with all my numbers," Alex said as he reached for his wallet and pulled out a business card. "Call me as soon as you know anything, please. I don't care what time it is, okay?"

Schlaeter started getting up, picked up the business card from his desk and stuck it in his front shirt pocket. "We should know something within the next six to eight hours. Hang tight."

"Thanks," Alex muttered. "I pray to God they're okay."

"We think we have something, Alex," remarked the agent at the other end of the line. "You're gonna want to see this. Can you get here ASAP?"

By the time Schlaeter's call came in, it was nine in the morning the next day. Alex had been unable to sleep a single wink. He'd tossed and turned all night as he retraced in his mind the last few days and tried to piece together the mystery of Gigi's disappearance. After leaving Schlaeter's office the day before, Alex had spent the afternoon with Gigi's family.

The entire day had been spent discussing the pros and cons of going public with the information. Alex had even suggested having a press conference, but Gigi's parents, being extremely private people, had not welcomed the idea.

Alex jumped out of bed, threw on a T-shirt and a pair of jeans, and raced to the urgent appointment. It took him less than twenty-five minutes to make it to Schlaeter's office, from South Padre.

"Follow me," indicated the special agent as he appeared outside the door behind the reception desk.

Alex bolted to his feet and followed the agent. "I appreciate you calling me and keeping me informed. I hope it's good news."

Schlaeter did not answer, but kept a serious demeanor. The pair walked into a media room with all kinds of gadgets and video equipment, and Schlaeter pointed to a chair for Alex to sit down. The agent then took a video disk with the words "Montemayor, Gisela" written on it and plopped it into a DVD player. A prompt screen came on, and Schlaeter clicked the RealPlayer icon on the screen.

"This is the video from outside the professional plaza on the day of Gigi's disappearance," said Schlaeter as the video began to play. "You'll be able to see cars coming and going and back here, on the top right side of the screen, you'll be able to see when Gigi pulls into the parking lot."

Alex immediately recognized Gigi's red Saab as it pulled into a parking space next to an older model Tahoe. Gigi got out of her car. There she was, fast-walking into the professional plaza. She was wearing her hair up in a ponytail, sporting sweatpants, a UT Longhorn windbreaker and tennis shoes. Alex noticed that she still looked as beautiful as ever.

Alex could feel his pulse beginning to race, afraid of what he was about to witness.

"I'm going to fast-forward it, okay?" said Schlaeter. "Although nothing happens for the next hour while Gigi visits the doctor, I want you to see what happens after she comes out of the clinic.

As Schlaeter played with the video machine and the fast-forward button, Alex made the sign of the cross and quietly prayed for a miracle.

"Okay," remarked Schlaeter, "here we go. Here she's coming out of the building." He hit the play button and the video resumed its normal speed. "Now watch what happens as she gets closer to her car."

Alex was glued to the monitor, the blood pressure beginning to build around his temples, his stomach tied in knots.

"Right here," snapped Schlaeter as he hit the slow-play button. The images showed a very pregnant Gigi on her cell phone, completely unaware of her surroundings, slowly approaching her car. Out of nowhere, a pickup truck suddenly came into view and blocked her car, while three men grabbed Gigi and pushed her into the truck as her car keys, cell phone and purse went flying. Two seconds later, the pickup truck was gone from view, but one of the men remained behind collecting Gigi's belongings from the parking lot grounds. He then got into Gigi's car and sped away.

"What the hell!" screamed Alex. "Oh, my God." He put his head down between his hands and began hyperventilating. "This can't be . . . she's pregnant, for the love of God. Who'd want to do this?!"

Schlaeter couldn't answer. As he sat there thinking of choosing his words carefully, all that came out was, "I'm afraid . . . it gets worse."

"What do you mean?" asked Alex. He was now white as a ghost.

"This morning, I got word from the *comandante* in Matamoros that they found Gigi's Saab."

"They took them to Mexico?!" Alex was now standing, pacing back and forth, going berserk. "And Gigi? Our babies? Are they okay? Did they find them?"

Schlaeter would not answer.

"Answer me. Is she okay?!" demanded Alex. "Have they found them?!"

"They pulled the car from an irrigation ditch outside Matamoros. There was no sign of your fiancée," explained Schlaeter.

"Nothing else to go on. I'm sorry. The *comandante* seems to think Gigi's parents will get a call soon . . . the abductors probably want money. They're letting the car dry out and then they'll run tests to see if they can come up with some evidence . . . hair, fibers, fingerprints, anything left behind by the assailants."

Alex fell to his knees, numb with pain, and feeling as if he was in a horror movie. "Please, this can't be happening. Please tell me it's not happening."

"There's more," interrupted Schlaeter. "We were able to trace the plates on the truck from the parking lot. It's registered to a guy with connections to the Mexican Syndicate, a gang that's known to work with some bad folks from across the border. And I mean bad people, Alex. They usually don't mess around with the public, which makes this kidnapping highly unusual."

"I can't believe this is happening!" screamed Alex as he stumbled over to a trash can next to Schlaeter's work station and began throwing up.

"If it's the gang I'm thinking of," continued Schlaeter, "you need to prepare her family . . . These guys take the money and still kill the victims . . . just for kicks. It's all a game."

"No, it can be!!!" pleaded Alex.

"What really bothers me, though," added the senior agent, "is the idea that they would target a female . . . with no known ties to any criminal organization. Usually, these gangs kill each other . . . for them to pick out Ms. Montemayor, at random . . . it just doesn't make sense."

"Can we help her? Call somebody? Do something?" begged Alex.

"I'm so sorry," Schlaeter said as he tried to help Alex back to his feet. He had fallen back to his knees. "Do you want me to tell her parents or do you want to do it?"

Alex felt the walls crashing down all around him as the floor opened up and started swallowing him whole. "I'll talk to them. Just let me . . . regain . . . my composure," replied Alex. *What can I possibly tell them? That this is all my fault? That I'm responsible?*

It was late March and Alex was sitting alone at Tino's Seafood Can-tina on South Padre Boulevard, debating whether he should have one last tequila shot and try to bury the pain or simply go home.

The first few weeks since the disappearance, Alex spent most mornings in Schlaeter's FBI office, working the phones, tracking down new leads, while the evenings were reserved for visiting and comforting Gigi's parents. Without new developments, it was real hard to keep their spirits up. He'd also been busy fighting the Mexican authorities for the return of Gigi's vehicle. The *judiciales* wanted to keep it because they needed their own forensic techni-cian to process the vehicle for evidence. At first, Mexican officials promised it would be just a matter of days before the car was returned. Two weeks later, Gigi's Saab was still sitting in the back of a junkyard, while the forensic evidence, whatever was left of it, slowly fizzled away.

Alex was dealing with his own issues as well. He felt respon-sible for Gigi's disappearance and the guilt was slowly consuming him, eating away at him. What made it worse was not having received a single call, note, anything from the abductors. The silence and lack of leads had everyone stumped, including Schlaeter and the two FBI profilers still working on the case.

The situation was even more unbearable for Alex because he'd witnessed Gigi's father withering away as he tried to cope with the mounting pressure. His pregnant daughter was abducted; Mr. Montemayor's little princess risked a horrific death, rape, torture, humiliation and whole bunch of other things too horrible to imag-ine. And, on top of it all, no one knew if the twins were alive.

"Can you close me out?" asked Alex of Vicky, the bartender with the body piercings. "I need to go."

"Here you go," Vicky said as she gladly handed Alex his bar tab.

Alex picked up his tab, reached for a fifty and threw it on top of the bar. He picked up his cigarettes, his keys and proceeded to walk out of the establishment. When the cold March air hit him, his limbs went numb, and the effects of the alcohol were magni-fied. He decided to walk back to the penthouse.

The island at this time of the year resembled a ghost town. With the exception of a few wealthy Winter Texans that could afford to stay on the island during the winter months, the locals enjoyed the quiet downtime, having almost the entire place exclusively to themselves.

Alex pulled out a cigarette, lit it, puffed on it a couple of times and exhaled. He was putting away the box of cigarettes and his Zippo lighter, the one Gigi had bought him with Lady Justice engraved on the sides, when his cell phone went off.

Without looking to see who was calling, Alex pressed the cell to his ear and muttered, "Hello."

"If chuu wanna see your girlfriend and twins . . . chuu follow instructions, understand?" said the caller in broken English.

Before Alex could even utter a word, another person got on the phone. This time, the caller spoke in perfect English. "We need an inventory of all your assets, bank accounts, U.S. and offshore, and a list of all your real estate. We also need you to give us the names of three of your close friends, their net worth, along with their phone numbers, home addresses, names of businesses, cars they drive and the names of the schools that their children attend. You better not screw this up. And don't you dare go to the cops. If you do, you'll never see your family. No one can help you, got it? Not the FBI, not BPD, or anyone else. You'll hear from us soon."

"Wait," screamed Alex, "don't hang up! Who are you?!"

"You know who we are," said the voice. "*No te hagas pendejo.* We're your worst fucking nightmare, asshole. You still like *pozole,* amigo?"

"Tiny? Is this you?" Alex demanded to know, not really sure what to think. "How do I know you're for real?"

"Hear this," said the voice. In the background, Alex could clearly distinguish two babies crying and whaling away. "How's that for real, *pinche pendejo*?"

"Please don't hurt my babies!" begged Alex. "Please, for the love of God. Listen, listen. I'll give you whatever you want . . . just don't hurt them!"

"No screwing around, *puto,*" said the caller, "you'll hear from us soon. And remember, you better leave Schlaeter out of this."

"Put Gisela on the phone!" demanded Alex. "Let me talk to her, please! I need to know she's okay."

There was no reply.

"Hello? Are you there? Answer me!" screamed Alex.

But the caller was gone.

"*¡Cabrón, hijo de puta!*" Alex yelled into his cell.

By the time Alex got home to the Contessa di Mare, his heart was beating as loud as a five-piece drum set. He picked up the phone and thought about calling Schlaeter, but quickly decided against it. He then got on his computer and tried to send Michael an email, but could not force himself to hit the send button. Finally, he dialed 911, but when the operator came on and asked him about his emergency, he was unable to utter a single word. He turned off his cell, went to the kitchen and poured himself a shot of vodka.

The truth of the matter was that he was absolutely terrified. The bravado and courage that once had brought him fame and fortune in the courtrooms of South Texas had all but disappeared. And what made the situation worse was knowing that soon they would be calling back demanding he produce the inventories, exposing his assets and net worth.

In the old days, folks in Alex's predicament would probably have picked up the phone and asked the FBI to get involved. Others would have called their friends down at BPD, and they may have lent a hand. Except lately the rules of the game had changed. These were the days when the drug and human trafficking organizations south of the border had turned on the government, and the henchmen were now in control. Doing whatever it took to make money, be it kidnapping, extortion, drug trafficking, alien trafficking, racketeering or money laundering. These guys didn't give a rat's ass about the FBI, DEA or the American cops. These rogue mercenaries had become so brazen that no matter how many new federal agents were relocated to the border, the violence now routinely spilled over into South Texas. Law enforcement, on both sides of the border, was completely helpless and utterly unprepared to cope with this new threat. Not unlike the politicians roaming the streets in Austin and Washington.

So Alex, not knowing what else to do or who to call at that hour of the night, dialed Romeo on his cell. "Romeo, are you awake?"

"Yes, boss, what's going on?"

"I'm in deep trouble, serious trouble. I need your help."

"Give me forty-five minutes. I'll be right over."

Alex met Romeo downstairs in the lobby area of the Contessa di Mare. He was holding an unlit cigarette in his right hand and the box of Marlboros and lighter in his left hand. As soon as Romeo finished signing the log-in sheet with the guard at the security desk, Alex motioned him to follow him.

The pair walked out of the Contessa di Mare, past the swimming pools, the tennis courts and down to the beach. Alex stopped to light his cigarette and offered Romeo a cancer stick.

Romeo declined, "Boss, do you mind telling me what's going on?"

Alex took a drag from his cigarette, looked around and made sure they weren't being followed. He pointed south, toward the jetties. The pair started walking in that direction when Alex spoke. "I think I know who kidnapped Gigi, Romeo."

Romeo's eyes got wide open. "Are you sure, boss? Are you going to call the cops? Let the FBI handle it."

"I can't. If they get involved, they'll kill her and the twins," replied Alex as the pair made their way down the beach, the surf quietly pounding the shore. The thought of Gigi and his children being tossed into a barrel full of acid gave Alex pause and made him sick to his stomach.

"She had the twins?"

"Yes, I'm pretty sure. I heard them crying in the background. Those were my kids, I know it. I could feel it."

"What do you want me to do?" asked a dismayed Romeo, looking at his watch. It was 3:30 in the morning. "What are you thinking?"

"I'm supposed to deliver an inventory of all my assets, every-thing I own. I'm going to do it. And you're going to help me."

Romeo thought about this for a while. "Did they leave a call back number? Instructions, a drop-off place, anything?"

"No, nothing. The cell showed 'Private Call,' that's all."

"What about Gigi's parents? Should we tell them?"

"I'll have to sit down with them . . . explain to them what's going on."

Romeo was scratching his head. "Well, at least it sounds like they're alive. That's good news." Romeo was now gesturing Alex to fork over a cigarette. "But what exactly do they want from you?"

"Everything," explained Alex as he handed over his lighter to Romeo. "All my cash, all the valuables, properties, vehicles, *todo*. Otherwise, I'll never get to see them alive."

"So they want ransom money?" Romeo followed.

Alex just stood there, shrugging his shoulders.

"Why don't we call the police, let the authorities handle it?"

"I can't take that chance," answered Alex as he kicked the sand around with his toes. "I already told you, they'll kill them . . . and I can't let that happen. These guys are capable of anything." Alex had to stop. "Have you read the Mexican newspapers?"

Romeo noticed his boss getting teary-eyed.

Alex then reached for another cigarette, lit it up and took a long drag. He held his breath, finally letting out a big cloud of smoke. "It's too painful to even discuss . . . "

"Are you gonna go along then?" Romeo was now thinking of a few stories he'd read in Monterrey's *El Norte* newspaper about thugs targeting the rich. As a result of this latest crime wave, most wealthy Mexicans were migrating in droves to San Antonio, Hous-ton, Dallas and even cities in South Texas, like McAllen and Brownsville. They were getting the hell out of Mexico.

"Yes. What choice do I have?"

Romeo was now puffing on his cigarette, also kicking the sand around. "If you had told me three years ago when we met . . . that things were going to turn out this way . . . Jesus freakin' Christ! *¡Qué pinche locura!*"

Alex scratched the top of his head. "I guess I pissed somebody off."

"Salamanca?"

"More like God. I let it all go to my head."

Romeo flicked his half-smoked cigarette into the ocean. "Well, I'm here. Whatever you need, *jefe*, okay?"

"We have to wait for the call. I'm calling my broker, asking him to liquidate everything."

"Did they give you a deadline?"

Alex turned and looked out over the ocean. Five miles out, he could make out the flickering lights from a British Petroleum oil exploration platform. "I don't know. The man who called said they'd call me back . . . I should have everything ready in a couple of days, maybe. I don't know."

"I'll do whatever you want me to do," declared Romeo. "Just let me know . . . whatever I can do to help. You can always count on me."

"Thanks," said Alex sounding completely grateful. He patted Romeo on the back, "you're a good friend, you know that?"

"I'm here for you."

CHAPTER 46

T HE CANDLELIGHT VIGIL for the safe return of Gisela María Montemayor and the twins took place on an unusually cold Saturday evening during the last weekend in March in Lanier Park. Despite the sky being overcast and the wind blowing in sporadic bone-chilling gusts, it seemed as if the entire community had come out to pray for Gigi and the twins.

The manicured grounds and architectural landscapes of the recently renovated city park covered some five acres right in the middle of the city. Located between Paredes Avenue, McDavitt Lane and Boca Chica Boulevard, the space was considered a mini version of New York's Central Park.

Alex had observed the vigil from a distance, not wanting his presence to become a distraction for Gigi's family or their friends. He'd been sitting in his Shelby with the car's top up, across the street at a convenience store. Alex was smoking, his eyes red from all the crying as he listened to Harry Nilsson's "Without You," again and again. He was about to push the replay button again, when his cell went off.

"Hello?" Alex answered as he lowered the volume on the car's CD player.

"Enjoying the vigil?" asked the voice without any hint of emotion whatsoever.

"Let's get this over with, shall we?" It had been more than two weeks since Alex had provided them with a copy of the inventory. "I've waited long enough," griped Alex, his heart racing. "Are my kids alive?"

"You have the money? The deeds to your ranch and the penthouse? What about the cars and boats? Have you endorsed the titles?"

"Yes, everything's set. Just tell me who I'm signing the deeds over to. I need a name. That way the property transfer can be recorded in the property records and the transaction can be completed."

"Don't worry about recording any deeds. We'll take care of that. How much money were you able to scrounge?" asked the caller.

"Sixty million. All cash. All in duffel bags," explained Alex, "five of them. Answer me this, are they alive? I need to know."

The caller disregarded Alex's inquiry. "Is that everything? I'd hate to find out that you kept a secret stash, somewhere."

"That's everything . . . unless you want the fifty bucks in my personal checking account at the credit union."

"Very good. I want the properties transferred to Fundación Santander. Once you've added the foundation to the deeds and you've notarized your signature on the docs, I'll give you instructions as to where to deliver the documents, the money and the keys to all your toys. You'll have two weeks to vacate your penthouse and take your personal things from El Caudillo. Got it? We also need the names of three of your friends, their phone numbers, home addresses . . . where they work, their kids' schools . . . everything."

Alex had hoped the kidnappers would forget about that request. "I don't have that other information, yet," said Alex, "still putting it together."

"You better get to work."

"I'll have it ready," lied Alex, "it's just taking me a while."

"Don't screw it up."

"Listen, there's . . . a . . . little problem," stuttered Alex as he tried to stall the discussions, maybe gain some extra time.

"What?"

"The babies don't have any papers, no birth certificates, no passports, nothing. How do you expect me to get them back to the

U.S.? It's just not enough time," cried Alex. "I need to apply for a special permit or visa, something . . . I don't know."

"I'm sure you'll figure something out."

"But, how do I know the mother and the babies are still alive?"

"Listen, you dumb shit," the caller was now quite annoyed. "I guess you'll just to have to trust us. You're not thinking of backing out, are you? You want me to deliver their bodies in a trash bag?"

Alex's pulse skipped a beat. He had no idea what to say, or even formulate some kind of coherent response. "It's just that . . . "

"*Mira, pendejo*," the voice continued, "I can have my associates go pick you up right now . . . at the Stripes . . . where you've been parked for the last hour. *¿Quieres eso?*"

Alex freaked out even more. These guys were very real, and very capable of putting a bullet between his eyes or worse, hacking him to pieces and feeding him to a pack of wild dogs.

"*Vale más que cumplas esta vez, pendejo.* If you screw this up . . . we'll find you . . . there's no hiding from us."

"Okay," stammered Alex, close to having a mental breakdown, "just let me know when and where you want to do the exchange."

The caller hung up.

CHAPTER 47

ALEX LOOKED DISHEVELED, thin and pale. He had barely touched the food on his plate. Across from him sat Lieutenant Governor Rene Yarrington, enjoying a healthy serving of *migas rancheras* with refried beans, bacon strips, sausage patties, *barbacoa* and hash browns. They were sitting in one of the booths in the back of the Toddle Inn restaurant, a tiny eatery made famous when Tommy Lee Jones, while visiting his South Texas ranch, proclaimed it had the best *milanesa con papas* in all of the United States.

"I'm sorry about your pal getting killed," started Yarrington, breaking the silence. "I read it in the papers. The thing I don't understand is this. What the hell was he doing in Matamoros, anyway? Were you aware that he'd gone to Mexico?"

Alex didn't know what to say. How could he begin to explain to Yarrington that he had asked Romeo to go and deliver his fortune, everything he'd worked for, in exchange for a chance to deliver Gigi, alive, to her family, and save his babies. How could he explain that he had trusted Gigi's captors to abide by their word? That he had been a coward and had been duped. And now he was destitute, homeless and broken inside? That he'd been responsible for Romeo's death.

"You know," continued Yarrington as he scooped up some *frijoles refritos* with a piece of flour tortilla he was holding in his right hand, "you should try the beans . . . they're amazing."

"Thanks," mumbled Alex, "I'm not hungry."

"Alex, son," said Yarrington, "I know Romeo was your trusted assistant, and I swear to God . . . I'll do everything within my power to help solve his murder. I've already had my staff put in a call to the governor of Tamaulipas. I'll schedule a meeting and we'll go see him. What do you say?"

"I don't know . . . "

"You don't think Romeo was involved in the business, huh? Running drugs or alien smuggling?"

Alex played with the Zippo lighter in his hand. "No, and that I know."

"Anyway, come with me to Ciudad Victoria . . . see the governor. This way you can demand, in person, that justice be done for Romeo and his loved ones. That way the governor will put his best investigators on the case. Anyway, did I tell you Cienfuegos got appointed to the court of criminal appeals in Austin?"

"Good for him. I wish him the best," Alex said in a sarcastic tone.

"Hey," snapped Yarrington, leaning forward and whispering, "that guy went to bat for you. Made you over a hundred million dollars, son. You should show some respect, or gratitude at least."

"He didn't do shit. I tried that case. I got it settled on my own without his help. The jury sent out the note that, ultimately, triggered the settlement. I put on a hell-of-a-case for the jury."

"Alex, you're so naïve. The reason the case settled was because Cienfuegos had the balls to write the jury note; it was manufactured by him, on his own. The real jury note that went out that morning had seven jurors for the foundation and five for you. The judge stalled and hid that note . . . to help your case . . . He replaced it with his. Cienfuegos gave you the push that you needed . . . and that's why he's now sitting on the court of criminal appeals. He played ball."

"You're fucking kidding me!" screamed Alex as the patrons in the restaurant turned to stare.

"Alex," whispered Yarrington, putting his index finger over his lips, "keep it down, son. I know it's hard to believe, but that's what happened. Thank God. The jury was so sick and tired of the case after hearing two months of testimony. Otherwise, we wouldn't be having this conversation. Anyway, Cienfuegos said you lost some of the jurors the very first day . . . that he could tell . . . something about your opening."

"It can't be . . . " mumbled Alex, feeling sick to his stomach. The cup of coffee he'd drank that morning was now working its way up.

Yarrington was grinning. "Pretty unbelievable, huh?"

"You're something else, ¿*sabes*?" said Alex.

"Why are you so surprised?" replied Yarrington as he leaned forward. "Stuff like that happens all the time. Look around you, son."

It all made sense. Yarrington's seemingly casual invitation to take the case. The carefully orchestrated replacement of Phillips with Cienfuegos. The denial of the foundation's summary judgment. Cienfuegos' pro-plaintiff rulings. The jury note. And why he'd failed to lose the case, which, in turn, had cost Salamanca the nomination to Roman Cardinal. This, of course, had made Yarrington very happy. And that, at least, explained why Salamanca may have had a hand in kidnapping Gigi, exacting revenge on his entire fortune and possibly killing his best friend, Romeo Saldívar.

Alex got up slowly from the table, his stomach churning with rage, despair and humiliation, while Yarrington continued to put food in his mouth, proclaiming that he alone would solve Romeo's murder and bring to justice those responsible for Gigi's kidnapping. He would also find a solution to the narco violence now plaguing the entire U.S.-Mexico border. And he would pass new legislation to eliminate the dropout rate in Texas high schools and secure funding for a new Regional Academic Health Center to be built on the campus of the University of Texas-Brownsville, all of this along with more insurance and tort reform while securing higher admissions for minorities at the state's universities. How, he alone, single-handedly, was going to figure out the solution to the immigration problem. And how he was ready to bring gambling to South Padre Island.

Yarrington's voice started fading away as Alex headed outside to catch some fresh air and try to find a way to make the pain go away.

CHAPTER 48

MARCELO GACHA BUSTED out laughing. For the last hour, Lieutenant Governor Rene Yarrington had been cracking jokes, sipping wine and telling tall tales.

The two fifty-somethings were sitting inside the Hitching Post II, home to the Hill Country's best oak-grilled steaks. They were surrounded by linen-covered tables, old ranch photos on the walls and hungry travelers from nearby Highway 71. Yarrington and Gacha were already on their third bottle of Llano Estacado Pinot Noir, after having devoured appetizers of grilled quail and artichokes, sixteen-ounce NY strips, with sides of rich truffle risotto and creamy scalloped potatoes.

Gacha, a rancher from Sinaloa in the drug and alien trafficking business, raised his wine glass. "Any other deals out there where we can make us some money?"

Yarrington raised his glass, as well. It was time to celebrate. Not a year earlier, Yarrington had helped Gacha with legislation that would de-regulate the Casas de Cambio, or currency exchange outfits operating up and down the Texas border. Making it, not only easier for Gacha to launder his own monies, but also to help the DEA launder profits for other cartels in what the DEA called operation "Rinse & Spin."

Gacha and the DEA had an understanding that the DEA would only use Gacha's Casas de Cambio, exclusively, for free, and Gacha would be protected and not be charged with engaging in any type of criminal conduct. The DEA needed Gacha's cooperation to follow the trails of drug money, while Yarrington needed Gacha's plentiful campaign contributions. In return, Gacha received protection from the DEA and Yarrington's assistance inside the Texas capitol. It was the perfect three-way marriage.

Yarrington downed the last of his wine. "You mean like the punk lawyer from Brownsville?"

"Yeah, that one. What was his name . . . Del Monte, Del Fuerte?"

"More like 'Del Dumbass,'" joked Yarrington.

Gacha busted out laughing. Finally, after several minutes of uncontrollable laughter and a few more sips of wine, he was able to continue. "I need to keep doing deals like that . . . to keep my men fed."

"What's the matter, the drug business too slow?"

"Well," Gacha cleared his throat, "if you must know . . . it's certainly not what it used to be. I mean, the Mexican military is putting a lot of pressure on us. And, of course, the politicians want their cut. It's getting tougher and tougher to make a buck. We need to diversify . . . a little kidnapping, extortion . . . you know . . . We could use a few more rich, unsuspecting targets."

Yarrington burped loudly. "Excuse me . . . sorry about that . . . now, wait, didn't Del Fuerte give you other viable leads?"

A waiter came by and poured more wine into Gacha's wine glass. When he walked away, Gacha continued. "Del Fuerte made everything up. He took those names straight out of the obituary section of the paper."

"That son of a bitch," exclaimed Yarrington, "unbelievable."

"Oh yeah," said an angry Gacha, "and he's got another thing coming."

"Well, I'll keep my eyes open and my ears to the ground . . . see what else pops up on the radar screen."

Gacha started playing with a pocket-sized, brown leather cigar case sitting in front of him. "You know us, we're not afraid to get our hands dirty. That way, you don't have to."

Yarrington switched topics. "Do we have confirmation that my cut was wired and deposited, as instructed?"

Out of the cigar case, Gacha pulled out a small, folded piece of paper and pushed it across the table. "There it is. Account number. Routing number. Location. Everything you need to access your millions. All thirty of them."

Yarrington pulled out his wallet and slipped the piece of paper into it.

"You never explained to me your reason for targeting this particular lawyer."

"Two reasons," Yarrington said, as he grinned broadly and shifted comfortably in his chair. "First, let me ask you, do you have daughters?"

"Yes, as a matter of fact I do. I have two little princesses. A fifteen-year-old and a six-year-old."

"Well, then, would you let somebody walk all over your little girls? String them along, then dump them, break their hearts?"

"No way."

Yarrington pushed his empty plate away. "Neither would I."

"And the other reason?"

"Because the piece-of-shit had to be knocked down a couple of notches . . . and somebody had to do it."

"I'll drink to that," said Gacha raising his wine glass.

"*Salud*," toasted Yarrington.

CHAPTER 49

A LEJANDRO DEL FUERTE sat in front of Romeo Saldívar's grave as the soft glow of the afternoon sunlight bathed the cemetery and its well-kept grounds. In the distance, he could see a couple of workers from the cemetery, digging up four new grave sites and setting up tents for the next day's burial services.

It was his first time visiting his old pal. He sat down on the cool grass to chat, in silence. As he relived the events of the past year, he realized everything about Alejandro Del Fuerte had changed. For starters, his appearance and good looks had gone to hell. He looked no different than Jackie, the homeless panhandler, from down the corner. He needed a shave, a serious haircut and an urgent dental debridement. From a 32-inch waist, he'd ballooned four pant sizes and now tipped the scales at 220. A far cry, from his once lean, muscular frame of 170 pounds. All courtesy of his daily consumption of 40-ounce cans of Olde English 800 beer and cheap breakfast tacos from the Stripes convenience store near his trailer park.

Not only had Alex's physical appearance changed, but his outgoing demeanor and go-getter attitude had also faded away. Perhaps it was the Paxil or the Abilify, but lately he'd been feeling jittery, afraid, even distrustful . . . paralyzed by fear and anxiety. As if somebody or something was lurking in the shadows, following him, watching him, ready to pounce on him. Living life on pins and needles was taking its toll. And he had no one to turn to. No one to share his feelings with, but for the counselor from Texas

Tropical. The one he saw once a month. Alex was alone and very much lost.

His life had been turned upside down. Gone were his dearest friends, Romeo, Fetzer, Astrid and Betty, including his fiancée, Gigi, and his twins. Gone was Grandpa César, who now lived permanently in a nursing home and had full-blown Alzheimer's. He cursed his luck. He wished he could go back and do things differently, undo the painful events leading up to this point, this very moment in time. He now realized he should have never answered Paloma Yarrington's phone call that fateful day in July. He shouldn't have agreed to meet Yarrington for lunch up in Raymondville. And, certainly, he should have never rebuked Bishop Salamanca.

Although Gigi's kidnapping and Romeo's murder had never been solved, officially, Alex felt certain Tiny and his men were responsible. He had no proof, no way to connect the dots, but deep down inside he had a gut feeling. Gigi had refused to discuss any details involving the kidnapping with anyone. Alex figured she'd probably been threatened with the life of the twins if she did. He could understand her not wanting to talk about it.

Sitting there on the cool grass, he tried to imagine how his life would've turned out, had he not been so stubborn and greedy. Right now, he and Gigi would be enjoying being new parents, relishing in the twins' milestones. Making a life together. Building a home, making beautiful memories. Romeo would be alive, and Alex would not be riddled with all that guilt.

Alex sighed. He reached for a Basic brand cigarette and found the Zippo lighter in his shirt pocket. He lit his cigarette and took a drag. He exhaled. Why was he still alive? Had Romeo suffered? Had he been tortured? Had Salamanca been involved? Who had given the order to wipe him clean? He wished he had the answers. The more he thought about everything that had happened, the more he'd wanted to end it all. Except he couldn't do it. He'd tried, once, without success.

"I didn't know that was you," said a soft voice, startling and jerking Alex from his depressing thoughts. He struggled to get up on his feet and slowly turned around.

Gigi then added, "I didn't recognize you."

Alex could not find the words. All he could say was a mellow and subdued, "Hey . . . I was just leaving . . . I'm on my way."

Gigi looked radiant. She was wearing jeans, a turtleneck sweater and shape-up tennis shoes. "I come here whenever I get a chance, to give thanks . . . Romeo saved my life, my babies . . . How've you been?"

Alex shrugged his shoulders, looked down on the ground. "My first time back . . . the guilt, you know?"

They stood there, trying not to stare at each other, not knowing what else to say, both feeling uncomfortable.

Gigi placed a fresh bouquet of flowers in an empty vase next to the headstone. "He was such a kind and brave soul, you know . . . I'll never forget what he did for me . . . talk about the ultimate sacrifice."

Alex managed to say some words. "It's all my fault . . . I should have gone myself and delivered the ransom . . . had I not been such a coward."

"Don't beat yourself up," said Gigi. "You did everything you could."

"No, I blew it."

"So, have you been doing okay?" asked Gigi, not wanting to relive the painful incident.

"So so," replied Alex, "I'm still working through some issues."

Gigi was kneeling down, fixing the flowers in the vase. "I'd been wondering if you were ever going to call? Ask about the twins."

"I didn't want you or anybody else to see me like this," said Alex, both hands in his sweat pants' pockets. "It's embarrassing."

"Are you living in town? I haven't seen you around?"

Alex had a hard time explaining, "Yes, a small house. Well, more like a trailer home." He finally confessed, "It's a little mobile home in a trailer park . . . on the outskirts of town . . . it's all right."

"Do you need me to lend you some money, Alex?" Gigi offered. "To get back on your feet?" She waited for an answer while she continued to stare at Romeo's tombstone. The only sound was that of the oak trees rustling in the soft wind.

"How's your grandpa?" she asked when Alex didn't answer.

"He's all right . . . but because of the brain injury, he did lose some of his long-term memory," explained Alex, "we've had to make some adjustments."

"I'm sorry. I hope he gets better."

"How are the twins?" gulped Alex, still in denial, unwilling to accept that the only family left, was practically gone. He wondered why was Gigi was being so nice. After all, hadn't he single-handedly shattered Gigi's dreams and deprived her babies of their father?

"César Alejandro is fine. He's got your eyes, your temperament . . . he's walking now, very independent. Suzette Adriana takes after me, likes pretty things, loves her dolls . . . she's a girlie girl."

"Do you have a picture?"

Gigi shook her head. "No, I don't. I'm sorry . . . after the incident, I learned to be super careful . . . I don't carry anything that might put their lives in harm's way."

Alex finished his cigarette, flicked the butt away. "I guess that makes sense."

"You want to meet them?"

"Would it be okay?" asked Alex, suddenly feeling extremely anxious. "Aren't you mad . . . for everything I put you through?"

"I'm still angry, but it's not the children's fault. Our issues are our issues. I'm still very hurt you cheated on me. You made me look like a fool in front of my friends and family, the entire legal community, the whole world . . . really."

"I'm so very, very sorry," muttered Alex, reaching for another cigarette. "I can't apologize enough. I threw it all away, and I have no one to blame but me."

Gigi stuck her right hand in her jean's rear pocket, as if looking for her car keys. "If you want to see your kids . . . come by the food court this Saturday . . . at the mall . . . they love to ride the carousel."

"What's a good time?"

"Noon."

Alex was digesting the words, making mental notes not to forget Gigi's cordial invitation.

Gigi was now staring out in the distance, looking as if she wanted to say more. She cleared her throat. "Hey, I never thanked you . . . the ransom . . . and giving up everything to save me and the twins."

"You don't have to thank me. I could never let anything happen to you . . . I just wish I could have saved Romeo. They wanted five more million for his return . . . and I didn't have it." Alex started sobbing. He had to use his T-shirt to blow his nose and wipe his face. "I'm sorry you have to see me like this . . . really." Alex tried to compose himself.

"Will you ever get back to the courtroom?" asked Gigi.

He let out a big sigh. "Don't know. My license is suspended for another year. I still need to finish picking up the pieces . . . and I've got to stick around, take care of Grandpa . . . he probably doesn't have long to live. What about you?"

"I'm thinking of moving up to Austin . . . I hear there's a need for Spanish-speaking criminal defense attorneys . . . Maybe I'll hang my shingle."

"And the twins?"

"That's what's holding me back . . . I don't think I can do it alone. So, we'll see." Gigi's cell phone started ringing. "I'm so sorry," said Gigi as she reached for her phone. "I've got to go. Mom and Dad worry too much. Got to get home . . . we'll catch up Saturday, okay?"

"Okay," sighed Alex.

Gigi turned and started walking toward her car parked in the designated area of the cemetery, at the far end of the property. She walked casually on the grassy pathways, her silhouette becoming smaller and smaller in the distance.

When she reached a pewter-colored Honda Odyssey, Alex heard the alarm disengage, and Gigi got in. She backed out of the parking space, turned the wheel and exited the cemetery. She merged with the heavy traffic flowing northbound on the frontage road.

Alex watched the vehicle until it faded out of view. As he stood there, he noticed he felt something he had not felt in a long time, a mixture of hope and excitement.

ALSO BY CARLOS CISNEROS

The Case Runner
Carlos Cisneros
2008, 368 pages, Clothbound,
ISBN: 978-1-55885-510-6, $24.95

Winner, 2009 International Latino Book Award—Best Mystery Novel–English

In this legal thriller set on the Texas-Mexico border, a young lawyer is caught up in a wrongful death case involving insurance fraud, theft and maybe even murder.

"There is a slightly subversive element here that gives the novel zip; it has all the same elements as a traditional legal thriller, but it's less predictable, more ethically ambiguous . . . keep your eyes on Cisneros."   —*Booklist*

The Name Partner
Carlos Cisneros
2010, 352 pages, Clothbound,
ISBN: 978-1-55885-594-6, $24.95

Named to the Texas Library Association's 2011 Lariat Reading List: Best 2010 Adult Fiction

In this hard-hitting and timely novel about a drug company that puts its shareholders' profits over safety, South Texas attorney Guillermo "Billy" Bravo struggles with his reponsibilities to his client, his family and his own personal ethics.

"This thriller lands firmly in John Grisham territory. But Cisneros makes the material his own."   —*Booklist*